I0578418

PRAISE FOR THE DANGEROUS ONES SERIES

"Madeline Dyer's *This Vicious Way* is an unyielding exploration
into the motivations of a young assassin. Inga's determination
to end the cycle of abuse that shaped her life makes for a gritty,
heartbreaking, and captivating story."
Sarah Mensinga, author of *Currently*

"*This Vicious Way* is brutal in all the best ways. It will suck you in
and tear you apart, put you back together and then do it all over
again. What a ride! If you want a fantastic dystopian world, with
unique and flawed (but totally kick-ass) characters—this is totally
the book for you."
Stacey Trombley, author of *Trial of Thorns*

"Dyer gives us a strong heroine, high stakes, vivid world-building,
and gorgeous writing all wrapped up in one package… What more
could you ask for?"
Kelley York, author of *Other Breakable Things*

"*A Dangerous Game* is an unputdownable story, a wild ride from
start to finish. This is a stand-out novel."
The Literature Hub

"This book is an adrenaline-filled thrill ride from start to finish,
where the only time you put the book down is to catch your
breath. Addictive, thrilling, amazing."
S.E. Anderson, author of the Starstruck series

ALSO AVAILABLE FROM MADELINE DYER

THE UNTAMED SERIES

UNTAMED
FRAGMENTED
DIVIDED
DESTROYED

THE DANGEROUS ONES SERIES

A DANGEROUS GAME
THIS VICIOUS WAY

COMING SOON...

THE THREAT OF THE HUNT

POETRY

CAPTIVE: A POETRY COLLECTION ON OCD,
PSYCHOSIS, AND BRAIN INFLAMMATION

THE DANGEROUS ONES
BOOK TWO

MADELINE DYER

INEJA PRESS

This book is a work of fiction. Names, characters, places, and incidents either are the product of the author's imagination or are used fictitiously. Any resemblance to actual events, locales, organizations, or persons, living or dead, is entirely coincidental and beyond the intent of either the author or the publisher.

This Vicious Way
Copyright © 2020 Madeline Dyer
All rights reserved.

Madeline Dyer asserts the moral right to be identified as the author of this work.

First edition, February 2020
Published by Ineja Press

Edited by Michelle Dunbar
Cover and Interior Design by We Got You Covered Book Design

Print ISBN: 978-1-912369-05-8
eBook ISBN: 978-1-912369-04-1

All rights reserved. No part of this book may be reproduced, transmitted, downloaded, distributed, stored in or introduced into any information storage and retrieval systems, in any forms or by any means, whether electronic or mechanical, without the express written permission of the author, except for the purpose of a review which may quote brief passages.

The author can be contacted via email at Madeline@MadelineDyer.co.uk
or through her website www.MadelineDyer.co.uk

*In memory of Tamara,
a truly wonderful and caring friend*

"YOU WON'T DO IT, WILL you?" Keelie grins at me, eyes sparkling, before she turns to Elf.

They're both in the water, and the waves lap against their knees. Elf's legs have gone red. He looks cold, but of course he doesn't say anything.

I stare at them, feel the warm sand under my feet, feel it press between my toes. I take a step forward, toward the water's edge. My stomach twists, and my heart races.

"Come on, you're *five* now," Keelie says. "We're five, and *we* can do it." She laughs.

"But you've been five for longer. You're older."

Keelie snorts, hands on her hips. She raises her eyebrows, then laughs. "I knew you'd be too scared."

I look back at the grassy bank where my mummy, Gweneira, Bea, and Caia-Lu are sitting. None of them are looking at us. They're weaving the mats. The other children are playing in the sand, a game organized by Kacey. Only Keelie and Elf are brave enough to go in the water—Keelie because she's fearless, and Elf because he does everything she does.

I turn back to Keelie, folding my arms across my

chest. "I'm not scared."

"Sure you're not." She smirks.

I take a deep breath and plow into the water. It's cold. Icy. My dress clings to me. I stutter and shriek, and Keelie splashes me. Saltwater and adrenaline. Heart pounding, I look at her, a grin forming on my face.

I cup my hands under the water, then throw it at her. The splash misses, and she runs deeper into the ocean.

I race after her, arms pumping.

"Get out of there!"

Mummy's voice. I turn back. She's standing at the edge of the sand, shaking her head.

"Inga, out now!"

"It's okay! I can swim. Aunt Lìxúe taught me!" I yell, just as Keelie splashes me again. I shriek, taste saltwater.

"We're having fun," Elf yells.

"Inga Lin, *out*."

"Yes, Inga Lin, *out now*!" Keelie laughs. "It's all right, Elf and I can have all the fun."

My skin tingles with the coldness, but it doesn't feel as cold now. No, there's a warm sensation inside me, mixing with my adrenaline and excitement, and this *is* fun. "It'll be fine, Mummy," I call back. Suddenly, Mummy seems farther away. "It's not dangerous. It's—"

Water splashes over my face, and I turn, spluttering.

Keelie grins wickedly and shrieks in excitement. "Come on! It's deeper out there!" She points behind her and then plunges farther into the water, swimming.

"Inga!" Mummy shouts.

I look back. Gweneira's by the water's edge too now, with her.

Above the crashing waves, I hear Keelie's laughter again.

My chest tightens.

"Don't," Elf says, his voice strangely serious. He's closer than I'd expected. "You're not as strong a swimmer as we are."

But I can do this.

I turn and dive back into the water, racing after Keelie. But she's fast. Still, I'm an okay swimmer, that's what Aunt Lìxúe told me. And she had to teach me in secret because Mummy is scared and won't let me or Gweneira near the water. Not since Gweneira nearly drowned when I was a baby. They've told me the story hundreds of times as a warning—how Gweneira got swept away by a current and they all looked and looked and couldn't find her. How they looked all through the night.

How they found her, washed up on the shore, alive, the next day. How Gweneira was subdued after that for a long time. How several of the adults thought the experience had traumatized both Gweneira and Mummy for life.

"I can't go through that again," Mummy said, and it's how she always ends the story. "Promise me, Inga, you won't ever go in the ocean."

I made the promise so many times, because I wanted to reassure her. And, at first, I had no intention of learning to swim. But then Aunt Lìxúe said it was stupid if I didn't learn how—and I found I liked it.

I plow through the water, adrenaline filling my limbs. This is fun. This is amazing.

Keelie and Elf and I swim out farther, until my lungs are burning. The sun is low, makes the water sparkle, and I think of the fairies in the story Caia-Lu told at the camp last night. I sat with Bea and watched her expressions as the fairies triumphed over the sea monsters.

Yes, water fairies.

I'm a water fairy, I'm a—

A wave crashes over me, around me, pushes me down.

I open my mouth, spluttering. Water down my throat, and—

Pain in my lungs. I can't breathe.

The water's too strong, too big, and—

Up. I need to go up.

My eyes sting as I try to see which way is up, and a murky shape flies toward me.

No. A sea monster!

I scream, letting more water in, and—

A hand grabs me.

I thrash against it and—

Light. Air.

I splutter. The surface. My throat burns, constricts. I hear my pulse in my ears, feel it in my forehead, heavy, and—

Keelie's eyes are wide, next to me. It's her. She's the sea monster, and—

"Are you okay?" Her voice wobbles.

"Get back here now!" Mummy roars, and I turn, throat burning, see her wading into the surf, knee-deep already. Her white dress floats in the water. "Inga Lin, now!"

Keelie pulls me back, helping me swim, and I feel stupid, silly. She's never going to want to play with me again. Sure, Elf will. But he's not as much fun. And I want Keelie to be my friend because she *wants* to be. Not just because we're cousins.

"What the hell did you think you were playing at?" Mummy screams the moment we're level. She grabs my arm, ripping me from Keelie, and hauls me closer to her. Water slaps against us. She's shaking. "You're soaked! You could've drowned. Have you got no sense? And after what happened to Gweneira, everything I've told you? And you promised you'd never swim!"

"I'm fine." I try to hug her, but she pushes me away, then pulls me back through the water, to the shore, where Gweneira and Bea are waiting.

"No. You're *not* fine," she hisses. "You're going to catch your death of cold, and we're miles from the camp! And I can't go back to get your other clothes— we've got to bring in the nets a little later, and I'm not making this journey again."

Her face gets redder and redder as she shouts, and the others on the shore are looking now. I want to turn my head and see what Elf and Keelie are doing, but I daren't. I bet they're laughing because my mum is the boring, angry one. Why can't she be more like Aunt Lìxúe?

"It's okay." Gweneira places a hand on her arm. "I'll walk back with Inga."

Mummy makes a sound deep in her throat, like an angry bull, before she nods. "Don't let her get away with anything." She shoots Gweneira a sharp look, and my sister nods before grabbing my arm.

Gweneira's grip is firm, and she doesn't even stop for me to put my shoes back on. Just marches me straight toward the trees, where thorns dig into the soles of my feet. I whimper.

"Not so brave now, are you?" But her voice isn't harsh. Gweneira is never angry. She's always there for me. "Don't worry, Mum will calm down soon. She just doesn't like the water, okay? Don't go swimming again."

The adrenaline in my body is leaving, and it makes me feel weak and shaky, silly. That and the cold. My wet skin goosebumps, and my hair drips watery snakes between my shoulder blades. I shiver. "I only wanted to play with Keelie and Elf." My voice is a whine, and I'm trying to appeal to Gweneira, even though she's not angry.

"There are some things we just don't do, Inga. And swimming is one of them. It upsets Mum too much. We don't do that."

I nod and wince as I stand on more thorns. Under the trees, it is dark, and our shadows are chopped up by trunks. Gweneira holds back a branch for me, and I duck under it. She doesn't duck low enough, and it catches her hair. She grimaces but doesn't stop to smooth her hair, so several strands stick out from her plaits. Gweneira's hair is dark, but not as dark as Aunt

Lìxúe's and Keelie's and Elf's and Bea's. Mummy and I are the only ones with pale hair. Sunshine, Caia-Lu calls it.

Gweneira smiles and squeezes my hand. I like holding her hand. She's got big hands, and she makes me feel safe.

"Come on, hurry," she says. "You're cold."

I'm shaking, but I tell her I'm not, and—

She stops, pulling on my arm to get me to stop too. Her other hand flies up in the danger motion—the first signal I was taught.

I freeze, look at Gweneira to work out where she's looking.

There.

I turn slowly.

Two figures stand in the trees.

Out of the corner of my eye, I see Gweneira's hand go to her belt—where she keeps her weapons.

"Shit," Gweneira says, and her voice sounds different and—and then I realize why. This is bad. This is danger.

The Enhanced Ones. The enemy. The ones we must always run from because they want to convert us. They want to take away our humanity and make us drink augmenters so we only feel what they want us to feel.

I swallow hard. Then I frown. I can't see any mirrors. Mummy and Gweneira and Keelie have seen the Enhanced Ones before and say their mirror eyes are usually the first thing you see. Little flashes of light. Unmistakable, apparently.

But I can't see any.

I stretch onto my tiptoes.

Gweneira lets go of my hand, then she steps slightly in front of me. "Stay behind me."

"Are they like us?" My words are breathless. "Untamed?"

"I don't know." A slight pause, and I stare at the floral pattern of her dress. "Okay, Inga. Okay. You're going to run back to Mum, okay?"

Okay. She says that word a lot when she's nervous.

I start to smile. Then I stop.

Then I smile again. "But if they're not Enhanced, they're Untamed, they're like us."

"I don't know," Gweneira says. I shuffle to the side and look up, see her frown. The blue of her eyes looks sharper, it always does when she's nervous. "You remember the traveler? He said about…" She shakes her head. "Just go back to Mum *now*."

"But—"

"That's not very welcoming," a voice says from behind us.

We both scream, turn, and—

A woman, right behind us. Normal eyes. Untamed eyes, and skin with patterns on. Images all around her neck and jaw, reaching up onto her face, all in electric blue.

Gweneira grabs me, pulls me close. My foot presses on something sharp, and I cry out.

"Yes, we'll have her," the woman with the patterned face says.

"No!" Gweneira yells, and she's shouting for help as she encircles me in her arms.

My heart feels too heavy, and I don't understand. They're not Enhanced, these people.

"Yes, dear. You must have heard of us," the woman with the patterned skin says.

Gweneira grips me harder. Her arm jabs under my ribs. She's holding me so tightly I can't get away.

The woman smiles. Yellow teeth. "And you must know this," she says. "We always get who we want. Now, give the girl to me."

"No!" Gweneira yells. Then she's screaming for our mum or anyone.

"Oh dear," the woman with the patterned skin says.

She lunges at me.

Hands grab me, just like Keelie's did in the water, only there are suddenly so many of them. More and more of them, all tattooed, with skulls on their necks, and they're wrenching me from my sister, and Gweneira doesn't fight.

She screams. A rush of air. And she looks scared.

"Yes, dear," the woman croons, "you're mine now, tiny one."

I cry out, twist around, try to get away from the woman with the patterned skin—

Something hits the back of my head.

I scream.

And then there is nothing.

I CANNOT HELP BUT SMILE as I stare at the man I'm going to kill.

He hasn't noticed me. Of course, he wouldn't. With a name like his, Hunter Devall never thinks he's the one who could be in danger. Head down, he walks hunched over, staring at the woodland floor. Dried leaves crackle under his steps. He's a lean man, but appearance doesn't fool me now. Hasn't done in a long, long time. Something to thank Bridie for.

I tread lightly, carefully, choosing bare earth to stand on, as I follow Hunter. My knife is in my belt. The blade itself is a little loose in the handle—has been ever since Falkes used it—and now I jiggle the handle, left, right, left, right, because it is a countdown. One movement for each step I take.

One movement for each step Hunter takes toward his death.

And he doesn't know it.

He wasn't even next on my list of originals, not that I stick to killing only them. All the new assassins have to go too. But the originals' deaths mean more to me. Hunter's always been near the bottom of my list because I prefer to take out the biggest threats first, the ones who have more Rijikarii energy. Safer that way. Since Bridie's departure, Brighid Berthold's the biggest threat, but she's going to be heavily guarded and difficult to identify, given that her Seer powers mean she can take on another's image. I've got no way to get to her yet, and so Zak and Clara have always been my next priorities, followed closely by Dylan and Taylor. Poor Hunter, right at the bottom with the other weeds: Gabi, Mark, and Luca.

But I'm not one to turn down a chance like this.

Sweat beads on the back of my neck.

I adjust the weight of the rucksack and bow on my back. The arrows are inside the bag—Amelia was repairing the quiver so I couldn't take it. Not that I'll need the arrows. I intend for Hunter to see me, so I will be close enough to use the knife. I want to see the terror in his eyes as he realizes his own weapon has turned against him.

I speed up. Faster, faster. My hammering heart cheers me on. Adrenaline spikes, and I step closer to a tree trunk, watch as Hunter slows his pace. He's still staring at the ground. I see a slight frown on his face. What is he looking for?

My eyes strain as I try to see. But there's nothing apparent.

Well, you've had enough time to find whatever it is you're looking for.

I jiggle my knife again in my belt as I make my way closer to him, but I keep the blade hidden. Walking silently is one of my strengths. Bridie Berthold trained all her children to have that ability. Pity she didn't train her adults in the same way.

My breaths are fast as I count the disappearing steps between Hunter and me.

Closer, closer, closer.

And I could do it now, I know. Throw the knife, and I'd get his back, easily. Possibly puncture a lung or damage a kidney. Enough to make him stop.

But I want him to look at me when he experiences his first pain at my hand.

The corners of my mouth twitch as I edge closer, closer, until I can see the tattoo on the back of his neck. A tiny, ornate skull, dead in the center, over a cervical vertebra. It mirrors the one on my neck perfectly, and my skin there prickles, before the sensation travels along to the sites of my other markings. That always happens when I think about the ways they rewarded me, branded me.

Time's up.

I allow myself one more smile, one more moment of reveling in the adrenaline coursing through my system.

"Hello, Hunter." My voice is smooth.

He jumps as he turns, and we are close—six feet apart. My gaze roves over his body, checking for bulky objects in his outline. I'd be a fool if I didn't check for any obvious signs of weapons.

Hunter's eyes widen, and his gaze is on my face in an instant, because that's what you always do. Knowing who you're dealing with, Untamed or Enhanced, is important. But the Enhanced aren't the only predators out here. Hunter and I may both be Untamed, but we are both killers, and, right now, we are more of a risk to each other than our supposed enemy.

The man in front of me hasn't aged well. Big grooves have been dug around his eyes, and his skin is dim, blotchy in places. His hair is graying, and he stands wonkily. He looks half dead. Odd. I haven't seen him in nine years, but I remembered him as being younger, full of vigor. But now, even his eyes, though still a fairly strong blue, look lifeless.

"Well, someone hasn't been taking care of themselves." My voice is low. "You look a mess. Seriously bad, Hunter."

The corners of Hunter's mouth lift. A strange laugh follows, then he clears his throat. He blinks, but it's not in the strong way he once blinked with.

"Inga." It's not a question, but he looks surprised. He may not have seen me since I was twelve—and oh so much has changed and not changed—but he knows me. "It really is you."

I smile. "Gods, you look ancient. What are you? Fifty?"

His upper lip curls. "I've been looking for you—for a long time."

"Haven't you all?" I laugh, feign carelessness, but my hand goes to the handle of the knife in my belt, and I hold it casually, confident he won't know it's there. He's not even looked me up and down, assessing for weapons. Error number one. Really, he deserves what is coming.

They all do.

Hunter lifts his hands in the air. For a moment, I think he's got a weapon—a pistol maybe—but his hands are empty. He's a fool not to arm himself.

"Petra said it was Oleta out here. But you—this is so much better." He's grinning, and he genuinely looks happy to see me. And that—well, that annoys me. No other way to say it.

My gut tightens. He was *expecting* Oleta. How many others of us are still out here? Still escaping the lives they put us into. Lives they want to trap us back into.

But don't pretend you didn't enjoy it, all that killing.

They made you what you are.

They awoke the world for you

There are snakes in my head, and they like to remind me of that joy.

I shift my weight from foot to foot. "Hunter." My voice is low, quiet. I rarely speak loudly. I don't need to. I may have a small frame and look innocent at first glance, but I have presence. Even my shadow is confident. I think that's why Minnow's little boys are so scared of me.

"It's not far," Hunter says. "Our truck's just over yonder." He gestures to his right. "I know you hate us, but we can forgive you for everything. No more blood has to be spilled—and you're coming back to us, we know you are. What happened was inevitable really, two strong girls pitted against each other, well, we should've realized. Bridie should've realized."

Yes, I think. *Maybe she should've.*

I think of the truck waiting, and I wonder how many others are there, and which of the originals on my list are there.

"I am so happy to see you again." Hunter steps toward me, closes the distance. "The others will be too."

"Likewise." I jiggle the knife in my belt again.

He holds his arm, indicating the way. For me to go first.

My feet are stone, and they hold me firm. "Tell me, who's still here then? It's been years."

"Oh, we've regrouped and expanded." He pushes greasy hair back. That's one thing that always annoyed me about Hunter and Luca, how their hair was perpetually greasy.

"And the original members?" I lean forward. "Zak and Clara? Dylan? They still there?" Most of all, I want to ask about Brighid—the daughter of the infamous Bridie, a fear-inducing woman I only saw once and never spoke to—but I've got to be careful. Don't want to make him suspicious, even if I do need to know what Brighid currently looks like, given she can change her countenance.

"Yeah, still going strong," Hunter says, and, really, it's worrying how relaxed he is around me. Does he not suspect anything? "But we got plenty of assassins now too, less pressure for you."

I bite my bottom lip slowly. "Still using children?"

He shakes his head. "You don't have to worry about that. We're not like that now, not without Bridie controlling everything. We're better."

Better. Huh.

I click my tongue. "I very much doubt that."

"Inga, careful." Like that, his tone has changed. The

switch has been flicked. "Remember who you are talking to."

"And remember who I am." I tilt my head to one side. "Remember who I killed."

He matches the tilt of my head with his. "Remember who trained you. And we're doing well now, Inga. You're one of us, and you should come back. Come back willingly, and you'll be fully compensated for your work with us."

"Compensated? Do explain, dear Hunter."

"We run things differently now. Like I said, we're not using children. Not the really little ones."

I make a deep noise in the back of my throat. *I* was one of the really little ones. Bridie's extremist group stole me from my sister's arms when I was five years old, raised me as an assassin, and sent me into the Enhanced Ones' cities to kill our enemy. Bridie thought that was the only way the Untamed could win the war against the Enhanced—those who are addicted to chemical augmenters that prevent them feeling negative emotions, but at the expense of their humanity. The Enhanced are soulless, robotic, and programmed to convert the rest of us, who they see as *wild and dirty and untamed*. Anyone who is bad and who is not controlled by them is a threat to their way of life.

Bridie said we needed soldiers in this war against the Enhanced, and we needed Untamed who were willing to fight rather than run and hide. So, years before I was born, she put together her own group, 'recruiting' children who her team trained to be the deadliest killers. And her group kept going.

"You know, you were always the best," Hunter says.

Liar. I don't know why I think that word, because I know it's the truth. I was the best. Better than Oleta, even. The best of Bridie's girls.

"And it's fate that I should find you here."

No, I want to shout. It's not down to fate. It's down to Petra—he's already said as much, even if Petra thought it was Oleta out here. Her sister. But Petra's looking for us, for them. That damn Seer. The Dream Land stopped giving her warnings of the Enhanced Ones' attacks on Untamed long before I joined the assassins, but she'd already developed her powers, and, apparently, the Gods and Goddesses couldn't take those away. She's a human tracker. She can find anyone she wants—or anyone she's forced to find. Given time.

Still, I'm surprised it's taken her this long to *not* find me. And they haven't exactly found me now. Hunter had no clue I was here before I made my presence known.

"Okay," I say, "let's go."

"Really?" Hunter's eyes widen. Shock. Huh.

Oh, you shouldn't wear your emotions so visibly. You've got to hide something.

"You're joining us again? Oh, Inga, Zak will be so pleased, you're all he talks about—someone's been coming after us for the last few years, and Zak wants you and Oleta back. Better chance of protection and—"

I pull out the knife. One swift movement. "You never were the cleverest, were you?"

Hunter falters. His eyes bulge, but he doesn't move, and, really, it's pathetic that he locks up like that. Guess that's what happens if you spend most of your life as an instructor and rarely actually face danger.

Makes it too easy to do this.

I plunge the blade into his heart.

Hunter's expression slackens. Then he screams.

I pull my knife out and stab him again, but the blade hits one of his ribs—damn, didn't get the angle right. He shoves me. But he's weak, and I'm strong. I kick him and he stumbles, still trying to fight me—because that's what we've all been taught. All of Bridie's bands. Even if his skills are pathetic now.

I punch him, feel brief pain spread through my fist, before I punch him again. His nose breaks, and blood squirts over me, thick and gloopy.

"Please... Please, Inga..." he pants, falling to his

knees. His hands go to the first wound I inflicted.

"Oh, Hunter," I whisper, crouching in front of him. "You shouldn't even be able to speak." I let mock sympathy fill my face, then I grab my knife again and slash his stomach.

He lets out a guttural scream, collapses onto his back. I stare at his feet; watch how they writhe as blood creeps along the ground to them.

Blood. A pool. It looks too dark though. Even his blood is bad.

But I stare at it. Wait for it. Wait for it to grow and form a figure. Keelie, Elf, and Bea—my cousins—are the usual ones. For a long time, I used to wait to see Gweneira, my sister. But it's never her. Still, seeing my cousins is a gift from the Gods and Goddesses—and it's how I know what I'm doing is right. They want me to do this, and, with every assassin I kill, I know I'm one step closer to finding my true family.

I smile as I wipe the knife blade on the grass and wait for my reward.

Twenty-seven down. Eight to go.

I BELLOW AT HUNTER'S BODY. Scream at the blood.

But it's too late. The vision didn't come, and it's not happening now.

I didn't see my family. And I won't—not with Hunter's body. The Gods and Goddesses mustn't have been paying attention. Maybe they were sleeping—or doing more important stuff, like turning more Untamed into Seers, giving them powers and prophetic visions so we can win the war.

Or maybe Hunter's death isn't worthy of a reward. No, I need to take out the originals who are higher up—Brighid and Zak and Clara—and any newcomers with status first, before I take out the weeds. This is proof.

But Hunter was here.

It was too good an opportunity and—

Something cracks.

I turn in an instant, see a figure hobbling toward me.

I grab my knife, but it's only Amelia Karnad. The woman who let me into her family years after I escaped the assassins. I turn my focus back to Hunter's body as I wait for Amelia to get here. She's old. It will take a while.

The muscles of Hunter's stomach are hanging out of one of his wounds and I don't remember doing that, but I probably did. It's what Bridie told us to do to the Enhanced Ones that we kill: *Pull their innards out, and even their augmenters can't fix the damage.*

Damn. I can hear her voice now. That gruff tone.

Amelia inhales sharply and hobbles closer, leaning heavily on her stick, until she's standing over Hunter's body. Her saggy face pinches in, her lips all but disappearing as she inhales sharply again—as if for dramatic effect. Only I know it's not. Her horror is real.

I watch her, from a few feet away. My back is against the smooth trunk of a tree, and there's something about leaning against it that grounds me. I breathe out hard. My rucksack is at my feet, along with the bow. There's a dead hare next to them. It ran out as I was waiting to see my family, and I am quick, swift. *Dinner.*

"Inga," Amelia says, but she doesn't turn to look at me. I stare at her side profile as she frowns, her gaze intent. She's a gnarled figure hidden in an oversized cardigan and waterproof trousers that the breeze intermittently puffs up.

She knew I was out here and what I was going to do, I'm sure, but at least she didn't stop me. She says she's my grandmother—by *soul*, not blood—and that she has a radar especially for me and her true daughter, Renee.

When Amelia turns to look at me, I step away from the tree and swing the rucksack onto my back.

"I didn't do it." My words are sharp, strong, and I'm very aware that my left hand holds the knife. I tuck it into my belt, wipe my hands on my already-stained jeans, then pick up the bow and rucksack, sling them onto my back.

The lie doesn't make me feel bad, because we both know that's what it is. I can't outright tell her it was me, because then she'd have to tell Falkes I did it when he inevitably questions her, but she can pretend she believes my lie.

And she's said it enough times—all the adults from Bridie's group deserve to die for what they did to me and so many other children. I've been doing it, over the last six years, taking them out one by one, cheered on by the Gods and Goddesses, and Amelia knows.

I pick up the hare. Amelia's eyes focus on the limp animal. She purses her lips for a long second. The movement makes the lines there look deeper.

"I know you didn't," she says, her voice low, gravelly. And by that, I know she knows. There's a spark in her eyes. An acknowledgement. "But they may have heard his screams."

"Did you?"

Amelia shakes her head, and her thin, gray ponytail swishes from side to side. I twist my head, look in the direction of our minibus and tents. The others I travel with are not in sight, and no one's rushed through the long grass and trees, alerted by Hunter's cries. Only Amelia is here, but chances are she didn't actually hear anything because she just *feels* that kind of thing. We're a good way away from where we made camp, and Falkes is exhausted. He said that enough times on the way here. He's not venturing any farther than he has to.

"They're not coming out here," I say.

Amelia nods and moves toward me slowly. Her waterproof trousers rustle, and I think I imagine her bones creaking. She's an old woman. Seventy-four, or seventy-five. She's not entirely sure which. But she's the oldest Untamed I've ever known. And it worries me sometimes, having her with us. Worries me in the sense that she can't run like she promised us she once used to. Her legs and arms ache, and she gets tired. Walking quickly sometimes makes her chest hurt, and her breathing gets fast.

But I can protect her, I know that.

I was made to be the best. And I owe it to her, for she and Renee are the only Untamed who seem to like me.

Who see beyond my past. And that's why I've stayed with Falkes's group, because of Amelia and Renee. I was ill when I first found them, needed medical help. I'd only planned to stay a few weeks at the most, but those two women showed me tenderness and love as they nursed me back to health. They gave me a chance when I believed no one would. So I stayed. And living in a group is safer, especially a group that has a healer. Falkes and the others may not like me, but I've got enough skills for them to keep me with them.

Plus, they think I'm a Seer. I had to lie. No Untamed would trust one of Bridie's Assassins, and I needed a reason as to why they should heal me, rather than just kill me. All Untamed worship and value Seers, want to have as many in their groups as possible, and, as it happened, a few days into my stay with them, I discovered Falkes's group had been Seer-less for a year.

"Let's go back," Amelia says.

Back. I grimace. No. I need to find the others. Hunter said their camp was nearby.

But you don't argue with Amelia. And something tells me she knows what I want to do anyway.

I swallow hard. There'll be time later. There has to be.

We walk back, Amelia and I, through the trees, to the other side of the woods where our shadows become long, drawn-out on the gravelly ground, distorted by the clumps of grass and low-lying vegetation. I swing the hare as I walk. Every time its bloodied fur touches my thigh, I feel more powerful, and it reminds me of the assassin Bridie and her men trained me to be. I was five when Bridie took me. Twelve when I escaped, and fifteen when Amelia and Renee took me in, against Falkes's orders. He just saw me as a blood-covered child who was screaming that she'd kill everyone if they didn't help her. But Amelia and Renee say they saw my heart under my fear.

Fear.

I wrinkle my nose. I was not afraid.

Only weak people feel fear.

"Give me the bow and the arrows," Amelia says as we reach the minibus. Minnow Atkinson is in the driver's seat, but she appears to be asleep. The two young boys stop whatever game they're playing in front of the bus and stare at us. "And your knife's hidden?"

I nod and hand the bow over and then retrieve the arrows from my rucksack and give it to her. I'm not supposed to have weapons. Not when I'm *dangerous*. That was Falkes's condition, all those years ago, on letting me stay, and he still goes by it.

Callum and Johnny, Minnow's boys, rush into the biggest tent, to where Falkes and Lexa will be. They always stop playing and hide when I get too close. When we're traveling in the bus, they insist on sitting behind me so I can't reach out and strangle them without them having warning, and Minnow never says anything about it. Just lets them get away it. My place is up front, next to the driver. Damn fools they are, thinking that would stop me if I wanted to hurt them. I could so easily reach across and stab Falkes as he drives, take control of the vehicle—and everyone in it.

"Give me the hare too," Amelia says.

I comply. Falkes will want to inspect it for illness and disease before we cook it. He's particular about things like that. Shame he's not as particular about ensuring I don't use anyone's weapons. He's divided all the weapons between the 'safe' adults—himself, Renee, Amelia, Lexa, Minnow, and Stephen, who's only just an adult, but still a crap shot. And really, Falkes is stupid, believing that Amelia wants a bow. She's our healer. She doesn't often hunt. No, she requests her own allocation of weapons because she knows the work I do is important. It's all about playing the system.

My hand feels empty without the hare, and I watch as Amelia disappears into the big tent.

From the other tent, I can hear Renee is working, so I head there, following the sounds of her flintknapping. *Chink, chink, chink.* Inside, it's humid and smells strongly of smoke. Renee nods when she sees me. Her black hair is tied tightly back, and she holds up the axe head.

"No," she says as she screws one eye shut and squints at it.

For a long time, I wished I had Renee's skills. I find it calming watching her shape a weapon out of nothing, to see how it's done. How death-makers are created. To know that the bluntest piece of stone can become deadly.

Renee picks up her hammerstone and strikes the axe head again. A flake of flint flies out toward me. It hits the side of the tent, where it drops down and joins others. I stare at that shard for a long time, so long my head starts to buzz.

"Kill anything interesting out there?" Renee's voice makes me jump. She always speaks loudly, mainly because Amelia's going deaf, only she now does it regardless of whether her mother's here or not.

"A sly hare," I say, depositing my rucksack in my corner of the tent.

Renee makes an approving sound and wipes sweat from her brow. Like Amelia, she knows what I do when I find members of my old group. And she says the Gods and Goddesses and spirits must be driving me toward them, encouraging me to right the wrongs of this world, because we stumble upon them a lot.

She's not wrong. The Divine Ones are definitely backing my work.

And Hunter wasn't alone. I grimace.

I need to go back out there. To Hunter's body, and beyond. He was with others. And I've still got eight more of the original assassins to kill. Eight more personal monsters out there. Chances are Hunter was with some of the originals, because they'll be the backbone of any new groupings, and without them, new recruits will just disappear, I'm sure. Hunter was probably with four, maybe five.

My mouth waters at the thought of getting so many together. My whole body buzzes with the need. They have to pay for what they did, they—

"I don't care," Falkes yells from outside, and Renee and I jump.

I hear Amelia's voice—fraught—and then Lexa's too.

I rush outside, Renee close behind me.

"And there she is." Falkes Hughes glares at me. He's an odd-looking man. Reminds me of a sick tree that's wizened and wilting in sunlight that's too harsh and powerful to cope with. He wipes sweat from his head—Falkes sweats a lot—then points at me. "Where is it then?"

"Where's what?" I glance at Amelia, but she's not looking at me. Her eyes are on Falkes.

"I told you, Inga sure as hell hasn't got a knife."

"There's one missing," Falkes replies, a muscle in his jaw pulsing.

"And Inga doesn't have it," Amelia says.

"Yes," Renee says, her voice loud and smooth, like a blanket. She's still holding onto the axe head and hammerstone. "Inga doesn't use weapons. We all know that."

I resist the urge to snort as Falkes's beady eyes narrow on me. The knife is still in my belt, but I've had it for weeks. This isn't a new thing.

"Has she got a weapon or not?" Lexa asks. Her short blond hair blows in the breeze. It would make her look angelic, if she didn't have the devil's eyes. Or if she didn't stink of alcohol, underneath the clouds of perfume she walks around in.

"No," I say, my voice hard.

"What *is* going on?" Minnow appears, bleary-eyed, her blue eyeliner smudged a little. Her normally-immaculate braid is a little awry, and she's got faint lines imprinted against her face from the minibus's headrest. She naps in there a lot. The two small boys hover behind her, clutching her tartan-print skirt.

"We need to search her," Falkes says, and he reaches out to grab me.

I duck, quick as lightning. "You're not touching me."

Falkes growls. "You'll do as I say. This is for the safety of my fucking group."

"But you're not listening," Amelia says, just as Lexa chides Falkes for his language in front of the boys. "Inga hasn't got a weapon. She hasn't done anything, she—"

"There's a dead man!" a voice cries out.

I turn and see Stephen Drake racing toward us. He's the final member of our group, a nineteen-year-old, who, judging by his looks, is definitely Fawkes's son, even if he isn't a Hughes by name. They both have noses that look too small for their faces, big, haunting eyes, and a shock of black hair which looks too dark against their near-translucent skin that seems to have them in a permanent state of blush. In the last eighteen months we've been traveling, looking for more Untamed—*good* Untamed—Stephen's crept up in height and muscle mass. He now easily surpasses Falkes's strength, and I don't like it now when Stephen stands next to me. There's something about his muscles that makes me uncomfortable. I may be a killer, but physically, I'm weaker than him.

Stephen waves those muscular arms at us. He's coming from the woods—the same direction Amelia and I went.

My heart sinks.

Stephen skids to a stop, behind Lexa, his aunt, panting heavily. "A body," he says. "An Untamed man…dead!"

Oh, damn.

Everyone turns to me.

Falkes steps closer, snarling a string of rotten words. "It was you, wasn't it?"

"Inga has not killed anyone." Amelia edges closer to me. "She was with me the whole time."

Her lie seems to tie itself around my throat, because it's what I've made her do—even if I didn't ask her to lie. My presence here has changed Amelia and Renee. Made them bad, like me.

Badness is like a disease. People catch it and don't even realize they have it. Not until it gets worse. By then, they're in too deep.

"And then she was with me," Renee says. "Still not killing anyone." She gives me a grin. The grin falls away when Falkes looks at her.

"Well, we'd better check out this body," Falkes says. "Could be Enhanced Ones about." But he glances at me, and he's not exactly subtle in his meaning.

I think of his words to me, two years ago: *You kill another Untamed and I'm killing you.* He'd been furious, screaming in my face, and he has a habit of spitting when he speaks. Or shouts. Especially if he's angry.

And he was angry.

It was his stepbrother I'd killed—the only Untamed life I've ended that wasn't linked to Bridie.

I'd been surprised Falkes had been that fair to me.

Still, Vincent may have been Falkes's stepbrother, but everyone knew what he was like. He thought he could beat anyone into submission with his fists. I wasn't the first one he'd attacked. But I was the last.

Falkes mutters something to Lexa. I miss the exact words, but I hear my name and some bad language, the kind of language Amelia would scold me for if I were the one to use it.

Falkes looks at Stephen. "Show me where the body is. Lexa, with me. Minnow and Renee, start packing in case we have to leave. Boys, get in the bus. And Amelia, keep an eye on *her*." He glares at me.

I glare back.

Falkes, Lexa, and Stephen head off. The boys climb into the minibus and sit in the back seat, eyes wide and on me. I mime claws at them, claws scratching, and they disappear, ducking down below the window. I snort.

Pathetic.

"You're not helping," Amelia says to me.

I shrug, then sit on the ground. May as well take the opportunity to rest.

"I assume it was you?" Even speaking quietly, Renee's voice is a bit too loud. She pulls out a box of cigarettes from the pocket of her overalls. Without fail, she always grabs them on raids, just as Lexa always get alcohol and perfume, and Minnow picks up eyeliner.

I look at the ground, really stare at it. I am tense, and my jaw starts to ache. I press my hands into the dried earth, then pull the stubby blades of grass until they come free. I toss them up in front of me, higher and higher, and watch as they flutter down.

"Inga?"

I look up at Amelia's tone. She's standing with her hands on her hips, a stern look in her eyes. Renee is behind her, a cigarette now in her mouth.

"What?" I pull up more grass. The snap of each blade as it leaves the earth is satisfying.

"You've got to help yourself here," Amelia says.

"Don't cause trouble. And don't be snarky with Falkes," Renee adds, fumbling with her lighter.

Trouble. I turn the word over in my mouth. Trouble was the first thing Falkes said about me when he saw me. *She's going to be trouble.*

"Inga." Amelia's voice is louder now. A warning.

"I'll be good," I say. Not that Falkes and the others can do much to me anyway—as far as they're concerned, I'm a Seer, and the Untamed worship their Seers. That lie makes me untouchable.

Or maybe it's not a lie. I mean, the Gods and Goddesses *do* show me visions—they're just not the usual type Seers receive. But if Falkes and the others think my visions warn me of danger to our group, I'm not going to dispute it. And pretending to be a Seer gives me power. If I tell them I have special powers and the Gods and Goddesses and spirits have shown me where to go, then I decide the route we take and where we settle down. And settling down is an impossibility until I've eradicated Bridie's originals and the new assassins.

I pull up more grass. *Snap. Snap. Snap.* And I continue doing it until the earth is bare and Falkes, Lexa, and Stephen appear again.

Their faces are sweaty, and they huddle together about ten feet from where I'm still sitting. Amelia and Renee are by the small tent's entrance, talking with Minnow. The little boys are still in the bus.

Damn. How is it fair Johnny and Callum are with their family and I'm all alone?

Sure, Amelia and Renee may believe they're my family now—but they're not. We both know that. The only family I see is thanks to the Gods and Goddesses. But it's been a while since the visions have worked. What if it's gone wrong? What if they can't show me Keelie and Elf and Bea anymore because they're dead? And what if that's why I've never seen my sister? Because she's been dead all this time? *Years....*

A lump catches in my throat.

No. None of them are dead. They can't be.

I have to see them again. Seeing my family is my reward for killing all the assassins. The Gods and Goddesses have practically promised me that. They can't back out on it now.

Determination sets hard inside me. I will see my family again.

I *will.*

Falkes beckons for Minnow to join him, and she does, yawning widely and picking up her long skirt so it doesn't trail in the mud. Really, the clothes she wears don't scream survival at all. Nor do her actions, not when she spends so long each day applying that blue eyeliner and making her hair look perfect. Always the same style, that braid, but she redoes it often.

I stare at the sky as they speak. It's beginning to darken now.

"No." Falkes's voice is loud, and I jerk my attention

back to them and—

His face is like thunder has slapped him. Anger that gets closer and closer as he marches over to me.

I jump up, adrenaline coursing through me. Fire glints in his eyes.

"No, Falkes, don't—" Amelia starts to say, but her words trail away as, in one swift motion, Falkes pulls a gun out of his belt and points it at me.

There's an intake of breath from the others behind him—Stephen and Lexa and Minnow.

"Did you do that?" His voice is a snarl. The Luger shakes in his grip.

I take a step back. My heel hits against one of the pegs for the big tent, and it throws me off even more than the metal barrel in my face.

"Did I do *what*?" I meet his cold eyes.

Amelia has always said my insolence will be the death of me. That and never knowing when to answer a question straight and not roll my eyes and not play up and not pretend to be the wild monster-girl they all think I am. But that's all they expect me to be—and we all know it's one of only two reasons Falkes keeps me with them. I'm good at killing the Enhanced Ones. I was made to be a weapon, and they use me as one.

Falkes presses the Luger closer until its cold metal kisses my forehead. "Don't fuck with me."

"*Language*," I mutter, my voice a perfect imitation of Lexa's tone.

Stephen stifles a laugh, then turns it into a cough.

Falkes flicks the safety off the gun. "The dead man over there. Untamed eyes. Did you—or did you not— kill him?"

I try to focus on Falkes's eyes again, but the gun is too close and the touch of it against me is a distraction. My vision blurs as I try to look at both the weapon and his eyes. I don't like it when people threaten me. Really, he should know better. Because one day, I might just snap.

"It's no good if we're looking for allies and you kill

every Untamed we come across."

Allies. Huh. I want to spit in his face. The urge is there, sudden.

"I did not kill that man. I'm a Seer." I make my voice louder. "I'm here to *preserve* Untamed life." Yes—and that's why Bridie's Assassins have to die. They hurt Untamed children.

"Seers aren't untouchable," Falkes spits.

"You really want to risk life out here without a Seer?" My voice is light, the lie wrapped tightly, securely.

Falkes glares at me. "Do you have a knife on you?"

I hold his gaze.

"I'm going to search you if you say no," he says.

I exhale loudly, then reach down to my belt, pull the knife out. He grabs it from me so hard the handle seems to bite me as it's yanked away.

"It's not good manners to snatch," I mutter.

Falkes presses the barrel of the gun even farther into my forehead, as if he's trying to break through my skull with it, but I don't react.

"You're lucky you're still with us," he says. "I don't have to keep you in my group."

I snort.

"And I sure as hell don't like you," he adds, as if those words are the final sting.

"Oh, really?" I raise my eyebrows. "And there was me thinking you *did* like me. What a mistake to make, eh?"

He growls—actually *growls*. Huh. And they say *I'm* the wild animal.

"One wrong move, Inga, and you're dead. Got it?"

I resist the urge to snort again. "And you'll be without an assassin to protect you." Not that I like calling myself an *assassin*, but it gets the point across. I'm too valuable to kill, if I protect his group.

His nostrils flare. "Do you get it?" He punctuates each word with a pause. "I'm not messing about here."

I count slowly to five, just to see the effort it takes him not to react. But he won't react. I know that. He's all talk. If he was going to kill me, he'd have done it when I murdered his stepbrother. Really, Falkes should've killed me then, if family honor means anything to him.

But it obviously doesn't, or then again, maybe he hated Vincent as much as everyone else did, and Falkes clearly likes having me about to kill Enhanced Ones whenever we get in a spot of bother—so I'm safe. The safest one here probably.

Just as he looks like he's going to explode, I nod. "Yes, Falkes, *dearest* leader. I understand."

He glares at me, then pulls the weapon away and spits at my feet.

I feel anger rising in me, anger kissing every part of my soul. Urging me on. I am dangerous. He should be more respectful.

But I don't do anything, because sometimes not reacting is the most unease-inducing thing you can do for other people, and Falkes wants me to react.

I rarely give people what they want. I've learned that's the best thing to do.

A moment passes, then Falkes steps back and looks at the others. "We're leaving. If she didn't kill the man, an Enhanced did."

Leaving? No. My heart slams in my chest. We can't. Not yet.

"It's safe here." I make my voice as strong as possible. "The Gods and Goddesses haven't sent me any warnings."

"Not a chance we can take," Falkes snaps.

I shake my head. I need to go back and find the other assassins Hunter was with. But if Falkes and the others believe there are Enhanced Ones around here, leaving is what they're programmed to do. Not go and hunt them down. Sometimes, I wonder how the Untamed survive at all. At least Bridie raised me to confront danger. Running away is a sign of weakness.

"Or that man could've been Enhanced and was killed by Untamed," Renee says. "Eye-mirrors fade after death. Or it could've been an animal attack. We know there are big cats around here."

"Big cats that have the ability to use knives?" Stephen snorts. "Those looked like stab wounds."

"Could've been claws." The sweat on Renee's dark skin catches the light a little.

"Staying is not a chance we can take," Falkes says. "Everyone, pack your things. We're leaving."

I flex my fingers as I watch him go into the big tent. Lexa, Minnow, and Stephen follow him, and the boys scrabble out of the minibus and follow too, each nearly tripping over his own feet in haste.

Amelia gives me a look—the *be careful* look—and heads into the other tent. Our tent, because Falkes never wants me sleeping in the same tent as him and the others. Oh, how precious they are.

I think they must be packing. We're all used to it. It's all I've ever known with this group. Some Untamed make permanent residences, others don't. Falkes has said if we find a big group, we may join them and settle, but for now, we have to keep moving. Chances are, there aren't any out there, especially not in this area. The only group we've had contact with in recent years is Taras's, but that dried up two years ago when our last radio was broken. Amelia used to be part of another group far to the east, but she left when Renee was a few years old and traveled for three years across land and seas until she found Falkes's group. Falkes says that's too far for us to go.

"Typical," Renee says. She holds up the axe head she was working on. "I was just getting started." She follows Amelia.

But I don't.

I linger near the big tent, the one Falkes and the others are inside. I hear their voices. Meeting voices. *Of course* they're having a meeting. And *of course* it's about me.

"It was her." Falkes doesn't bother to lower his voice, and I suspect he knows I'm listening. "I don't care what Amelia and Renee say or think. Inga is dangerous."

I snort. Well, of course I am. I'm special because I've got Rijikarii energy in me. Only a few people have it, and it makes me headstrong and defiant and a killer and bad and dangerous and all the words that Falkes loves to use to turn the others against me. My Rijikarii is part of me though. It's why Bridie recruited me. Recruits who have higher Rijikarii levels make natural assassins. And I'm not scared of killing. I revel in it.

I did so much better than all the other assassins. Some of them barely had any Rijikarii.

"We can't afford for her to kill any more of us," Falkes continues.

"Well, this man wasn't actually one of *us*," Minnow says.

"Doesn't matter," Falkes says.

"Yeah, she's still killed other Untamed," Stephen adds. "Regardless of whether it's been her killing those people recently, all of Bridie's lot have killed at some point. We know that."

"Yes," Falkes says. "And Inga doesn't care about the distinction between the Untamed and the Enhanced. She was trained as a killer, and that's all she is."

My blood pounds in my ears. That's not true. Give me any Enhanced, those soulless robotic automatons who are wiping out humanity and converting us into them, and I'll kill them first. No hesitation. The Untamed deaths…well, that only happens to those who deserve it.

"It's only a matter of time," Falkes says, "before she kills one of us. You've all seen that vicious look in her eye. That's not normal. She's messed up. Who knows what really happened to her before she came to us? No. I said it at the time, we should've never let her into our ranks. All it's caused is bloodshed."

I hear the sounds of movement, and I shrink back, melt into the shadows.

"We need to do something about her before it's too late," Falkes says. "Something should've been done a long time ago. I made a mistake letting Amelia talk me into accepting her into the group. Inga's bad news. These recent killings prove it."

"So we're going to kill *her*—in cold blood?" Stephen asks.

I raise my eyebrows and wait. Whatever reply Falkes gives isn't verbal.

THREE

"YOU MUST CALL ME MOTHER." Bridie's voice is low, careful. Her head is lowered toward me and the bars of my cage. Her matted, gray hair hangs in greasy strings, partially covering her eyes so all I can truly see of them in the dark is the spark in them. The danger.

"You must call me Mother," she says again. "And you must always do as I say. Do you understand?"

I jolt as I look up at her. My eyes sting and my chest aches from crying, and my arm hurts. I want to scream and cry more, look for my mummy, but I am scared of this woman in front of me because when I cried earlier she was angry. So all I say is, "Yes, Mother." And I try not to cry.

Bridie's lips peel back as she grins, revealing too much gum and rotting teeth. It makes the hut seem darker, full of secrets and bad things, not like my mummy's hut.

"You must never question me," Bridie says. She's got a tattoo on her neck, a bird flying from flames. It's nicer than the circular patterns on her face.

I just watch Bridie and press my lips together.

"Mothers always know best, and mothers keep their children safe. My rules will keep you safe, so you must never question my decisions or instructions. Just as you *must never question the commands of the band leaders, for I guide them too, and all of this is to help you and keep you safe. Do you understand, Tiny Inga?"*

I nod and edge closer to my bars. They're cold under my hands. Out the hut's window, I can see the other children playing outside. I want to be out there. Maybe Mummy is out there....

"Inga?"

"Yes...Mother." I gulp. She's not my mother. I want Mummy.

"And you must never rise against me. For that would be a great crime, punishable by death. Or worse." Her eyes glint.

I don't understand what could be worse than death, but I nod, feel the corners of my eyes and the bridge of my nose burn as tears form. "Yes, Mother."

Bridie smiles and turns around. A man appears from the shadows of the hut, and I freeze. Has he been here all the time?

"Yes," Bridie says. "She'll do well. Brighid and Petra both agree that she's got high levels of Rijikarii. We'll start her training next week, when band three is back."

"Band three? Fi's squad?" the man says. "But Zak's is lower in numbers."

Bridie nods. "That is true, but Fi is getting old. The rankings within band three will shift in a few years, when she's out of the picture, and the band needs flesh blood, more littles... Apart from Oleta, there's not much Rijikarii in that group. It needs more." She glances back at me. "Keep her in the cage until band three is back. Limited food, water, and contact."

The man nods and smiles.

FOUR

I WALK AWAY FROM THE big tent, a strange sense of power and confidence growing inside me. They think they can kill me. It's almost laughable.

"Can you go to the river?" Amelia appears in front of me, and I jump, hadn't realized she was no longer in the small tent. She thrusts several bottles at my feet. They're the large ones we stole on a raid a little while ago. "My back's hurting, need some more water for the hot-water bottles." She grimaces. "Bet it's those spirits."

Amelia's been saying there'll be a Turning—the time when the seasons change and the spirits become more active and even deadlier—for a good few weeks now, but no one, other than the odd Seer, can predict the Turnings. Not even her aged back. And, really, I'm glad—because if we had as many Turnings as Amelia hints at, we'd never have a moment's respite, and I'd constantly be reliving the nights at Royston's Rock, the scratchy blanket over my face: Caro's and Oleta's hands, warm in my own, squeezing, reassuring as they whispered to me, but I could never make out their words, because all I could hear were the shrieks outside as the spirits fought. The sounds of the battle terrified me. Or at least they did until Bridie discovered my fear.

She made sure to burn that out of me.

I touch the scars on the backs of my legs. Little round marks. The hot poker—because I had to learn and none of her children would be scared of the Turnings.

Amelia taps one of the bottles with her stick.

I nod. "I'll get the water."

The river's that way…by the trees, near the body. I look at Amelia, and I *know*. She knows I have to go back. She *wants* me to.

It's going to take Falkes, Minnow, and Lexa at least an hour to take the big tent down and get it in the minibus as Lexa likes everything folded neatly. She gets stressed if there are creases, and given that her sister—Stephen's mother—disappeared a couple of months before I joined their group, presumably caught by the Enhanced, Lexa nearly always gets what she wants else she turns on the waterworks. The disappearance was six years ago, and she still milks it for all she can.

Actually, I've probably got a lot longer than an hour. They're not going to work quickly when they don't feel under immediate threat from an outside force. If there were Enhanced Ones nearby, they'd assume I would have received a vision and told them.

Huh. If only they knew safety is only ever an illusion.

And really, how stupid are they? Don't they know the Gods and Goddesses would never choose me as a Seer? I've killed Untamed. In the eyes of the Divine Ones, I am a traitor. No way would they bless me with the powers to keep Untamed safe.

And yet they give me visions of my family….

But Falkes's group is lucky to have me, whether I'm a Seer or not. I was made to kill Enhanced Ones. I was made to protect my people. And if they want me to protect them, they should be nicer. We all know who the strongest in this group is.

I push my hair back. An hour or so gives me plenty

of time.

Amelia heads off to the big tent, and I set the plastic bottles down on the ground, then duck inside the small tent. Renee's packing her things, and she looks up at me, doesn't say anything as I rifle through Amelia's belongings until I find the Glock she keeps hidden. I check how much ammunition is in it, then pick up a new magazine as well. We're getting low on this—the ammunition—but we're low on food too. Falkes will have us go on another raid soon.

I tuck the Glock into the back of my belt and retrieve my rucksack. I check the supplies in it, the survival kit. Doublecheck for the bandages and antiseptic, in case someone removed them in the last hour or so. A long time ago, I got shot on one of these missions. My self-appointed missions. It wasn't a bad wound, but it's taught me to always have medical supplies in my bag when I'm going after them.

I know the assassins are in the area, and they'll be waiting for Hunter to return with Oleta. They'll be suspicious by now, on guard.

"Be careful," Renee says.

Her concern touches my heart. It's strange having people who care for you because they *actually* care. Not because they care whether you come back and whether you can still do your work. I'm still not used to it, and it makes me feel wrong.

I leave the tent, grab the bottles, and start back toward Hunter's body. It doesn't take me long to reach him. I skirt around his form. Two flies buzz above the open wounds of his torso, and I imagine how his blood will congeal, how the cats in this wood will tear his flesh with sharp teeth. I almost wish he was alive when that happens. So he can feel the pain. Some people deserve to be eaten, and some deserve to be alive when it starts.

A grin stretches across my face, and I turn right, heading deeper into the woods.

I am good at navigating. Always have been. Put me

in a wood, and I can orientate myself in a matter of seconds. Amelia calls it my sixth sense. But it's more than that. I hear things others don't. My soul is so in tune with the world, I can feel where others are. Maybe that's why it's easy for the Gods and Goddesses to reward me with visions of my cousins, even though I've not been chosen to be a Seer.

As I walk, I wonder which others of Bridie's children are still out here. Oleta and Samira got away, as did Harmony, and many of the littles. But they couldn't run as fast. I didn't stay to protect them. We all just scattered. I'm sure the surviving uncles and aunts rounded most of them back up within a few days.

I walk for ten, fifteen minutes, before I see smoke. The trees are thinning, and the smoke is wood-smoke. A campfire.

I edge closer, more cautious now. The gun in my belt whispers reassurances to me with every step I take.

A truck is visible first—white paint stands out against the darkening trees. They should've painted it a darker color. I slow my steps as I hear their voices, count the figures that appear through the trees. All adults. I'm close enough to see the marks on them: signs of status, killings, rewards, and punishments— as well as the identifying symbol of the skull on the one whose back is turned to me. Bridie's favorite marking. It was always she who tattooed the marks on us at our camp. Or scalded our skin with pans of boiling water when we'd been bad.

Only Bridie's gone, so someone else must have taken over, be etching the marks into skin, because these people I do not recognize. They're all new, joined sometime since the day I and the others escaped.

I shift my weight from foot to foot. There has to be one here who's the same. An original. Hunter said there were other originals—but did he mean in this group? How many groups are there? I'm out of touch with how big the organization is—or isn't—now.

And I need to kill the originals. The men and women

who trained me to kill, who kept me in line: *Zak, Clara, Dylan, Taylor, Gabi, Luca, Mark.* And Brighid, Bridie's infamous daughter, the hooded and cloaked figure I only saw once.

And then there's Petra—the Seer never raised a hand to me, so she's not on my actual list—but she is another original and still part of the assassins' group. Those on my list aren't the only ones I'm going to kill—no, all the new assassins have to die too—but the originals are the important kills. Their deaths mean more to me.

But Petra—can I kill her? When she's just as much a victim as I was?

Then I frown. Petra told Hunter he would find Oleta here. Her triplet sister. Not me.

Would Petra really make that mistake?

Unless Petra knows it's me who's killing them, and so she sent Hunter into my path? Could Petra be on my side? She never did hurt anyone. Bridie took her and Oleta at the same time, when they were eleven, already Seers. The third triplet was not taken. I don't know whether it was intentional, or if Anita had been taken by the Enhanced Ones at that stage. It's a bit of a gray area, and not something that Oleta or Petra would ever speak about. Still, the assassins got two of the sisters, but it was only Oleta who was trained to kill. Petra was nice—though strange, I remember that—and maybe Bridie knew she'd never be a killer. Still, she's got other powers. Tracking powers—skills that were just as valuable to Bridie as assassination.

I frown, my forehead tingling. Maybe Petra sent Hunter to find me, bring me back, and stop the assassins' numbers decreasing. She may have been on our side before, but she didn't leave with us, and who knows what brainwashing she's had?

But why would she get my name wrong on purpose and make Hunter think he was going to find Oleta?

Concentrate on the here and now, Inga.

I focus on the people in front of me: four men. Three

move between their truck and the campfire. The other grills meat over the flames.

I set the plastic bottles down, then head nearer, and crouch behind the base of a tree, kneeling in its debris, feel bits of dirt and twigs imprinting on my knees, through the thin fabric of my worn jeans.

I wait and wait, because someone else has to appear.

My disappointment is a flame inside me that doesn't die down.

No. It is just the four unfamiliar men.

I spit at the ground. It's not fair.

The hairs on the back of my neck rise. Maybe Petra and the other originals are somewhere else, and they sent Hunter and his men down here to collect Oleta. Hunter never actually said Petra was with them at their camp and spoke to him in person, did he? I try to think. Petra could've passed the message onto him via other means.

I wonder when these men will realize Hunter's not coming back. If an original was here, they'd all be suspicious by now. But these men are relaxed.

Maybe one or two of them will head out as the night properly draws in. Maybe I'll kill them—bang, bang—as they do. The gunshots will alert the others, as well as my own group, but who cares? I'll get the other assassins easily, and Falkes is *already* gunning for my blood. Why not give him more reasons to kill me and see if he follows through, especially after that conversation I overheard?

My eyes narrow on the men. They're all sitting around the fire now, talking as they wait for the meat to cook.

My upper lip curls.

Let's do this.

Shooting them in cold blood, without them realizing I'm here, would be no fun, even if I don't recognize them. They'll know I was one of them. Bridie marked her team for the world to see, and my shirt has no sleeves and a low neck. My marks are proud and clear.

I count to ten under my breath. It's a habit left over from Bridie's training, and, as much as I hate all these habits, it's one I can't break. Because it does make sense. It calms me, and being calm is vital.

Then I ready the Glock and move toward them.

"Hello, boys." I can't help but smile. I love calling men like these boys. I can almost see their feathers ruffling.

I wait until all of them have seen me—and my assassin marks—and then I pull the trigger.

A scream. A man falls, and the others jump up. Birds fly from the trees as I get numbers two and three in quick succession. Spurts of red fly.

The fourth starts to run toward me, and he screams a war-cry, but it's pathetic really. He doesn't even reach for a weapon. Unarmed?

Bang. I get him easily.

One of them by the campfire isn't dead—his hand is moving—so I shoot him again, and the sound burns through me. The trees seem to take the gunshot and twist it, magnify it, and I hear the shot over and over and—

He's *here*.

His face. In the sky. This was enough? These deaths, even though the men weren't originals.

But they were still assassins.

"Elf," I breathe.

I've watched him and Keelie and Bea regularly for the last few years, and I know the visions are true. This is him now. Elf. Even the first time the Gods and Goddesses gifted me with visions of them, I recognized each of them even though they looked older.

Elf always has the same eyes. Eyes that bore into me.

Keelie's grin is always infectious.

Bea's stare is always slightly curious and slightly shy. Once, I saw another girl with her—a child—and she had the same curious look in her stare. A daughter or a sister, I guessed, but I know soon I'll be able to ask her. Ask all of them. We'll be united soon.

Now, Elf stares at me, and I am talking to him—I realize that, and I can't process what I'm saying, but that doesn't matter. I stare at his face. He's got a cut on the side of his face, a deep one. Looks new. I look harder, and there's pain in his eyes. Pain and anguish, and he mouths a word. A name.

A name I immediately feel inside me, as if it's *my* thought, me thinking her name.

Keelie.

I inhale sharply, because I feel his emotions—the crashes of despair and anguish shaking him.

Something has happened and—

Elf disappears.

My breaths come in short, sharp bursts. My forehead hurts. And, a moment later, I come to my senses, focus on the Glock in my hand and the dead men lying around me.

I haven't got long. Falkes and the others will have heard the shots, likely be coming for me. With pitchforks and knives and guns.

Pitchforks. I laugh.

I push my hair back, tuck my firearm back into my belt and head toward the new members of Bridie's Assassins. I wonder if they still call themselves that. Maybe Brighid's in charge now, and they are Brighid's Assassins. She'll now have the phoenix tattoo, the symbol of the leader, because she is the natural successor to Bridie's leadership.

I don't like *Brighid's Assassins* though. Hasn't got a ring to it. And something tells me they're not going to dishonor Bridie by renaming her group, even though Bridie isn't with them anymore. They'll still be terrified of her, though pretending they're not.

But Bridie terrified everyone, to some extent.

People never left Bridie's clutches—until we did. Me and Oleta, the two she'd turned against each other because she knew, together, we'd be a threat to her. And we were. Oleta and I had become enemies, but then we united, along with Petra, and went for Bridie and freed the other children.

I stare at the unseeing eyes of the men I have killed, and I imagine their spirits begging me to say the Spirit Releasing Words, to let them break free and make the journey to the New World easier for them. Huh. As if I'm going to do that.

"Inga the Killer does not do kind things," I say, and the words make me feel powerful. "Not for people like you."

I step over their bodies and reach for the meat speared on the stick over the flames.

Looks about done.

I pull a chunk off, wincing at how hot it is. Wave it around in the air to cool it. Charred smoke wraps around me.

Lightning flashes, makes me jump, and a few seconds later, I hear the rumble of thunder. Strange. It's not raining. I look up at the sky. Dark clouds.

But no rain. I've got time.

I chew methodically as I stare at their bodies. Two of them have their mouths open, and there's the urge in me to take their teeth so I can drill holes in them and add them to the chord around my neck....

No. My hand slaps at bare skin.

I do not wear that necklace anymore. I threw it away after I drove the knife into Bridie's chest, over and over.

I do not collect teeth.

I killed the four men, but this meat doesn't taste as sweet as I thought it would. Because they're not originals. There are still eight of them out there.

Eight lives to wipe out.

It is my purpose.

The voice in my head told me.

And I have to do it.

So drive off and do it. You can take their truck, their supplies. And you'll be alive—not traveling with a group that largely wants to kill you.

I stare at the bodies. Would Falkes really kill me?

Stephen and Minnow? Lexa?

I sincerely doubt it. None of them have got the backbone to do it. They're all words, no action. Just say the stuff that makes them feel better.

And Amelia wouldn't. Renee wouldn't.

Amelia. Renee.

My chest tightens. How can I leave Amelia and Renee? The only women who have shown me kindness? A grandmother and mother, of sorts—though I have never called them by those names.

You should leave them—you can't risk Falkes killing you and you not killing those who deserve death.

I press my lips together as another bolt of lightning flashes. The thunder's louder this time. I curse at the distraction, because I need to think. Would Falkes *really* kill me?

No. He wouldn't do it. Seers really are too important.

I bend down and pick up a twig and twirl it round and round in my hands. Its bark is smooth.

I look at the truck. A white Volkswagen Amorak.

Just leave them. You don't owe them anything.

I sigh. I've already got enough faces haunting me. Amelia's and Renee's on top of those aren't going to make a lot of difference.

I shrug. Yeah. I need to find the other assassins and—

Lightning, around me and—

Pain, my body. Everywhere. Too intense.

I try to scream, but my throat—too raw.

White light. Too bright. Eyes, burning.

Heat floods my body, too hot and….

And then there is nothing.

AN OLDER GIRL LETS ME *out of the cage on the fifth day. She's got long black hair, and she speaks in a throaty voice.*

"Do as they say, and it will be easier. Remember, never question Mother," she says.

Her fingers are clamped around my upper arm, painfully tight, but I can't say anything. I just nod.

We reach the doorway of the hut, and I blink as bright light fills my eyes. The sun—it's so strong. I try to lift my other arm to shield my eyes, but it's painful. I can't remember what happened to it. Something when these people took me from Mummy.

My mummy. My real mother.

Tears fill my eyes.

"Don't cry," the older girl warns me. "Mother punishes us all if anyone cries." She glances down at me. "We have to stick together, Inga. We look out for each other. Okay? You can be my little sister. I'm Oleta. Oleta Alanis. Just be strong, and you'll be fine."

Oleta?

But I have a sister: Gweneira.

I don't want to be Oleta's little sister. I'm not Oleta's

little sister. I don't need Oleta.

But she's here, and Gweneira isn't. I look up at Oleta, and she gives me a quick smile. And then we're by another hut, and I'm dragged into darkness again. My skin goosebumps. It takes my eyes a moment to adjust, but I already know the hut is full of badness.

Oleta gives me a little nudge forward, then leaves, and I stare at the woman seated in the hut: Bridie. Her gray hair is tied up this time. Her collar is high, and all I can see of the tattooed fire-bird on her neck are the tips of its wings, reaching up, from under the edges of the collar. Bridie tilts her head from side to side, inspecting me. I feel my knees shake, feel weaker and weaker. I'm going to fall over. My vision wobbles. Tears and—

No. I think of what Oleta said. Be strong.

"Do you know what this is, Inga?" Bridie speaks in a low, careful voice. "Come closer."

I step forward and see she's cradling a gun in her hands.

"You do know what it is, don't you?" Bridie's voice is a whisper.

I look at the gun, how her fingers curl around it like it's an extension of her. Of course I know what it is. I'm not stupid. Part of me wants to say that, even though I know they don't like it when I speak like that. The side of my face still stings from one of the other women's slaps this morning when I said I wanted more food.

I watch Bridie and nod, once. My eyes are on the gun. I remember my mum holding her gun. And Aunt Lìxúe had hers. They stood back to back once, posing with the guns as Aunt Ramna—their other sister—painted them, and I thought they looked amazing. Powerful. Like the women in Caia-Lu's stories. Afterward, Keelie picked up a gun, her eyes glistening.

"Don't touch it," I whispered, hovering in the hut's doorway.

But Keelie was already holding it.

She laughed as she turned to me, dark hair whipping in front of her face. "How are we supposed to kill Enhanced Ones if we don't touch the guns?"

Keelie laughed and laughed as she pointed the gun at me. She stopped laughing when my mum rushed in and screamed. She wasn't laughing, hours later, when Uncle Owen was giving her a stern talking to about respecting weapons.

Now, Bridie laughs.

She does not sound like Keelie or any of my family. Or any of the people from D'Elinous.

I watch Bridie carefully. I do not like her. But they say I'm with Bridie now, that I should be happy she noticed my potential. That Bridie's going to help me become the best.

Bridie reaches for my hand with her grimy fingers, smiles, and says something about my chubby baby hands. "They'll never suspect you."

She strokes the back of my hand. I want to wrench my hand away. My fingers aren't chubby, and I'm not a baby. I'm five, and I can climb better than Gweneira, and she's a lot older than me.

I am not a baby.

"Come with me."

Bridie pulls me swiftly out of the hut. I see Oleta watching from the doorway of another hut, her dark hair partly obscuring her face.

"This is Royston's Rock, our northern-most camp, Tiny Inga," Bridie says. "Do you understand?"

"Yes, Mother."

"We have several camps, and I am Mother to all the people in my camps. But we have a hierarchy—little steps connecting each of us. I am the most powerful woman here, but I won't be looking after you. We have aunts and uncles for that."

Aunts and uncles?

Bridie guides me into the next hut. There is a lot of stuff inside this hut. Blankets and bed rolls and containers and curtains strung up. The smell of herbs hangs in the air, and a scrawny dog is asleep on a cushion.

I don't notice the person inside at first. She blends in. An old, old woman sits on a wooden stool. I stare at her wrinkly hands. Her skin looks like crumpled paper.

"This is Fi, one of our aunts," Bridie says. "Fi, this is Inga Lin." She looks back at me. "Each of the aunts and uncles has their own little family, Inga. And you are going to join Fi's. You must listen to her at all times, for she will look after you. But you must do as she says. If she asks you to do something, you do it, else she won't look after you. See? It's all about exchange, trust, and respect."

I stare at Fi, but she doesn't speak. She stares coldly at me. She's wearing a metal crown, and it looks a bit silly, like she's playing dress-up.

"You will belong to Fi's family," Bridie says. "Band three, we call this family. Fi is in charge of everyone in band three. If you can't find Fi, then you find Yvette instead, because she has the next highest ranking after Fi. She's the second-in-command for band three. Do you understand?"

I nod, but I don't know who Yvette is. I stare at the dog. I think she's awake now, but she hasn't moved. She looks thin. I can see her ribs. I want to stroke her.

"You are doing great, Tiny Inga. And you are now part of the littles—the little children—of band three," Bridie says. "The littles are the youngest, and you are lowest in the hierarchy—until you grow and pass the tests and train hard and become a higher. Those are the older children. Oleta and Caro are the highers in this group. It is important you learn this hierarchy and respect it," Bridie says. "Everyone must know their proper places in order for this to be a peaceful and loving environment."

Bridie pushes me forward. My bare foot catches on something sharp. A blade. The pain is sharp and big, and tears come to my eyes.

Fi glares at me, her whole face tightening inward as she shakes her head ever so slightly. Oleta's words come back to me. We don't cry here.

Bridie touches my shoulder. "Fi will see that you settle in and learn our ways, Inga of Band Three. I'll leave you to get settled. The other littles will be back shortly."

I turn and watch as Bridie strides away, then I look back at Fi. The old woman hasn't moved from the wooden stool.

After a few seconds, Fi shakes her head again, then touches her necklace. "Not another one." Her voice is low. "May the Gods bless you, child," she says, her voice tearing like tissue paper. "You're going to need it."

SIX

"*NO!*" A VOICE CRIES, AND the voice is screaming the word, over and over. "*No! No! No!*"

I recognize the voice…distantly, from a time long forgotten….

…and white… there's whiteness all around me.

I blink. My eyes feel scratchy and….

…and I am swimming through fog, but I have no body. Weightless, and—

Caia-Lu looms in front of me. But I'm not here….

I'm….

I don't understand.

My head.

My head hurts.

"Not her as well!" Caia-Lu shouts, and the world darkens.

Slowly, I open one eye.

My vision blurs.

I'm lying down. Lying down? Why am I lying down?

I sit up gingerly, and my head thuds. I blink at the pain, reach to touch my forehead, and—

My hand. I stare at it. Surface-level burns cover my fingers, angry-looking welts, but they don't hurt. Not particularly.

My eyes widen. My other hand is the same.

The lightening. The storm.

I frown. I'm drenched. Rain? It rained? I don't remember rain. And it's not raining now.

Not her as well.

Caia-Lu's voice rings through the air, broken, fragmented. I frown. I saw her… I did.

No. I look around. I'm the only one here.

I can't have. I was hallucinating. But her, of all people? The elderly Seer back at the village I was born in?

I blink and look down at my body. My bare arms, my jean-covered legs. And I frown.

What happened? Was I walking back to Amelia and Renee? There was the storm…and lightning.

Lightning.

I was hit by *lightning.*

And I'm alive.

I swear under my breath. No. I wouldn't be alive. I look at my arms. No new marks on them, or burns. Lightning would burn more than just my hands, wouldn't it? And surely my hands would be agony? But they're not.

There's a ringing in my ears, and I bend my fingers, make a fist. It barely even hurts.

I frown, then take a deep breath. Whatever happened, I need to move.

I pull myself up, see the truck. The white truck. The Amorak. I stare at it for a moment, grounding myself as everything comes back.

Yes. The assassins. Those new ones. I killed them,

and I saw Elf.

I push my hair behind my ears. A few tufts of it seem different. A more brittle texture, or shorter. Something. I frown, confused.

Damn, I must look a mess.

I take a deep breath, then look around properly. How long have I been lying here? I need to get back.

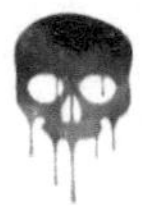

The Amorak's engine roars as I drive it through the woods, only stopping for a few minutes to fill up our water bottles and place them next to the assassins' supplies in the truck bed.

When I pull the truck into the clearing where Falkes and the others are, they point weapons at me—and this is me being nice, not leaving them to get killed by the Enhanced? Huh.

Through the grimy windscreen, my gaze catches on the gun in Renee's grip. Think it's the Kimber Eclipse Custom II. Next to her, Amelia holds a knife. Her Glock is tucked into my belt.

I snort and stop the truck, its brakes squealing like a spirit. I throw the door open and jump out, only wincing slightly as the backs of my legs ache.

"You can put those weapons down," I yell, and I feel better now, almost back to normal. The drive back pretty much cleared any remaining dazed feelings from my head.

Renee and Amelia lower their weapons. I don't hear whatever it is that Falkes says to Lexa because my truck's engine is still running. With my confused state, I'd had a little trouble getting it started after I'd found the keys in one of the dead men's pockets, but the Amorak clearly needs a good service. Given that we should all be leaving here very soon, I won't turn the engine off.

Minnow and Lexa lower their weapons too. The two boys hide behind Minnow's long skirt, their eyes wide. Stephen lowers his gun a moment later, his eyes clearly showing his interest in my new truck. Only Falkes remains as he was, his firearm trained on me.

See? He wants to kill you. You're a fool for returning.

"Where the hell did you get that?" Falkes barks. Whether he's talking about the truck or the gun in my hand, I don't know.

"Were those gunshots yours?" Amelia asks. Her eyes hold hurt—that I'd taken her gun without her permission, and, for a fraction of a second, I feel bad. She's always saying to me that I just need to ask.

Then I push that thought away. Just because Amelia's one of the only people who has overlooked my past and is nice to me, doesn't mean I owe her anything. I need to remember that, get that into my head. And, anyway, she knew where I was going.

I nod. "Yes. I killed some Enhanced Ones." The lie comes easily, and it's better to say that than who they really were.

"There are Enhanced *nearby*?" Minnow asks. She touches the end of her braid—a nervous habit.

"Not anymore," I say. "Anyway. I packed up their supplies. They're in the back." I point to the pick-up's bed. "Along with our water. And don't worry, I've checked the vehicle for tracking devices." I pause, remember how it took me longer than normal to check it all. I kept forgetting what needed checking. Because of the lightning? But I *can't* have been hit by lightning.

"So we're good to go," I continue. "We ready? Amelia, you riding with me?" I look toward her, feel the sense that I need to appeal to her, get rid of the hurt in her eyes.

"Woah. Hold on," Falkes says. "We don't need another vehicle."

"You're turning it down, really?" My gaze is scathing, but I look past him, at the evening sky. It's a strange color—a darkened streak runs across it. I frown. Is the Turning close after all? Was that what that little storm was about? A warning of the danger that is to come?

"Twice the amount of fuel," Falkes says. "Twice everything."

"Everything?"

"Engine oil, pure water, all the maintenance. We've got a perfectly good vehicle we can all use."

"Then let me worry about this one." I flex my fingers. "It's my truck." I need a vehicle of my own, if Falkes and Stephen *are* planning to kill me. I doubt Minnow and Lexa would do anything, and I know Amelia and Renee wouldn't, so the men are the two to watch. "Now are we leaving or what?"

Falkes doesn't look happy. But this is brilliant. One of the assassins' trucks. I cannot stop smiling as I get back in the Amorak's driver's seat. God, even the seats are comfy.

And it's mine. This is my truck. I feel a connection to it as I breathe in the air of the truck. Sure, it's a bit damp-smelling. And it smells of them—the assassins, but it's a smell only I can detect. I learned that long ago when I killed one of Bridie's men, shot him dead inside his car. Renee had been with me, and she'd been nervous but had checked the vehicle over as we discussed whether we should take it. I'd thought the interior smelled bad, but she couldn't detect anything. In the end, when we returned minus the car as it was a wreck, Amelia put down the strange smell that only I could smell to all that I've been through. That and some souls are more intuitive than others.

Amelia climbs into the passenger seat next to me. It takes her a moment because there's no running board on that side—been taken off for some reason— and she's old. She grimaces a little as she sits, and I watch as she shuts the door, her hand shaking with the effort. She leans her stick against her legs, and the door behind me opens. In the mirror, I see Renee sliding in.

"How many were there?" Amelia asks as she settles into the seat. She reaches for the seatbelt, then finds it's been cut away. They all have, apart from the driver's, and I'm not sure why the assassins would do that. We didn't used to. But a lot of the interior of the Amorak is in bad nick.

"Four." My voice is low. I stare at my hands on the wheel. My skin is dried and cracked around the burns, but there's a smudge of blood on my left thumb. My own blood, from the burns? But it doesn't look right.

"And how many is that now?" Renee asks. In the rear-view mirror, I can see she's taking off her hiking boots. She groans, and I get ready for her to complain about the legroom in the back. Out of our whole group, Renee's the tallest.

I shrug. "I don't know how many of the new recruits I've killed."

It's just the originals I keep count of. And with Renee, well, I can never tell how she truly feels about me killing the assassins. Amelia is always quick to say those men and women deserve to die whenever they come up in conversation, but Renee is quieter, less easy to read. Maybe part of her agrees with Falkes—that I shouldn't kill them, because they're Untamed, even if they are bad.

The minibus's engine chugs to life, sounds even rougher than usual. A quick glance tells me Falkes is in the driver's seat. Minnow, Lexa, Stephen, and the boys are inside with him, and he points at me then makes some complicated gesture.

"He means you're to follow him and not lead," Amelia tells me.

I grunt. "I'll do what I want."

But I keep my place behind the minibus. I need to think, work out where I want Falkes's group to go next. Of course, I could go off on my own after the assassins, now I've got a truck, but it pays to have other Untamed around. I glance at Amelia—especially someone trained in medicine and healing. And Falkes and Lexa are decent shots.

I've got a map, Bridie's map. I left her clutches with it, right after I killed her. She'd marked the various assassins' camps with little red crosses, but, in the last two years, I've led Falkes's group around those and taken out every assassin I could find. The remaining assassins aren't sticking to known places. Makes sense really. I think of what Hunter said: they know someone is searching for them, killing them.

A smile tugs across my lips.

In the minibus's back window, the two boys press their faces against the glass, so their noses go all upturned.

I curl my fingers into claws and give them a small wave.

They duck down.

Amelia tuts. "They're still terrified of you, you know. And all this killing doesn't help."

"Killing the Enhanced is what keeps us alive." I give her a look as I steer the truck forward, one foot ready on the brake. Falkes has an annoying—and dangerous— habit of braking suddenly, when he doesn't need to, and crashing into the minibus is the last thing I need. Wouldn't exactly make them like me more—not that that's important anyway.

"Yes," Renee says. "If they *are* Enhanced."

"And I'll have my Glock back, thank you," Amelia says.

I let out a soft laugh, as I pull it from my belt and pass it to her.

"You know, would've been safer if you'd given it back to Ma when you weren't driving," Renee says, but her voice is light.

We drive on. None of us speaks any more, but the atmosphere feels nice. Soft. Welcoming.

I look around the interior of the truck. The three of us could just drive off... I wouldn't have to say goodbye to Amelia and Renee then. Just take them with me.

No. I can't take them away from their group. I can't. I am trying to be a good person.

But Falkes wants to kill me. But how *would* he kill me? He's weak. I'm an assassin.

No. It's just talk.

"Hey." Renee's voice is tipped with excitement. "Are these heated seats?"

Amelia reaches for the control panel. "That they are."

"Whack it on then," Renee says. I catch her grin in the rear-view mirror.

"Think it's only the front seats," Amelia says, eyeing one of the broken control panels. "And they might not work. Doesn't look the best of conditions in here."

"Still beats the bus any day."

"And it's ours," I say.

Ours? Don't you mean it's yours? *You'll have to drive off and leave them if you're not bringing them with you.*

I grip the wheel harder. But....

And that's why you shouldn't have let yourself become close to them. That's why—

Amelia screams.

I jolt. Red lights, the minibus. It's braking. Hard.

I slam my foot on the truck's brake, fly forward with the momentum. The seatbelt grabs me around the neck, sharp pain, and—

Amelia screams as she's thrown forward, and I throw my arm out, try to stop her hitting the windscreen, end up jabbing her in the ribs. Weight hits the back of my seat—Renee.

Tires screech, metal on metal. We're not going to stop in time.

I wrench the wheel to the left. Gravel flies up. More metal on metal, scraping and—

We slam to a halt, next to the minibus.

"What the hell is Falkes playing at?" I yell and—

And then I see it—what's in the road.

A shape.

A body.

My heart quickens.

Amelia looks at me. "Did you do this?"

"No." It's not one of mine. It's a woman. Her hair is long and glossy, looks like liquid tar spilling on the ground illuminated by our headlights in the almost dark.

I look to the right. Minnow's in the passenger seat at the front of the minibus, and she gestures for me to wind down my window. We're a foot apart, if that.

I wind it down, and Falkes leans toward me, pushing Minnow back with his arm.

"Why the hell were you driving so close?"

I stare at him. "You're asking me *this* when someone is lying in the road?" I gesture at the body. The woman.

I open my door, bang it against the minibus as I get out. Falkes yells at me, but I'm not listening.

I'm running, skidding. The ground is wet—wet with blood.

Blood.

I skid to a stop, shingle flying up and onto the woman.

She's not moving, face-down in a pool of blood, black hair fanned out. Her dark arms stick out at angles that aren't natural.

Behind, I hear a vehicle door slamming shut.

"Inga, get back!" Renee shouts.

But I ignore her and look at the body. The back of the woman's head.

"Untamed or Enhanced?" I ask her, as I reach out. One hand with the pistol, the other bare. I touch the woman's shoulder. Warm.

I flinch, then tell myself to get a grip.

Untamed or Enhanced?

I roll her over. Her left arm slaps into the blood, sends splatters over me and—

Eyes open. Untamed. No mirrors.

And....

Tattoos on her face. Circles and a crow in electric blue.

THIS VICIOUS WAY

My own skin prickles.
A skull for graduation.
A circle for each important kill.
A bird for the status of an aunt.
No… No….
My mouth dries.
It's *Oleta.*

I CAN'T MOVE. I'M STARING at her.

Oleta. Oleta is *here*.

That's…that's….

She can't be….

She blinks. She's *alive* and—

"Move," Amelia barks at me as she hobbles to my side.

I stare at her. Her medicine bag hangs from her arm, making her stance lopsided. She's out of the truck? When did she get out of the truck?

Amelia turns and shouts at Falkes and Lexa who are also out of the bus, standing in front of its harsh headlights. The tips of their shadows drip into Oleta's blood.

I back away. Oleta is *here*.

"Inga, come back over here." Renee's voice is too loud, as usual, and I flinch a little.

My heart pounds. Hunter expected to find Oleta. But he found me. But Oleta *is* here. Petra was right?

Petra was never wrong when I knew her. My vision blurs, and I step back again. The trees. Those woods? I bring a hand to my chest, try to quieten my heart as I recall where the site is that I murdered Hunter at. Oh Gods. Yes, if I hadn't been there and he'd kept walking in the direction he was going, he would have found Oleta.

I look back at Oleta, on the ground. Amelia does her best to lean over Oleta's body, but the woman's old. She leans heavily on her stick, using it for balance as she tries to crouch.

Oleta's foot moves, and I think she's trying to get away or fight or something—only she's weak, can barely move. I stare at her trembling foot. Like her arms, her ankle is tattooed with blue circles, the marks of many important kills visible under the wash of blood. My own skin burns as I stare at them, as if my tattoos can tell that more are near. Magnets, drawn together. It's been a long time since I've looked at these symbols on another and *not* wanted to kill the person. The originals and newcomers all have them, but Oleta's got far more. She always had the most, was rewarded more often than anyone else by Bridie. Even more than I was, despite me being superior by the end.

I jolt. Oleta's not wearing shoes… She's not wearing *anything*. And the blood—she's covered. What *the hell* happened to her?

I feel sick. The blood. It's the blood. I can taste it. And it's not right. I shouldn't be reacting like this. I'm one of Bridie's Assassins. I kill people. I see bodies all the time.

No. I *was* one of Bridie's Assassins.

But I still am. It's *who* I am. I know that and—

"Hell, no." Falkes shakes his head as he strides toward Oleta, and the movement jolts my full attention to him. "Amelia, get away from her."

Amelia turns, her eyes narrowed. "This woman is injured."

"No," Falkes says, and he's pointing at her arms—the marks on them are clear, despite the blood. "She's one of *them*. We're not taking another." He glances at me for a moment. "Leave her."

"Leave her?" I nearly explode. "What the *hell*, Falkes? She's injured, she's—she could die and—"

And she's *Oleta*.

I push past him, kneel next to Amelia, look at Oleta's face. It's her. Really her. My heart does a stuttery thing that makes me feel sick and—

Oleta's eyes widen as she locks onto my gaze. Recognition? She remembers me?

Of course she remembers you. What you did was....

She opens her mouth, but only a rasping sound comes out, then her face twists in a grimace. Her breathing deepens, grating and heavy.

"What's happening to her?" I stare at Amelia.

"Possibly blood is in her lungs," she says, her voice crisp. "Renee, can you get my other bag?"

"What are we doing?" Lexa asks, stepping forward. She massages the back of her neck for a second, then pushes her spiky hair away from her forehead. She's got tattoos on one arm—normal tattoos. Not signs of monstrosity. "We can't stay out here. Whatever's injured her could be watching us."

Whatever's injured her? I stare at Lexa, aghast. She's talking like it's a monster that's attacked Oleta. That's half-killed her. Not a person. But it has to be a person, doesn't it? I breathe deeply. Those new assassins I killed—did they do this? Was their group bigger than five? Had they already sent others out to look for Hunter before I got there? Maybe there are more assassins in the area now, alive? Ones who did this to Oleta.

Brighid.

The roof of my mouth dries. Realistically, Brighid is the only assassin—original or not—who I can imagine could take out Oleta. I only met her once—a cloaked and deadly figure—but she's the one who's going to be problematic for me, when I find her. Not easy like the others.

So did Brighid find her and did Oleta refuse to join our old group? Or maybe it was Zak and Clara who found her? Together, they'd probably equal Oleta's skills, and if Oleta was already weak or injured….

But why didn't Oleta heal herself? I'd have thought that would be instinct, self-preservation? Healing is her Seer power, and it's the obvious thing to use. Unless there were children with her and she didn't want to risk harming them, due to the side effects of her powers. Even the most hardened assassins aren't heartless all the time. And if Oleta's haunted by what happened before, even to half the extent I am, there's no way she'd heal herself if—

Something explodes behind us.

I whirl around. "What the—"

The air's suddenly hazy, thick with smoke and debris and flying fragments. Grit hits me, stings my arms. I blink, vision grainy as I try to see. Is something on fire?

A loud creak sounds. Wood. I inhale sharply. The trees. See them on the left, partly glowing orange. Embers and—

They're going to fall!

"Back in the bus!" Falkes yells at Lexa, and—

A gunshot cuts him off.

I blanch, duck and throw my weight down, try to work out what is happening. I lift my head up, tasting sand at the back of my mouth. My heart pounds as I scan the area. Who's got the gun?

"Under fire!" Amelia yells.

My head spins.

Oleta.

My heart hammers. A distraction. She's a distraction. No!

I turn my head. The bus. The boys. Is this the assassins' new plan? Because we had loads of plans, ways we'd distract Untamed groups so we could get their children.

But the assassins are not getting Johnny and Callum.

I jump up, run back to the minibus. Grit slaps against my legs, and the air feels wrong. I see Minnow inside the bus, with the boys. Both of them. Johnny and Callum. Still there.

I breathe a sigh of relief, but I don't understand. Oleta's not bait? This isn't a ruse?

Something shrieks, a high-pitched whine, and heat blasts over my back. I turn to see the blazing trees falling. Orange sparks jump into the sky. And there's more, more trees burning. They're going to fall, spread more flames, and—

"Enhanced!" Lexa screams.

Enhanced. Poison runs through my blood at the name.

My neck cracks as I look to the right. And—and they're *here*. The Enhanced Ones loom up. Six of them. The soulless beings who are taking over humanity, trying to wipe us out because they think a life with no negative emotions is better. Their mirror eyes—the signs of those who take augmenters—flash.

Our enemy is on the right, the burning trees on the left. They think they've trapped us, think we'll surrender with nowhere to run. But I feel it—feel the training Bridie had drilled into me. The urge to kill the Enhanced. Because that's my purpose, that's what I'm made for: killing the Enhanced.

My hand slaps against my belt. The movement is automatic: reaching for a weapon. But there's nothing there. Amelia's got her Glock now. But I don't need weapons to kill them. My bare hands are enough and—

A Seer would've foreseen an attack.

I inhale sharply. Falkes and the others—they're going to know, have any suspicions confirmed. And they're not moving. Just standing there, while Enhanced Ones are approaching. With guns they shouldn't have.

The Enhanced don't believe in violence—or at least that's what they say. But we steal our guns from them. Supposedly they have them for sports. But, well, this proves otherwise.

They're full of lies.

"Run!" I scream at my group. Sparks fall over me, burn my skin. I hiss, my arms jolting as I try to get

Falkes's attention. "Get in the truck."

If they're quick, they can drive back around the way we came, before those trees catch fire too. And they have to get away. In a close-up fight with the enemy, they'd be useless. I pull in a quick breath, do the calculations. Can I get Oleta to safety before the Enhanced reach us? Get her in the truck bed and make sure my group's safely in our vehicles and away, before I kill the Enhanced? Kill them right here, push them into the flaming trees, and get away myself?

"Leave the woman!" Falkes shouts.

Oleta. *No.*

My head spins. The Enhanced are closing in us, but they're not fast ones, these. Haven't taken the right augmenters. And that gives us time. Gives me time.

"Get her in the truck!" I yell, and I run—run toward Oleta and the Enhanced Ones' figures behind her. I can do this, if I'm quick.

"Surrender, Untamed Ones!" a voice yells.

"Inga, no! Leave her!" Falkes screams at me. I don't know why he cares about me getting caught. He wants me dead. Or maybe he doesn't want me converted. I'd be a deadly Enhanced One, even though the enemy is supposedly against violence. "It's a trap!"

A trap. But it can't be. Oleta's Untamed and—and the boys are still safe and it's the Enhanced Ones who are here, not the assassins.

I can't think. Too much is going on.

But the Enhanced can't get us. Can't get her. I won't let them. Oleta's part of my family. My assassin family. And I won't let the Enhanced Ones force an augmenter—a vial of colorful liquid—down her throat that will convert her into one of them. We've killed too many Enhanced to join them easily.

I slip my hands under her shoulders, drag Oleta back two feet or so as she screams and tries to wriggle. Smoke billows toward us, gets in my eyes. My vision burs as my eyes smart, sting.

"Inga!" Amelia screams.

A gunshot sounds—another one. They're using guns. They're not supposed to use guns.

Lexa shrieks as the Enhanced shout at us. I catch glimpses of guns flashing in the light before there's rapid gunfire. But it's both ways this time. Falkes has got his gun. And Stephen and Lexa.

Damn fools. What are they doing? They're not trained for this. They need to give me the weapons and run and—

The Amorak's headlights blind me as I drag Oleta with me. Her skin is slippery with blood. Then Renee's at my side, helping me lift her. We run the last few feet to the truck with her, duck down just in time to avoid a barrage of bullets, then throw Oleta into the truck bed. She's not moving now, completely limp.

"Why are they using guns?" Lexa screams. "They shouldn't use guns!"

"Give me your gun!" I yell, twisting around, see her in the front of my truck. I may be able to kill with my bare hands, but I'm not stupid. Guns are preferable.

"Just get in!" Renee shoves me up at the truck bed.

"No! Got to kill them!" I twist, shove her back. "Give me a gun!"

"No, you've got to stay alive and with us," Renee hisses, then she pushes me over the side of the truck.

Her action catches me off guard, and the edge of the truck wall scrapes my stomach and chest hard, knocks breath from me, then I'm in the truck bed, too, next to Oleta. Landed on my shoulder. Pain grabs me, and, for several seconds, it's all I can concentrate on.

No, get a grip.

I fight it, sit up, crash into something. Containers. Our water containers. And the assassins' supplies.

"Inga?" Renee's holding onto Oleta. Not much space with the three of us in here and all the supplies.

I pull myself to the edge of the truck bed, look out. Three of the Enhanced are running after us. Only three? Did we kill the others?

But killing three isn't enough.

"Give me a pistol! I can shoot from here!" I shout at Renee.

"No," she yells. "What's happened to your head?"

"What?" I reach up, touch something wet and sticky on the side of my face. But I can't concentrate on that now. The vehicle lurches forward, rumbles, faster and faster. "Where's Amelia?"

"The bus," Renee pants. "Is her bag in here? I don't know what to do for this woman."

For Oleta....

I stare at her. She's still not moving. More wetness slides down my head.

If Amelia's in the bus, then who's driving my truck? I twist, look through the window of the back of the cab, see short spiky hair. Lexa. But—the bus? Where is it? I can't see it. Amelia and Falkes and Minnow and the boys? Stephen? Did he get out of the bus at all? I can't remember seeing him. But he hides when he's scared and—

Headlights, suddenly on my right. Another vehicle. The minibus? No—there's a rumbling to the left too. Shit. The Enhanced have a vehicle here too.

Something hits the metalwork on the opposite side of the truck bed. Oleta screams. She's conscious again, and her eyes latch on me.

"What the hell?" she says, and her voice is the same. Low and gruff, and I don't know why I'm focused on that, when we're being chased and there are Enhanced after us and—

Oleta's eyes widen as she looks down at my leg.

My leg.

I become aware of the pain in my left leg. My thigh. Blood. So much blood. More than what's running down the side of my face.

I see the bullet embedded in the side of my thigh. Red and raw, just like when I was nine. When I saw my flesh like that, when... Gods, what had happened? I can't think.

My breath comes in sharp bursts. Oleta was there

and Bridie was arguing with her, trying to get her to heal me.

My vision fogs. Someone else was there, weren't they? I don't know.

Then I see no more.

"Inga? Inga?"

I blink. A shape above me. Oval.

Gradually, it turns into the outline of Amelia's head. Her eyes appear, then her nose, and her mouth.

"Inga? Inga, can you hear me?"

I blink through the pain and—

It comes back to me, all at once.

I jolt, sit up. I'm on a foil blanket, on coarse grass. "Where are the boys? Are the boys okay?" My lips are too heavy, so hard to move them. Can't tell if I got the words out....

"It's okay. They're fine," Amelia says. She's sitting in one of our fold-up chairs, her stick balanced against its arm. "We all got away."

All.

All of us. I breathe a sigh of relief. Then I look down at my leg. Thick, bloody bandages wind around my left thigh. My jeans have been cut away around it— the denim hangs loose below my knee, only attached to the rest of the leg on one side. One of my walking boots has gone.

I look at my hands. The burns from the lightning seem more prominent. Or maybe these are new burns, from those sparks and the burning trees.

"Well, Falkes got shot," Amelia says. "But Oleta's healing him now. Incredible Seer powers. She says she'll heal you after him—he insisted he was first." Her gaze is dark, but I don't think it's because of

Falkes's decision. No, Amelia's been displaced as the healer by someone who doesn't have to rely on herbs and first aid.

The *healer*.

My expression slackens. No. Oleta… She can't heal, she….

I struggle forward, crawling, nearly blind with pain and—

"What is it?" Amelia asks.

"Stop!" I yell at Falkes. Can see his figure and a person in front of him, twenty feet from me. *Oleta.* "Stop! Oleta!"

I move faster than I thought I'd be able to, but it's not fast enough.

Falkes turns and looks at me, and I see past him, into Oleta's eyes. Oleta—perfect now. Not injured, not….

I'm too late. Falkes's wound is barely there.

I shake my head, back away. Waves of pain threaten to take me, and I look at Oleta. I see it in her eyes.

No… No!

But it's already started.

"Yes, Oleta's a Seer," I say to Amelia and Falkes, my voice low. "Like me. Only she can heal as well."

"I have heard that healing *is* a rare Seer power," Amelia says.

I nod. I'm lying on the ground, exhausted and in pain. My leg is on fire, and my words are labored. Above, the clouds are moving too fast, and it makes me dizzy. "But when Oleta uses her healing powers, other things happen."

I turn my head. Minnow's standing a little way away with the children, and I think Lexa's in the minibus with Oleta and Stephen. Oleta wasn't happy when I told her to stop healing Falkes, and neither was Falkes, even though she'd apparently already finished, but I told Falkes it was important. I used my Inga the Killer voice and was ready to use my Seer card, but they listened.

"Other things?" Falkes frowns.

"Really bad things. Like—like earthquakes. Bad ones."

"Coincidence. Seer powers can't affect tectonic plate movement," Falkes says, and he says it like he knows. So confidently, it annoys me, because he can't possibly comprehend the fact that he *can't* know something. Even though he's pretty ignorant to life.

"And other stuff too. Things would—people would die." *Children* would die. They'd get sick. I've seen it happen. "Look," I say. "I'm a Seer. You shouldn't doubt me on this, believe me."

"Believe you?" Falkes's eyebrows lift up until they seem to touch his hairline. "You didn't warn us of that attack."

"Seers don't see everything," I say. Irritation fills me and I'm staring at my bird tattoo. A snowy owl, on my right arm, given to me when I became the best assassin and took over the role of aunt for band three. I've never liked the owl's eyes—the only part of the tattoo that's in gold, rather than the usual blue. These eyes see too much, and they make sure I know it.

"But they should." Falkes's glare has meaning.

"You're changing the subject." I turn my arm, so the owl isn't watching me and try not to show I'm flustered. "*Oleta*. Oleta is what we need to focus on. And her powers. She mustn't use them. It's too dangerous."

"The Gods and Goddesses and spirits wouldn't give Oleta powers if they harmed our children," Falkes says. "No Seers' powers are harmful to us."

"What about the Enhanced Ones' Seers? They use their powers against us." And it makes me angry, even thinking about their Seers, because all the Enhanced

Ones' Seers were originally Untamed Seers. The only way to get Seer powers is to be Untamed—the Gods and Goddesses and spirits wouldn't gift an Enhanced One with the abilities. But there's no guarantee that Untamed Seers won't be converted by the Enhanced into one of their own—or that the Untamed Seer won't willingly surrender to the enemy.

"But they're not *Untamed*," Falkes says.

"But *all* Seer powers are unpredictable." I fold my arms. "There are side effects. Damn it, the powers come from the Gods, Goddesses, and spirits—and you know the spirits attack us. And—" I lower my voice. "Oleta's not stable."

No one with Rijikarii energy is. But her powers are bad. They mustn't be used. We found out that the hard way, under Bridie's command.

At first, Oleta's healing powers were great. They didn't seem to affect anyone at all. But then the littles started to get ill. It was just colds and sniffles at first—until it wasn't. Until it was much worse than that, and every time Oleta healed someone, those particular children would get worse.

Until they died.

I look toward where Minnow is now sitting with her boys. She's rubbing her neck a lot, looks pained.

"Oleta using her powers could affect Johnny and Callum," I say, and, again, I tell Falkes and Amelia what I know.

"Just a coincidence," Falkes says.

"You want to risk this?" I stare at him. "You want to ignore what a Seer is telling you?"

"Risk it?" Falkes snorts, looking toward the bus. "There's nothing to risk. Oleta is safe."

Anger unfurls in me. It's taken me years to get to this level with Falkes, and Oleta's already got him defending her? Already?

I look back at the bus, and I see her. Oleta's now sitting on the steps of the minibus's open doorway. She's curvy and feminine. Her hair looks well-looked-after, glossy, and she's got big eyes. Her top is lowcut and her skirt is short.

Oh.

I feel sick as I look at Falkes. "You've got no chance with her. And if you're thinking her healing powers can't be harmful because she's beautiful, that's just wrong. You'd put all of us in danger."

"Danger?" He raises his eyebrows. "Inga, I think you are jealous."

"Jealous?"

"Because she is pretty and a Seer. And you are ugly and a Seer." His lips curl in a smile of sorts.

"And you *hate* assassins." I glare at him.

He shrugs slightly. "Maybe it's just *you* I hate. You killed Vincent." Fire glows in his eyes. "But she didn't. Oleta has a clean slate in my eyes, and we'd be stupid to ignore her healing powers. Those could be invaluable."

A clean slate? I never had a clean slate. Never. The moment Falkes saw me, he'd decided. And maybe it *was* that very first moment that did it because I was screaming and covered in blood and vowing to kill them all. I was messed up. I'd been surviving on my own for three years after escaping Bridie's group. All Untamed groups I'd come across had rejected me as soon as they saw Bridie's marks on me. They all hate the assassins because they take their children. No one trusted me. Some Untamed even tried to shoot me before I had a chance to speak, and it had made me distrustful.

I'd been determined to survive on my own, but then I'd become feverish. I needed a healer. Needed medicine. And I stumbled upon Falkes's group.

Right from that first day, Amelia and Renee saw something in me—even though my delirium had me threatening them all, saying I'd kill them if they didn't heal me. Thus, my first interactions with Falkes weren't my calmest moments. But Falkes's first glimpse of Oleta was nothing like that. She was unconscious, naked, harmless, injured, and beautiful.

But even dangerous ones have quiet moments, and this is wrong. Bad. I can feel it.

I turn to Amelia, my eyes begging her. Falkes just wants to use Oleta, but Amelia's fair. She has to be.

"We will keep an eye on the situation," she says.

An eye on the situation? I want to scream. What use is that?

"Now, I need to check the oil in the bus," Falkes says.

I watch him leave.

"You know, you could've stuck up for me," I mutter to Amelia.

"Inga, I pick my battles with Falkes carefully. As should you."

I lift my arms up, then drop them. "But this isn't right. Her being here. She's an assassin. She's one of Bridie's."

"But so were you. And we gave you a chance."

"This isn't about giving her a chance—because we're doing that. She's with us. This is about her healing powers. You know what Falkes is like, and he's going to use her to heal every little cut and graze now. And it *will* have repercussions." I shake my head.

It's not just Oleta's healing powers that are bugging me. It was what she was like. And sure, Bridie made her like that, just as she made me like it too. But there was something extra about Oleta. She almost *lived* for killing.

But how can I explain this to Amelia without sounding petty? When I get my own buzz from killing? What's the point? Amelia won't get it. Of course she won't. She wasn't there. I breathe out hard.

"Just make sure she doesn't use her healing powers again," I say. "Otherwise bad things are going to happen."

Amelia gives me a look. "Inga, you need to trust that the world isn't as bad as you think it is."

I stare at her and shake my head. The world *is* a bad

place. It's all around us. It's she who's too trusting.

And those who trust too easily are always the first to die.

EIGHT

"IT IS TIME FOR LESSONS." Fi's voice is low, and she rounds up me and the other littles, herds us out into the open area at the side of the camp. "This will be an important lesson, so you must listen carefully. If you fail your lessons it will reflect badly on me. And we don't want to make Mother angry."

I nod and tell Fi I will do my best. The other two littles do the same, but I think they're just saying it because I did.

The littles from bands one and two are also here, but we don't mingle with them. I know that now. We stick to our own bands, our families.

But I look at Fi and then I look at the other littles. They don't feel like family.

Only Oleta and Caro—the highers, the older children in band three who've got the skull tattoos on the backs of their neck—are nice here. They talk to me, and Caro gave me some of his food yesterday while Oleta told me stories about the spirits and the rewards they give to good people.

"Sit down," Fi tells me and the littles.

I sit on the dusty ground, and the other two littles sit next to me. Samira is only four and sucks her thumb. Nathan, the other one, doesn't seem to know how old he is, and it *makes me feel superior.*

"Good, we're all here," a deep voice says.

I look up at the man. I've seen him around the camp. One of the instructors. A couple of days ago, Fi explained who the different adults were, pointing to the instructors, the recruiters, and those on the logistics team. I still don't know what the logistics team is. But it sounds important, and everyone on that team seems to do secret work. Caro said he heard them huddled around the campfire late again last night.

"I am Instructor Mark, and today you will learn an important lesson," the man says.

One of the littles from band two looks like she's going to start crying. A woman frowns at the girl—I think the woman's name is Clara, and she's the aunt of band two because she wears a crown with the number two on it.

Instructor Mark clears his throat. "What you will learn today is a lesson that the Untamed don't tend to teach you until you're much older, and only then if you want to learn it. But we do things differently here. We believe that a lack of skills and insufficient knowledge of self-defense is a death sentence, and all of you have been chosen by Mother to survive." He smiles. "Today, my children, you will learn how to survive. You will learn the first steps in killing the Enhanced Ones."

WE DRIVE FOR AN HOUR or so, Renee steering my truck over rough ground as she follows the minibus, and then we stop. Oleta's done no more healing, thankfully, but my thigh's getting worse. The pain is growing, taking over more and more of me. I stay half-sitting in the truck bed while the others are outside. They're probably going to be talking soon about where we're going to go next, trying to work out which direction to go in, rather than just driving aimlessly, which seems to be what Falkes is currently doing. It's a conversation I should be steering, as I need to find more of the originals—and the newer assassins too—but right now, I can't move. And I hate it. Hate being trapped. And what if Falkes chooses this moment to try and kill me? I won't be able to fight back easily or run.

Is he still going to try and kill me?

I scoot to the left, look over the edge of the truck wall. We're in fairly open land that sweeps down toward a valley. Little cover to speak of, mainly shrubs, not many trees. Just the odd clump.

Falkes is talking to Oleta. She's smiling at him a lot.

She's got some of Lexa's clothes on, but Oleta's bigger, curvier, and the top is too tight. It boosts her breasts up higher.

Anger rolls through me again. Falkes is being so nice to Oleta. And he can *see* her marks. They're all over her arms and face, her marks clearly visible, just like mine.

"How are you now?"

Amelia's voice makes me jump. She's standing at the tailgate, and then puts her medicine bag on top of it. The zip's undone, and I can see all the little bottles and pouches inside.

I pull a face at her that's mostly a grimace. "I've been better. I—I need to see Oleta." I shift my weight, and something digs into the back of my thigh. Renee gave me a pair of her overalls to sit on, but there's something in the pocket. I unzip it, find a small flake of flint.

"Not yet." Amelia's voice is crisp.

"But—"

"No, Inga. I need to look at your wound again first. Sorry. It's going to need cleaning again, and it's going to hurt. Renee's just getting some of the water-purifying tablets from Minnow."

I nod, and my vision fogs over a little. Then Renee's here, and they're unwrapping the bandage.

"Lie back down," Amelia instructs. "You're looking pale again."

I lie back and stare at the sky, at how it's broken by branches. In the distance, I can hear voices—Falkes and the others—and I concentrate on them as I bite through the pain as Amelia and Renee tend to my thigh. But, after a while, their voices fade away, and it's just me and the sky.

There are shapes in the sky. Dusty white clouds flit around, faster and faster, moving back and forth. I watch as the clouds form images.

I smile as a woman's face appears. A woman with kind eyes and blond hair. She smiles and tells me to trust her.

Trust.

Her face looks kind. Beautiful and—

It's my *mother*.

I scream as the full force of the pain hits me.

"Sorry." Renee's eyes are suddenly over me, where my mother was, and....

My mother?

I blink, shake my head, then tense as the pain comes again.

"Just a little more to do." Amelia's voice is distorted, and all I can really hear is the thumping in my head. The pounding. My pulse, too fast, heavy.

I grit my teeth.

"You're doing great," Renee says, and her voice is loud enough to drown out my heartbeat, but then her words become all I can hear. Repeating and repeating, and I'm caught in the echo, trapped, twisted inside it. *You're doing great. You're doing great. You're doing great.*

I can't escape the words. They're everywhere. Haunting me.

Because it's not her voice, not Renee's voice.

It's *Bridie.*

Why didn't I realize? Oh Gods. I normalized it. Thought it was....

And I stare at Renee, at her figure, silhouetted, the evening sun behind her. The sun? But, no, it was already dark and...and it's not Renee, because this woman has longer hair, and her nose is smaller....

She turns to me, and my mouth dries.

Bridie.

Bridie is *here.*

No. She can't be... She....

I open my mouth to scream, but there's something in my throat. My voice is thick, stuffed with feathers, and I'm pulling feathers out of my mouth—so many of them and—

I am running. My thigh is burning, and sweat drips into my eyes, makes them sting. And I'm running,

running away from her.

But she's at the top of your list. You have to kill her.

But she's not at the top of my list, she's not on my list at all. She's already dead. She's—

And I'm running away—I never run away! But I am, I am and I....

"Oh, Tiny Inga, do not be afraid. You don't ever need to fear me."

I turn toward her, and my thigh burns. I see her. Really see her. Not just silhouetted, but in all her depths. Lank, gray hair. Dark eyes. White skin that looks almost shiny. Bridie's lips are painted red, but not very well. The color's smudged around her chin.

It's blood.

I stare at her hand and—an arm. She's holding an arm. A child's arm.

She's eating the....

I swallow hard. My stomach roils.

Run!

"Don't be scared, dear," she whispers. "For I am your mother, and you must never be scared of your mother."

"No!" I scream. "You're not my mother, you're nothing to me—"

"Inga!"

I blink, and Amelia's here, wiping sweat from my forehead with a damp washcloth, and there are spiky branches in the sky above me. We've moved? I don't remember.

I struggle to sit up and Amelia tells me to be careful. It's brighter. The day is....

"You were asleep a long time," Amelia says. "How are you now? The fever's gone down."

A long time? I was asleep a long time? My eyes smart and my vision wobbles. There's a dull ache in the back of my throat. A fever?

"How long?" I ask. I squeeze my eyes shut for a moment. My eyelids feel too heavy.

"Nearly two days."

Two days? I stare at her. No. It can't be… It was only minutes. An hour, at the most.

"Are you in much pain with your leg?" Amelia's voice is odd, restrained, and she's not looking at me. Not making eye contact.

"Uh, not like before." I look at my leg. My jeans have gone, and I'm wearing leggings, over what appears to be the shape of a bandage. My nostrils wrinkle. Minnow's leggings. The ones she wears under her long skirts when it's cold.

At least the jumper I've got on is my own. And my own boots too—both of them, this time.

"Good," Amelia says. "I suggest you just rest."

"Is Oleta still here? What's happening? I need to see her."

"Oleta is still here, but she's busy helping Johnny and Callum. Now, Inga, don't do anything to annoy Falkes."

"What? Annoy Falkes?" I raise my eyebrows. "Why would I do that?"

"I mean it." She hunches forward a little, as if she's trying to disappear into her huge cardigan. It's the one she always wears, and stains cling to its fibers. "I overheard him and Stephen talking about stabbing you. I told them exactly what I thought of that, and I don't think they're going to hurt you—"

"Oh, it's okay. I can handle myself."

"You can't when you're unconscious. And they could've got you easily." She gives me a stern look.

I yawn, then straighten my back. "It's fine. They won't do it. They've been talking about it since I killed the man Stephen found, and they've done nothing. Haven't got the balls."

Her eyes narrow. "You never said anything."

"Because they're not actually going to do it," I say.

She frowns. "Your life isn't something you should play with. Don't annoy them. I mean that. Oh, and stay out of Stephen's way completely. He's still shaken up from the ambush by the Enhanced Ones.

Always thinks he's going to suddenly see his mother, Enhanced, coming for her him."

I frown. Yeah. I remember the last time we encountered Enhanced. Maybe four months ago. Stephen behaved really weirdly afterward, and I heard him tell Falkes that he'd had nightmares in the days after about his now-Enhanced mother turning up and forcibly converting him. Falkes had tried to comfort him, pointing out that they didn't know what had happened to his mother, that they had no proof she'd been taken and converted. And it wasn't likely anyway. After all, the Enhanced wouldn't have only taken one Untamed woman from the group. They'd have been greedy, taken everyone. And Stephen's mother just disappeared one day, so I'm told.

"Okay, but what else has been happening?" I ask Amelia.

She shakes her head. "Nothing for you to worry about." And then she disappears.

I must still be losing time, and I blink, shake my head, as if I can shake the problem away. Shake away the badness.

I breathe deeply. I'm sitting up, and I stare at my leg, then check under the leggings. The bandages are tinged pink and a sickly yellow color. I peel back the outer layer, see something sticky and pale oozing out. One of Amelia's poultices. A vague memory of her applying it flits through me. That was earlier, wasn't it? It takes a few moments for its smell to reach my nostrils, and then I grimace. It's not pleasant.

"That's going to take ages to heal, you know."

I look up. Oleta's leaning over the side of the truck. Her black hair is dead straight and falls in a glossy curtain down the inside of the truck bed. She rests her arms horizontally on the edge of the wall and props her chin on her wrists. The posture draws attention to the glowing ink of the crow on her left upper arm. Each aunt got a different bird, one that suited their personality, according to Bridie. The crow is a good fit for Oleta, a symbol of bad luck, death, and intelligence.

Oleta's eyes fix on me, and I suddenly feel inadequate as she looks me up and down. I pull my leggings back up. Oleta always looked so perfect—even as a child. And that hasn't changed.

Oleta. The girl who tried to usurp Gweneira by being my sister.

But Oleta *was* my sister—I know that. Sister, of sorts. She was there, all those years.

She kept an eye on me when I was young. She would call me Little Sister. And I'd feel safe, in a way. Sure, there were the years we hated each other, fought constantly, and tried to hurt each other without Bridie finding out—but there was also the final year. The year we came together to take Bridie out of the equation.

We were close. We had to be to survive. But I still hate that I think of Oleta as my sister now. Sister, in a way.

That's the complicated thing about family when it spreads beyond blood: you get all these extra relations, and they compete for your loyalty, when the only ones who should truly have it are those you're related to by blood. My loyalty should only be to Gweneira and my mother. My cousins, too.

Blood is stronger. That's what I told myself after I left the assassins. I wouldn't construct a new family as then I'd be forming connections and loyalties that aren't based on blood, making myself vulnerable to others' bad intentions. Blood is the only thing that can keep me safe—my own family—and everyone should be careful about who they let in.

I didn't want another substitute family, people who could hurt me, but then I got Amelia and Renee. Their blood isn't toxic, not like Bridie's, so maybe I was lucky there, even if Falkes and the others aren't the kindest.

But now Oleta's here. She's a reminder of my assassin family, a reminder of the monstrosity. How much poison has her blood absorbed that will now try and seep into my blood? Seep into Amelia's and Renee's and the others'? Because she's worse than me.

But she's also like me, and no matter what I tell myself, I know Oleta's part of my family still. I made the decision to save her from the Enhanced, to bring her into my new family. And it wasn't even a decision I had to think about.

"You're going to be out of action a while, Inga." Oleta's voice has a slight drawl to it. "You sure you don't want me to heal it?"

My eyes narrow. "How can you risk it? You know what happens when—"

"I've got a better grip on my powers now. It's safe." She laughs. "No one's been sick since I healed Falkes, have they?"

I shake my head. "But it's not a risk I'm willing to take."

She rolls her eyes. "So, you'd rather be useless in an attack then?"

"I'm not useless."

"Oh, yes. Because you're a Seer. When *are* you going to tell this group that's a lie?" She raises her eyebrows. "It's been so interesting hearing about you from them, but surely they're going to wonder why you've never used any Seer powers? Especially if we get attacked." She lifts her palm and a ball of white light bulbs in it. "This is a pretty handy attacking power. Every Seer has it, I'm told."

I glare at her. "I *am* a Seer."

"Sure." She laughs.

"No, really, I am."

She snorts. "The Gods and Goddesses wouldn't choose you. Not when you've killed Untamed. I mean, if they *were* choosing now, they wouldn't even choose me, and I've killed less than you."

She stares at me, a challenge in her eye. She can't know I've been killing the assassins across the last years, can she? But we both know who the first Untamed I killed was.

I shrug. "Well, the Gods forgave me. It was for the greater good. And now I'm a Seer."

"A Seer who didn't foresee the Enhanced Ones attacking? Falkes told me all about that. I mean, I did cover for you, but—"

"Seers don't see everything."

"Exactly. That's what I told him."

I size her up. She still looks strong, though she's got more weight on her now. Looks healthier. "What's been happening with you? It's been years."

Her eyebrows are still raised, and she looks like she's been frozen. Then she shakes her head and laughs. "Why?"

"Why do I want to know what's been happening with you?" I frown. "Oleta, we were family." I hate saying the word, but I need to change the subject away from my lie, and I know she thought of us as family.

"No, why *pretend to be a Seer*? You hate Seers." She flicks her hair back.

"No. I don't."

"You hated me." Her eyebrows get even higher.

I shift my weight a little. "How can you think that? I never hated you. Not really." I twist my hands together.

"So, you're jealous of me then?" She snorts. "So jealous you now pretend to *be* me?"

"Not you. Just a Seer." I sigh. "It gives me points here. Among Falkes and the others—but I don't get why you're so focused on this."

"Points? Come on, Inga, you're going to have to explain yourself here—if you want me to keep your secret." Her eyes are sly. "We can always catch up later."

This is a test. Would she really keep my secret?

My sigh gets lower. "Look, if they think I'm a Seer, then I decide where we go. I have that authority— and they're not going to question me or make us go somewhere else."

My shoulders tighten, and the pain from the bullet

thrums through my thigh. Huh. That's the thing about Oleta—she has a way of making people give up their secrets.

"And why would you need to decide where you all go?" There's an angle in her voice that digs under my skin, but this is exactly what she does. If Oleta wants to know something, she finds it out. Just like if she wants something done, it gets done, whether by her hand or not. She steers both conversations and actions when she's got an agenda, and this isn't anything like how I imagined our first talk after finding each other again would be. She has suspicions, her suspicions are nearly always right, and she knows this—she wants me to confirm it.

"You know what I've been doing, don't you?"

Oleta laughs. "It had to be you. I've heard about your work—a lot of people have. News travels fast among Untamed. The *good* Untamed. Ha, not that many will talk to me, but still. I knew it had to be one of us—a former assassin. And some of those deaths, there are only two people who could do those. You or me. And, well, I knew it wasn't me. So, congratulations, Inga, you're the Night Slayer."

I look back at Falkes and the others. They're far enough away, and I lean in close to Oleta. "Is that what they call me?" I snort. "The Night Slayer?"

She grins. "How many have you got then?"

"Twenty-seven originals. Eight more to go. But there's all the new members too."

Interest flickers in her eyes, sharp. "There's only eight of those bastards who tortured us left? Which ones?"

"Brighid, Zak, Clara, Dylan, Taylor, Gabi, Luca, and Mark."

A strange look passes over Oleta's face. "How many new assassins are there?"

"I don't know. The recruits aren't just children now. Many adults have joined. It's not like how it was when we were there." Then, adults didn't join. Not that I knew of anyway. Numbers were boosted by children being recruited and growing up in Bridie's system. She already had her loyal adults.

But *of course* the remaining assassins would have to recruit adults now as well. I wonder what made other Untamed join them.

A shadow falls across Oleta's face as she nods. "Okay." She looks up at me, makes direct eye contact. "Are you going to kill Petra?"

The question throws me, and I shrug. "I'm still undecided. She's not on my list of originals, but it depends on whose side she's on when I encounter her."

A dank taste fills my mouth. Petra is complicated. She didn't hurt us ever, she wasn't like the others, but she didn't escape with us. She didn't even try to leave, just believed she couldn't. Fear meant she chose to stay, to let the assassins use her Seer powers for their own gain. I breathe deeply. Who knows what her current state of mind is or how much brainwashing they've done to her since? She may not even be anything like the girl I remember.

But Petra is also Oleta's sister. Triplets, with their other sister. I don't know how Oleta feels about Petra, who chose to stay and work with the assassins over leaving with us. And it never made sense why she stayed, when it was Petra who helped Oleta and I with the plan that took out Bridie. And it worked—the plan worked. Bridie was dead, so Petra could've left. There was confusion at the camp and plenty of time for Petra to leave with us.

"I'm in," Oleta says.

"In?" I look at her.

She leans in closer, over the truck wall. "You're not the only one of us Bridie ruined. You got the big kill, but I want to wipe those smug smiles off those bastards' faces. I'm joining you, Inga. Two of us together, we've got a better chance of defeating them."

"Hey—my chances have been just fine."

"Doesn't hurt to have someone have your back." She looks down at my leg. "But we really do need to heal you. So, you ready, Inga?"

"Ready?"

She smiles, and then she's climbing into the truck bed next to me. Sympathy is painted on her face, but I can't tell if it's genuine or not. "To be healed. You have to stay still."

I pull back from her, dragging my weight across the truck bed. My shirt snags on something, maybe a nail, and I jolt, then wince as the movement sends a fresh bout of pain through my leg. "No, you're not healing me."

"Well, what else are we going to do?" She glares at me.

"You could answer my questions for starters," I say. "What's happened to you? You looked dead when we found you."

Oleta shrugs. "Think it was a tiger. Something attacked me in the dark. Used my powers, but I didn't think I'd survive. But, anyway, don't change the subject." She waggles her finger at me as she leans against the rolled-up blankets that are strapped against the wall. "You know we have to do this. You're a protector, Inga. Not just because we've got men we need to kill. But these people—the ones you're with now—they count on you to kill for them, to keep them safe. But you can't do that now. You're weak."

Weak.

I don't like being weak. I grit my teeth.

"And there's no risk with me healing you." Oleta smiles. "Not anymore."

"But there is, and it's my choice."

"This is stupid. Look." She points to my right, and I follow her gaze, see Johnny and Callum playing together, with sticks. *Thwack,* as they connect. "See? They're fine. I told you. it's not happening anymore. That was just because I was young, inexperienced at using my powers. I healed Falkes again, last night, and those littles are still alive. Nothing bad happened."

I stare at her, feel blood drain from my face. "You healed Falkes *again*—after everything? How could you risk it?" She did it when I was out of it? Slept for nearly two days… How many other stupid things has she done that I don't yet know about?

"After everything?" Oleta makes a simpering sound. "Always so dramatic, Inga. But, look, it's fine, and we need to be in strong shape. We need to be ready if the Enhanced attack. And what are you, currently? You're weak, Inga, and a liability. If they attack, you're not getting away. You won't be able to fight the Enhanced. The only thing you'll do is join them. You won't be able to avoid it." She reaches out and touches my face. Her fingers clamp under my chin, and she tilts my head up so I'm looking directly at her. "They'll make you take augmenters. You'll become the enemy. Or if it's the assassins who find you, they'll make you join them again. All because you're too scared to let me heal you. Who would have thought the Night Slayer was scared?"

"I'm not scared." I glare into her eyes.

"Oh, but you are." She lets go of my face and shakes her head. "You're pretending it's because you're concerned for the boys. But they're fine. You've got proof, look. The real reason you don't want me to heal your damn leg is because you're scared. You've always been scared of Seers."

"I am not scared of Seers."

"Then prove it." Her eyes hold the challenge so strongly, like turbulent water.

I turn to look at the boys again. Their game's getting a bit violent now, and Minnow and Stephen are heading over to them. I watch as the two adults stop and have words with the boys, hear the boys' whines as Stephen takes their sticks. As they all walk away, Minnow trips over her skirt, and I suppress a laugh.

To the right, by the trees, Falkes is sitting by a small fire. He looks healed. A lot better.

I turn back to Oleta.

"Okay," I say.

She grabs my hand and—

And I feel it.

The energy.

She's healing me. My leg and—

This is wrong! This is bad!

I inhale sharply, pull away, break the contact. Can't help it. It's just instinct and—

Oleta rolls her eyes. "You are such a wimp."

I glare at her, then check the bandages, under my leggings. I unwind them. My thigh's tingling. The bandages come away sticky and wet with the poultice and some blood, but the wound itself looks about three months old. Not a couple of days old. I press my fingers against my skin. There's slight bruising.

"Well, you could've let me finish it," Oleta says. "Probably still hurts a bit, right? But you should be able to walk. And fight."

I look up to see her eyes spark. Is she expecting an imminent fight?

No, of course she's not. But we have to be prepared. That's always rule number one.

"Who are we going for next?" Oleta asks me. "I want Zak, by the way. Gods, I hate that man."

"He's joint-second on the list, with Clara. Right after Brighid. I've ranked them by status and power, and that's the order I want to get them in."

Oleta nods. "Chances are he and Clara are together, right? When we find them, you take that bitch and I'll have him."

Irritation curls through me. She thinks she can choose who she gets? This is my list, and I want Zak. I want to make him pay. I've dreamed about it for years. Oleta can think what she wants, but she'll be lucky if she gets the weeds to take out.

"I don't know where any of them are though," I say. "They're not using the usual settlements now. I've been to all of them. It was a coincidence I stumbled across Hunter the same day we found you. You know, he was looking for you. Petra had sent him out there, said you were in the area."

Oleta's gaze darkens. "She did?" She clicks her tongue, but I can't tell what she's thinking. "They're using her, making her work for them."

I watch Oleta carefully. Is she pleased her sister is looking for her, even if it's to recruit her? I think of Gweneira, how I'd do anything to see her again. But under what circumstances?

"We're going to have to drive around and search for the assassins, try and track them if we see any signs," I say.

Oleta nods and touches her shoulder. I think it's the one all the blood was coming from when we found her—the tiger attack—but now it's perfect.

"I can use my powers." Oleta throws an arm around my shoulder. She smells of lavender, and I don't like it. "I'll do some searching."

I sit forward a little more. "You think you can find them?"

She taps her temple. "I always know where Petra is."

My eyes widen. "It's not just her who can track people? Why didn't you say anything?"

"It only works with Petra, and it's not always totally accurate. Mainly just a communication link. But, still, I wasn't going to tell dear Mother Bridie all my secrets. Healing isn't my only Seer power. And Petra can tell us everything we need to know. Locations, everything."

I frown. "So, you're in contact with Petra?"

"On and off." She shrugs. "Her powers are weaker at times, when they hurt her."

"Okay, but the assassins are using Petra—you just said that. Won't she tell them where we are, if you're in contact with her?"

She folds her arms. "You either trust me or you don't—and that means you either trust Petra or you don't. We've got eyes on the inside, Inga, with her.

She's still one of us. *Sisters* stick together."

"Even if she's compromised?" I want to mention the other sister, Anita. Oleta and Petra don't trust her, not now she's Enhanced, so how can Oleta still *absolutely* trust Petra? Or is she just desperate not to lose her last remaining sister? I lower my voice. "Oleta, Petra may not have wanted to, but she *did* send Hunter after you."

"Because I was injured. Something attacked me, and I needed help. Petra knew that."

"And that would've been worth you rejoining the assassins?"

Oleta glares at me. "You either trust her or you don't. And don't we need this intel if we're going to kill them?"

"Okay." I swallow hard. "Ask her where they are now. All the assassins. I want specific locations. But don't mention me. Don't tell her that we're going to kill them. The less she knows, the better."

"She's trustworthy."

"But they're using her. We don't want them getting any info out of her. Contact her now."

"In time," Oleta says with a smile.

"What?" I stare at her.

"Give me a chance to enjoy my new life first. Just a taste of it, eh, Inga, before it all gets messy again?"

Before I can answer, she moves to the end of the tailgate and jumps to the ground. "Hey, Johnny! Callum! Want to play a game? I can get those sticks back from Stephen, and we can play swords!"

The boys grin and yell with excitement. And I feel it. The rush of envy. At how everyone likes her, when they hate me.

But she's worse. I know her. Oleta is so much worse.

TEN

I STAB THE AIR AS hard as I can, force all my anger and frustration into it.

Stab, stab, stab.

"Good, Inga," Instructor Hunter says. "Tighten your grip on the dagger, and put more of your weight on the balls of your feet."

All the littles are in the training arena with Instructor Mark, Instructor Hunter, and Instructor Gabi. All of us littles are wearing our freshly washed training kits: shirts, shorts, and running shoes. The first assessment is later today, and I'm going to do well. I know I am. Aunt Fi isn't watching the training, but the aunts and uncles of bands one, two, and four are here, watching over their littles with smirks and knowing glances.

This morning, Fi rubbed her temples when I asked if she'd be coming to watch us. She didn't answer, and it had annoyed me. I've trained for the past year, and I'm doing well, and I want her to see this.

I glance at Nathan and Samira, the other two of Fi's littles. Nathan is shaking—he always shakes when we're out here—and Samira's frowning with the effort of paying such close attention to her work.

"Concentrate, Inga," Instructor Hunter says.

I concentrate and swipe the air with my dagger.

"Pull back a bit," Instructor Hunter says, then instructs me more and more, tells me to change my angle.

A little way away, I see Oleta and Caro. They both give me a smile and a thumbs up, and I grin back, wonder if they know how good I am. Because I am good, Instructor Hunter is always saying that. I've got spark, apparently.

And I'm going to do this. I haven't been training for the past year just to fail this test. I'm going to be in the top three. I'm going to make Aunt Fi and Mother Bridie proud.

Instructor Hunter and Instructor Mark have us practice for the next few hours, and then Mother Bridie arrives. With her is a girl who looks very much like Oleta. Same dark skin and hair, but she's skinnier than Oleta and has a narrower face. It's the other Alanis Seer. Petra, I think her name is. Caro told me about Petra in low whispers a few weeks after I joined Aunt Fi's family. Oleta had returned, angry, one evening, and I'd asked him why she was worked up. He said Petra is her sister, but she's kept locked away most of the time.

The metal cuffs are still around Petra's wrists, a short chain attached, and she flinches as Mother Bridie tugs her along. Now, Oleta's gaze is firmly on Petra, and the two sisters stare at each other, almost as if messages are passing between them. But I know that's wrong. Oleta just has healing as her Seer power. Nothing else.

"Hello, littles," Mother Bridie says, and her gaze slips over all of us. There are eleven of us, from across all the bands at this camp, and this is a competition. The three who do best will get more points meaning we're closer to starting the training that will lead to us graduating, becoming a higher. And the top three will get a reward, a reward that Mother Bridie has promised will be amazing.

And I want it.

I'm going to get it. I'm ready to go out on missions, proper missions. I want to be like Caro and Oleta and the other highers. The ones who get out of this camp, who go on missions and return glowing and whose necklaces grow heavier and their skin more inked with each accomplishment.

"Hello, Mother," we all say.

Mother Bridie talks with the instructors and the aunts and uncles for a few moments. Caro and Oleta both give me encouraging smiles.

"Let's see what you're made of," Mother Bridie says.

A little from band four, a tall girl called Grace is to go first. Instructor Mark is her examiner, and my heart thuds as I watch. The hand-to-hand combat is first for her, then the dagger throwing. I'm strongest at the dagger throwing, but most of us are. Combat is always harder for us, as we go up against the instructors, and though there are rules about which moves they can do, given their size, they're still adults. Still strong.

Grace breathes out hard, rugged breaths.

"Loser!" a boy from band one shouts, and the uncle of that group—a man called Zak who I don't like at all—smirks.

Grace glares at the boy from band one, and then the combat begins. It's like a dance. A swift dance full of fast moves. All too soon, it's over, and I'm not sure how she's done.

My heart thuds as I watch her in the dagger-throwing. She hits the board, but misses the crosses on it, I think because the boy from band one shouts again.

"Next will be Inga of Band Three," Bridie says. She's sitting in a chair to the side of the arena. "Inga of Band Three is blessed with Rijikarii, so this should be good."

I frown. Rijikarii. They keep mentioning it around me, linking it to me, but I don't know what it is. The most Mother Bridie has told me is it's a type of energy, and Oleta's said she's got it too.

"Good luck," Caro yells. The sun makes his blond hair look almost white.

"Kill it, Little Sister!" Oleta shouts.

All I can hear as I walk to the arena is the blood pounding in my ears. I flex my hands into tight fists, try to ignore how numb they now feel. I can do this.

Instructor Hunter gives me the dagger—apparently, I'm being tested on that first—but as he did the majority of my training for this assessment, I know his moves too well so either Instructor Mark or Instructor Gabi will be doing the combat with me afterward.

But, for now, it's the dagger-throwing.

I can do this.

"Ready?" Instructor Hunter asks.

I nod, my smile tightening. Mother Bridie likes it if we smile as we demonstrate our abilities, that's what Caro and Oleta told me last night when they gave me all their tips. I didn't hear them helping the other two littles in our band, and it made me feel good. They see something in me.

I test out the weight of the dagger and then look at the target on the other side of the arena, twenty feet away, that's how far away I heard one of the men say it is. A badly drawn man's body, with two crosses on it. One over the heart, one in the center of the forehead.

I lift my dagger carefully. I can see the mark on the board where Grace got her dagger—in the right shoulder. At least she hit the board though. I know for a fact two of the littles from band one can't, including the boy who called Grace a loser.

"Any time you're ready, Inga," Mother Bridie says, her voice dripping with expectation.

I tense my muscles, then I throw the dagger. Adrenaline pumps through me.

It hits the cross on the forehead of the target. There's an intake of breath, and Oleta and Caro whoop loudly.

"Full marks," says a low voice, and I turn to see Aunt Fi standing behind the other adults—instructors and those in the logistics team.

My heart warms a little.

"Now for part two," Mother Bridie says. "Let's see what other skills Rijikarii has given you."

Instructor Mark steps forward. He's got his combat gloves on. Leather. He's the only one of the instructors who wears combat gloves, but the littles who trained with him say leather smacks hurt more.

I take a deep breath and face him. I make sure my face shows no weakness. I fix my smile in place and wait for the bell.

All I've got to do is get a minimum of two punches into Instructor Mark's torso and stay on my feet for the whole two minutes.

Instructor Gabi rings the bell.

Instructor Mark advances toward me. His steps are heavy, but he's favoring one leg. I glance at his feet. One shoe's falling apart. Okay. I can use that.

Always notice everything about your opponent, that's what Instructor Hunter told me to do.

Instructor Mark and I skirt around each other. He's not as tall as the other men, but I'm still a child. He won't put in his full effort, I'm sure of that. Wouldn't want to permanently injure me. Mother Bridie likes me too much.

My breathing is heavy.

"Come here," Instructor Mark snarls, hands reaching out. He's backing me into the corner of the arena, where the chain-link fence is the highest.

I scream my ear-piercing scream—the scream that Instructor Hunter said was my secret weapon—and Instructor Mark winces. That moment is all I need.

I kick and my foot connects with his thigh. His weaker leg. He stumbles, and I slip under his arm, run back to the center of the arena. I am fast. Nimble, Instructor Hunter called me.

I pull air into my lungs so fast I feel sick. Adrenaline tries to make me dizzy.

Instructor Mark rounds on me, speeding up, and I keep running, zigzagging.

He reaches a hand out, and I duck and—

His other hand grabs my shoulder.

I twist around, sink my teeth into his leather glove. He shoves me away, and I stumble, but I am fast, and I do not fall.

I skip away, eyes on him. A laugh escapes me as a metallic taste spreads through my mouth. Instructor Mark watches me. He's breathing hard. Two contacts with him—two that I've got in, the kick and the bite. I've passed—so long as I stay on my feet for the rest of the time. All the instructors are allowed to do is grab us and pull us to the floor. They can't kick or bite or punch us, but they're allowed to use their strength.

I size him up. He's considerably stronger than me, I know that. When we first started training, Samira said it was unfair to have adults against us, but the instructors were quick to point out that when we become highers, we'll be sent to the towns to kill Enhanced Ones. Adults. And we'll still be children.

"But being a child doesn't make you weak," Instructor Veronica had said.

Instructor Mark grunts, and the littles from band one shout words and try to distract me.

I glance toward Mother Bridie and the sand-timer. Looks about halfway through. Just got to stay on my feet.

And get another contact in—sure, my dagger-throwing was the best, and I've got the required two contacts, but I want three. I'm not settling for the minimum amount. I need to prove to Mother Bridie that I can do this. I will be the best.

I run to the right, toward the edge of the arena, leading Instructor Mark with me. He reaches out for me, and, again, I duck. Only this time I don't run under his arms, I yank myself backward instead. Instructor Mark skids, and, before I can think about what to do, I kick him in the back of the knee.

I am good at kicking.

He yells, and I run, twisting around and—

The adults leap forward. From all around the arena. Instructor Hunter and Instructor Gabi and Mother Bridie and—

No. The time's not up.

I frown and look back. Instructor Mark is sprawled on the floor, groaning, dust swirling as he grabs his knee.

"Broken it!" he shouts. "She's fucking broken it!"

"Don't be silly," Mother Bridie snaps, her voice dark, but when she looks at me—just for a second—she's smiling. "Get up."

Instructor Mark shouts something, and then the other two instructors are helping him.

Mother Bridie turns to me. "Well, well, well. Exceptional. Looks like you've got full marks on this one too." She directs me to sit with Grace at the side of the arena, and the taller girl gives me a look I can't quite comprehend.

I rub my hands together, count to ten under my breath to try to calm my racing heart as Instructor Mark is led away. Five minutes later, the assessments continue. Instructor Hunter and Instructor Gabi do the rest of the combats, and I watch with interest in particular for the dagger-throwing. No one else's scores even come close to mine.

When all the littles have been tested, the adults confer for the results. Petra, the Seer, stands with them. One of the aunts is holding onto her chain now.

"You're going to win this," Caro says to me, slapping my shoulder. "Gods, you'll be a higher in no time."

A higher.

A grin spreads across my face.

"Is Instructor Mark okay?" I ask.

Caro shrugs, and we all look at the hut that Instructor Mark disappeared into. No doubt, Oleta will heal him later.

Aunt Fi approaches us. "Come on, you're going to miss the results."

The four of us head back to the side of the arena. Mother Bridie is now inside it, in the center, with Instructor Gabi next to her. Both of them are wearing long, dark cloaks made of qiviut.

"This examination was quite the entertainment," Bridie says. "But we must remember its true purpose, for these tests reveal when our littles are ready for the transition into greater work, to begin their real training that will prepare them for graduation, so they can serve us and all Untamed."

An elbow shoves against me, and I turn to find Zak, the uncle of band one, glaring at me.

"You just remember your place," he says.

"Excuse me." Aunt Fi's voice is low and deadly. "There's no need to take your jealousy and frustration out on a member of my band."

Uncle Zak grunts, and then we all look toward Mother Bridie.

"Top of the board are Inga of Band Three, Harmony of Band Two, and Grace of Band Four," Mother Bridie says with a smile.

My breath catches at my name, and then Caro and Oleta are pulling me up.

"Little Sister, you did it," Oleta says, smiling—but her eyes are cold, yet I can't focus on that because Caro pulls me into an embrace.

It's warm and nice, the feeling of his arms around me.

And then it's over too soon, and cold air wraps around me again.

"Follow me," Mother Bridie says to Grace, Harmony, and me.

The three of us follow her out of the arena and back through the camp, around the little huts and shacks, until we get to the caves. The caves that are out of bounds. No one must go in the caves, that's what she told us, because the connection to the Gods and Goddesses is strongest in caves. That's why Petra's kept chained up in one most of the time. She has to do her work there.

Two of Mother Bridie's men guard either side of this cave entrance, and they each carry spears. Mother Bridie nods to them, and they step back as she walks into the cave and—

Someone screams.

A scream from inside.

I falter. Harmony looks at me, her eyes wide. Grace lets out a whimper.

"Come on." Mother Bridie's voice is sharp.

We scurry after her.

It's dark in the cave, and I blink several times to keep sight of Mother Bridie's shape. The fragments of light are from small cracks in the walls, the ceiling. I look up. What if the roof falls in on us?

The screams start again. The hairs on the back of my arms rise. My heart speeds up.

We follow Mother Bridie to the end of the corridor-like tunnel.

I can hear breathing—heavy breathing. Breathing that isn't our own.

"Let us out, now," a voice snarls, and I jump back, catch my hand on something rough and hard. The stone wall. I'm right by it.

"You are savages," another voice cries, a lower-pitched one, this time.

My chest tightens.

"Move back!" Mother Bridie yells. "Do as I say! Move back, or we'll hurt you."

"You'll hurt us anyway," the first one yells. Are there just two of them?

"Move back."

I hear movement. Next to me, Harmony trembles and—

Light. Sudden. I blink. Retinas burning and—

A flash, in front of me.

In an instant, I'm alert. Weapon. I need a weapon. They're Enhanced! They're in this cave and—

A rock. On the ground. The size of my hand. There's only one rock; the rest of the floor is smooth.

I lunge for it. The moment it's in my hands, I feel better, and I look at the Enhanced Ones, look properly now. There are chains on them, chains that rattle, just like Petra's. No augmenters around here? I check quickly, but I see no colorful vials.

"Excellent, Inga." Mother Bridie's voice is a purr, and I look up to see she's smiling. Her lips are painted a brighter red, or maybe it's the torchlight that's doing it. Even though it's not shining on her. She looks at me and Harmony and Grace. "Killing adults requires practice. But there is knowledge that needs to be gained before practice can be effective, in honing your skills."

She taps her foot twice.

"Smell them," she says. "Smell the fear on them that they deny they experience. Do it. Inga, you first."

I step forward. No choice. There are three of them, three of the enemy. The nearest Enhanced is the oldest woman. She looks angry.

"She cannot hurt you—she's tied up, and you've got a weapon. Don't dally, you shouldn't be scared. My children are not scared, are they? I do not have weak children."

I step right up to the woman, and I'm still holding the rock.

She's the first Enhanced One I've seen close up. When I was at D'Elinous, Keelie told me how she saw one close up and described to us all how monstrous the person looked.

But this woman does not look monstrous.

She looks angry.

She's shaking.

And she looks like us. Except for the eyes. Her mirror eyes.

"Smell their fear, smell it all, for it is proof they lie, and we hate liars." Mother Bridie is smiling. I can tell by how her words curl at the end.

I inhale, my face right by the woman. She can't move. The chains are too tight.

Mother Bridie directs Harmony to smell the Enhanced, and then Grace too. Then she hands us each a dagger and gestures toward the Enhanced Ones with a playful smile.

I stare at the dagger in my fingers. It's a close-range weapon. Instructor Veronica taught me all about the weapons used to kill Enhanced Ones a few months ago, and she said that guns are always preferable. You only get close to the enemy if you have to.

I look at Mother Bridie. "We're not using guns?"

"Oh, Tiny Inga." Mother Bridie laughs. "You have to be prepared for anything. And gunshots are not stealthy. Stabbing requires more than just coordination and a steady hand. You need upper body strength and knowledge of anatomy."

Harmony lets out a stifled gasp. "No," she whispers.

"Yes," Mother Bridie says and glares at her.

"Get away from us," the Enhanced woman nearest me cries and—

Bridie slits the woman's throat in one quick movement. The other two Enhanced women scream.

"Not so calm now, are we?" Mother Bridie laughs. "Inga, you'll have the redhead, and Harmony the brunette. Grace, you'll practice on the dead one. But, first, come here." She beckons us forward with her long fingers, and then wipes

the blade on her jeans.

I stare at the blood pooling by the dead woman's feet.

"Time for an anatomy lessen," Bridie says. She reaches for my hand with her free one, then guides me to touch the woman's chest.

I freeze up, and Mother Bridie jerks my hand forward. The woman's chest is warm.

"See there? That's where the heart is. But it is protected by the ribs. Want to see the ribs?"

Harmony makes a choking sound.

"See the ribs?" I stare up at Bridie, only partly illuminated by the torchlight. The torch is on the ground now.

Bridie's lips curl. "What better way is there to know your opponent than to really understand how the body works?"

The other two Enhanced scream as Mother Bridie cuts open the dead woman's chest. Harmony retches. And I... I don't. I just stare. I feel numb, my vision glassy. And... And I expect to feel things—revulsion and fear and disgust.

But I don't.

I am calm.

I am fascinated.

Mother Bridie nods at me, approval in her eyes, as I step closer.

"See, that's where the ribs are," she says. "You need to get your dagger in at this angle—just like that. There, see, it directly pierces the heart."

Blood squirts out in a minutely thin line. It hits me, marks my arm.

"Now, time for you to do the work. All of you." Mother Bridie points at the other two Enhanced women. "Take one of them each, and stab them in the hearts." She stands up. "I'll be watching you carefully. Remember, precision is key. And you have to be quick. Remember, in the wild, it would not be like this. They would not be tied up—but we all have to start somewhere."

Grace falters. "I don't want to."

I look across at Grace and frown. Her Enhanced One is already dead, and the heart's exposed. It's not even like she's got to kill her or slice her open.

Mother Bridie raises her eyebrows. "Do you not want to be fed tonight, Grace? It would be a shame if you went hungry, given you did place third in the examination and the food is rightfully yours."

Grace turns watery eyes toward Mother Bridie.

I inhale sharply. No. She can't cry!

"Oh no," Mother Bridie whispers. She looks back at me and Harmony. "You two, wait here. Grace, come with me."

My chest tightens as Grace follows Mother Bridie out of the cave. I watch their shadows grow longer and longer, then disappear entirely.

"Let us go," one of the Enhanced Ones says.

Neither Harmony nor I answer her. We both just look at each other, as we hear Mother Bridie's raised voice from outside the cave. Then a slapping sound and high-pitched cries.

When Mother Bridie and Grace return, Grace's face is red on one side, and she holds onto her arm, awkwardly clutching it to her side.

Mother Bridie beams at Harmony and me, and, for a moment, I think we're going to get the punishment too. That's what Oleta warned me about before: if someone cries, Mother Bridie doesn't just punish that person.

But Mother Bridie doesn't raise her hands to Harmony and me. She just continues smiling. "Let's continue with this lesson."

"YOU LET HER DO IT, then." Renee nods at my leg, then points at it with her knife.

I nod. "Yes. Yes, I did."

We're skinning three hares that Stephen caught in snares, and I concentrate on getting the hides off in one piece. It's something I always like to do. A challenge. And then I often stuff the empty hides with long grass or leaves and sew the skins up, so the hares look like they're still alive, though deranged, and I leave them next to the boys' seats in the bus because they're scared of hares.

"So Oleta healed you, and nothing bad has happened to the boys?" Renee asks.

I make a noise of agreement deep in the back of my throat and reach for a slightly sharper knife. Ahead of us, Oleta is playing with Johnny and Callum. They really like her. She races round with them, and they're all shrieking with excitement.

I look down at the dead hare in my hands.

Maybe the problem is me, not who I was. I always thought my past as an assassin automatically made me the enemy, but I never actually tried to be the boys' friend, to play with them in a way that wasn't designed to scare them. I thought that my role of protector for them was enough, that I didn't need to be nice as well, not when I take their safety seriously. Because those boys are never going to be snatched, not under my watch.

I breathe out hard. Falkes did say it was *me* he didn't like—and he seems fine with Oleta. But how much of that is because of her looks? Is her past automatically redeemed because of that? Or is it really just my personality that makes me an enemy in his eyes?

"What are we doing now then?" I ask Renee. "Just traveling still?"

"Are you trying to change the subject?"

"I'm being practical." I give her a look. "We need to know where we're going." I glance at Oleta. She needs to find out from Petra where the assassins are. But I also need to know if Falkes and the others have been making plans, know whether there's likely to be any opposition to a plan to keep traveling.

Renee nods. "Falkes is determined to find other Untamed—oh, I've messed this one up." She stares at the hare she's working on. "You'll get that one's hide off in one piece, right? Ma wants to make gloves out of them… But yeah, Falkes… He's not going to settle with just *us*. Heard him saying the other morning that the Enhanced must keep records on where they think we are. Said we should raid one of their towns and try and find that info."

I process that information as I stare at the hare. Its eye looks glass-like. Knowledge on where other Untamed are would be helpful—the Enhanced think we're violent, so they're bound to have notes on which groups are the most violent, more of a danger to them. And Bridie's group is the most violent I know of, especially toward the Enhanced.

"What's the nearest town or city to here?" I ask, then make a flaying cut in the hare's neck. A little blood oozes out as I get ready to skim the blade along, keeping it parallel to the meat. The hides are always attached more firmly than I expect and typically I put too much strength in and end up hacking off the hides in sections.

"I don't know." Renee grunts. "I lost track of where we were long ago. You'll have to ask Ma that."

Yes. Amelia's good with locations and directions for the cities and towns, whereas I'm better at navigating woods, wild places. Amelia's got maps, too. A lot of them, some hand-drawn, some printed. She's marked on them little things to remind her of places, where things happened. The place of Renee's birth is on one, as well as marks indicating where she thinks there are other settlements in the other regions. We're one of the last Untamed groups in this area—if not the last, since contact with Taras's group ended after the last radio got broken—and, for a long time, Amelia has wanted to cross the sea to find her family, even though Falkes says it's too far to go.

"Do you think we've got enough numbers to start a new settlement ourselves?" Renee asks. "You know, if we can't find anyone else?"

I grimace. "There's, what, ten of us?" I count on my fingers to make sure. Yes.

Renee nods, then frowns at her knife. She runs the pad of her thumb over the edge of the blade then grunts. "We're not going to survive many generations with just us."

"I mean, technically, it could work." I shrug. "You and Amelia are one bloodline—the Karnads. The Atkinsons are another. Then there's the Drakes—Lexa and Stephen. But he's also most likely Falkes's son, so he could count as a Hughes too. So if we call that one two gene pools, then I bring the fifth, and Oleta's the sixth."

"Is gene pool the right word?" Renee asks.

"I don't know. Thinking of it as family trees really, by blood." I remove the rest of the hare's hide. It's predominantly in one piece. I glance at the hare

Renee's already skinned. It's better than that one, anyway. "Who knows? But it would work."

"But Falkes and Stephen are the only available men, and they're related." Renee wrinkles her nose. "Oh Gods. You and Oleta would get Stephen because you're roughly the same age. Which means Minnow, Lexa, and I get Falkes. God, I wish I'd passed the menopause like Ma. Going to be all sorts of little Hughes running around."

"Do you think they'll do it like a rota?" I ask—because I can't imagine ever wanting to sleep with Stephen. I shudder.

"Like we're breeding stock?"

I shrug. "Guess so."

But maybe there's not even any point in trying to reproduce to keep our numbers going in this area, when we are dwindling. The Enhanced are winning—in this land. If we're going to try and keep our people going, we need to move. Maybe we should travel to the east, try and find the lands Amelia's original group came from.

"This is a bloody weird conversation, Inga." Renee shakes her head. "If we do make a new Untamed settlement, we'll have to recruit more people."

Recruit. I don't like that word.

"But, well, I don't want to bump uglies with Falkes." Renee laughs. "So I sure as hell hope we find others."

Bump uglies. I can't believe she just said that.

"There's always stragglers around, right?" Renee says.

I look at Oleta. "Apparently."

"So long as you don't kill them." Renee gives me a sly look.

I pretend I didn't hear her and continue working on the hare. May as well gut it and butcher it too.

After a quick meal of boiled hare and wild carrots, during which Renee talks about percussion flaking and the differences between flint and obsidian, I volunteer Oleta and I to refill the water bottles. Falkes's eyes are narrowed, and I know he's watching us as we head off, down the valley toward the river.

"So have you done it?" I ask, once I'm satisfied we're a sufficient distance away. I'm carrying both bottles and I tap them against my thighs as I walk. My injured thigh only hurts a little.

"Done it?" Oleta's eyes are sly. "Come on, Inga, be specific." She laughs.

"Don't," I warn her, my voice low. She knows what I'm talking about, and I need her to know she can't mess with me. She may be older, but here, I am in charge. I am Inga the Killer—the Night Slayer, as they apparently call me. *Me.* Not Oleta. And this is my mission. She's just a helper.

She pushes her hair back. It falls in a perfect curtain, dead straight. "Yes."

"And?"

"Petra says they've got a lot of men now. Just in the last few months. New ones. Made four different camps, not counting the group Hunter was with. Apparently, none of Hunter's team returned last night, when they were due back. Amazing, isn't it?" Oleta nudges me. "How does Bridie's group just keep going, even without her? Blows your mind." Oleta flashes me a look I can't quite read. "Petra says the group she's with is at Royston's Rock."

My breaths speed up. They're back *there*? But no, they can't be.

"No. That's wrong," I say. "I've been there twice. First time, I killed Veronica and two other originals. They were the only ones there. Second time, two years later, it was deserted. Didn't I tell you before? I've been round all the known settlements, and none are being used now."

Oleta's eyes narrow. "Well, you're wrong. They're

back at Royston's Rock."

"Are you sure?"

"Are you questioning the intel my sister is providing? Because I don't see you getting any information. Face it, Inga. They're using their old camps again."

Royston's Rock. Probably the last camp I want to visit again. I grimace.

I may not know for sure where we are, but, even so, that site has to be a day or so's worth of driving away from here. And to get there, we'd have to go near the Enhanced Ones' cities. I know Falkes wants to raid, but he's always been adamant that we choose small towns and avoid their big cities. If I claim we've got to go nearer to where the enemy is, he could get suspicious.

I'm going to need to be very convincing.

"How many assassins are at Royston's Rock now?" I look at Oleta. "And the children?"

She straightens up a little, and the movement emphasizes her cleavage. "Seventeen adults, at the moment. Petra's not as clear on the children, but thinks there are seven, but more are likely to arrive soon, adults and children." She clenches her hands into fists, then grabs a few strands of long grass and tugs them clean of their roots as we walk. "Petra's kept locked up most of the time."

"Most?" *Most* is an improvement on when Bridie was in charge. Petra was in chains permanently then, even when she was taken out of the cave. And I had the key—right at the end, I had the key and I could've let her out.

But Petra told me not to, said she wasn't coming with us.

Maybe I should've told her not to be stupid and brought her anyway.

But then you wouldn't have eyes on the inside now.

Hmm. If she really *is* our eyes.

Oleta and I reach the river and dip the open bottles under the water's surface. They make a *lug-lug* sound as the water fills them up.

"So, we going to Royston's Rock?" Oleta asks, heaving one of the bottles up to her side. "You going to tell them you've had a Seeing vision? Because if you are, you need to tell me. As far as Falkes is concerned, his group has two Seers now, and surely if the Divine Ones send one of us a warning, they'd send it to us both? We need our stories to match at all times, else they could get suspicious."

I don't think that's how visions work for multiple Seers, but I nod anyway. "So, if you get a proper vision, you tell me too?"

"Deal." Oleta smiles, flashing teeth that seem too perfect. Not like my ones. They're wonky.

"Okay," I say, stepping closer to her. "Here's what we're going to do."

TWELVE

"A WHOLE GROUP OF UNTAMED?" Falkes stares at me. His eyebrows look bushier than usual, and they knit together as he frowns. "An Untamed group, just days away from us?"

His eyes flicker over to Oleta.

She's leaning against the side of the minibus, her arms folded and her ankles crossed over. She nods. "I got the vision too." She draws the words out a little longer than she usually does.

I shoot her a look.

"What's this?" Minnow asks, stepping over to Falkes. Her braid falls in front of her shoulder as she touches his arm lightly.

Falkes points at me, then Oleta. "They say they've seen another group. Been shown them in Seeing dreams."

Behind them, Renee and Amelia step up.

"Another group?" Amelia's eyes light up, and I feel a momentary flash of guilt. "Where are they? How close?"

"A couple of days away, the girls reckon," Falkes says.

Girls. Huh, Oleta and I are women.

"Is it Taras's group?" Amelia's eyes are imploring, begging me.

Falkes grunts. "Could be. Could be anyone. There's got to be pockets of Untamed surviving like us. Those big tribes—those ones that people haven't seen in a while, what are they?"

"The Zharat and Mariballii," Lexa says.

"Yeah, them." Falkes yawns. "Could be them. Or what's left of them. Maybe people broke off."

Amelia's eyes shine. "It could be my own people."

"They wouldn't be this close, Ma," Renee says, but she's speaking loudly, even for her, and excitement pulses through her words. "They're across seas, remember?"

"I didn't know the Dream Land could guide us to other groups." Minnow frowns.

"The Dream Land is there to aid the survival of the Untamed." Oleta tosses her hair back. It seems extra glossy now, shiny, and somehow draws attention to the electric blue of her tattoos. "And everyone knows you need numbers to survive."

"We need to go then." Amelia clasps her hands together. "This is—this is wonderful! The best news I've had in years."

Another flash of guilt pulls through me.

"Yes," Falkes says. "Where's the map?"

"We don't need a map," I say. "I can drive my truck, lead us."

He gives me a withering look. "You're in no fit state to drive. Your leg may be healed, but we're not taking chances. My bus is leading, and I'm not having the truck crashing into the back of us as your reactions aren't quick."

Anger uncoils inside me, and I want to reach out and shake him, squeeze his throat, watch his face turn purple. The desire is just there.

He knows nothing about my reactions.

And, anyway, *he* shouldn't drive so cautiously and

brake so much. No wonder Minnow and Lexa always seem to be rubbing their necks or complaining of pain. The amount of whiplash they get is ridiculous. Maybe we should offer them a place in the truck….

"And I want Oleta in the bus with me," Falkes says.

"Why?" Oleta's tone is sharp.

"Two Seers. And we don't put all our eggs in one basket in case there's an accident. Oleta, you know the way? Good. You can direct me. I'm driving. And Renee, you drive the truck."

Amelia and Renee sit up front, with Renee driving. I'm behind them, in the central seat of the second row. Just the three of us. I look at them. My family, for now. Until I'm reunited with my cousins. And my sister and mother—if they're still alive.

"Falkes hasn't said anything more to you, Inga?" Amelia asks after a while. "No more threats that he's going to kill you?"

"No." I don't feel that threatened by him though. I mean, if he was really going to kill me, he had plenty of chances when I was unconscious and injured. That would've been the time to do it.

And even if he does try now, I am strong. I can fight him. And that's *because* of my thigh being healed. Because of Oleta. As much as I hate to admit it, it would be a different picture if I was still injured and plagued by fever.

"Good." I see Amelia's brows tighten in the mirror on the passenger's visor. The sun is low now. "Just keep an eye on him. I've got a bad feeling."

"Ma, when do you ever *not* have a bad feeling?" Renee smiles.

"It's listening to my gut that keeps us safe."

We stop when it's nearing full darkness, because moving headlights in the dark are a dead giveaway to any Enhanced Ones who could be watching. We've driven out into yet more forest tundra—cold lands scattered with trees and some low vegetation, mainly rushes and the odd forb. Not a great deal of trees in this part though.

"Seen anything more?" Lexa asks me, then Oleta. We're sitting outside. My truck's sidelights are on, and moths hover in front of them, bathing in the streams of light.

Oleta shakes her head, and I do the same. Lexa grunts. There are two flasks of whiskey on the ground next to her, along with a bottle of something else. Maybe wine. She persuaded Falkes to let her have more of it earlier, said she'd been thinking a lot about her missing sister and needed something to dull her senses. Of course, Falkes agreed, as soon as Lexa turned tearful.

"I think we should sleep in our vehicles," Falkes says. "Too late to get the tents set up properly." He glances at Amelia and Renee. "You coming to the bus?"

Amelia glances at me. "Inga's truck is fine for me."

Inga's truck. I smile.

"And me," Renee says, cigarette in hand. She fumbles with her lighter for a moment.

"Are you sure?" Falkes's voice is loaded, and I frown.

"I'm sure," Amelia says. She smiles at me, and, for some reason, I find myself smiling as we get back inside.

"Oleta, in with us." Falkes's voice is sharp.

I glance over my shoulder, see her halfway toward my truck. Our eyes meet, and, in the dim light, I think she widens hers at me. I frown, but then she's turned back, laughing at something Falkes says as he guides her into the bus, one hand on her shoulder.

I frown as Amelia, Renee, and I lower the seats in

the truck, try and work out what it is Oleta was trying to tell me. That wide-eyed look isn't one I know on her. But how much have we both changed in the last nine years?

"What are these Untamed like?" Amelia asks me.

"A big group." My voice is strong. "But the Dream Land didn't show me much." That's the secret to lying—not giving too many details that they can catch you out on later.

Renee mutters something under her breath, and I look at her.

"What was that?" I ask.

"Nothing," she says, then smiles. There's something about her smile that doesn't stick right with me though.

"I've been waiting for this all my life," Amelia says. "To find my people again."

"Ma, it's not going to be them," Renee says. "We're too far away. Different lands."

"Describe them, Inga. What did they look like, the people the Dream Land showed you?"

I busy myself with getting the blankets. Someone moved the bundles into the back of the cab earlier, but they're still all tied together. "They just looked like Untamed. Regular Untamed." I hand Amelia a blanket. It's one of the assassins' blankets. There's a lot of their stuff still in the truck.

"I guess we'll soon see if they're friendly Untamed," Amelia says. She's smiling. "Good night, my dear girls."

We listen to the sounds of Falkes and the others. Doors of the minibus slam. One of the boys is shouting something, and then we hear Minnow telling him to quieten down. He whines back. Sounds like an argument.

But, in here, I can shut myself off from them. I have my own space. A truck, solid walls—so much safer than a tent where anything could rip through, hands could pull back the drape. But here, Amelia and Renee and I are locked inside it.

Safe.

And I will keep us safe. I *will.*

I close my eyes, but sleep doesn't come. I listen to Renee's and Amelia's breaths, how they get deeper, fuller as they fall asleep. Renee snores a little.

I'm always jealous of how easily they sleep.

How easily all of them do. But they don't have haunting eyes in their minds, or the sounds of death spun into their souls, or monstrous memories seared to their very beings.

I look through the window, and, in the minibus, I see Oleta. The only face at the window. Her eyes look sad, lit by moonlight. The sadness is the first thing that strikes me. And I know—I know that look. The nightmares, the flashbacks, we both have them.

I am not alone.

None of us are. We're bound by the horrors.

"PATHETIC." MOTHER BRIDIE'S WORD IS *a whisper,
but she may as well be shouting. The whole camp can hear
her. "Utterly pathetic."*

*Ty, the child in front of her, whimpers. He's a new recruit,
a little in band one. Poor Uncle Zak gets all the weak'uns.*

*"You thought you could maim yourself and be excused
from your work?" Mother Bridie asks.*

*I lean around the curtain in the doorway, my heart
pounding. Ty is holding onto his arm, tightly. Red has
already pooled by his feet. He sways a little.*

*Behind them, I spot Caro. He's in the shadows, watching
the boy. The longer I look at Caro, the more details of him I
can pick out in the dim light. I see the way his eyebrows are
furrowed as he frowns. He's watching the boy and Mother
Bridie intently. His hands are clenched into tight fists.*

*After a moment or so, Caro's eyes look up and meet mine.
As Mother Bridie and Ty argue, Caro makes his way to me.*

*"Don't watch this," he says, and he tries to pull me away
from the doorway, but I can't move.*

*"You are not getting out of this, Ty," Mother Bridie
shouts. "You're doing this. You're learning how to kill,
because that is who we are. A little injury like this isn't*

going to stop no one."

Mother Bridie turns, and I duck down, my heart pounding. Did she see me?

"Oleta!" Mother Bridie's yell is loud.

I breathe a sigh of relief. She didn't see me?

"It's always easier if we don't watch," Caro says, pulling me farther away from the doorway. His hand is warm. "It's wrong, I know, but there are some things we just have to pretend we don't see, else we all get hurt. And it's not like anything we can do will change things for the better, for us."

I frown and clench my hands together, focus on the callused skin covering them. The signs of the training they made me do. There has to be something we can do. You have to stand up to bullies, that's what my mum always said.

My mum. The memory catches me in the throat, and I startle a bit. When was the last time I thought of her?

Outside, there are more shouts. What's happening? I start to move toward the door.

"Watching won't make you feel better," Caro warns. "It'll just make it worse. You won't be able to unsee it. Believe me."

"But I can't not know what's happening," I say.

My heart hammers as I slowly look back out, around the edge of our hut's curtain. Oleta is there now. Her black hair is tied up high, and she looks scared. I've never seen her like that before.

"Heal him," Mother Bridie barks.

Oleta shakes her head. "No."

Mother Bridie lunges for her, slaps her hard. Oleta falls back in the dust. I inhale sharply, and I want to go and help Oleta, but I can't move. My legs are frozen. I am made of stone. Stone that watches as Mother Bridie hits Oleta over and over.

"No!" Oleta cries. "I don't want to hurt anyone with my powers."

"I tell you what to do," Mother Bridie snarls, standing over her. "And I said **heal him.**_"_

Caro writhes in pain. My arms are around him. He's too hot, sweating. It was him this time. It's always one of us — never an adult.

Anger unfurls in me.

No. Not Caro…not —

He moans. The sound tears holes through my chest.

"It's all right," I say, but my voice catches, and I don't know if it will be all right. Because each time now, it's worse. How soon before Oleta's powers inadvertently kill someone?

And not just anyone.

I look at Caro. His eyes are shut, but under his lids I can see movement. I try to hold him tighter, but his skin is slippery, slick with sweat. A rancid smell radiates from his body.

The door opens, and Yvette steps in. She's a quiet woman, rarely speaks. It was her nineteenth birthday yesterday. She drank a lot then, and now her eyes look bleary as she glances at Caro and I, then Oleta.

Oleta is in here too, in Fi's hut. She's sitting in the corner. Her eyes are glassy. Earlier, she was muttering about the Goddess of Justice, but now she doesn't say a word. She never does, not after. But we all feel what she feels, because it wraps around us. It becomes a second skin over me that I want to shake off, wash away, along with Caro's sweat.

But it's stuck. It can't be washed away.

It is a reminder that we are bad now.

FOURTEEN

I WAKE, SWEATING. THAT DREAM, that nightmare. *Caro.* I mouth his name and tears pierce the corners of my eyes. I fight them, my heart rate rapid. My breaths shudder. It's not the worst nightmare, the worst flashback, I've had about him, but remembering Caro sick and in pain like that still gets to me.

Pull yourself together.

I take a deep breath and count to ten silently. Amelia and Renee are still asleep. I watch them for a moment, but their breaths are suddenly too loud, and it's too warm in here. I blink quickly as more tears burn my eyes. No. I need to get out, need to calm down. No one can see me like this. And this is pathetic.

I grab my jacket and open the door. Cold, morning air sweeps into the truck as I slip out and shut the door softly. It's still dark, and a heavy mist hangs over the land now, but the night is lifting away. For a couple of seconds, I stare at the bus. It's parked next to the Amorak. There's no movement from inside either.

The jacket rustles as I put it on, and I pause, tightening the laces on my boots, before heading to the right. There's a patch of trees there, just about visible in the early light, rising out of the mist.

Trees have always grounded me, and, as I approach them, just seeing them with their gnarled, twisted forms, beaten by the wind, makes me feel better, in a way. Because they're still standing, still here, no matter what. There are five trees in this group, and their branches are forever reaching out to the right, reaching for something more, something invisible but known to them. I touch the dry bark of the nearest trunk, feel its callusy texture under my fingers. Only a couple of leaves cling to the branches, and I breathe deeply.

My breaths are deep, and I imagine them as cleansing, purifying, getting rid of *that* nightmare. That flashback.

I press my fist to my mouth and squeeze my eyes shut.

It's okay. It's okay.

I breathe slowly, concentrate on filling my lungs. Ridding myself of the memory. Yes.

I'll feel better soon. I will.

This is just a weak moment, and I will not be weak for long.

I count to ten again.

When I open my eyes, I feel calmer. It is over. I am safe.

Safe.

That blasted word.

I head back toward where the minibus and truck are parked, and, just as the vehicles appear to emerge from the mist, I freeze.

A sound. A stick cracking—under someone's foot?

I whip my head around, my eyes wide, searching for movement. See moths in the air, the blades of grass wobbling, dancing slightly in the breeze. The breeze and—

Breathing.

My eyes narrow. Someone is here.

Behind me.

I turn.

A figure appears in the fog and haze and—

A *person*?

My eyes widen.

There's a woman in front of me. Looking kind of… silvery.

This is…this isn't right.

A *Goddess*?

That's my first thought—and damn, it's stupid. Ridiculous. It can't be a Goddess because I'm not a Seer.

And they wouldn't make a Seer.

Oh Gods. Oleta. I need to find Oleta. She's a Seer, she'll know what to do. I'm just a fraud, I'm just—

"Hello, Inga," the silvery woman says.

No.

My mouth dries.

Move! Every muscle in my body begs me, screams at me to run. Run to the truck and drive away. Get everyone away. And my body's trying to, trying to do it without me telling it to.

But I…I can't.

All I can do is stare at her, feel my blood turn to ice as she gets nearer and nearer with heavy steps that seem to shake the land.

She lifts her head, and tendrils of lank, gray hair fall to either side of her face.

Her eyes are bluer than in life, and they dive inside me.

"Hello, Inga." Bridie smiles. "I've been waiting a long time to see you."

FIFTEEN

I—I CAN'T BREATHE.

I can't move.

Bridie….

My breaths come too quickly, one after another. I'm choking. My throat—it's closing, restricting and—

No. Bridie *can't* be here.

I can't be with her. Not here. Not again.

She's *dead*.

Bridie takes a step forward, pushes a clump of her hair over her shoulder. She looks the same. The same as always. That's all I can focus on, and, suddenly, it's like the last years—those of freedom—haven't happened. I'm back in the hut, with her and her adults and the other assassins and the children she kidnapped and trained, having her lecture us, discuss tactics for the upcoming assignments. Having her hold my hand, stroke my palm, tell me I'm gifted, an important one to her.

But I wasn't.

We were all just weapons.

"This isn't real." My words are muttered, and I curse myself. I need to sound strong. I force myself to look her right in the eyes and lift my head higher, though my feet feel numb, like I could fall over at any second. "You're not real."

Damn, what's happening to me? Madness? Huh. This is madness. This isn't real. It can't be.

"I'm not real?" Bridie laughs. I hate her laugh with every bone in my body. "Well, my dear, I must say, this isn't the reunion I was hoping for." Her tone is careful, like she's poised.

Of course she is. She's always ready to strike. Even in my imagination.

The roof of my mouth dries. Pain flits through me, and I feel it—the anger, the adrenaline rising inside me, and how it crashes against the walls of my souls, demanding to be let out, so it can burst free and burn everything, get its revenge. Make her hurt, make her pay.

"Tell me what's been going on," Bridie purrs, reaching for my hand.

Move!

But I can't.

I never could. Not when I was little. Not now.

I grit my teeth as she makes contact. Her touch is hot and clammy, and I'm powerless to stop it. I am frozen.

"What happened to you? I thought you'd be the one to take over. To continue my legacy. But, no, you're running around with a bunch of hideaways."

Hideaways.

No. The thought of her having watched us all makes a rancid taste spread behind my front teeth. She's seen Amelia and Renee. Does she know Oleta's here too?

I stare at my hand in hers. I am pale, but she is ice.

"Oh, Inga, do you not have a voice? Did I flatten you into total submissiveness?" Bridie laughs. "I always knew you'd be easy." She meets my eyes slowly. "Easy to control."

I wrench my hand back. "I am not easy." My voice shakes. It's not me. Not the current me. It is the five-year-old me. The me who was scared, right from the moment I met Bridie in the woods, when I clung to my sister *and* tried to pretend I was strong.

"You've already proven you're easy to control." Bridie tilts her head to the side. "And it was so easy to find you."

"No, you're dead—"

Her lips twist into a savage smile. "No. I'm *free*," she whispers. "The New World was waiting for me. It's a lovely place."

The New World—the Untamed afterlife. I gulp.

"You're visiting from there?" I stare at her. Her hand, it felt real.

"I know Seers, and Seers know how to make things happen. Channeling, they call it. It's usually between families, but then again, we are family, aren't we?" Her grin gets bigger, garish.

"No." My word is a bullet. I stare at my hands— don't know why I do. Because this can't be real. This is a nightmare too. Not a flashback, a new construction.

"Call me *it*," Bridie whispers, and her whisper is both soft and sharp. Gentle and deadly.

"No."

Run!

But I can't move. I am shaking. Move, and I fall. My body is a traitor, and my mind isn't far behind. I can feel the flashbacks. They're close, like birds in the sky, swooping in.

Nausea threatens to become something more as I stare at her.

I need to turn around and get away. Need to shout to Amelia and Renee and Oleta and Falkes. We all need to get away from here.

Bridie's lips peel back. Even her teeth are the same— several missing, several streaked with yellow and brown marks. Her gums are black and shiny in places, only dulled slightly by the eerie, misty light.

She steps closer. "Call me *Mother* now."

My heart beats too fast. I try to step away from her, but my legs, they're still not working, still not mine.

And this can't be real. She can't really be here. Not her…ghost.

My stomach roils.

"Oh, you've always loved me, Inga," Bridie whispers.

Her words are like daggers, and I'm cut open, bleeding, raw. I am pouring out of me in huge rivers only I can see.

"I never loved you." I speak through gritted teeth. "I hated you. I still hate you."

She smirks, pressing her lips together so a huge expulsion of air exits her nostrils. "Keep telling yourself that, but the world knows." She lifts her arms up around us, and the moonlight catches her skin, makes her look like she's glowing. Like she's pure.

She is the least pure person I know.

"We belong together, Inga. We make the best team."

"No." I shake my head, feel the anger rising again inside me. "No, we didn't. You kidnapped me. You controlled me. You saw me as nothing but a machine you could control."

"We were saving the world. We did gallant things."

"No!" I yell, and I see someone behind her, stepping out of the mist.

It's Hunter.

There are more behind him: Bridie's men and women, the instructors, aunts and uncles, the logistics teams. The ones I've killed and… They're here too—*of course* they're here. A herd of evil, being channeled here from the New World? I thought I was free of them if I killed them, but… How did the Gods and Goddesses and spirits let them into the New World? They're evil. The New World is supposed to be a safe place.

But they're not Enhanced.

They're still Untamed.

And they're shouting. Shouting my name, shouting threats—but they stay behind Bridie, don't get any closer. Because Bridie's told them that I'm hers?

"We're not the bad ones, darling," Bridie says, her

voice like smoke as her men close around her. *"We never killed an Untamed individual."* Her eyes bore into me.

"Liar," I mutter. I shake my head. A harsh laugh escapes me. "You killed Fi. And what you did to Yvette—"

"Was deserved. Just as what you did to Vincent was. Perhaps we're more alike that you realize. There was a reason, after all, why I chose you. I know everything about who you are, who you can be."

"You know *nothing*," I snarl.

"We know everything," one of the men says.

Bridie laughs. It is not a good laugh. It is the laugh of the worst kind of person. Then she steps closer. Darkness swirls inside her eyes. "I know, Inga. I know exactly what happened."

My chest rises and falls too quickly. "Know *what*?" I hold her gaze, refuse to be the first one to look away. I am stronger now. She has to see that. She has to know that.

I am more than what she made me into.

So much more.

And all because of Amelia and Renee. They taught me to be human again, to feel.

"I know you killed me." Bridie's voice is low. "And I know you think you've got away with it. *Oh, clever Inga! Clever Inga who killed Mother and set all her brothers and sisters free!*" Her eyes flash. In the distance, I hear thunder. "But you're not so clever, because everything has consequences. And this—" She points at her heart. "*This* has consequences."

The men and women behind her stare at me. Venom drips from their gazes, and it burns me, drips on my skin.

"I look forward to the consequences playing out," Bridie says.

The *consequences*?

She smirks. "You, Inga, your days are numbered. Remember that. Don't get too comfortable." She steps back, nods at her adults. "Let's go."

"We'll be seeing you," Hunter say. His voice is dry. "You can count on that."

"We don't break our promises," another of the men says.

I watch them leave, walk away, my heart pounding so fast I feel sick. I run my hands through my hair. It's sticky. Sticky with sweat. I'm sweating loads, shaking and—

No. Bridie can't do this to me. They can't do this to me.

I won't let her or them have this control over me. Not when Bridie is dead. All those people are. They're not real.

I take a deep breath, watch as they disappear into the mist. I hold the air in my lungs for as long as I can, until my vision starts to darken, then exhale. My eyelids burn as I turn and head toward the truck and minibus.

Everything has consequences.

SIXTEEN

"YOU ALL RIGHT?" OLETA'S VOICE is low as she corners me outside the truck.

Everyone else is up now. Minnow and Lexa are nearby, sorting through weapons and ammunition, while Falkes arranges the food supplies, cataloging everything. Amelia's humming to herself as she shakes out her cardigan, and Renee's set up a small work station for her flintknapping.

Stephen announces to anyone who's listening that he's going for a piss, and Johnny and Callum burst into giggles.

"Inga?" Oleta's eyes are wide.

I nod, don't say anything. How can I say anything? Admit that I'm going mad? Because I have to be. Bridie *wasn't* there. She *wasn't* visiting from the New World. Nor were her men and women, the assassins I've killed. They can't have been. I killed them all, they wouldn't just *threaten* me with consequences. They'd act there and then, I know it.

That was all my imagination.

Because you're scared of her.

And I am. I still am. Admitting it, even to myself,

feels like a dagger ripping through me.

I curse, and Oleta's look gets sharper.

"What's going on?" she asks. "We not going to Royston's Rock?"

I take a deep breath. "We're going. We're going to kill every last one of them."

Oleta looks around quickly, and I realize I've said the words a little too loudly. Lexa and Minnow are the closest, but neither has reacted to my words.

"You don't look so good," Oleta says. She's wearing one of Stephen's T-shirts this time. It's big on her, and very bright orange—makes me feel giddy. "Nightmares?"

"You don't know the half of it," I mutter.

She holds out her hands, as if she expects me to take them. Huh. Like I'm going to do that. I keep my hands to myself.

"Talk to me, Inga." Her voice is soft, like liquid silver. A wave of lavender washes over me again. I can't believe Lexa's sharing her perfume with her because that's sure as hell not a scent clinging naturally to Stephen's shirt.

"There's nothing to talk about." My gaze is like steel.

"Oh, there's *everything* to talk about, Little Sister." Oleta's eyes are sharp. "We have to talk, Inga. We have to stick together. The things we've seen, we need to let them out. If we don't, they'll eat us from the inside out."

I roll my eyes.

"It's true. Don't look at me like that. The longer we're quiet, isolating ourselves, the more broken we get. Talking heals, Inga. It really does."

"So who've you been talking to?" I shiver, pull my jacket around me tighter. The wind's picking up.

A vacant look fills her face. "Do you ever think of what we could've had?"

"Changing the subject?" I raise my eyebrows.

She flicks her hand at me, as if batting away my question. "Like, how life could have been different—

you know, if Bridie hadn't chosen us? I just… I keep thinking about it, Inga. And I remember my parents, my brother, and life with my sisters, before all the bad stuff happened. I remember it all."

Her words make me uncomfortable, because I don't remember much of my life before. I was five when Bridie and her cronies took me. Ripped me from Gweneira's arms. I remember that moment, and, right before it, how angry my mother had been at me because I'd been swimming with Keelie and Elf, and swimming was something she'd forbidden, but I haven't got loads of memories. I can't even remember why we weren't at our village, what sort of trip we must have been on to be near the ocean. Or maybe we lived near the ocean anyway. I can't remember. But it was the last time I played, and the sea monsters were the monsters striving to reach me—until they weren't the monsters.

Until the real monsters came.

I was freshly five years old, but Oleta told me she and Petra were taken when they were eight. And those three years, they obviously made all the difference. Oleta would tell me about her old village a lot, when we were in Fi's band.

I stare at Oleta. She looks lost, like she's fallen inside her memories. I need to get her out of there. I know that feeling.

"What's been going on with you since we left the assassins?" I ask. "You've barely spoken of it."

She flinches and looks down. "Nothing much."

"Nothing much?" My tone is incredulous. I let out a long breath. Out the corner of my eye, I see Stephen returning to the bus. "Seems I'm not the only one who doesn't want to talk then."

Oleta's gaze darkens, and then she turns away. I look at the tension in her shoulders, how it's visibly building up.

She shrugs. "I fell in love, okay?"

"You fell in love?" I stare at her back, wait for her to

turn back around and smile and laugh, to tell me she was joking. Because we don't love. We're assassins. We're deadly. We don't experience soft feelings like love.

But Oleta doesn't say she's joking, and she doesn't laugh. She turns slowly, and I see depth in her eyes. Depths I'm not used to.

"They killed her," she says, shakes her head quickly. "Her name's Sasha. She… I went a bit wild after we escaped." She swallows hard. "I joined other groups, but they weren't very trustworthy. The men mainly saw me as a conquest—the whole *dominate an assassin* thing."

I wrinkle my nose. "Really, that's what they said?"

Oleta nods. "I didn't trust anyone for so long, except my…" She looks down. "When I met Sasha, I was a mess. But she was there for me. She listened. And she was the kindest person I knew."

"That's great," I say, but I'm very aware of how she's using the past tense to talk about her.

"They killed her, Inga. The assassins. Zak killed her. And it makes sense, given what we did. What Bridie made me do and—" She takes a deep breath. "The Goddess of Justice always punishes those who do wrong." She closes her eyes.

"Hey," I say. "The Goddess of Justice was just something Bridie made up. All those stories she told us? Those were just to keep us in line."

Oleta looks at me through narrowed eyes. "The Goddesses and Gods are real. Bridie may have used them to scare us, but they're still real." She shakes her head. "I was out hunting. Sasha wasn't well. She hadn't been for a time, she said, but right before we met, a lynx had attacked her. It was really quick, us falling in love. Just weeks, really. But it felt real. We both said it. But her wounds were infected, and no matter how hard I tried, I couldn't heal her." She takes a shaky breath. "I don't know why. It's not like they weren't working, because I healed myself at one point. They just wouldn't work on her…" She looks down. "Anyway, Sasha was injured, so she'd stay where we'd made this shelter, and I'd go out hunting every couple of days. She told me to leave her. Said she knew she was dying, but I wouldn't.

"I was out hunting, and when I came back, she'd been stabbed." She wipes her eyes, angrily. "That's how I knew they were tracking me, the assassins. They knew what Sasha meant to me, and Zak took her from me because we're not supposed to love. It only leads to pain."

I swallow hard. "You…you saw him?" My mind ticks. Where was this? How close was Zak to her, to me?

"I didn't see him," she snaps. "But I know it was him."

I turn over the words I want to say in my mouth, but I don't speak.

"I'd told Sasha everything in those few weeks," Oleta says. "Absolutely everything." She blinks at me. "It freed me, Inga, it really did. And you need to be free too. So, come on, talk to me."

"Talk?" I stare at her. "Now?"

"Yes." She folds her arms, looks impatient. "Tell me how you're feeling."

"How I'm feeling?" I burst out laughing. She wants to know how I'm feeling? I snort. What a lot of shit this is.

"You've gone soft." My tone is harsh.

Oleta's brows furrow. "And you've become a bitch."

"Look, we need to get going. We've got to get to Royston's Rock as soon as we can. We don't know how long the bands are going to stay there."

"Petra will tell me where they go. We've got time to talk, Inga." Her tone is stern, sharp.

"But why give them the opportunity to run, to hurt more people?" I stare at her. Another wave of lavender drifts toward me. She really has gone soft.

I turn away from her, see Falkes walking to the

minibus. "We ready to go?" I shout to him.

He nods. Doesn't say anything. Just nods.

We drive for most of the day, skirting widely around the perimeter of an Enhanced city. The back of my neck feels prickly, and I don't join in with Amelia and Renee's conversation. My head is too…busy. Feels like my thoughts are wading through stickiness, sugar that tries to weigh me down, hold me back, stop me from thinking about what I really need to think about—which is the plan. How Oleta and I are going to take out the assassins.

Questions burn through me.

How many will be there? How many children will they have imprisoned? How many of those children will actively fight against us, under misguided ideas of what is right? What's the best way to strike? How do we keep Amelia and Renee and Falkes and the others out of the action? We can't have them rushing in. They're not trained. They'd mess it all up.

My nose wrinkles as I think about Oleta—is she still capable of fighting? I think of the state we found her in. A member of Bridie's Assassins shouldn't have ended up like that. Even against a tiger… Especially a Seer. What about her white-light power for attacking?

Huh. She really has gone soft.

Maybe that's what love does to you.

I wrinkle my nose again. I'm never going to get soft like that. Never going to fall in love.

But don't you want it?

No. I don't want that. I don't want to become soft like Oleta.

SEVENTEEN

"YOU LET THEM GET AWAY? How could you?" Mother Bridie's eyes flash. "It was an easy set-up! The easiest! Is that who I've trained you to be? Are my assassins cowards?"

I take a step back. My foot catches an exposed root, and I fall back, land heavily on the dry earth. Dust flies up. "No, you don't understand—there were too many of them! They had guns."

"Did you not have a handgun?" Mother Bridie stands over me, a bowl of hot water in her hands. Steam rises from it, makes the air shimmer in front of her face.

I curse myself, curse how I froze out in the field. I could've been taken by the Enhanced so easily, because I showed weakness, let them know that I wasn't a skilled killer like the rest of band three.

The first time I was supposed to kill—to really kill an Enhanced One who wasn't bound, who wasn't expecting it—and I messed up.

Mother Bridie lifts the steaming bowl above me. My chest hitches, and I remember the pain—the pain of it before, when her scalding water met my skin. How long it took to heal.

"No, please, please!" I shriek, try to roll out of the way, but her foot is suddenly there, digging into my ribs.

"You know what happens if you disobey orders. You need to be tough. I will not have weak people in my bands. My assassins are feared by all. I will not have you ruin my reputation. Tiny Inga, you have to learn. You cannot be a coward. There is no other way. I am sorry."

I stare at Mother Bridie. She's not sorry at all, but still, I beg her, over and over again as she holds the bowl over my head. I look up, see the corners of her mouth twitch.

"Please," I try again, but I know.

It is useless.

"I am only doing what the Goddess of Justice would do," Mother Bridie says.

"I'll do better next time!"

The bowl shakes, and I don't have time to move. All I manage is to bow my head and try to curl up, protect my face, before the scalding water pours down.

It hits me. Instant pain. My neck, my back, my shoulders, and —

I am devoured by my screams.

EIGHTEEN

IT'S EVENING WHEN WE STOP. Royston's Rock is in the distance. There is just enough light left in the day that I can see the shape of it against the horizon: a huge, oblong-shaped boulder. I can't see any signs of the actual camp from here; it was always on the other side of the boulder, out of sight from this side.

"How are we going to play this then?" Oleta sidles up to me, chewing on the end of a strip of dried meat. She's got Lexa's puffer coat on, and her breath fogs the air. "Petra says they're still there."

I peer into the gloom. Do the assassins have any notion that today will be their last? Has Petra said anything? I lean back against the side of the truck and feel the coldness of the metal through my denim jacket. "We'll go tonight."

"The two of us?" Oleta's eyes flash. She glances over to where Falkes and the others are sitting, then looks back at me. Something lurks in the depths of her soul, something I can't quite read. But she can't be scared, can she? Or has love really got inside her?

I give her a look. "We're more than capable."

"I know." She bites off another bit of the dried meat,

chews it loudly, her mouth open.

I watch her carefully. She used to be the fire, the first flame. But now the dynamics are off between us. Time changes people, and the both of us are no exceptions.

I hunch my shoulders a little, so the jacket collar will warm my ears, but instead it catches against the rough patches of skin on the back of my neck. I lift my hands and touch the area. The skin is a strange texture mostly, but eerily smooth in other parts. I slide my finger across the smoothest bit. It's just slightly off center of the back of my neck, to the right of my skull tattoo. The asymmetry of it annoys me.

They've all seen my scars—Amelia and Renee and Falkes and the others—but they've not asked. No one does. Even Callum and Johnny don't ask about the scars. They've asked about my tattoos and the killings, and even made up a story about the owl on my arm, but the scars are off-limits. I'm glad. I don't want to tell them about the scalding water. I don't want their sympathy.

"Well, I need a cool name then." Oleta shrugs and licks her lips.

"What?" I stare at her, but I'm focused on the shrugging movement more than her words. Shrugging—that's uncertainty. I don't get her now. Yet other times I *do* know her. It's like she's two different people. The one she used to be, and this one. And I never know which one she'll be.

She wipes her fingers on Lexa's coat. "You're the Night Slayer, Inga. I'm not just going to be your assistant." She laughs.

Something about her laugh bothers me.

"You sure you're up to this?" I look for any sign of softness in her face now, but I can't find any.

Her eyes darken. "Don't question me."

There. That's the Oleta I know.

I hold her gaze for a while. "Don't give me a reason to."

"Don't speak to me like you're in charge." Her voice

is low. "We're working together on this, Inga. We're *equal*."

Equal? She doesn't want to be superior?

I frown. She stares at me, eyes wide, waiting for my answer. I keep my lips pressed tightly together. She's back? So what was that earlier, that shrugging?

"I'll contact Petra again and update you in a bit," she says.

"And ask her to drug as many of them as possible."

"You need them drugged in order to kill them?" Oleta raises her eyebrows and inhales sharply.

"No. But there are going to be a lot. We don't want one screaming as we kill him and alerting the others. Best to see if she can drug everyone."

Oleta makes a noncommittal noise. "Well, we need to work out what we're going to tell Falkes and the others."

"Tell them?" I glare at her. "We're not going to tell them anything."

She raises one eyebrow. "They'll notice us sneaking away."

"No, they won't. They—" I pause as Renee walks over to the truck, tells us she's just getting another blanket for Amelia.

"Oh, is she cold again?" Oleta asks.

Renee laughs. "Ma's always cold."

I wait until Renee is back with the others again. They're sitting by the bus, on the fold-up chairs that Falkes keeps in the minibus. Renee drapes the extra blanket over Amelia. She'd wanted to make a fire when we stopped, but Oleta and I had stopped her. Smoke would alert others to our location, and though they think we're nearing good Untamed, I was quick to point out that smoke can be seen for miles and we don't want to risk the Enhanced seeing us from a distance.

"Falkes and the others will be asleep," I tell Oleta. "They won't notice us sneaking away."

"We're not taking chances. Don't want to have one

of them wander after us and ruin everything. We need to warn them." Oleta gives me a stern look. "We're going to rescue children, Inga—we're not killing them. We're bringing them back, and Falkes and the others need to be prepared. Can't just surprise them with a bunch of half-trained killers."

"The hell we are bringing them back!" I stare at her. We can't bring any children back. Doesn't she realize that?

"We're not killing the children." Oleta's eyes flash. "They didn't choose that life."

"I didn't say we were killing them." I lower my voice. Even I'm not that heartless. "But they're not coming back here with us."

"What are you saying? We kill the adults and leave them?"

I nod.

"Some will be *babies*." She shakes her head. "You can't leave babies out there, alone."

"They'll have older children with them."

"We don't know that," Oleta hisses. "There could just be newborns for all we know."

"Then find out from Petra." I stare at her. "But we can't bring any back here."

"What if there's just one toddler or something?"

"There won't just be one," I say. "And there will be older children who can look after the littles. We'll kill the adults, and, without leaders guiding them, they won't become as bad as we are. With time and care, they'll find their true selves again. Find families."

I think of Caro. If all the adults at our camp had been killed, he'd have taken care of all the littles, made sure they didn't grow up to become what Bridie wanted us all to be.

Oleta's upper lip curls, but before she can say anything, I cut her off.

"This is final," I say. "I mean it. We're not bringing any children back with us. And don't say a word to Falkes or anyone. Not unless you want them stopping us from going completely."

Despite what Oleta says, we're not equal. *I'm* in charge, and one thing I've learned from living with Falkes all these years is that you don't give him warning of anything. That gives him power, gives him the chance to stop you or change your plans, make his own decisions. And telling him what we're going to do would have him tie us both up or something. He doesn't want trouble.

He doesn't want me killing anymore Untamed, regardless of who they are.

And he won't want more wild assassins in his group. No more little monsters.

No more little monsters who will scream and fight them—because they won't all be older and pretty like Oleta. And not all the children will be like how Caro was. Hell, I wasn't. And some will have discovered they like killing. Some will be loyal to the assassin way of life. And I am not endangering this group.

"Contact Petra now," I tell Oleta, ignoring the glare she gives me. "Get the latest intel. Numbers."

"The children," Oleta whispers.

I roll my eyes. "Then we'll finalize the details."

Two hours later, I am a ball of energy. All different types of energy. Excitement and adrenaline and anticipation—the good kind of nerves, because I'm not weak. No.

I find myself smiling at the outline of the truck. This is it. I can feel it. We're going to wipe out more of the assassins. Get most of them tonight in one go. Oleta reported from Petra that the majority of the assassins, thirty-five of them, are now at Royston's Rock, along with children of all ages. Only a small band, led by a new recruit, is out north. It's a small setback that not all the assassins will be present, that I can't take them all out in one fell swoop, but we're going to make progress. Big progress.

And we reckon the eight originals are at Royston's Rock. I clench my jaws. We're going to have to be careful. Especially with Bridie's daughter, Brighid, around. And if she teams up with Zak and Clara to fight against me and Oleta, the three of them are going to have more power.

Still, if Petra's free of her chains and able to fight alongside Oleta and me, we have a fighting chance.

I breathe deeply as I imagine seeing the originals again. I can picture them perfectly: Zak and Clara, the deadly aunt and uncle siblings; Brighid in her cloak of darkness, moving too quickly, her face a constant moving blur of others' countenances; Dylan and Luca, the seconds-in-command of Zak and Clara; and Taylor, Gabi, and Mark, the instructors—assassins who aren't skilled enough to fight alongside the aunts and uncles, but skilled enough to teach.

I know it's silly that I'm putting so much emphasis on eradicating the world of Bridie's original gang, when they've got new recruits, but the moment the world is ridded of the original assassins, I'll feel better. I know I will. The weight from around my shoulders will be removed. I'll be able to breathe again— properly breathe.

"So we'll reach our new people tomorrow?" Amelia's face is hopeful, illuminated by a sliver of moonlight. She's sitting a little way away from me, huddled up in blankets.

We're all out here still. Lexa and Renee are smoking. Minnow's napping in her chair, one hand over her face—no doubt smudging her carefully applied eyeliner. Callum and Johnny are playing a complicated game of tag with Stephen in the dark. Falkes is half-lying, half-sitting against the stump of a tree, after he complained the fold-up chair was giving him backache, and he's now using a twig to pick the dirt out of his nails. Every so often, he digs too deeply with the twig and yelps as he jabs himself in the soft nail bed.

"Yes, ma'am," Oleta says, a small smile on her lips. She's on my other side, the closest person to me. "Very soon we'll be with other Untamed."

I catch her eye, give her a look, but she just smirks.

"I bet it's Taras's group," Amelia continues. She exhales a long breath. "Has to be. My, I wonder if I'll recognize Marina." She turns to me. "It's been a good thirty-five years since I've seen her. She was a wee lass last time, when me and Adesh saw her."

I tune out her words as she reminisces about Adesh Karnad, her late husband and Renee's father, because whenever she mentions him she goes on to talk about her love for him, how amazing they were together, and I don't want to listen to that kind of soft talk now. I need to stay sharp.

"I think it's time to turn in," Oleta says, faking a yawn. "We're going to have a busy day tomorrow."

"You got a feeling about that?" Lexa calls to her, then looks at me as well.

I nod. "Seer powers."

Oleta smirks, but soon enough, we are all heading back to the vehicles.

I climb into my reclined seat and wait for sleep to take Amelia and Renee. Oleta's in here now as well—Falkes didn't stop her with some crap about not putting all the eggs in one basket—and her eyes are sharp beacons in the dark.

"Ready?" I whisper against the backdrop of heavy, sleeping breathing.

Oleta's eyes glisten.

NINETEEN

"WE'RE KILLING ALL THE ADULTS," I tell Oleta as we walk through the dark. "Don't discriminate between originals and newcomers. They've all got to go."

Earlier, before we sat with the others, Oleta and I finalized the plan after she'd been in contact with Petra. We should both know what we're doing, but I know Oleta—or at least I knew her when she wasn't unpredictable like she is now—and I'm not taking any chances.

"With the exception of Petra, of course," I add. "She's the only one we bring back—so long as she doesn't try to harm us."

Oleta nods. "And the children. We're bringing them back."

My shoulders tighten. How many times do we have to go through this? "No. They'll have been brainwashed, just like we were."

Her jaw visibly tightens. "But they have to come with us. We can't just leave them. They're *us*, Inga. And we're bringing Petra back anyway, so we bring them too."

I feel anger rising inside me. "The more goals we have, the weaker our overall results will be. If we're trying to rescue children and kill the adults, we'll end up doing neither well. And eliminating the assassins is our priority."

She glares past my shoulder, and I pause for a second, before swiftly walking on. I know that look. She's going to disobey me. Cause trouble there? If she doesn't stick to the plan for killing the assassins and do her part, it could make me more vulnerable.

I sigh. "Look, this time we kill all the adults, okay? But we'll go back and get the kids later. Once we've warned Falkes that our group's going to grow a whole lot."

She kicks at the long grass. "What's the point in splitting it into two journeys though? We're going to be at the camp tonight. Why leave the children, then go back for them?"

"Because we'll need Renee and Amelia and everyone with us to help with children. Probably take the minibus. And we can't tell the others now, else we'll be stopped from going altogether—I can guarantee that. Then we get no children *and* we kill no assassins. This is final, Oleta. This is the plan. No arguments."

She glowers at the darkness. "I don't believe you have any intention of going back for the children, ever. You just want to kill the adults and leave the littles to die."

I let out an exasperated gasp. "Look, they wouldn't die anyway—they're half-trained killers. And we could be doing a lot worse to them. But we're not. We're *not* killing them, are we?" Well, so long as they don't try and kill us, stop us from doing our work. "Focus on that, all right? And we *will* go back for them once we've warned the others and made plans. If we suddenly turn up with them, Falkes could very well kill them, say they're too dangerous, going to stab us in our sleep or something. No, we've got to play this carefully."

And we need to assess whether they're safe to bring back at all. Hell, this whole idea about going back for the children later was just a spur of the moment thing to get Oleta to comply with the plan.

But it is a promise I've made now, and I hate breaking promises.

I swallow hard. We need to plan out something as big as bringing back a bunch of children, and get Falkes and the others on board. I guess it'll help that most of our group members are parents; we can really play on their emotions to get them to agree with the rescue. But that's it—the rescue has to have all of us involved. Whereas the killings just need me and Oleta on board.

I flex my fingers, then they automatically go to the two guns—Amelia's Glock and Renee's Eclipse—and the knives in my belt. It was easy to get them.

Oleta looks at me. "How can we just leave them though, really? The children? They're going to be scared when strangers have just murdered their families."

"Murdered their *captors*," I correct. "They're not their families."

"The assassins are all about family," she says. "And we're part of that family too, no matter what, and we'll be leaving these children alone."

"Just for a day or something," I say. "Maybe not even that." My head spins. How quickly can we get the others on board? I think of Falkes. How realistic is it that he will agree to this? And if he doesn't? Well, Oleta's going to do it anyway, I know that.

She lets out a long sigh. "Fine. But—"

We see it.

My breath freezes in my lungs as I stare at the signs of life in the darkness: the shapes of the hut are visible by the moonlight, and the embers of the central fire glow.

I breathe in deeply, feel a little winded. The roof of my mouth is dry. I touch the handle of the Glock in my belt, for reassurance.

I don't know what I expected to feel—or that I would feel different seeing the camp this time than I did before, only years ago, when I killed originals here.

But I do.

Because it all comes flooding back. And maybe I felt like this last time, but I didn't linger on those feelings. I was more savage then, having freshly escaped the assassins. I was focused on killing and killing only, not half-formed plans of saving children.

Royston's Rock is the camp they trained me at, and suddenly I think about my childhood there. Out of the two camps I lived at under Bridie's reign, it's the one I remember the most. My formative years were spent there.

I have memories embedded in the very soul of the place. Good and bad. Memories seared on my skin.

And it looks the same.

New life has been breathed into it, but it looks the same. I resist the urge to laugh. After all these years, they haven't made it any different. I wonder who's in the central hut now. Which pathetic 'leader' has been given the task of overseeing the camp.

Anger boils through me. My gut tightens.

"Ready?" I glance at Oleta.

Her mouth is set in a long line—her determined face. She nods.

"Right. We go in and take out all the adults. We secure their weapons. Where's Petra meeting us?"

"First Hut." Oleta rolls her shoulders, then points, even though it's not necessary. We both know where First Hut is. Too many memories. At least that means Petra's not in the caves.

"I don't know that she's agreed to the drugging though," Oleta adds. "She wouldn't say."

I stare at her. "*What*? What do you mean? Why didn't you say this earlier?"

"Didn't seem relevant."

I curse her under my breath. "No, you must know what Petra's going to do."

"I don't."

"She must have said yes or no as to whether she's helping us."

"We know she's helping us." Oleta's tone rises. "She's told us who's here, and she's not told anyone about us."

That we know of. I want to add that, but I don't. It wouldn't help.

"But you don't know if she's actually drugged anyone?"

"I don't know."

I roll my eyes. Oleta could've found out this info if she tried. I look at her sideways. There's no point in me saying anything else, but is Oleta totally up for this? I frown. She used to be like fire, but now she's ash. Sometimes hot—scaldingly so—but burnt out. Different. A shadow that can sometime bite, sometimes melt away.

My heart pounds. If Petra's being awkward and hasn't drugged anyone at the camp to make our job easier as we take them all out, how much of the information she's given us can we trust to be accurate? A dank taste spreads across the back of my mouth. Even if Petra's being completely honest with us, there could still be more assassins here than she knows about. And if none of them are drugged, how realistic is it that Oleta and I can take them all out?

For the first time, my gut twists.

But, no, we have to do this. We have to—

Something rustles behind us.

I grab the Glock and turn in a flash, eyes narrowing at the darkness.

"What was that?" I hiss at Oleta.

She's turned too, a knife out ready in one hand, a pistol in the other. "I don't know." Her words are slow, careful.

I don't turn my head to look at her, but from my

peripheral vision, I can tell she doesn't look at me either. I just keep staring. There was movement. I know it. An animal or a person?

"Are we being followed?" Oleta asks after a moment.

My eyes are so wide the cold of the night makes them ache. I look out for Falkes's shape or Renee lurking. But there's no one.

The night air whistles. I look at the sky. Small streaks of color—orange and navy—have merged into the darkness. But they're visible, setting the stage for what's to come.

"Shit." I let out a long breath and look at Oleta. "The Turning."

My hands shake. I don't like the Turnings—the times when the seasons change and the spirits are most active. The spirits are deadly—things I can't fight and kill. Not when shooting one just shatters the spirit and causes the rest of the flock to attack you.

I may be an assassin, but I'm not stupid enough to take on forces beyond my control.

Oleta looks at the sky for a long moment. "Could just be morning dawning."

I shake my head. "That's not a sunrise. And it's too early. It's the Turning coming."

"Well, we've got time," she says, her voice crisp.

We have? I bite my lip. The Turnings come in quickly, most of the time, and we've not had one for a long, long time. I frown. Longer than usual. The spirits must be restless. They're not going to wait for us to finish our work.

Unless they help us?

I frown. It's not unheard of for spirits to help, but that tends to be only if we're fighting the Enhanced. Will they understand the assassins are worse than the Enhanced, forcing Untamed children to be killers? Destroying their lives?

But your life wasn't destroyed.

My jaw sets. That's because I'm strong. But I think of the Atkinson boys, Callum and Johnny—they'd be destroyed if they were recruited. And with less Untamed about now, the assassins can't be as picky with which children they take.

"We won't have another chance if we don't act now," Oleta says.

"Okay, now."

I push my hair back and slip my Glock back into my belt, then take my biggest knife out. If the men and women are sleeping and not drugged, then death by the quickest and quietest methods is preferable. And I know all the techniques.

I am smiling. I can't help it. Adrenaline pulses through me, the sweet promise of what is to come: death.

I am an assassin—doing just what they raised me to do.

"Okay. Signal system," I say. "No signal means everything is fine with each of us. The call of the female Eurasian eagle-owl means there's danger, that you need my help or I need yours." Huh. Not that that will happen. "And find out from Petra if they are drugged. The call of the male eagle-owl means they're not. No signal if they are."

Oleta nods, and I signal to her to start the plan as soon as we reach the camp.

We separate. She goes for First Hut, where Petra will be, to get her so they can work on securing all the assassins' weapons and gathering the children into a safe place, before joining me.

I skirt around the edge of the camp, my steps light.

Start on the outskirts and move inward.

Bridie's own instructions—one of the ways of taking out a whole village. She taught us well. All the silent assassination methods.

The first hut I come to is small. The entrance panel flaps slightly, only tied down by one small piece of string. Flimsy. Just asking for trouble really.

My knife is in my hand, and I cut through the string silently. I lift the panel and look inside. Darkness. Of course. I hear breathing—heavy—as I wait for my eyes to adjust. The night air cools my back as I peer inside. Three women. I can see their shapes. Dark hair.

They're not any of the originals. My shoulders sag. Why can't they be?

I know it doesn't make a difference whether the first assassin I take out at this camp is an original or not—because every adult here is going to die, and quite probably all the children too—but it matters to me, a small part of me is caught up on it.

I step in, my feet silent. The best predators are silent.

I do another quick sweep of the hut. No children in here. Good. None of the women have stirred. Drugged or just heavy sleepers? I'm not a heavy sleeper. Not when I was raised by Bridie, and she and her adults could come for us at any moment. I never liked that, that feeling of never being safe. Close your eyes, and your guard goes down, makes you vulnerable.

I stare at the sleeping women. Oleta hasn't alerted me with the call of the female owl, so that means yes, everyone is drugged. I wonder what the women are dreaming about. Do they dream of murder and crying babies and other atrocities? Or have whatever drugs are in their system blocked it all out?

I slit the first woman's throat before she even stirs. As blood gushes from her neck, she opens her eyes, sees me, but she's choking. She tries to speak, and her hands go to her neck, trying to stop the waves of red.

But she can't.

A smile tugs my lips.

A squeaking gasp grates against her teeth, and—

The other two women jolt awake.

Shit. Not drugged enough. Or at all?

Not that that's a problem.

I am quick.

I stab the next nearest woman in the abdomen and kick her down. I am swift as I stab her twice more.

The third woman watches me, eyes wild. She doesn't make a move to protect herself or attack. Just stares at me.

"Please," she whispers.

Please? I stare at her. What kind of wimps work for Bridie's gang now? Damn, Bridie would be turning in her grave if she knew this woman had taken on her legacy.

I snort.

As if I'm giving any of them chances.

The pleading woman looks to be a few years younger than me—eighteen, nineteen, maybe—and suddenly Oleta's words come back to me. What if this woman was a child who grew up here? I didn't know all the littles and highers—Bridie's Assassins was a huge organization, spread over several camps.

What if this woman never wanted to be this person?

What if she is me?

No.

I see the marks on her. The killing marks. The trainer marks. Whether she wanted it or not, it doesn't change what they've made her into or the fact she hasn't escaped.

She doesn't stop me as I slit her throat.

I wipe her blood off my knife, onto my leggings—or rather, Minnow's leggings, they're hers—then assess my work. The woman I stabbed in the stomach and chest is moving feebly. I slit her throat too. Minimal noise. Good.

Before I head back out, I listen for sounds outside. The air feels thick, heavy, like it's working with Oleta and me to help us.

Oleta. Is she getting the children? I can't hear any cries or shouts. Are they drugged, even when these women weren't? Was that why Oleta didn't signal to me that the assassins were drugged? If she found the children clearly drugged wouldn't she just assume Petra had done it to everyone? And what about Petra? Is she helping? Or is she not?

I move onto the next hut. Two men and a woman. All sleeping. None are originals.

Adrenaline floods me as I stare at the woman.

I go to her first and plunge the knife deep into her neck, getting the artery. Blood sprays out. She gasps, chokes, brings her arms up, tries to fight me. Nails scratch me, but I'm quicker.

"No!" a voice screams, and something hits me across the back.

I stumble to the right, but I haven't lost my balance completely. I kick out, catch the advancing man in the side. He falls back. I tighten my grip on the knife, and then I slash it across his abdomen, before turning back to the woman, finishing her off.

More figures come at me, and it is a dance of death and revenge and righteousness as I move from hut to hut.

Because this is right.

This is it.

And they fall down, dead.

There are shouts in the camp now. Shit.

But it means I can use the firearms now, if they know I'm already here. Quicker and easier. I swap my knife for the Glock.

I wipe sweat from my forehead as I move onto the next hut.

Empty.

I frown.

What?

My breath pounds through me. Where are the others? I've taken out nine. There's got to be more. They're grouping together somewhere?

Oleta and Petra should've secured all their weapons now, and be gathering the children Oleta deems as not a threat—probably all of them—to set them aside, out of harm's way. But are they complying? The shouts I can hear sound like they're from adults, but they're meaningless to me. A different language?

I frown, and—

A man launches himself at me. My Glock flies from my hand and—

Luca.

An original. *Yes.*

I see the fire in his eyes—fire that a weed like him doesn't normally have, but it ignites my own, or maybe it was still burning from the last kill, because this is easy.

He is weak—surprisingly so—and my hands go to his neck, even though I've got the Eclipse and two knives in my belt. Killing with my bare hands is always more satisfying—and he's weak. I can do this easily. Even if it means my hands touch his long, greasy hair.

Luca tries to knee me in the chest as I squeeze, and he should be using his arms, his hands against me, if he really wanted to fight. But his arms flail at his sides as I choke him.

His eyes bulge as I slam him against the wall of a hut. His face turns a flat gray in the moonlight.

"Why aren't you trying?" I yell at him, but he goes limp, and I'm supporting all his weight.

Limp?

Playing dead?

I let him fall, and I am ready—ready for him to strike like the snake he is.

But he doesn't.

I wait, feel the hairs on the back of my neck stand. Cool air kisses my skin.

Luca doesn't move.

So I lean over him, and I snap his neck with my bare hands. It's a technique Bridie taught me and—

And I am waiting—where are Elf and Bea and Keelie? Why aren't the Gods and Goddesses showing them to me? I need to see them, I have to see them, and—

"Well, well, well," says a slow voice.

I turn and see Gabi.

She looks awful. A lot thinner than when I last saw her, and she's clearly lost all her muscle mass. Hasn't been training. Or she's been ill or injured. Her eyes narrow as she stares at me.

She makes the first move: a clumsy attempt at a punch which I block effortlessly. My other arm shoots out, and I strike her upper stomach. She grunts, and reaches for me, for my neck.

I bite her fingers, and she screams.

Use the other gun.

But I don't reach for the Eclipse. Or even the knives. My hands close around her neck, and she's shaking as I snap her neck in one swift move. Her body slides down mine. I step over it.

An owl hoots, too close, too loud, too drawn out. The female call.

Oleta's signal.

Trouble.

I turn, grab the Glock from where it lies on the ground a few feet away from Luca's body, and I run, suddenly more aware of the blood that splatters my clothes.

Oleta signals again—the call for danger and requested help.

My sister needs me.

Sister. A sour taste fills my mouth as I think the word.

No. *Gweneira* is my sister.

But Oleta needs me.

I plow on. She saved me. I won't let her down.

My breaths come in short, sharp bursts as I spring forward.

Oleta calls again, and I hone in on where the sound is coming from.

I fly into Second Hut, ready, adrenaline pumping through me and—

It takes me a moment to see the scene. A woman lying across the floor. Dark hair and—

Oleta.

I inhale sharply. No sign of Petra, but Oleta's bleeding, and—

"Oh, Inga too, how lovely."

My gaze jolts upward.

Another assassin, one I don't recognize. Short, cropped blond hair, and skinny arms and legs. Looks a bit like Lexa actually, but taller. Very tall, especially for an Untamed woman. She's not armed.

I line up the Glock. It will be an instant death. Loud—but they know we're here. And maybe Falkes and the others will hear it, but they'll understand. And it's too late for them to stop us.

Oleta wheezes something at me, but I can't make out the words.

The blond assassin hasn't moved. My finger over the trigger flexes.

"No!" a voice cries. "Not my mother!"

I jolt as a weight hits me, just as I pull the trigger.

The gunfire sounds as I fall to the side, crying out and—

Stephen's face, against mine, sweaty and—

He wrestles me to the ground.

Stephen?

He's here? What the hell?

He punches me, but there's only so long I can stay shocked for.

I ram my fist into his upper stomach. He grunts, but he's strong—muscles bulging as he pins me down, his hands over my wrists. I can't move my arms, can't get to the weapons in my belt. And the Glock—where's the Glock now?

I yell, and see Oleta moving. Shapes and—

The woman—is she dead?

Is she Stephen's mother, Lexa's sister? I try to think of her name, but I don't know it. I never met her. But she was assumed to be dead or Enhanced—that's what Amelia told me. Not with the assassins.

I bring my knee up, hard and quick, and get Stephen's crotch. His eyes widen, watering, but he screams at me, spittle splattering my face. And he doesn't fall away, doesn't double up. Damn. He's strong.

I fight against his arms, got to weaken his grip on

me. Need to get my hands free.

"I'm going to kill you!" he roars, and I see a glimpse of the woman on the floor. Definitely dead. His mother? She looks like Lexa. Drake blood clearly shapes her features. An *assassin*....

Another assassin gone, dead, and I'm trying to lift my head, trying to see Keelie or Bea or Elf, because the Gods and Goddesses have to show them to me, they have to. My family. Unless they're all dead, and that's why I can't see them....

"Should've killed you a long time ago," Stephen hisses, still red-faced and panting, and—

Oleta screams. I look to the right, past Stephen's ear. A knife's blade flashes, and it happens quickly.

Stephen screams, gurgles, his weight collapsing on top of me as Oleta stabs him in the back. His muscles pin me down, and I hear Oleta's barking laugh.

She pulls me out from under him. She's shaking—the kind of tremors that arise from adrenaline. She doesn't look weak now, and she's not bleeding anymore. Had time to heal herself?

My head spins, and I'm free—losing time, I don't know. Everything's happening too quickly.

Oleta stabs Stephen again and again and again, grinning as she does.

Death.

Death.

Death.

I've never seen her eyes so alive, and I wonder if that's what I look like when I kill. Oleta looks high, wild, as she turns back to me. Is she seeing her lost family, her parents and brother? Do we *both* get rewarded by the Divine Ones?

Stephen gurgles. His fingers twitch, reaching out toward me. "Please..."

Oleta stamps on his face. "Come on," she yells at me. "You know we've got to do this."

Killing Stephen is weird.

I do it, but I don't feel present.

Not in the way I normally do as I slash his throat, and then his stomach and chest for good measure.

And I want to say it's because he's not an assassin. Only he's not the first Untamed I've killed who isn't an assassin.

His nose cracks under my boot. A spur of the moment action.

And then it's done.

"Wow," Oleta looks at me. "Was Stevie-boy an assassin too?"

I shake my head. "I don't know..." Maybe she's right. Maybe... I mean... His own mother... His own mother was one of Bridie's. Maybe he was in contact with her the whole time? He knew she was here. And that we were here....

Unless he followed us, saw this settlement, and then found her?

"What do we do now?" Oleta is breathless. "If Stephen's here, Falkes could be too. They all could be."

Falkes. My shoulders tighten. Is he in on this too? He's Stephen's father, I'm sure of it. So was he in love with Stephen's mother, still in contact with her? Still—

Footsteps. Outside.

Shit.

I see my Glock, a few feet away. Must have fallen in the fight with Stephen. I grab it, feel in my belt for the Eclipse but find it's not there. Just got one knife too now, no idea where the other is, and—

The drape of the hut is pulled back.

Harsh light. A torch.

A woman, there.

Dark hair, a petite frame, and vivid, blue eyes. Somehow, I see her eyes, even in this light.

My eyes widen.

No....

The tattoos on her....

"Hello, sister," Gweneira says.

I STARE AT MY SISTER and hold onto the Glock even tighter.

Time seems to stop. We have all frozen. Nothing is happening. Nothing *can* happen, except my heart pounding and me staring.

Gweneira is here?

"Gweneira?" I think I say her name out loud, but she doesn't react. Doesn't move. Still frozen.

She looks older. But she would do. Her hair is a dull brown, plaited and braided, two snakes hanging over her shoulders.

Still, her eyes are the same. It is comforting.

"You're in charge here?" Oleta's voice is low, but it breaks through the rushing sounds in my ears.

"I'm not just in charge—I'm the leader." Gweneira's voice is soft.

The *leader*?

And then I see them. See them properly in the torchlight. The tattoos on Gweneira's arms. The eagle on her left shoulder—the symbol of her aunthood— and the *phoenix* over the base of her throat. I inhale sharply. It's Bridie's phoenix: the sign of the leader, the one who rises and lifts the Untamed back to superiority.

And the phoenix is on *her*? My sister? She's the new leader? Not Brighid Berthold, Bridie's daughter? Is Brighid dead?

Oleta looks from me to Gweneira and back again. And then they share a long look. A look I can't decipher. I think Oleta nods at Gweneira, but I'm not sure. My vision, it's....

I shake my head, stand up. I don't remember crouching by the bodies of Stephen and his mother.

Oleta and Gweneira. No. They shouldn't meet. Not my sisters—

No, Oleta's not your sister!

"Give me the gun if you're not going to do it," Oleta says, and she's *asking* me, not yanking the firearm out of my hand, that's important. And she's not springing forward to kill her with her bare hands, or with a knife. Has she still got one on her?

"No!" I yell the word too forcefully. She can't use it on Gweneira, she can't.

"So, sister, you're the Night Slayer," Gweneira says.

My sister doesn't sound like herself. That's what I focus on. It's not her. It can't be.

"Inga, we have to kill her."

"We can't."

"We kill *all* the assassins."

"But not *me*," Gweneira whispers. Her whisper is a blanket over my mouth, pressing down, suffocating me. "That wouldn't be a nice reunion."

"Why?" I yell at her. Fury pulls through me. The Glock feels hot in my hand, like it's burning me. "Gweneira? Why are you their leader? Is it... Were you looking for me? Joining them only to—"

Gweneira laughs—a savage sound that cuts me. "Is that really how you want to spend this time, trying to pretend that I'm not Bridie's successor?"

Bridie's successor. My stomach twists.

"And, oh, sister, I don't know what all the hype is

about. You're not a big, bad wolf. You're pathetic. You could've killed me ten times over in the last few minutes, but you've done nothing but stare."

She's… They've got her. Got my sister. She *must've* joined to find me, but they've messed with her head and—

Gweneira lifts her hand. A pistol, in her grasp. I see it at the last moment.

Oleta screams.

I try to move, but my legs are stone, and I can't.

Gweneira smiles at me as she pulls the trigger. "Sleep well, sister."

"THEY'RE GOING TO KILL US *if we can't do this.*"
Samira is shaking.

"It's fine," Caro says. "You can do this."

"But it's the test tomorrow." Oleta's brows furrow.
"Group-test." She shakes her head and looks at me, then
Samira, then Nathan. "You three better not let me and Caro
down."

Me and Nathan and Samira? Her and Caro? I stare at
Oleta, feel heat rush to my ears. She's grouping me with
Samira and Nathan? What the hell? I'm nearly seven years
old, and I'm close to being a higher! Samira and Nathan are
still at the bottom of the littles, haven't passed the test in
the top three to even allow them to start training with real
Enhanced. Last time, Samira was fourth. But fourth means
she's still too far down the list. And Nathan's always been
close to last.

My skills are closer to Oleta's and Caro's than Samira's
and Nathan's—yet because of my age, Oleta thinks she can
just lump me in with the babies?

"It's okay," Caro says. He places a cooling hand on my
shoulder. "We'll all be fine."

I swallow hard.

"We work as a group," he says. "We cover each other. We've always got each other's backs."

"You mean we look after them." Oleta doesn't even try to hide the disdain in her voice. Her words drip with it, and I imagine it as venom, venom that trickles on me, that burns.

"Hey, I don't need looking after," I say.

"Oh really? So, you didn't freeze when you were out in the field and needed us to save you?"

"That was months ago."

"And that's the only field practice you've had," Oleta snaps. "We don't know what the group test will be! It could take place in a town or anything."

"It wouldn't," Caro says. "Not when Samira and Nathan haven't left the camp yet to train."

"But they should've by now—plenty of time," Oleta says, glaring at Nathan. "And that doesn't mean Bridie's going to give us an easy test."

"I'm more skilled than the other littles." I rub my arms and find myself looking at Oleta's arms. At the marks on her.

The rewards.

I look at my own arms. Bare.

"We're going to do this," I say.

"If you want your marks, you've got to prove you're a good killer. Our group has to win tomorrow," Oleta says. "My group does not fail. And that means you and Samira both need to do your jobs and one of us had better bloody well hope that Nathan doesn't need saving more than usual."

She talks as if Nathan's not standing right in front of her, and he glances at Caro, probably trying to work out what to do or say that won't make Oleta more angry. She doesn't look happy. Of course she doesn't. Group tests are unpredictable, that's what I've learned. It's the first time our band has had one since I've been here, and there seems to be no structure about when they pop up or which bands are tested. Band one has already had three. But this is the first one for Fi's family, and all we know of it is that only the highers and littles are involved. That's all Bridie's told us.

When Fi and Yvette heard this, a strange look passed

between them, before Fi looked relieved.

Samira's eyes are shiny. She's close to tears. I resist the urge to make a snide comment. But, really, if she wants to be respected more here, she needs to act less like a baby. It's common sense. Anyone will tell you that.

"And Caro and I shouldn't need to carry any of you," Oleta continues. "You need to learn to do this yourself and—"

A scream cuts through the air.

The five of us jump up.

I stumble to the doorway, ahead of the others. Cold air blasts over me as I see men and women rushing around. A scurry of movement. And shouts. Lots of shouts that I can't make out and—

A gunshot.

I flinch.

"Are we under attack?" Caro's voice is breathless.

"No, don't go out!" I grab his arm.

"Don't go out?" Oleta sneers. "We don't run away from threats." She turns scathing eyes on me and—

And that's when it happens.

Out there.

"You thought you could challenge me?" Mother Bridie's scream is loud.

We turn and look outside.

There is a gun on the ground, a few feet away from a woman on her knees. Fi. It's her…and there's another body, a little farther away. A woman stirring feebly. Yvette.

What? They turned on Mother Bridie?

My heart squeezes as Mother Bridie picks up the gun and—

Bang.

My ears burn.

Fi falls. Slumps down. Dust rises.

She doesn't move.

She's…she's dead?

Mother Bridie killed one of us?

One of us.

My breath catches in my throat, and I look at Yvette. Yes, she's still alive. But no one's going to her, and I can see the ground around her is turning red with her blood.

"Anyone else?" Mother Bridie yells, turning. Her gaze locks onto mine, across the dusty ground, and my soul turns to ice. "Anyone else want to turn their backs on our good work?"

I flinch. Caro grabs me, pulls me to him.

"What about Yvette?" I hiss at him.

"She won't be part of this band now," Oleta pants. She's got Samira and Nathan crushed to her sides. It's instinct. The five of us are squashed together, our beating hearts shaking. My breath is loud in my ears, and Samira's elbow jabs into my side.

Slowly, I lift my head away from Caro's chest and look back outside.

There are more people out there now. The other bands. Men and women stand, looking at one another. No one has gone to Fi or Yvette, still.

"This is what's going to happen from now on." Bridie's voice is loud, but I can't see her. "Anyone who betrays me or does not try hard enough is being removed. We do not tolerate weaklings."

Her words seem to echo, over and over, overlapping with each other, as if they're replicating and filling up the camp. Samira stifles a cry.

And then suddenly Bridie's in the entrance of our hut. She casts her eyes over the five of us, huddled together.

"Oleta, you are now the head of the family. Find me in an hour, and we will discuss your new position as aunt."

Oleta nods, and I am shaking. More words are exchanged, but I can't think, can hardly concentrate.

"Come on," Oleta says roughly, pulling away from Caro, Samira, Nathan, and me. "We need to practice."

"But—" Samira says.

"No buts!" Oleta yells. "Did you not just see that? The group test is tomorrow, and I am in charge! With the mood Mother's in, we're all going to lose our lives if you can't hit a simple target."

TWENTY-TWO

I AM NOT DEAD.

That's my first thought when I open my eyes and—

Stephen's face, his expression captured in death. Next to me.

I scream, jolt, and—

Weapons. My hands reach for them, but my belt is empty.

"Inga?"

I turn, my heart pounding, see Oleta.

We're both alive.

My sister… Where is she?

"Have you got your gun?" I ask Oleta. "A knife?"

She shakes her head. "They took all of ours, before they left." She's holding onto something—it takes a moment for my eyes to adjust and see the hand. A child's hand.

Oleta's got one of the children *here*? My head spins. The girl is dark-haired, with skin a few shades lighter than Oleta's. She can't be more than five years old.

And we're still *here*.

Then I frown.

"They?" I say. There was more than one assassin—

more than just Gweneira?

"Petra and Gweneira, plus a few more newbies. And the rest of the children."

I don't like the way she says my sister's name. She's not allowed to say Gweneira's name. She's not allowed to be Gweneira.

But…but my sister is not my sister now. She's….

I startle as another child unfolds from the shadows behind Oleta. A boy with blond hair. His skin looks gray.

"It's okay," Oleta says. "There's four of them."

I pick out two more forms.

"They're still pretty heavily drugged, so that works in our favor for getting them back," Oleta says. "Seems Petra only drugged the children."

I frown. So we don't know what these children are like? How skilled they are? Whether they'll turn on us?

Then I look at Oleta. "Wait. So, Gweneira and other assassins left? Why did they leave their children?"

"I don't know. But we've got to go, it's getting light," Oleta says. "Come on."

I glance at Stephen's body and the other assassins we killed.

"I only saw Gabi and Luca, of the originals. Killed them both, of course." I look up at Oleta. "Did you get any?"

"Taylor," she says. "Dylan was here, but I only saw him in the distance. He got away."

He got away—and then he left.

I frown.

"Why?" I look at Oleta.

"Why what?"

"Why did they leave? Why are *we* alive? No. *How* are we alive? My sister had a pistol. She shot me? What the hell?" I stare at my body, search for the wound, the—

"I healed you when I came around. Healed both of us."

My head is fuzzy.

"But we've got to go now, Inga. I've had a look around. Falkes's body isn't here. None of his group are, only Stephen. Unless Falkes joined the assassins, he'll be where we left them. But he's going to realize Stephen's gone, if he hasn't already, and we can't be here when Falkes gets here—because he's going to search the area and find this." She gestures at Stephen's body.

"Yes. We can't be here." My head buzzes as we move. Pain hovers in front of my eyes. There are too many things that don't make sense, and I don't like it.

Gweneira never intended to kill me? She shot me, yet she must've just wanted to stun me. That's the only assumption I can come to as we walk. And she left Oleta alive as well. Of course, she'd have noticed the tattoos on Oleta too. She's left us alive, even though I'm the Night Slayer and I'm targeting her people?

Her people. My stomach twists at that thought. My sister is leading the assassins. How didn't I know this? Does this mean Brighid's definitely dead? And Gweneira left with the assassins...but left some children behind?

I stare at the children, then realize I'm holding two by the hands. I don't know when I got hold of their hands. My head is blank, my mind foggy. Is this the effects of being shot and the healing? I frown. It wasn't like this before, with my leg and the healing...and that was a gunshot wound too.

I turn to look at Oleta, then stop. She's got the other two children, a boy and a girl, just like I have. "This doesn't make sense. Gweneira is leading the assassins. My own *sister*. She shoots us but doesn't kill us, leaves us to just wake up and leave. And she makes sure none of the other assassins kill us? *And* leaves us with four of the children."

"You're forgetting Petra's a powerful Seer," Oleta says. "And she's on our side."

Powerful? So powerful she couldn't break free of

chains and was too scared to leave with us before? Or even this time. "No," I say. "I don't buy this."

"We shouldn't question our luck," Oleta says.

"But it's not luck." I'm sure of it. I loosen my grip on one of the children's hands, but he starts to sway and my instinct kicks in to hold onto him.

Huh. Is that what feeling maternal is like?

"Look, we got what we came for. We killed most of the assassins, and we rescued some children."

"But we didn't kill *all* the assassins, and the children—we can't take them. They're too dangerous. And it's too suspicious as to why they've been left with us. Wait, they left *four*." My tongue feels strange as I speak. "That's a manageable number. Petra's tracking them. That's why they left them, to keep tabs on us through them. They think we're with others. No, they *know*! Petra's told them about Amelia and—"

Oleta's eyes narrow. "Petra is on our side."

"Is she though?" My chest feels strange. "She left with Gweneira, that's what you said. No. We can't take these children. They're spies."

"Look, Petra doesn't need these children with us to be able to track us. She can track anyway. And if she was going to track anyone, it would be me," Oleta says. "We've got a connection. Or are you going to throw me out of your group too?"

"We've got to kill them," I say through gritted teeth. "It's too much of a risk."

"Hey! I'm not killing them." Oleta pushes her two behind her.

"Okay, I'll do it then."

The blond boy and red-haired girl look at me with brimming eyes. My throat closes up as I try to let go of their hands, so I can do it. I've got no weapons, but my hands are enough.

Only I can't. I can't let go of their hands.

My frown gets deeper, and—blond hair. The boy's hair is the same shade as Caro's.

Caro.

My gut tightens.

I swallow hard and look at the boy, at his big eyes that look up at me. His bottom lip wobbles. Fear. He's scared.

He wouldn't hurt anyone. I just feel it—and I don't know how I feel it, and none of this is right. But he's clinging to me. And he trusts me.

The last time I held the hands of children like this was when I was recruiting them. Under Bridie's orders, I took part in three recruiting missions over the years. I wasn't a natural choice for recruitment, not when I was trained as an assassin, but occasionally a good opportunity would present itself when a roaming group of Untamed neared our camp, and Bridie would only have days to make a plan and sometimes our camp's recruiting team was already out on a different mission, far away.

I breathe hard and concentrate on the feel of the little hands in mine. They're clinging to me. Is that the way I once clung to my mother? I blink and try to think, think of her. Sara. I know her name and the color of her hair and eyes, but I can't remember much else about her.

Anger unfurls and crawls through my veins. Bridie took that away from me. She took my childhood, my family. And I look at these two children. More lives the assassins tried to ruin.

I imagine them playing with Johnny and Callum, laughing and shrieking, having normal childhoods. They'll race into the river and splash each other. They'll have fun.

And these ones are young—four or five years old, I'd say—so how skilled in assassination can they be? Especially when the new adult recruits weren't that good at fighting.

"I knew you couldn't." Oleta gives me an approving nod. Maybe she was right all along: we have to save them. These children haven't become us yet. They need protecting.

"It's on you if they're spies." My voice is low. "We need to go."

I make my way to the door, bringing the children who are squeezing my hands way too tightly with me. I look outside. The sky is still angry. Looks alight in places.

But there's no one about. The assassins really have gone?

"We need to go now," I say. "The Turning's closer. We've got to get back before then."

"So, what the fuck are we going to tell Falkes?" Oleta clears her throat as the vehicles come into view, silhouetted against the sunrise and angry sky. "What's the plan?"

I frown, don't understand her annoyance, her aggression. Bringing children back was what she wanted.

The small blond boy whose hand I'm still holding giggles then repeats Oleta's swear word. It's the first sound I've heard from any of them, and I stare at him for a moment. His eyes look a little glazy. Were they worse than that earlier? Is this him coming around? Is he going to turn on us, violent and out of control?

"Inga?" Oleta's voice is sharp. I can't work out her tone now, whether she's annoyed or not—but that's what Bridie taught us to be like. *Never wear your heart on your sleeve.*

"Nothing," I say, hunkering my head a little. There's rain in the air, and a chilling bite to the wind. No spirits yet, but the sky's preparing for them. "We tell Falkes nothing."

"*Nothing?*" She stares at me. The changing light makes her look more severe. "Uh, he's going to notice his son isn't here and that these sprogs are. I don't think we can hide four extra mouths."

I shrug. Why's she talking about this like it's my idea? "We don't know anything about Stephen's death. Okay? We try and figure it out with them. But we make sure they don't go that way." Because any dead assassins they find, well, they're going to know it was me. And then they'll see Stephen's body. And Stephen's mother too.

"Um, don't they know that we were heading that way this whole time? They think there's an Untamed group waiting for them over there." Oleta clicks her tongue, then she leans closer. "And what about the littles?"

"We'll say we found them. We heard them playing or something, and we got up early to go and look in case Enhanced Ones were about."

"No, I meant they saw Stephen's body." Oleta keeps her voice low.

The children's hands seem to get heavier in mine. "They were drugged," I say. "They're not going to remember. And you've got Seers powers. Just make them forget."

Oleta snorts. "Are you really that stupid thinking you can get away with this?"

"Me? It was both of us."

"You were the one who killed Stephen. Just like you did Bridie and—"

A high-pitched screech cuts her off.

Damn. A spirit.

I turn, whirling round, pulling the boy and girl with me. A shape hurtles through the air. A spirit. Then rain lashes down, ice-cold.

The blond boy tightens his grip on my hand, whimpering. Instinctively, I push him and the girl behind me, then slip a little, but regain my balance. The girl's hand disappears from mine, but I've still got the boy's. And where's the girl?

My eyes smart against the rain, and my vision blurs.

A spirit hisses. Too close.

"Shit," Oleta says.

"Run!" I yell.

We all run. The wind howls, and something flashes a deep purple above me, stings my eyes. My clothes are sodden, molding to me.

We reach the bus and truck. No one else is out, no one throws the door open.

"Come on!" I yell at the children, as I yank open the driver's door of the truck. They're all behind me, the children and Oleta. "Get in!"

"Inga? What the hell?" Renee's voice.

But there's no time to answer. I lift three of the littles up, shove them inside, my heart pounding, then I'm climbing in too, into the driver's seat. Oleta is behind me, the fourth child wriggling in her arms.

"Go on, through there." I push two of the children over the center console, toward the back seats where Amelia and Renee are both shouting now, then I slide myself across to the passenger seat, to make room inside for Oleta and the other child. My leg crashes against the gearstick as I climb over. "Shut the door!" I yell at Oleta, just as she slams it.

The truck rattles. My pulse pounds in my ears. Outside, a spirit hovers in front of the windscreen.

"Inga?" Renee shouts.

"Found some children," I say, breathless. I turn to look in the back. My hair drips water down the back of my neck, under the sodden jacket collar.

Amelia rubs her eyes, her face bleary. She frowns as one of the children jabs her with an elbow. "What is going on?"

"Come on, quick," Oleta hisses. The land flashes. The spirits. The Turning—happening quickly now we're in safety. A coincidence? Or were the Gods and Goddesses holding it back?

But, no, they're not involved in the Turnings….

"What is going on?" Renee hisses.

"We need to get the covers up," Oleta says, pointing

to the windows. "The Turning!" Flashes of light zoom across the sky. "Where are the blankets?"

"What about the bus?" Renee asks. "Do they know it's the Turning? Where are the weapons? My tools?"

"They're asleep in the bus. It's fine," I say. But I picture Stephen. Dead. "And your tools are in the truck bed." Not that Renee can use her hammerstones and flints against the spirits. And the weapons are in the truck bed too. Well, Oleta and I lost some of them to the assassins, but not all. We've still got those I took from Hunter's group. And Amelia's bow and arrows too. Probably a knife somewhere as well. It's just the pistols we've lost.

"But if Johnny or Callum wake and look at a spirit…" Renee doesn't finish. We all know bad things happen if you look at a spirit. Very bad things.

I lean across and beep the horn.

The sound makes Amelia and Renee cry out, but looking through the windows, I see movement in the bus.

"The Turning!" I shout at them, and then I see Lexa's face pressing against the glass. Good. She's seen the sky. She'll know what to do.

I try not to look closely at the spirit—a mesh of eyes and hair—that flies past us. It zooms in on the bus, and my mouth dries.

"Come on, people, blankets!" Oleta shouts.

"Here," Amelia says, pushing the blanket she was sleeping under to the front.

Oleta grabs it, then she's stretching it across the windscreen. "Tape?"

Renee hands a roll to her, then we're all working on blocking out the sight of the spirits, while the children sit numbly together on the backseat, all four squashed up together.

"Is this one going to be strong enough?" Renee asks. With the windows all nearly blocked now, it's darker in here, but I can just about see her leaning over two of the children as she points to the blanket covering the back window that looks out over the truck bed. "It's the window that's cracked. Think I can risk running to the back to get the guns?"

"No," Amelia and I say at the same time.

"If any spirits get in, I'll blast them with power," Oleta says.

"Me too," I add, but my voice catches.

And what the hell am I doing letting my voice catch? I'm not weak. I'm not shaken up by what's happened. I'm not.

Oleta leans closer to me for a second, her mouth by my ear. "The others are going to know Stephen's not there now."

Her whisper is barely audible, but I jolt as if it's deafening.

"Right," Renee says, turning around. She scoots the children over a bit so she and Amelia can sit down properly in the back again. "That's all the windows blocked. Inga, what the hell is going on?"

"Who are these children?" Amelia asks. "What about their parents? Are they still out there—in the Turning?" Alarm fills her voice. "They're from the Untamed group we're heading for, aren't they?"

"No," I say.

"We rescued them from Bridie's group," Oleta says.

I turn to her, my eyes wide, shoot her my best glare, but I don't know if she sees it.

There's a sharp intake of breath. I can't tell who it's from. If it even is one of us, and not a spirit outside.

"You did *what*?"

Hell, I could kick Oleta right now.

"Oh, and Stephen's dead," Oleta says. She shrugs her coat off, catching me in the side. "Here, Amelia, can you hang this on the back of the seat? We got soaked."

Amelia doesn't move to take the coat.

"What?" Renee's eyes widen.

Something screeches outside.

"Inga killed him," Oleta says.

My hands turn to stone. What the hell is she playing at?

Oleta twists around. I think she's hooking the hood of her coat over the headrest of her seat. Water droplets spray out, hit me, and I jolt.

"Stephen tried to stop us getting the children," Oleta says. "He was going to kill these sweet cherubs. Inga did what she had to do, so don't blame her." But her tone is off. I can't fathom her out.

"Stephen's dead?" Renee whispers. For once, she's not speaking loudly.

"Yes," I say.

"And you've rescued children that Bridie's group were training?" Amelia asks. Her voice sounds strange in the darkness. A flash outside lights up the blanketed windows. "Because that was who we were headed for, wasn't it? Not a *good* Untamed group… Okay." She exhales in one long hiss. "Right, well, we have to go. We have to leave."

"What, Ma?"

"If Stephen's dead and Falkes finds out, then…" Amelia glances at Renee before pointing back at Oleta and me. "All of us, come on, now. We're going. We're starting afresh, away from them." She looks at the littles. "We're giving these four a better life. We're giving all of us a better life."

All of us? I stare at her. She's including Oleta? And the four littles? Just like that?

But Oleta's not the one who Falkes is going to hate….

But leaving them? Falkes, Lexa, and Minnow, I don't care much about—but the boys. Johnny and Callum? I protect them. They need me to keep them safe.

"We can't stay here," Amelia says. "Oleta, drive."

"But it's the Turning," Oleta says, and as she says it, rain batters down harder, a thunderous sound on the roof.

"Falkes will kill you and Inga, and the babies too," Amelia shouts. "And I'm not having that fate for any of my children."

Any of *her* children?

But Oleta's *not* Amelia's, and the littles definitely aren't. Amelia's only done the stupid granddaughter-becoming ceremony with me. I'm her granddaughter, these children aren't hers. Oleta's not hers!

"We are not risking anything, and Falkes is going to go crazy when he finds out Stephen's dead. Oleta, drive now."

"I can't drive through this. And we've only just got the blankets up."

"If we wait, we're waiting for Falkes to kill our family."

"We *can't* drive through this," Renee says firmly. "Else we're all dead."

Amelia makes a frustrated sound. "Then we leave as soon as it's safe."

"If we leave Johnny and Callum, they'll be dead or Enhanced," I say. "Falkes, Lexa, and Minnow can't protect for shit."

Amelia makes an exasperated sound. "What do you suggest then? Or do you want Falkes killing you and these kids?"

"We could say Stephen was killed by the spirits." I say. "He'd never have to know the truth. Stephen went outside in the Turning and—"

"And how do we explain the children?" Amelia grabs the arm of the blond boy and even in the dark, I see his eyes widen in fear. "They've all got scars—just like yours. And Falkes will find Stephen's body—and the assassins you killed too," Amelia says. "We're not lying to Falkes. Lying is bad."

"But we could say Stephen went there on his own," I say.

Amelia shakes her head. "No. We're going. Our truck's leaving as soon as the Turning lets up. No arguments. I'm the oldest, I'm in charge." Her voice cracks, but it's not weakness—it's lightning. It's energy. It's decision.

"Where are we going to go?" Oleta asks after a long

moment.

A spirit shrieks outside the window.

"To find other Untamed, of course," Amelia says. "Someone's got to be out there. Taras's group or someone."

Oleta nods. "Okay, well we should sleep now. The Turning's going to last hours, I can tell. We need to be rested."

"Good idea," Amelia says.

Good idea? What the hell is Oleta doing? I stare at her, but she's smiling as she stares straight ahead.

This isn't… Something's not right with her. We can't just leave and go and find another group. We can't! Oleta and I need to go after the assassins, after my sister. We have to end it, once and for all.

Even if it means killing your sister?

I grit my teeth.

Gweneira's not my sister now—I don't know her.

But I don't know Oleta either now.

I just… Nothing makes sense.

I can only trust myself. Things were going fine when it was just me going after the assassins. But since Oleta's been involved, it's gone wrong. *She's* wrong.

I look at her, and I can feel it. There's something off about her, and something tells me things are only going to get worse.

TWENTY-THREE

ONCE THE SOUNDS OF THE spirits have died down, and I haven't heard them for a good twenty minutes, I peel back a corner of the blanket from my window. My clothes are still damp, and moving in them feels horrible, but, yes, the Turning is over.

I wake the others. The adults—not the children. The blond boy is asleep, now stretched out across my lap. I watch his chest rise and fall for a few moments.

Leaving is the best decision. I'm sure. For us and these four children anyway. Not for Johnny and Callum. But this is for the sake of the lives of four children over two, and I try to tell myself that this means it's okay. That it's the right thing to do.

But leaving two innocent children—children I vowed to protect—isn't okay, and I know it. But what else can we do?

"Any movement in the bus?" Amelia asks as we take down the blankets.

I turn my head. The bus still has its blankets up. "No."

"Excellent."

"They may follow us when they hear our engine,"

Renee says.

"But our truck can go faster than the bus," Amelia points out. "And they've got to take down all their blankets first. We'll get a good head start, and they'll be looking for Stephen anyway."

"I need the toilet," Oleta says, her hand reaching for the door handle. "We've got time, right? Before we leave?"

"No," Amelia says. "Don't open the door. They'd likely hear it shutting again. We drive away first, give them no warning—"

"But I really need to go."

"Just wait. We'll stop in a bit. Need to get the weapons out from the back and check what supplies we have."

Oleta groans. "I don't know how long I can wait. Really am bursting, here."

"Well, you can use the Sheewee and a bottle." Amelia turns to one of the children who is now awake and murmuring something. "What, dear?"

Oleta's eyes widen as she looks at me. "You have one of those? A Sheewee?"

"It's Renee's," I say, and Renee chuckles.

"Just drive now, Oleta," Amelia says. "And put your seatbelt on. You've got one, so you may as well use it."

The air seems fragile as Oleta turns the key in the ignition, and then the engine's too loud, makes me think of the thundering rain on the roof earlier.

"Go, go, go!" Oleta mutters as she floors it, promptly waking the rest of the children.

They startle and cry out. The tires squeal, and the engine strains as the truck bounces along.

"It's okay," I say, trying to soothe the child I'm holding, but my tone is blunt, and even I know I'm not maternal. I try to calm him, but then Amelia's speaking to them all in a soft voice.

"It's okay, my darlings, we've got you now. You're away from those bad, bad people."

"What's happening with the bus?" Renee asks,

glancing in the rear-view mirror. "Any movement?"

I look in the side mirror. "Nothing." It's just still. Still there. Hasn't changed. I frown. They're not going to come after us? Have they somehow not heard the engine?

But they must've.

As we drive away, I watch the bus for movement. There's nothing.

"Do you think they're okay in there?" I ask.

Renee snorts. "You're not usually worried about Falkes. Hey, Oleta, whack the heating on?"

"It's not just Falkes in there," I point out. No matter how much I tried to scare the boys with dead hares, I still promised myself long ago that I wouldn't ever let assassins recruit Johnny and Callum. They need to have better childhoods than me and Oleta did. Better, by far.

But what about these children we're now with? How damaged are they really? I look at them, look for clues, but of course there's nothing. And we don't know what the training methods are like now.

I don't like the indecision, the not knowing. It's weak. I need to be strong and in control.

"So," Renee says after a while. "How'd you find the assassins?" In the rear-view mirror, I see she's got one eyebrow raised.

"Coincidence," I say, just as Oleta says, "My sister told us where they were."

"Hey!" I yell at her, but she's smirking. What is up with her? What is her game? To literally tell them everything?

"Your sister?" Amelia says, eyes on the back of Oleta's seat.

"Yes, Petra is with them. She's giving us intel on where they are—and so we went and killed the adults and rescued the children. Well, that was the plan. Only got these four out, and we didn't even get to kill that many adults. So, they're still out there." Oleta's eyes narrow, and she grips the steering wheel tighter.

"Can we stop yet? I still need to pee, badly."

Amelia's eyes are wide as she looks back at Oleta and me. "Have you two got a death wish?"

"It's important work," Oleta says. "And my bladder is kind of important too."

"It's *my* important work." I glare at her. "I'm killing them—it's my list."

"Yeah, you have a list, but you're killing any assassins you come across," Oleta says. "The list may as well go out of the window."

I hold her steely gaze. "I'm killing everyone on my list." And it's going to be me who does the killings. Oleta's already taken out one who was on my list—Taylor—and she's not getting any more.

"You'll do no such thing." Renee's voice is sharp. I look back and see her knuckles are white as she grips the corner of a blanket. "I am *not* a part of this. And neither is Ma."

"And neither are you two," Amelia says. "Not anymore. You will stop, and we're going to find other Untamed."

"What?" I turn on her. "I can't—I have to do this."

"We've got babies with us now. Babies—who knows how affected they are? And if they're going to turn out anything like you two, then you need to do everything you can to reverse it. Inga, I mean this—you're leaving that life behind. We're looking for other Untamed. You're one of us now, so stop clinging to your old life."

"But someone has to do something," I say. "The assassins are expanding." My own sister is leading them. And I still don't understand that. My head spins. "Amelia, you don't get this—but we have to take them out. Do you want them taking more children?"

"I don't want you getting us all killed."

"I won't," I say.

Renee clears her throat. "Stephen's dead."

I let out a frustrated sigh.

"And there's going to be no more talk on this matter. Understand? Both of you." Amelia's eyes are wild—

the wildest I've ever seen them—as she looks from Oleta and me. "Do you *understand*?"

I glare at her. "I'm not agreeing to this." I look to Oleta for support, but she just nods, eyes on the land ahead.

"We should avoid the assassins, yes."

"What?"

Oleta reaches across and touches the arm of the boy who's on my lap. "We have to protect them now."

I stare at her. "You're backing down?" Unless she's just saying this because Amelia and Renee are here? I frown.

"And so will you," Amelia says. "Inga, you've got children now." She points at the blond boy snuggled against me.

"He's not my child," I say. "None of them are."

"*Of course* they are. You and Oleta are their mothers. That's how this world works. Inga, you came to us, and Renee and I became your mother and grandmother. Now, you've brought those children into our lives, so you damn well better look after them. And that means being around. Not going after them people and getting killed."

The moment we stop, I follow Oleta out of the truck and over to where there are trees. Renee and Amelia hover at the back of the truck.

"Seriously?" Oleta stares at me. "You're going to watch me piss?"

"No." I glare at her.

"Then what are you doing? Because I already said I'm desperate to go."

I glare at her. "What are you doing? Why are you telling Amelia and Renee everything? And please tell me you're joking when you said we're avoiding the assassins now?"

She raises one eyebrow, then turns away.

"Hey? What are you doing?"

"Trying to find some privacy," she snaps back. "We can have this conversation once my bladder is no longer screaming."

She retreats into the cover of trees, and I wait. When she emerges again, she's smiling sweetly.

"Well?" I fold my arms.

"We have to be honest with our group."

"What the hell is that supposed to mean?"

"One of us has to be honest. We have to tell Amelia and Renee everything. Tell me, Inga, when are you going to tell them your own sister is the assassins' leader? That dear old Gweneira is the new Bridie?"

I breathe hard. "Don't say her name," I growl.

"Because you're pretending it's not true?" Her voice is high-pitched. She's mocking me.

I swallow hard.

"We need to be *honest*," Oleta says. "Honesty is how we survive."

"But telling them about the assassins is just going to stop us killing any more of them."

"Which is good."

"What?" I shake my head. "Amelia and Renee are not in listening distance now. We can make plans."

"We have no plans. Except to protect the children." Her voice is sharp, loaded, and I don't understand it.

My eyes narrow. "What is going on? All that talk before about killing all the assassins? But now you don't want to—you're just interested in the children."

"Yes, children are the future. And these ones are weak at the moment. I bet they don't know shit. Not properly. They won't know how to fight, how to protect themselves, so we have to keep them alive and with us. Safety is in numbers, and we will teach them to be the best fighters and survive."

I inhale sharply. "No." I shake my head. "We're not

using any children against the assassins." I frown. That's why she wanted to get the children? "*No*. We're not stooping to Bridie's level. I mean it. These children are free of that life, of any fighting, now."

Oleta laughs. "How naive are you?"

Her question unnerves me, because danger and power radiate from her body in waves. Waves that are threatening me, and I don't understand her agenda.

"What do you want?" I frown. She's dangerous, I know that. Of course she is! We both are. All assassins that Bridie trained are. But Oleta and I are more dangerous; Bridie selected us because of our Rijikarii energies. We're strong and dangerous, and we deal in death.

I can't sense Rijikarii myself, but something tells me it's swelling in Oleta, getting stronger and stronger. And soon, it will burst. I frown. I need a Watcher Doll. They can sometimes reduce the effects of Rijikarii. But, then again, you need a Seer as well. Spirits need to be called to the Watcher Doll, spirits who can siphon off some of the energy from the person's soul. And I can't see Oleta agreeing to such a plan.

"I want to keep these children safe and alive," Oleta says. "And that means keeping them away from the assassins. They're going to have a red alert out for us. Kill us as soon as they see us, and they'll take the children back. But if they can't find us, they can't do that."

"So you want to run and hide?" I stare at her. "That's not the Oleta I knew."

Her eyes flash. "I want to raise our next generation and teach them how to be even more deadly than us. I want a group, a large group. When we've got the numbers, I want to burn the assassins' camps to the ground. But that can't happen now. Not soon. We need to get stronger first."

"And then there'll be more," I say. "More assassins. Look at how the numbers have grown since we left. I'm not giving up now."

"I'm not telling you to give up. I'm telling you to delay, to plan this out."

"I'm not giving them time to get stronger." I shake my head. "I've got my list, and I'm killing everyone on it as soon as I can, plus everyone else."

Oleta grabs my arm and—

Pain. Her fingers. I wrench my arm away, panting.

I hiss something under my breath. Her Seer powers. "You think you can threaten me into running away?" I let out a laugh. "I'm not letting them take more innocent children. And I'm surprised you want to give them time to ruin more lives. This plan of yours won't work—and you know it." I point at her. "No, you're giving the assassins time to get away. All that talk about wanting to help me kill the adults was lies—just so you could get some of their children, supposedly to fight the assassins with, yet you also want to give the assassins time to get stronger?" I frown. It doesn't make sense. "You on their side?"

Oleta steps closer, her hand held up. Anger flickers in her eyes. "I hate the assassins more than you do."

"I find that hard to believe." I size her up.

"Inga, Oleta, get back here," Renee yells.

I look back to see her getting into the truck. Looks like Amelia's already in the driver's seat.

"Coming," I shout. Then I lean closer to Oleta. "We're not using the children to fight them when they're older, and we're not letting the assassins get away. I'm killing them as soon as I can."

"But—"

"Aside from the fact they're *children*, we still don't know why Gweneira let them leave with us. They may be babies, but we know the assassins want as many babies as they can get their hands on, and we don't know what is going on."

Oleta makes a *hrmf* sound deep in her throat then turns and walks to the truck. I follow her.

"All right, girls?" Amelia's voice is careful.

"Fine," I say, climbing in.

The babies are still sleeping. And I stare at their small bodies.

We shouldn't have taken them. I'm sure of that. This isn't right. What is going on? What danger are we bringing with us?

"So," Renee says. "When were you going to tell us that we have no guns with us now?"

THE ENHANCED CHILD IS IN the corner.

There is no escape.

We both know it.

My hands feel too heavy, like they're not mine.

I'm going to drop the gun.

"Please, no!" the Enhanced child cries, and I see myself in her eyes. It is disorientating, because I am not me. I am her too.

I am all of us.

"We go for the children first," Mother Bridie reminded us all before she dropped us off in the city. She said the words just like how she said them in every training session before this. "Always the children, because then they can't grow up. We wipe out a new generation before they're even adults."

I thought it would be easy. She made it sound easy.

But this girl has blond hair like me. Like my mother.

My hands shake.

"Please…please…" Tears run down her face.

Tears run down my face.

"I have to," I whisper, and it's true. I've got to kill her and find Caro and Samira and Nathan as soon as possible. As the aunt of our band, Oleta's no longer involved in the group-

test, and Caro told me I need to make sure I do the killing because he said I'm more capable than the other littles.

"I'm sorry," I whisper to the Enhanced girl as I pull the trigger.

"It's okay," Caro says. "We passed the test, it's okay."

He wraps his arms around me in a way that reminds me of my sister. The sister I told him about, because we speak about our families, me and Caro and Oleta. Our real families. Families who aren't the three of us, thrown together. Families who aren't Mother Bridie and the aunts and uncles. We talk about our real families, the ones who get us into trouble with Mother Bridie and her men and women if we mention them.

I am shaking. For hours, I have been. Everything hurts, but it's not physical pain. It's inside me, my soul. Because of what I did. My fingers are curling, and they feel wrong. I remember the feel of the Enhanced girl's teeth in my sweaty palm, how they clumped together, as I ran from the room. How I tried to wipe the blood from them before handing them over to Mother Bridie.

How Mother Bridie inspected the five teeth I had clenched in my hand.

"Only five," she whispered. "We always get ten, Inga. Ten. You know this."

I nodded. I did know it. Ten, because it's Mother Bridie's favorite number. And because the killer keeps one, Mother Bridie keeps three, and the other six are added to the protection gate around the caves in the camp. Protection against the Gods and Goddesses.

It was easy to get the girl's teeth after I shot her. To slam a chunk of stone against her mouth. She was dead; she never put up a fight.

But I could only do it enough to get five out.

My hand wouldn't work when I tried to get the sixth.

And so I ran without finishing the work.

Bridie wasn't happy, and she gave me less food—only enough to account for the five teeth. Not the full ten.

"It's all about exchanges," she said.

I swallow hard. Maybe I should've just got the extra teeth. The Enhanced girl was dead anyway. And maybe now I wouldn't feel as shaky if I'd had a full meal.

Or maybe my shakiness is nothing to do with the contents of my stomach.

"It will be okay," Caro says. His voice is an anchor to me now, in this moment in the dark hut where we hide and wait and hope they don't come. Oleta was supposed to be here too, but she's been called to a meeting of the aunts and uncles.

"We won't be here forever," Caro whispers.

I see the dead Enhanced girl when I blink.

The first group-test, complete. I may not have got the right number of teeth as the trophy for Mother Bridie, but she was still pleased. I heard her say that on the way back, when we were in the cab of the truck and one of her men was driving. She said it was enough for us all to pass and for me to become a higher.

I don't want to be a higher now.

I stare at Caro. The outline of his face in the dark. I have to concentrate on that, otherwise I see the Enhanced girl's body.

The girl who's dead because of me.

And the girl—her smile still haunts me. I see it. The smile, how she greeted me in her clean clothes. She was eating sweets, and she offered me some, started talking of her parents, saying they could help me.

Help.

I want help.

I want to be her. She wasn't scared and hungry and alone.

And now she's dead.

Because of me.

"I did it," I whisper. "I'm a murderer."

"Because you had to. Because Bridie made you do it."

He doesn't call her Mother Bridie or just Mother, and it shocks me.

Caro takes my hands in his. His touch is both cool and warm at the same time. "Inga, it wasn't you."

"But it was—"

"No. This isn't you. The people Bridie shapes us into are not who we truly are. They're the people she molds us into, but we're still here, underneath. We have to be. We—"

Something clicks on the other side of the hut door.

"What was that?" My voice is a whisper. My stomach churns. I'm going to be sick, and the thought makes me even more nervous. Mother Bridie doesn't like it when we're sick in here. She makes us clean it up.

Caro and I stare at each other. My heart pounds, the sound filling my ears, until it's all I can hear.

The door flies open.

"What are you doing?" Instructor Mark snarls, several others behind him. "Filling her head with nonsense!"

I scream as they grab Caro, as they haul him out.

Caro yells and yells, but I can't make out his words, and I can't move to help him. I'm locked in place. My body won't work, and I cower against the wall, feel pain in my chest, my head.

"Inga!" Caro screams, and then—then they lift him off his feet. He's twelve, and he's the biggest of Bridie's child assassins, but Bridie's men are men. They carry him away, out of sight, and I'm left here, shaking.

I can't move.

Everything's just….

They heard him, heard us. They were listening, outside? They suspected Caro would speak badly of Mother Bridie?

I hear a scream: Caro's.

Footsteps.

Near.

Getting closer.

"Hello, Tiny Inga," Mother Bridie's voice is cool and calm as she steps into the hut.

She shuts the door. It doesn't do much to block out the screams.

I am shaking, and I look at her.

"You did well today, don't forget that," she says. "Don't let Caro's lies fill your head with poison. Poison is bad. It tries to make you hate yourself, make you think that you're not who you are. But you are this, Inga. You will be my best assassin. It is what you are destined to become."

I try to say something, but only a squeak comes out.

Mother Bridie laughs—only she's not my mother. Not when she'd hurt Caro, because he's my friend.

No. She's just Bridie. She's not family. She means nothing to me.

"You just remember how pleased I am with you," she croons. "How well you did. I said you would be my best one, did I not?" She smiles and reaches for me. Her arms go around me for the coldest and hardest of embraces, but then she strokes my hair. "We'll get your tattoo sorted tomorrow, then you'll officially have graduated, be a higher."

"What's happening to Caro?" I whisper.

"Oh, Inga! You don't need to think about Caro, anymore," Bridie tells me, and her words, though quiet, are somehow enough to drown out his screams.

TWENTY-FIVE

"WE NEED TO STOP," AMELIA says, squinting through the windscreen. "Think we've got a flat. And I've got a bad headache."

She pulls the truck over and kills the engine.

Oleta points ahead at where there are animals grazing near the top of the hillside in the distance. "Reindeer."

As we drove, the forest tundra steadily turned wetter, with more boggy areas and patches of lying water. Trees are more plentiful now—mainly firs and Dahurian larches—and the autumn colors look pretty, but there are still more open-areas of grassland every now and again, particularly on the hills and around the valleys at higher altitudes. That's where the herd of reindeer is.

Renee frowns. She's in the passenger seat at the front. "Think we should get one of them?"

"Definitely. They'll be moving onto tundra soon, won't they?" Oleta says. "And I'd rather stay in the warmer areas for as long as we can."

Renee nods and glances at Amelia, no doubt worrying about the effects that the chilling winds of the tundra would have on her.

It's cramped in the back, with Oleta, me, and all the children, and I lean forward so I can see. The reindeer are a couple hours' walk away. We've got spears in the truck bed, and a carving knife, thanks to Hunter's group.

"Some of us can go and hunt while we get the tire changed then," I say.

"I'll stay here with Amelia and *our* children," Oleta says with a glance at me. Her arms are around one of the girls. "I can change a tire, easy. Should probably put some fuel in the tank too. There's still a can of that in the back, right? Good. Inga and Renee, you go after the game."

My head snaps toward her. "Why?"

Oleta gives me an odd look. "Because you're not going to want children tailing you when you're hunting."

I shake my head. "No. I think you should come with me. We can do the hunting together."

"Hey," Renee says. "You two aren't going off on your own. Else we know what you'll do."

"What will we do?" Oleta asks, the picture of innocence.

"Go on a murder spree, no doubt." Renee clears her throat. She's been doing that more and more the last couple of hours. I wonder if she's coming down with something. "Inga and I will go hunting. Oleta, you change the tire and sort the fuel. Amelia, keep an eye on the kids."

"You don't need to tell me what to do," Amelia says. "I'm quite happy to learn more about our new group members." She smiles as she turns to look at the four children. They still look dazed, half-asleep, even the one on Oleta's lap. One of the boys is leaning against me, and my arm's starting to feel numb. The other two are squashed together in the middle seat.

Why aren't they talking and crying and screaming and doing the other things that children do? What have the assassins done to them? They can't *still* be drugged.

"I still think Oleta should come with me," I say, my eye on her. "And not because we're going to go on *a murder spree.*"

"I can hunt just fine, you know," Renee says. "You don't need to doubt my ability as a hunting partner."

"That isn't what I'm worried about." My focus is still on Oleta and the children. But it's not the children I'm worried about. It's Amelia. I care about her, and I don't yet care about the children. I've got no attachment to them, but I have to Amelia. And there's something off about Oleta. Really off. I don't want to leave Oleta with Amelia.

Something is going on.

I glance at the children. At the boy with hair the same color as Caro's, and my heart tightens.

Caro.

Bridie had him lashed for six hours. By the time I saw his body—barely moving—it was strung up like a piece of meat in the middle of the camp. Caro's eyes were blackened and swollen, and his face didn't even look like his.

On the third day of Caro being nailed to the post, Oleta and I took him some food and water. Samira kept watch as we fed him, and she talked the whole time about how someone else must have been feeding Caro and giving him water because he was still alive. Still strong.

But the next morning, when I woke early and went to see him, he was dead, and Bridie was disappointed.

"Weak!" Bridie bellowed through the camp. "That boy was weak, he wasn't one of us!"

I didn't find out until much later that Caro wasn't supposed to die. He was supposed to endure that torture for a month, before being welcomed back into the ranks. Bridie had spent years training him, after all.

Tears threaten my eyes, and I blink quickly and look away from the blond boy next to me.

He's not Caro.

But what if it's his body I return to see?

But Oleta wouldn't…would she?

"You'd better go now," Oleta says. "Before those deer get away."

"No, I don't think we should." I make my voice as authoritative as possible, because she's up to something. She has to be. Rijikarii is strong in her. "Oleta and I should stick together. We've got more power that way."

"No, it makes sense to have a Seer with each of us," Renee says. "And like Ma said, you two aren't going off together. Now, come on, Inga."

I glance at Oleta, and she smiles at me. A smile that anyone else would think was innocent—only I know her, and I know it's not.

"I'll just get my jacket." I maneuver the sleeping boy away from me, then stretch over Oleta to reach it. It's been hanging by the opposite window to dry a bit more, though the denim's going to take ages. When my mouth is by Oleta's ear, I whisper, "What the hell are you playing at?"

Then Oleta grabs my arm. Her fingers are cold. "Do as I say, or they'll find out you're *not* who you say you are. I wonder what punishment they'd have for a fraudulent Seer? I wonder if Amelia would still be so kind to you if she knew the truth?"

I freeze and stare at her, hear my heartbeat in my ears. "You do anything to Amelia, and I'll kill you," I hiss back.

"I don't doubt that. Here's your jacket."

She passes it to me. I don't relish the thought of putting it on—it's going to be cold enough outside as it is, and damp denim against my skin won't help.

Oleta laughs, and it's that laugh that seems to follow me as Renee and I get out and sort through the weapons in the truck bed. They're tied to the side in a bundle, near to where I was lying down when injured, though that space is now occupied by the small tent.

It takes us a few moments to separate two spears from the bundle, and then I swing Amelia's bow and the quiver of arrows onto my back.

"I really don't think we should leave them," I say to Renee, careful to keep my voice low. I can see Oleta through the back window. She's not facing me, and shouldn't be able to hear me, but who knows what Seer powers she has?

"Why?" Renee says.

I shift my weight a little. The ground is spongey. "There's something off about Oleta."

Renee glares at me. "Oh, for the Gods' sakes, Inga, I am absolutely fed up of you two. Don't whine to me just because you're not getting your own way."

"That's not what it is."

"Oh, really? So, it's jealousy, is it? You're jealous that you can't hog me and Ma to yourself now?"

I grit my teeth. "That's not what I'm saying."

"We are a group," Renee shouts. "A *group*, Inga. We make decisions together. As a whole group. We have to trust each other. And, right now, I don't trust you and Oleta if you two go off on your own. You've already done a calculated attack on the assassins once when you pretended we were going to find an Untamed group, one we'd join—and that was an attack that got Stephen killed. You're not doing that again—you're not. We have to protect each other. Do you want assassins to kill me and Ma? Or those children?"

I shake my head at Renee, then wait until she looks back up at me. "No. Believe me, that isn't what this is about—look, it was Oleta who wanted to bring the children back. And we didn't kill all the assassins, and they could've killed us, but they didn't. They let us live and escape *and take* their children. And Oleta was determined to take them, right from the start. It's Oleta I don't trust. And those children, I don't trust them either. We shouldn't have brought them back."

Huh. I should've trusted my gut instinct that they're

spies or something. Instead, I got soft.

"They're *babies*." Renee gives me a disgusted look.

I let out an exasperated sigh. "There is something off about Oleta." I think of how I was sure I saw her nod at Gweneira. Yes. There's something really off about her.

"It'll be fine," Renee says, her voice gruff. "Anyway, it's not like Ma can't hold up her own in battle."

"But Amelia's old," I say. "And if Oleta goes for her—"

"Hey, Ma is still a fighter. And don't try and turn me against Oleta, just because you're jealous." Renee chuckles and plunges her hands into the pockets of her overalls. She produces a chunk of flint and momentarily looks surprised, before depositing it back into the pocket. "Now, come on."

We go to the front of the truck. Amelia winds her window down and tells Renee and me to be careful.

It's not us who needs to be careful though. I'm sure of that.

In the back of the truck, Oleta is still smiling, her arms around the children. I want to whisper to Amelia, try and warn her, but Renee's glaring at me. Instead, I just ask Oleta if she's going to get out to change the tire.

"Of course." She gives me a look. "That's why we've stopped, after all."

"There's plenty of time for that," Amelia says. "Let the girl rest a bit first."

Hmm. I press my lips together so firmly my gums start to throb.

Renee and I leave with the hunting weapons.

We work out which way the wind's blowing and discuss tactics, where we're going to approach the herd from. The route we decide on means walking round and approaching the reindeer from the left side—adding quite a bit onto our walk. But there are plenty of larch trees for cover.

"Let's hope they don't move in the meantime," I say.

We set a brisk pace, and it's just as well Amelia's

waiting in the truck. I think of how frail she looks at times. Well, she is old. It's normal to look frail when you're old, isn't it?

"Do you think we'll end up with Ma's people?" Renee asks as we wade through long grass. "If we can't find anyone else?"

I shrug. "It's a long way, across seas, right? Like weeks or months of travel?"

The thought of meeting more Untamed who'll judge me doesn't exactly fill me with joy. My heart feels heavier. I look at Renee. I like being with her and Amelia. Just the three of us. They were the only reason I stuck with Falkes's group, because most of the time, the others ignored me. But with Oleta tagging along—and now the littles too—everything is going to change.

Maybe we won't be able to make the journey or find another group.

And I do need to finish what I started—with the assassins. Even if Gweneira is leading them. I can't do that if we're overseas.

But I don't want to go off on my own with just Oleta. I can't leave Renee and Amelia and risk never seeing them again.

"Be fun, though, to meet my relatives," Renee says with a shrug. "I never really knew my dad well. But apparently the Karnads are a huge family."

Relatives.

I try not to think of Gweneira, but I can't help it. I'm glad she doesn't look like our mother though. Gweneira never did, not really. I can't really remember my mother, except her hair was as light as mine. Gweneira was the odd one out. Dark hair.

Like *Oleta.* My other sister.

But, no, Oleta's not my sister. And Gweneira—maybe she isn't either. Not anymore.

But Gweneira is blood. My closest blood relation? And is our mother still alive? My father is just a gap. A gap where a memory should be, but isn't. I don't even know his name. At least I know my mother's: Sara.

As the land gets steeper and we climb the hillside, Renee and I breathe deeper. We don't talk, except to refine our strategy for hunting the reindeer. We have to change our plan when the herd starts to move, the beasts heading across the top of the valley, toward a thick patch of trees. We decide that we need to get to those trees first. We can't have the herd disappearing in there. Aiming with the spears and arrows will be easier if we've not got trees to block us. At one point, I think one's seen us, and we have to remain still for a long time until we're sure we're good to continue. It takes just under an hour to reach the larches on the far side of the herd.

Now we're here, I can see these trees seem to be the edge of mountain taiga—a coniferous forest that sweeps across the next valley and up high after, where dark, rocky summits rise into the sky.

The sun is considerably lower now, casting long shadows, and I place my spear at my feet, choosing to use the bow and arrows.

"They'll probably head toward us and the trees as it gets darker," I say. Or at last, I think they will. They'll want cover for the night, right, a warmer place? But these are reindeer. They also live out on the frozen tundra. "I reckon we've got half an hour before they move toward us. And they shouldn't smell us on the wind. It'll be easier to get them if we wait them out."

Renee nods.

My stomach rumbles, and I try to ignore it. We've not had much food since leaving Falkes and the others. Most of it was in the minibus.

We wait. It seems to take ages, but the herd moves closer and closer.

Renee gives me a small nod, the spear ready in her hands. "I'm going for the nearest doe."

I load the arrow onto my bow. "I'm going for the stag."

A small smile edges onto my face, despite everything, my worries about Amelia, my certainty that Oleta is bad news.

Renee nods at me.

I fire at the same moment she throws her spear and—

I see it all in slow motion. See my arrow fly through the air. See it turn, like it's hit an invisible wall, get redirected—redirected toward Renee.

I scream, the deer scatter, and Renee's eyes widen. Somehow, I see her pupils. They're so big, too big.

She tries to move, run, but she doesn't. Not in time.

The arrow dives into her side. Renee makes a startled, choking sound, and stumbles backward. Her eyes lock onto me. Then she falls.

TWENTY-SIX

I LIKE KILLING.

I like it a lot.

"Yep, we can take them," Oleta says, leaning forward. *The tips of her dark hair touch the paper map. "No problem."*

Zak frowns.

"Are you sure?" *one of the logistics men asks. I don't know his name, but the team changes a lot, the individuals often being rotated between the different camps.*

I know what the men and women in the logistics teams do now: they coordinate strategies for attacks on the Enhanced Ones' towns and cities, working out which places are the best for us to attack and when. They secure trucks for us, getting us the transport we need, as well as weapons.

I've been in band three for four years now, and I can see the bigger picture, how what we're doing is right: it's the only way the Untamed can beat the Enhanced Ones. We have to be killers, and we have to be coordinated.

Bridie isn't just the Mother of a few bands and camps, like I'd thought for a long time. No, last year we had a gathering, and there are twenty-four bands in total, split across six camps. Bridie oversees all of them, of course, but she's more hands on with her own camp. The other camps are run by a great aunt or uncle that Bridie really trusts.

We're no longer at Royston's Rock, but have set up at Bluejay, swapping with bands eleven, twelve, thirteen, and their logistics team. Only two of their instructors still remain at Bluejay. I still wonder if the swap was because Bridie doesn't want to see the sites where Caro and Fi died, but the camp here is nicer than Royston's Rock in many ways. That's what Bridie gave as the reason for the move, and there's been a lot more game about, and the winters are warmer here than they were at Royston's Rock.

"I'll have Inga with me," Oleta says with a grin, looking back at me. "She's a good killer."

The logistics team turn to stare at me, and I can't help but smile. I am a good killer. And I like killing.

I like the rush.

"Who else?" one of the women asks Oleta. "Can't just be two of you taking on the west side of the town. You need more numbers."

"I'll take our other highers too," Oleta says. "That's three."

Three including Harmony who transferred across to band three a few months after Fi was killed. We needed more numbers, and Bridie never allowed Yvette to rejoin us. She was the only one from Royston's Rock who didn't come with us here. She's still there, and I wonder what the new bands there think of her, every time they see her finger-less and tongue-less.

"We need another band out there as well," Zak says. "I'll bring my highers too."

Oleta doesn't look happy, but she doesn't argue. She's the youngest aunt, and she told me before it's about playing nice for the most part, while not sacrificing your authority.

"Wonderful," the head of the logistics team says, wrapping up the meeting. "Gods, at this rate, we'll be ready to combine with the other camps and take back a whole town. Then it'll be cities too."

Cities.

I smile.

That's a lot of killing.

Good job I like it.

TWENTY-SEVEN

"NO...NO...NO." I SHAKE my head. I don't know how it happened. I do not know. I don't know!

That's all I can think as I stare at her. Renee. With the arrow in her side and—

There's blood. So much blood, bubbling out, pooling.

"Inga…" Renee's voice is weak, and her eyes are wild, and how did it happen? I wasn't aiming at her—I wasn't! The arrow *moved*. It moved!

It wasn't me. I—

I retch, spew the little contents of my stomach onto the ground. Mainly acid and bile, but some half-digested food too. It lands on the bow and the quiver. They're on the ground too. When did I drop them? I can't think.

"Inga, help…me," Renee rasps.

I drop to my knees, straight into my vomit, and look at her. I reach out, as if to touch her, but I can't do it. I can't touch her.

She's dying.

A deep sound bursts from me, and I clap my hands to my mouth, try to cram it back in.

I've done this to her. Me. My arrow. *Me.*

"Inga, help me." Renee's words are short, sharp, like her breathing. Her breathing that's so quick now. Her chest rises and falls too quickly.

I am Inga the Killer, the Night Slayer. I kill people. It's what I do. I know it's what I do. The Enhanced, the assassins, Falkes's stepbrother, Stephen....

But *Renee*? No....

My vision wobbles, blurs. I reach out. My hand's shaking. It never shakes, but it is. I am. My fist closes around the arrow, and then the shaft of the arrow's trembling, and the arrow's point is trembling inside her, gauging more and more of her flesh.

Renee groans.

I pull my hand back sharply.

"I don't know what to do."

"Get...get..." Renee whispers.

"Get what?" My voice is too loud. "Renee, I don't know what to do. I didn't mean to do this, I'm sorry, so sorry, and—"

Her body shudders, the whole length of it. I stare at her fingers, the way they curl. Curl toward me. Pointing at me: Inga the Killer.

I let out a choked scream and jump up.

Need to get away.

Have to get away.

No! I can't leave her. I can't! I—

I stumble backward.

Renee's lips are moving, but there's no sound apart from gurgling. *Her* gurgles. The arrow pierced a lung?

I stare at the blood accumulating around her side.

She goes still.

"Renee?" My voice sounds strange. "Renee?"

I take a step closer, then bend down, say her name again.

I touch her arm. Warm. But she doesn't respond.

"Renee?"

I'm shaking her, and I'm crying and shaking her again. I feel her wrist, try to find a pulse, and—

And I can't. I'm shaking too much, can't do it, and—
No. Concentrate.

I take a deep breath, then lower my ear to her lips. Listen for her breathing.

There's…there's nothing.

A strangled sob escapes me, and I jump back up. Adrenaline courses through me, and I run. Run blindly. I can't see. I just run.

My foot catches something, and I fall heavily, hit the ground hard. Pain shoots through my leg. I scream—but not because of the pain. Because of what I've done.

I've killed Renee.

The woman who was like a mother to me.

The only woman beside Amelia who trusted me.

Amelia.

My mouth dries. My chest feels like it's caving in. How do I go back? How do I tell her what I've done?

What *have* I done?

A rancid taste fills my mouth. I try to spit it out, but I can't. I dry-heave, on all fours, staring at the ground. The stubby blades of grass. My hands, and my wrists, with my killer marks.

Nothing can ever be the same again.

Night falls. I am walking through swampy forest. I don't remember picking myself up and moving from where I fell, but I must have. I'm in the taiga now. Don't think I've climbed toward the mountainous area, but my feet are sore and I must have walked far.

I've got the bow and quiver on my back, and I'm carrying the two spears. My one and Renee's. And Amelia and Oleta, where are they? Why haven't they driven over here?

Because Oleta's done something to Amelia?

No. I feel sick. I'm the only bad one here. I killed Falkes's stepbrother, and Stephen, and now Renee.

I reach a river. Wide, rushing water separates the conifers. The air is hazy, though it is dark.

And—

And there is a person in the water.

A body.

I flinch, drop the weapons, then I'm plunging into the water. Ice-cold, frigid.

I reach out for the body and—

It moves.

He moves.

My breath catches in my throat as I see his face. "Caro?"

It's him—looking exactly as I how I remember him, the same as he was, injured, the day he died.

"You shouldn't be here," he says. And his voice is shrill—not right. "This isn't your place."

And then—then he's gone.

Gone.

Everyone goes.

I don't know where that thought comes from, why it seems important.

Not everyone goes, do they?

I've still got—

No. I haven't got anyone.

I am alone.

Inga the Killer is alone.

Feeling floods back into my legs, and I run back through the water, splashing it over me until my leggings are soaked.

My breaths try to burst my lungs, and there is pain in my head. I reach the water's edge and kick up dirt and mud and small rocks, and I'm running so far, so fast and—

The conifers thin out and, I see Renee's body, ahead. I am back *here*. I've come back in a circle. The circle of life and death. I don't know why I think that when I'm staring at her body. At the blood around her.

She looks so little now.

Just her *body*.

I jolt. Renee needs sending off. The Spirit Releasing Words, they have to be said. Or is it too late? How long has it been? I can't think, just push my hair backward. My hands are sticky. I look at them. Blood.

I step up to her. "I'm sorry," I whisper. A tear trickles from the corner of my left eye and runs down my nose. From there, it drips onto her chest. And I wait for something to happen, as if my tear can bring her back.

But it doesn't.

Nothing happens.

I gulp and then lift my hands. I make the signs of the Journeying Gods and Goddesses over her body as I whisper the Spirit Releasing Words. And then…then it's done, and her body needs sending off. Not just her soul.

There was the river earlier. The water I saw Caro in.

I frown, look back, try to remember where it was. Then I scoop my arms under Renee, pick her up. She's heavy, and I stumble.

I half-carry, half-drag into the taiga, to the river. My lungs burn fiercely and I don't know how long it takes me to get there, but then we're here. Her body makes a huge splash as I throw her in the water. I get soaked, but it washes off some of the blood on me.

Yes. I need to wash it off.

I scoop ice-cold water over me, feel it bite my skin as I scrub with my hands. As I get rid of the evidence. As I—

The spears. And the bow and quiver. They're all on the ground. I left them here, earlier? I pick them all up, feel numb. And then I'm walking back, to the open grassy area, where the trees thin out and the air has a stronger chill to it.

My feet are numb. I am numb. So numb—and it's the only thing I can think of, how numb I am.

This is… I blink. My head is heavy, and it feels like

things are happening too quickly. Like there's no pause in between.

I breathe deeply.

Renee is gone.

Because of me.

Gone.

My throat seems to get thicker. It's constricting. I gulp, and then there are lights in the darkness. And it's dark, so dark now. But it's a vehicle. Headlights. It's my truck. It's Oleta and the littles and *Amelia.*

My heart sinks. I am shaking, I am too cold, I am falling—only I'm not. I'm stock-still. I can't move.

Oleta is driving, and she pulls the truck level with me, winds the window down. "Inga?"

I stare at her. My eyeballs feel like they're frozen.

She's not the bad one.

That bad feeling I had. That sense of danger. Of one of us being bad news.

It wasn't her.

It was me.

In the front passenger seat, Amelia frowns and then looks around me, peering into the night. "Where's Renee?"

"I…" I swallow hard, clench my hands into tight fists. "I don't know." The lie is a snake around my neck. But I can't tell her. Can't tell her what I did.

She'd kill me.

No—Amelia wouldn't. She's not a killer, not like me.

But she'd abandon me—and she wouldn't allow Oleta or the littles to be with me. I'd be alone. And I've always said I don't need anyone, I'm better on my own, but looking at her and knowing the prospect of being banished is so very real, I can't say the words.

I just can't.

And saying them won't bring Renee back. Nothing will.

Amelia frowns. "You don't know?"

Oleta's staring at me, a knowing look in her eyes.

But that's ridiculous, she can't know!

I shake my head. The tears in my eyes stretch the shape of the truck and Amelia's head. "The deer stampeded us. She ran...and I can't find her." It sounds pathetic. She has to realize I'm lying.

Amelia's eyes narrow. Oleta doesn't do anything. I know because I'm staring at her mainly. Waiting for her reaction. But the muscles of her face don't do anything. They don't slacken or tighten.

The snake around my neck squeezes tighter. I feel sicker.

"Well, we'd better look for her then," Amelia says. "Put the spears in the back, then jump in, Inga."

TWENTY-EIGHT

MY HEAD IS KILLING ME.

I need to lie down, but I can't let them know I'm ill. Not now. Not in the ceremony, when the overall best assassin will be announced as well as any changes to the rankings of the bands.

Last year, I was promoted and became a second-in-command to Oleta's leadership, the same rank that Yvette had held under Fi, and I'd been looking forward to the ceremony that would lift me above the other highers. At first, Oleta hadn't been keen—she'd ruled the band without a second for a while—but nothing really changed.

And now nothing will change. The littles will stay littles. They're not good enough to graduate yet. We've only got two highers in our band: Harmony and Samira. Nathan died of injuries a few months ago, and even Oleta's powers couldn't save him. We've got three littles, and though our band is smaller in numbers than some of the others, nothing's going to change. Not until the recruiting team finds new blood that runs with Rijikarii and gives good skills for assassination. Bridie tells me she's got people studying Rijikarii and its organic formation within some Untamed groups. Her daughter Brighid is one of them, out in the field, observing a powerful woman that they believe Rijikarii originates from, while Petra's still being trained to improve her skills for sensing Rijikarii too. But, so far, I've heard no news of any potential recruits who have Rijikarii.

And, right now, all I can concentrate on is my pounding head.

We are standing in a row. Me and the others. Oleta is to my left, and the jeweled crown sparkles from her head. She's been wearing it the last few evenings, like she's trying to get as much use out of it as possible, even though it's obvious she's not going to lose her position as aunt. The only person who could've beaten her is dead.

The space where Caro should be is still empty, has been for over two years. Two whole years without Caro. I try not to look at it, but of course I see it. We always leave his space when we line up for the yearly rankings, even though we're at a completely different camp now. Caro never made it to Bluejay.

If the adults have noticed the space we leave for him, they don't say anything. No one ever mutters his name, but I think of him every night. I don't want to lose my memories of Caro—they're the only places I know for sure he's alive.

I don't want to forget anyone. I've even been trying to learn the names and personalities of the littles around here. The new recruits. The pudgy two-year-old boy who has what seems to be a permanent scowl and the identical twin girls who can only be four years old at the most. I'm not even sure what Bridie saw in them, but she vets all the potential recruits and often leaves our camp to go on the recruiting missions to ensure she gets who she wants.

Bridie told me once that she watched me for nearly two years, following many of the excursions I went on, before implementing the plan that recruited me. She still knows where D'Elinous, my old village, is, and I have dreams sometimes where I'm torturing her, getting the information out of her, and returning.

Bridie emerges from the hut, the last of the adults. She's got her cloak on and face-paint streaked across her cheekbones. Her matted gray hair is tied up high on her head in a knot almost the same size as her head. I find myself staring at the shadow of it as she steps forward and stops in front of us. She looks like a two-headed monster. One head on top of the other. I imagine the second head to be full of gnashing teeth. Needle-like.

Behind Bridie, Hunter beats the drum, a slow, thrumming pace.

"Let's begin," Bridie says. She points at Oleta. "You are the reigning best assassin and you have been for six years." She's always abrupt in these ceremonies. "Just as you have been the aunt of band three for the last two years."

Oleta curtsies low. When she straightens back up, she's standing at a slightly different angle, and a beam of harsh sunlight blasts my eyes. I blink, squint, and step back.

Bridie smiles. "But the end of Oleta's era is here."

There's a collective gasp.

"The best assassin is determined by the Rijikarii energy levels within individuals, as well as other factors, including their death count, and the best assassin is now Tiny Inga." Bridie doesn't put any effort into making the words dramatic. She says them all so matter-of-factly, so casually, like it isn't a big moment. "Oleta, give her the crown." She points at me. "I am making Inga the aunt, and you, Oleta, will be her second-in-command."

My legs feel too heavy. There's a rushing in my ears. No one is speaking.

I realize they're all looking at me. All the adults. The world's eyes are on me and —

No. I must've heard wrongly. Bridie can't be swapping mine and Oleta's positions.

"Her?" Oleta exclaims. I see the malice in her eyes as she sweeps her gaze over me. "She's nine."

"The aunt of a band is the most gifted, the strongest, and most effective of my assassins," Bridie says. "Inga is nine years old, yes, but her Rijikarii surpasses your levels now."

I look at Oleta and the pretense of us being sisters lies shattered at my feet, sharp shards pointing toward me. She wants blood. There is a promise in her eyes.

"No," Oleta says. "I'm older! I am fourteen." She casts

me a scathing look. "No. I'm way better than her."

I stay silent. I want to say I'm sorry—I want Oleta to like me because I know we've got to stick together. But I can't say I'm sorry. Not when Bridie and the others are here.

Only weak people say sorry.

"The crown, Oleta." Bridie's words drip with venom.

Oleta grabs the crown from her head, snatches it so quickly she grabs several strands of her hair with it, and shoves it at me, at my face. I turn, and the crude spikes scratch my cheek.

The metal is hot to the touch, warmed by the sun and Oleta's scorn. I put it on quickly because Bridie's watching me. I don't like the way it feels.

"We shall announce the rest of the rankings," Bridie says, her voice dry.

With a flick of her wrist, Petra is by her side. She's wearing her full Seer get-up. A long black cloak and face paint, but it's a different design to Bridie's.

Petra gives Oleta what I think is supposed to be a comforting look, and it's strange, watching the two Seer sisters. One of whom is never allowed to be a Seer in the true purpose. That's what Bridie said. Sure, if Oleta gets a vision, she can tell her. But she's not to try and speak with the Gods and Goddesses and meditate and learn the ways of different energies and whatever else it is that Bridie has Petra do.

No, Oleta's got the opposite life in a way—but both sisters are still prisoners.

Bridie runs through the rest of the rankings for the bands. One of the littles from Zak's group is third from the bottom. His eyes fill with tears, and he turns away. We all know he's stayed at the bottom way too long now. We're only given so long to improve and already newer and younger recruits are overtaking him.

After the ceremony, Bridie calls his name and beckons to him with a curled finger. He shakes as he follows Bridie into the hut.

"You think you're going to get away with this?" Oleta snaps, makes me jump. She's suddenly right in front of me.

Her eyes are ice shards that dig into me, and just her tone sends shudders through me. "You're going to pay for this, Inga."

TWENTY-NINE

"WHY ARE YOU SOAKED?"

Inside the truck, Oleta glances at me, then turns the heating on. Hot air blasts over me. But it doesn't make me warmer. Nothing can now.

"Fell in the river," I say—because Caro can't have been there. He was just a figment of my imagination. Has to be. Just like Bridie was when I saw her and—

Gweneira.

I inhale sharply. Did I imagine her too? Because she wouldn't lead the assassins and—

No. Oleta saw her too. Even two crazy people don't imagine the same thing.

Oleta grunts as she steers the truck forward. "You keep looking that way for Renee," she says, and then she's telling Amelia to look the other way. She even gives the children instructions, but I can't bear to turn around to see if they're more active—more childlike— now. I just stare straight ahead.

I look for Renee's figure as we drive, skirting around the edge of the forest, the engine straining as the land gets steeper, and part of me really expects to see her. She'll be walking toward us, illuminated by the lights in the darkness. We'll stop the truck, and she'll get in, and then we won't have to drive around with the headlights announcing our presence. Because anyone can see us.

Only it doesn't happen. We don't find Renee, and we don't stop driving.

I grip the edges of my seat so hard my knuckles throb, and I look at Amelia. The muscles around her mouth look tight. Her lips are firmly clenched together, and she's frowning as she squints ahead.

"Keep looking that way," she snaps at me, but then her gaze lingers on me for a second too long before she returns her gaze ahead.

My heart hammers against my ribs. Does she know? Does Amelia know what I've done? I look at her, and, suddenly, she's not the kind and loving Amelia I know. She's the woman who's going to kill me when she finds out.

And she will.

Her pretense that we're family will melt away.

No. Amelia's not like that.

But anyone can be like that if circumstances dictate it.

My stomach twists. Nausea rises. I need to get away.

"How's your headache?" I ask.

Amelia replies, but I can't make out her words, and I don't ask her to repeat them. Something in me doesn't want to get into a conversation with her, because then I'm inviting more questions. Questions I can't answer. Not truthfully, and I want to be truthful. For the first time, I feel it, a powerful urge within me, to be completely honest and straight with Amelia. To prove that I'm trustworthy. That I'm part of her family.

Only, now, I can't.

I lean my head against the window, feel sicker than ever, like the whole world is spinning faster and faster, but I'm not moving. I'm stuck, watching, and I can't keep up.

We don't find Renee. Of course we don't. And then the truck's engine stutters, makes a roaring sound. I can't think how long we've been traveling in circles, wider and wider. We're in the forest now, have been peering into the gloom of the trees for what seems like hours. It's still dark and the clock on the dashboard doesn't work.

"Low on fuel," Oleta says. "Very low."

"Any more in the back?" Amelia asks.

I shake my head, then realize she won't have seen my answer. "No." My voice cracks. I know we only had one spare can, and Oleta already put that lot in the tank.

Amelia makes a slight hissing sound. "Will have to search for her on foot soon then."

Search for her on foot.

I swallow hard, feel sick. I can't remember how close we are to the river where I sent Renee's body off to aid her journey to the New World—if I said the Spirit Releasing Words soon enough. And I don't think I did.

I peer into the darkness. The confiders seem ghostly. Is Renee trapped between worlds now? In pain?

I shudder.

Oleta stops the truck, and we get out. My legs feel too soft, insubstantial, weak. And I shouldn't feel like this. I should be strong. I am an assassin. I have strength.

"Take the tent," Amelia tells me and Oleta. "Renee might be hurt, and we might not be able to move her back to the truck until morning. Though what use the truck will be now, I don't know." She frowns. "Best take as many supplies as we can. We may not come back here at all."

"So we're all going?" Oleta asks.

Amelia nods as she goes to the back of truck.

"But shouldn't we stay in the truck?" Oleta says. "We've got the littles with us. And it's sheltered in there."

Amelia shakes her head. "No, we don't know we're coming back here. And we've all got to stick together."

I nod and—

I freeze.

I can hear water. It's close. The river? My chest rises and falls too quickly. What if the river's washed up Renee's body and she's lying on a bank and we find her? Amelia will know instantly it was me. I just *know* she will.

And then what will happen?

I'll lose her.

Just leave now, a voice in my head whispers. *You can outrun Amelia, maybe even Oleta too. Just make a run for it.*

But I can't make my legs to do that. My brain won't make the command, and I know that, even if I did, my body wouldn't obey. I'd fall.

Oleta and I get the tent out of the truck bed while Amelia assembles the supplies into rucksacks. I shoulder the tent and a small bag. Amelia has her medicine bag, a rucksack, and a spear—which she uses in placement of her walking stick—and Oleta takes the bow and quivers. We divide the knifes up between us adults. There are quite a few of them, once we've searched the whole truck for anything useful. The little children have no weapons. I see Oleta making sure of that. We both know what Bridie's children can be like. And—and there's something off about these children. They're still not behaving like children. How long does it take for drugs to wear off? It's been over twenty-four hours now.

I follow Amelia. She's walking at a fair speed, barely putting any weight on the spear. I suppose that's what fear for her daughter has done for her.

The blond boy decides he wants to walk with me. The other three children huddle around Oleta.

Through the gaps in the trees, I see the sky is a heavy charcoal, not quite as dark as it could be for nighttime. A little moonlight to guide us, but there's something about the light, the quality of it, that reminds me of an evening at Royston's Rock, of how my skull necklace slapped against my breastbone with every step I took as I trekked around the camp in secret, with Caro and Oleta. The rhythm of the necklace was like a heartbeat. I remember it, and the feeling, well.

Being alive is important.

Amelia points to the left. I slow my pace, looking that way, eyes narrowing as I try to pick out shapes between the trees. I think we're far away from the site Renee died at.

"That way?" I shift the weight of my load as I look, test the slipperiness of the ground with one foot. The terrain is softer, but only slightly.

She nods, and we head deeper into the forest. The ground gets wetter, boggier, and water sloshes around my hiking boots. I lift the blond boy over a particularly wet part.

We don't speak more. I listen to Amelia breathing, note the raspiness, how some breaths are louder than others. Was her breathing always like that? Damn. She is old.

Our pace slows, and, every now and again, the hairs on the back of neck lift, and I look back. I don't know what I'm expecting, who I'm expecting to see, because Renee's gone and Stephen's gone, and I know Falkes and Lexa and Minnow and Johnny and Callum aren't in this area. They can't be. There's no one else here, watching us.

It's just us. Us placing one foot in front of the other. Three Untamed adults and four Untamed children, breaking off on their own. But I am broken off from them, a heavy secret between them and me.

"You'll get better, you know." Amelia's voice

startles me.

"What?" I look at her. We've walked for hours. Above, weak, morning light illuminates the sky. Something about it reminds me of the milk and honey drink she and Renee gave me when they first took me in.

"Bridie," Amelia says. "You won't always be thinking about her. About what she's made you into."

"I wasn't." There's a hard edge to my voice. One sharp enough to cut.

I look toward Oleta. I don't think she heard Amelia's words.

"Because you're more than that." Amelia runs a hand through her hair, then gestures that she needs to stop.

I help her sit on a rock and get the rucksack off her back, and she touches her chest for a moment. Alarm pushes through me. I can kill the Enhanced in a thousand different ways, but I don't know the first thing about illness and old age. Amelia's the healer, not me. And Oleta can heal injuries, but what about old age?

"You are an amazing and intelligent young woman," Amelia says. "You burn brightly, and I am proud to call you my granddaughter."

My throat feels tight as I stare at her. A fierceness burns in her eyes. Behind her, the lightening sky looks thicker, heavier than the trees of the forest.

"Thank you," I say.

Amelia nods, then she gets up.

"Renee!" she shouts, using her hands to funnel the sound from her lips. "Renee!"

But Renee doesn't answer.

Renee will never answer.

THIRTY

I DREAM OF RENEE. OF course I do.

She's standing over me, and she's sweating. Her sweat is crimson, and it falls onto me, marks me. It burns my tattoos and scars.

"Coward," she whispers. "Coward, coward, coward."

But then she changes. Her face gets younger, her skin paler, her eyes lighter, bluer.

"I know what you're feeling," Gweneira says. "Don't fight it. Embrace it. It's not just you who is destined to be a killer."

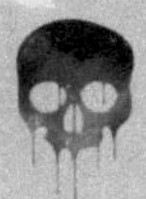

I wake, panting, drenched in sweat. Sweat that burns and burns and burns.

Coward.

No. My skin isn't burning.

I rub my hands up and down my arms.

There's a bad taste in my mouth. My chest rises and falls too quickly. The darkness is thick around me.

It takes me a moment to remember. How it's just me and Amelia and Oleta and the littles in the tent.

My chest hitches. My stomach feels empty, but I'm not hungry. Couldn't eat earlier when the others did, diminishing our supply of food even further.

Renee.

I turn my head. The coarse fabric of the tent drags against my cheek. I can see Amelia's shape on the groundsheet. We set the tent up once it got light. We'd walked through most of the night and were exhausted. Now, Amelia's breathing is deep, slow. She's wrapped up in two blankets.

I push my shoulders back and reach for my knife, where it sits by my feet. I stare at the crude marks in the handle. We got it when we were raiding last, when Falkes led us into New Vitaliz and we took supplies and weapons.

I lie back down, listening to the lemmings or mice or voles or whatever-they-are outside. Hear their scurrying feet, the pitter-patter of their steps. *Food.* But I don't get up to try and catch them or set any traps.

I just lie here, unsleeping. Waiting, just in case. Because something tells things can only get worse.

When we move again, Amelia and Oleta take the rucksacks with the blankets, the water pouches, the large weapons, whatever food we still have left, and the medicine bag. I take the tent—our *home* now, fabric rolled up, the frame folded—and the spare clothes, bundling them all together. One T-shirt, two pairs of cotton trousers, two jumpers, a pair of Renee's overalls, one broken sandal, a couple changes of underwear, and some spare laces for walking boots. Turns out most of our spare clothes were in the minibus. Amelia, Oleta, and I each have a knife in our belt.

I notice the blond boy's eyes sparking when he sees my knife. The other three children ignore it.

"We'll check over there." Amelia's voice is rusty, and her breathing is already loud. I look at her, but she shakes my question away. Because we both know talking about it doesn't do any good. Talking won't magically produce medication, doctors, or treatment. "We'll find Renee today. I can feel it in my bones. Always easier to find someone when it's light."

I shield my eyes from the streaks of sun breaking through the forest canopy and look to my right. More forest, the foliage so thick it doesn't look like foliage. Just a wall.

"Let's go, Inga," she says. "That way."

"Where the forest is thicker?"

"Renee might have crawled in there for cover during the night. She could be injured and too weak to come back out now."

I lead, my knife moving fast as I cut back vines and shrubs. It is slow-going and hard work, but we make our own pathway through the forest.

I feel the way sweat lines my back, makes my shirt stick to it, and I become aware of my odor and dripping underarms the longer I cut. My face feels grimy, dusty, and the constant movement works the tie in my hair loose. Twice I stop to redo it, lifting my matted hair from my hot neck, while Amelia gets a water pouch out. We take two sips each—two sips is always the rule when we're low on water—and then I grip the handle of my knife harder with my sweaty fingers.

"We will find Renee," Amelia mutters, and it's a promise, and Karnad girls never break their promises, that's what she says.

Karnad. That's the name she and Renee said I could use. But *Inga Karnad* never sounded quite right to me. Because no matter what I tell myself and what they tell me, I'm not one of them. But I'm not Inga Lin anymore either. I'm Inga the Killer. Bridie's marked me, and I can't escape my past. It's who I am. And I can't take the Karnad name when I took Renee's life.

I swallow hard.

You have to tell Amelia.

But I can't. No.

But what are you going to do? Keep pretending to look for her? Spend the rest of your life doing this?

Amelia's stomach rumbles from behind me as I cut our way through the forest, but we don't tuck into the last of the food. That's for when we're desperate, and Amelia says we're not desperate yet, even though Oleta and the children are complaining of their hunger. I wonder how many dizzy spells Amelia will need to have before she considers herself desperate.

We pass a bush with a meager number of berries that Amelia says are edible, and as Oleta and I forge a path ahead, she and the littles collect them and carefully fold them into a scrap of cloth. We eat three each when the sun is at its highest. The juice is bitter, tart on my tongue, leaves a strange aftertaste.

"I'm hungry," the blond boy whines.

"We need meat," Amelia says, her voice low. "Protein. Renee will need energy when we find her."

I nod. We always need meat, calories. That doesn't change just because we're on our own. And so we collect berries and look out for food, while calling for Renee, until Amelia needs to stop again.

It's mid-afternoon, judging by the position of the sun, and we find some dry ground to sit on. The terrain's got steeper, and we've been heading up a mountainside for the last hour or so.

"I just need to rest my legs," Amelia says to me. "You should sleep, Inga. You look beyond exhausted."

Part of me wants to argue with her. I'm the one who should be looking after Amelia, staying awake to protect her. But I haven't got any spare energy for such an argument. My body feels like it's humming.

I settle down, and she takes one of the blankets out from her pack, drapes it over me.

I think of Falkes and Lexa and Minnow and the boys. I wonder what they're doing. What they're saying about me.

Then I feel myself drifting off, a heavy slumber overtaking my body, the kind of heaviness that could absorb several hours in a fraction of a second.

When I wake, Amelia is standing and—

There is a woman in front of her.

"What?" I yell, jumping up and grabbing my knife—because Renee, it can't be Renee. She's dead and—

This woman is not Renee.

Adrenaline pounds through me. Need to protect Amelia, have to protect her, have to—

She's Untamed. The woman is *Untamed*. Beautiful, dark eyes. Dark hair. A face that says she's seen things. Bad things.

My breath catches in my throat, makes a rasping sound. My chest hitches. An *Untamed* woman. My head spins. There are other Untamed here?

The woman looks at me. Her eyes narrow as she stares at me, there's a fierceness in them that recognizes something in me. She's wearing a tie-die shirt that's several sizes too big for her, and a necklace dips under its collar.

"Inga, what is it?" Amelia turns to me. She's got moss and lichen in her hair, and there's grime on the right side of her face, folded into her wrinkly skin.

"*What is it?*" I stare at her, then point back at the woman, and—

There's no one there.

It's just Amelia and me. Oleta and the children are a little way away.

I look around again. There really is no woman, no one else here. Oh Gods, I'm more sleep deprived than I thought. Because that's the only explanation—the woman isn't a family member *and* I haven't just killed an assassin. And, well, I can't be becoming a Seer for real.

"I thought I saw a woman," I say, and I try to swallow away the bad taste in my mouth. Damn, my words sound pathetic. Make me sound mad. Crazy.

You're just a stupid little girl. Bridie's words, from long ago.

"Enhanced?" Amelia's voice is sharp.

I shake my head. "No. Untamed. She was..." But as I try to recall her appearance, a strange feeling slips over me. My forehead tingles, and I can't remember any specifics about her. "I must be over-tired," I say, rubbing my forehead.

Amelia makes a *hrmf* sound and nods. "Get back to sleep. Maybe you'll see more of our people and can relax in your dreams."

I wasn't asleep when I saw her though, I want to say. That woman was here. But I don't utter another word. I keep it to myself because I know how unconvincing it would sound when I tell Amelia that I can't remember any specifics about this woman.

Even the color of her hair's gone now.

I just remember the eyes. Dark and Untamed.

And I know, somehow, she was real.

A twig cracks, and I look to the right. I see Oleta. She beckons to me.

I sigh and get up.

"Not here," she says.

I follow her through the trees, until she stops and looks at me. There's a bright glint in her eyes.

"Go on, then, spill." Amusement tugs the corners of her mouth up. "What did you do to Renee?"

THIRTY-ONE

OLETA WATCHES ME ALL DAY, all night. Every day, every night. It's all she's been doing since I took her place. Even when we went out on a recruiting mission, she paid more attention to me than the children we were taking. Every time I looked in her direction—as we approached the Untamed settlement, as we waited for the playing children to stray a little farther from their huts, as we grabbed them and knocked them unconscious, as we ran back to where the trucks were—her eyes were on me.

Now, I return the action and inspect her. The hairs on the backs of my arms stand on end, and the crown feels heavy on my head. I hate it. And I hate Oleta, putting me on guard all the time. Even now.

Because that's what we're doing, watching each other, when we should be enjoying the celebrations. Many of the assassins from the other camps and bands are here, and people are having fun.

But not me.

"Have a drink, Tiny Inga." Bridie hands me a glass of rancid liquid.

"Thank you, Mother." I knock it back quickly, ignore the way it burns my throat. Behind the fire, I can see Oleta *watching me. Her eyes are cold, and her threat runs in my ears again:* You're going to pay for this, Inga.

But what would she do? Kill me?

"Perhaps I should not call you Tiny Inga anymore," *Bridie muses. I see the dancing flames of the fire in her eyes as she observes me for a moment.* "But you are so small and that is to our advantage. Tiny, but mighty."

Someone beats a drum, and then people are singing. Bridie wanders off, and the moment she does, a group of littles swamp me. I think they're from band nine, and of course, they all want to talk to me. Clara warned me this would likely happen, said that I'm quite the topic of conversation among the other camps. An aunt at so young an age.

"It's a lovely crown," *one of the littles says. Her eyes are eager, full of longing.*

"Maybe you'll be the head of your band one day," *I tell her.*

The girl's eyes light up, and I want to tell her how much I hate wearing the crown, how it's always either too hot or cold, how it pulls my hair. And how the weight of the scorn that comes with it is a predator following me.

In the dim light, I catch the smirk on Oleta's face. When I stare at her, she mimes a gun with her fingers, points it at me.

I ignore her. A reaction is what she wants. And she can't really hurt me. I know that. Any assassin who turns against another has Bridie to answer to. And Bridie doesn't always kill traitors. Though Yvette's not at this gathering, I know she's still at Royston's Rock, tongue-less, trying to please.

No. Oleta's got to be very careful and clever if she wants to hurt me.

The other aunts and uncles start to congregate by the lake at the southern side of Bluejay, so I head over there too. I stand next to Clara. On my other side is one of the aunts from another camp, and she gives me a disdainful look.

"Are you old enough to be an aunt?" *She turns to her side, to the others.* "I thought Oleta was too young, but this one? She's just a child."

I take out my dagger and press it to her side. Not hard

enough to cut, just enough to be felt. "Don't be so quick to judge. Age means nothing."

From the other side of the congregation, Bridie approaches.

The aunt backs away from me, and, for the most part, no one else bothers me. Of course they wouldn't. Just as Oleta has to be careful around me, so does everyone else.

The night draws on, and people continue drinking and dancing.

I don't drink any more though. One was enough. I need my senses alert. I need my surroundings sharp—Oleta is still watching me. Every time I turn around, she's there in the shadows.

"Have you heard from your daughter recently?" one of the instructors asks Bridie. "She is studying Rijikarii, correct?"

I turn to look at Bridie and see her nod.

"Brighid is still in the field, studying our sacred energy, that is correct." Bridie takes a long drink. "But she will be visiting soon."

"How long has she been out there?" the instructor asks. "Eight years now?"

"Approaching ten." Bridie looks proud. "She is dedicated to our cause, and she's a powerful Seer, able to send messages to our resident Seer to provide updates on Rijikarii."

"What kind of updates?"

A smirk crosses Bridie's face. "Wouldn't you like to know? My dear, secrets are power, and Rijikarii energy is the biggest weapon of all."

The instructor looks a bit miffed and turns away. Bridie sees me looking and gives me a strange look. I turn away quickly, heading back toward the food tables.

I grab a bowl of shchi, add a pinch of fresh herbs to the top for garnish, and dig my spoon in. Whoever made this soup was extremely generous on the garlic. Can barely taste the cabbage or meat in it, it's so overpowering, but it's still good.

Just as I'm finishing the shchi, and considering getting more, I catch another glimpse of Oleta. Still watching me.

Anger rises in me, a hot flood. I set my bowl down and

head toward her. My grip is firm when I grab her arm.

"You going to do it?" I yell at her. "Make me pay?"

"Now?" Her voice is a simper, and she shrugs herself out of my grip. "Where would be the fun in hurting you when you most expect it?" She shakes her head softly, mock-sadness on her face.

THIRTY-TWO

"YOU KNOW," OLETA SAYS. "IF we were still with Bridie, she'd give you top marks for this."

I tighten my fists. "I haven't done anything."

"Oh, Inga. We know each other better than anyone else knows either of us. We were raised together, by that woman, so trust me when I say that I know when you're lying. Look, just tell me. We have to stick together. We are the only one we can trust."

Trust? She's talking about trust now?

I take a step back. A twig breaks under my foot and the leaves of the trees whisper. "I didn't do anything to Renee."

And I didn't—well, not intentionally. And that's what Oleta's asking. We were raised to kill, to execute, and she's asking if I murdered Renee.

And I didn't.

I don't even know how my arrow got her. It wasn't supposed to. Not at all.

"I did not kill her."

And I didn't—it must have been a spirit or something. A spirit in the air, redirecting the path of the deadly point.

Oleta snorts. "Really? You're not taking the credit for this?" She shrugs. "Shame."

"Shame?" I stare at her.

"She was always prattling on about flint and the best way to strike rocks." Oleta laughs, startles a bird in a nearby tree. "I mean, it's not hard to make a weapon, is it? And she was *so* annoying."

My eyes narrow, and, suddenly, the air feels too hot. "What did you just say?"

Oleta laughs. "Getting protective of Mummy Dearest, are you?"

I punch her. One quick movement, and she stumbles backward. Then there's fire in her eyes as she leaps toward me.

I am ready, and I duck under her swinging arm and spin, get a kick into her side, just as she punches me with the other hand. Right in the face. The momentum throws me off, and I stumble, breathing hard, feel something wet sliding down my face.

Blood. I taste it, and I stare at her, my breaths loud in my ears.

Oleta pounces on me. She's bigger than me, and I struggle with her weight, before she slams me against a tree trunk. Pain reverberates through me, and I grunt.

Her hands go to my throat. Squeezes.

"I think we both know who the best assassin is right now." Her voice is low.

"Yeah?" I glare at her. "Then how the hell did the assassins take you out? I saw you, lying in blood in that hut with Stephen's mother."

Darkness swirls in her eyes. "Don't test me, Inga. I'm on your side."

"Really?" I yell, and my voice sounds strange, thick. "Because I don't know who you are anymore or what the hell you're doing." Saliva flies with my words, lands on her face. She doesn't wipe it away, because to do that she'd have to remove one hand from my neck.

She just holds my gaze, smiling slightly. "I think

you're getting weak, Inga. I think you killed Renee in a fit of anger and now you can't cope with it. You should've been able to beat me easily. But you're preoccupied with guilt." She inhales sharply. "So, here's what's going to happen. You're going to back my plan. We're hiding the children until they're older and stronger. You're not going to go looking for any of the assassins. If you do, I'll tell Amelia you killed her precious daughter. And, not only that, I'll kill Amelia too." She squeezes my throat harder. "Got it?"

I stare at her, my breaths coming too hard, too quickly. My nose is going numb. I think it's still bleeding, but my face feels weird. "So, you're going to let the assassins grow stronger?" My voice is raspy. "Let them take more children?"

"I already told you. Petra's on our side, working from the inside. We've got a plan, Inga, and the next bit is solely down to Petra. We are taking a step back, for now."

"Petra is not reliable," I say. "She said all of the originals were at Royston's Rock, and they weren't. Brighid wasn't there."

Oleta just smiles. She knew that? She was lying to me?

"Still four originals left, Inga," Oleta says.

I nod. *Zak, Clara, Dylan, and Mark.*

"They will die. I promise you that. But not yet. You have to trust me and Petra. Leave this to us. We're not some stupid girls who've thought up a quick plan. This plan has been in the works for a long time. Do you understand? Because I mean it when I say I'll make sure Amelia finds out the truth about Renee's death. And you know I am not averse to killing."

"You can't prove I killed Renee," I whisper.

"Can't I? I'm a Seer."

"You still can't prove it."

"Is that something you want to test?" She laughs, a harsh raucous sound and—

"Olie," says a voice.

Oleta and I freeze, then look back. One of the littles. The dark-haired girl. She rushes over to us, jumps over a small, fallen branch, and then Oleta's scooping her up.

"Olie, Amelia says we're to leave again now."

Olie? I stare at Oleta.

"Good," Oleta says. "Inga and I were just practicing. You can never practice combat enough." She turns on her heel, strides away with the girl in her arms. She looks back at me. "You'll want to pinch your nose. It's bleeding everywhere."

I wipe blood from my face, and then follow them. Huh. If Oleta thinks she can take over my mission, and stop me from killing the remaining originals, she's got another thing coming.

When we set off again, I ask the littles what their names are, and Oleta and Amelia look at me in surprise.

"We know what their names are," Amelia says.

"No, they haven't said."

Amelia frowns, then points at each of the children who are walking ahead. "Zita, Kam, Michaela, and Joshua."

Kam. That's the only name I take in though. The blond boy. He smiles at me, and I feel warmth inside me. Until I remember what I've done.

"We've been talking to them for a while," Oleta says. "Are you feeling okay?" Her voice positively drips with mock concern. "You're not still hallucinating, are you?"

"Hallucinating?" Amelia's voice is sharp.

"I think she got kicked in the head or something when those deer stampeded," Oleta says. "Or maybe it happened when she walked into that tree earlier.

Did you hear about that? Gave her a nosebleed and everything."

"Then heal her," Amelia snaps, stopping. "We don't want a head injury complicating things."

Oleta nods. "This won't take a minute."

I glare at her and imagine all the ways I'll kill her as she wraps her hands around my skull.

She doesn't call on her magic, even I can feel that. She just counts to ten, then steps back, smiling sweetly at Amelia. "All done. She won't hallucinate anymore."

THIRTY-THREE

I PULL OLETA'S HAIR AS hard as I can. She shrieks and turns on me, and everyone's watching. A planned fight, a display for the littles. A bit of entertainment before the big celebrations begin. And of course I volunteered the two of us as soon as I heard that Bridie wanted some sort of exciting act for everyone to watch.

Oleta was grinning at first, when we started in this arena, half an hour ago, but now she's not. Because no healing is allowed—that was Bridie's rule when we set up this fight, and Oleta's not going to break that rule with Dear Old Mother watching. Not that Oleta would start healing herself, leaving her vulnerable to attack while she does it. Not with me standing here.

And I am the better fighter, by far. I'd say it's pretty embarrassing for her really.

I shove Oleta against the wall of the arena, and she lets out a small gasp, before fire fills her eyes.

There's cheering all around. Eight bands are here so far, including Brighid. I saw her briefly, Bridie's infamous daughter, when she arrived earlier for the fourth day of the gathering. She strolled through the camp with confidence, barely exchanging a word with anyone. She went straight for Bridie's hut, her head bowed under a thick hood, a long dark cloak, similar to the one Bridie makes Petra wear sometimes, flowing around her.

Oleta mutters something dark, before throwing herself at me. Our bodies connect, and her fist gets me under my ribs. I exhale loudly, but I'm already moving, twisting, shoving her back. She's weaker on her right side, and I jab her there.

Oleta staggers backward, and I get another swift kick in. More energy builds inside me, and I strike her again.

"Aw, are you tired?" I whisper as she falls. "Poor, Oleta. Guess I really am the strongest." I laugh. "No wonder I'm aunt and you're not."

More fire rears in her eyes, but she doesn't speak.

I punch her face. Break her nose. Feel the clean snap of it.

There's an intake of breath from the crowd. I lean closer to Oleta. "Have I proven myself?" I whisper. "Because I am by far the strongest based on combat and kills, and those are what Bridie places a lot of value on. I'm the aunt—and you can't change that. And this game you've been playing is twisted and sick. So you're going to stop this vendetta you've got against me, or I won't hold back next time."

She glares at me. "If you kill me, Bridie will kill you."

My upper lip curls. "You want to take that chance?"

Oleta looks away.

"No? Thought not." I grunt and look away. "In any case, I've won this fight."

"We'll see," is all she says.

THIRTY-FOUR

WE KEEP MOVING—ME AND Oleta and Amelia and the four children who barely act like children—covering more of the mountain taiga, getting higher and higher. The mountainside is ragged, and twice we get to sheer drops, where the siltstone rock just falls away, plummeting down thirty, forty feet in a cliff.

"Don't want to fall off one of them," Amelia says to the children. "You wouldn't survive a fall down a rock face like that. You've got to respect mountains, always be wary of your surroundings, else the cliffs will get you."

When night falls, we set up the tent again. Oleta and I do it wordlessly while the children gather berries, and Amelia sits at the edge of our little camp—it's just the area where we've got the tent and our supplies, but she calls it a camp. Makes it sound more exciting for the littles.

The *littles*.

Something's up with them. Even Kam, the one who sticks closest to me—there's something not right about him. I don't like them being with us.

Isn't it just that you don't like children because of what they remind you of?

No.

It's not.

It's the danger that radiates from them.

This is wrong.

But I can't say anything. Not to Amelia without her questioning me. And definitely not to Oleta. But I know we shouldn't be around them.

I could just leave, but I'm not leaving Amelia with Oleta and the littles. And she won't come with me willingly. And I want her to do everything willingly, especially after what I did to Renee.

We settle down for the night, inside the tent. I'm first on guard, but I don't plan on waking Oleta up to take over at all. I don't trust her. I don't know when I'm going to sleep, as Amelia wants us all searching for Renee again tomorrow, but that's a problem to face then.

I watch the rise and fall of Zita's chest. There's a little moonlight filtering in, through the hole in the tent's roof. Zita's red hair is splayed out like a sun around her head, and she holds a cone close to her chest. The cone is green. She must've pulled it from one of the larches. She looks peaceful.

A Ural owl calls somewhere in the distance, and then another one answers. It makes me smile, makes me momentarily forget the pain of my nose, the way my face is burning, how the pain of it is getting strong and stronger.

I grit my teeth and hold the tensed muscles of my jaw until pain throbs through my gums. I concentrate on that as much as I can, try to ignore the pain and—

Something cracks outside.

I'm super alert. I hold my breath and listen. Amelia's deep, raspy breaths and the slight rustle of her clothes as her chest moves up and down proves she's still asleep.

But there's no noise from outside.

Yet there *was* a crackling sound.

It will just be a lemming, I tell myself, and I say it in Amelia's voice in my head. It will just be—

Another crack fills the air. Closer.

Footsteps.

Someone's outside.

My heart thuds, delicious adrenaline, released. I grab the knife from the foot of my sleeping area. I placed it there earlier, keeping it as far out of reach of the children's hands—and Oleta's. She's on the other side of the tent, her arms around Joshua and Michaela. Her snores are loud.

Amelia is next to me, and I reach out with my right hand, shake her leg. My eyes aren't on her—I'm watching the doorway of the tent—but I think she's still awake.

"There's something out there," I say. "I'm going to look."

Something? No, it's someone, the voice in my head corrects.

"Renee?" Amelia's voice is hopeful, and, for a moment, I'm sure it *will* be Renee. Renee, back from the dead, here and—

No. Someone else.

Because it can't be her.

But I have been seeing people who aren't actually here. Bridie, the assassins, Caro, that Untamed woman who I can't remember... And are there more? Have there been more?

What if I *am* hallucinating now, and Renee is there, and—

Amelia sits up. "My boots—pass me my boots."

"No. You just stay here. I'm going to check it out. Could just be a deer."

I crawl forward, keeping my weight light on my knees and hands. Something brushes against my side. The spare blanket.

My fingers burn as I reach out with both hands to undo the fastening of the drape. The blade of the knife scratches against the fabric.

I pull it back and—
Movement.
I inhale, sharp.
A mouse runs away.
Just a mouse.
I stay where I am, on my knees in the entrance of the tent, staring. Staring into the woods. The trees look like people, and there's something about them that makes my stomach tie itself into a tight knot. A knot I shouldn't have, shouldn't feel, because I'm not scared.

Tiny Inga is never scared. Bridie's whisper.
I breathe deeply.
"Is Renee there?" Amelia's voice.
"I can't see her… I don't know what it was that I heard. But I'm going to have a proper look." I crawl out of the opening. Something in my back moves and clicks as I unfurl myself, stand straight. It's cold out here, and I feel my skin goosebump. I pull my jacket closer. It's beginning to smell now, needs washing properly to get all the blood and dirt off it, and the stench clings to my nostrils.

I look around, at the trees, walk a few paces forward. The darkness is full of shadows, and the trees are the biggest shadows of them all. After a few seconds, my eyes adjust more to the dim light. The moonlight catches most surfaces, but in broken patterns, makes everything look like it's fragile.

I look into the sky, see the moon, its face fragmented by branches. A silver beacon, fractured by dark thoughts, that makes the sky around it even darker. But there are clouds, clouds floating. I don't think they're rainclouds.

Good.
I look left and right again. There really is no one here. No one at all.
I walk around, to check, and—
Amelia screams.
I jolt, and I'm running, eyes burning. The tent? There it is. Amelia? Can't see Amelia.

I reach the tent, skid inside it, and—

A long-fingered hand. A flash of orange somewhere, and a torchlight burns, and—

And they are *inside* the tent.

The Enhanced Ones.

"Surrender, wild ones," one of them says, just as there's movement to my right.

A flash of light—Oleta's angry face.

I grab my knife, plunge it into a torso. It goes lower than I'd have liked—hits the lower stomach, but the man screams. I pull my knife back toward me, but someone knocks it from my hand. I curse, and everyone is screaming.

"Stop at once!"

"Get the augmenters in them!"

"No!" Oleta yells. "Not the children!"

One of the littles shrieks, and then there's chaos. Too many shouts—the Enhanced shouting at us and to each other and Oleta and Amelia and me. And the children? Where are the children? I turn, try to see them. Little shapes, huddled at the sides of the tent, crouching down—is that them?

There's not enough light. Too dark.

Blood pounds in my ears. "Kam!" I yell, and I'm reaching out—his hand? Is that his hand?

"Drink this up, sweet child," a voice says.

I whirl around just as a figure drags one of the children across the tent. Michaela, the black-haired girl.

"No!" Oleta screams.

I shout, leap forward. And there's too much movement. Oleta and I are both about to strike. Amelia too. And the Enhanced are moving too.

"Where are the other children?" Amelia yells.

I punch an Enhanced One, and he falls back, but another catches him. Arms and legs, everywhere. Too little space, and—

Pain. My head.

I blink, see bright white lights as I turn. A garish

smile. A fractured mirror. I kick out hard, but haven't got the space to do it properly. My movement catches Amelia, and—

Blood splatters over me. Warm.

I turn, heart pounding. Someone screams. A man. Not one of us.

A ripping sound fills my ears, and then there's light—moonlight. The side of the tent, ripped. Oleta grabs Michaela and throws her through the gap.

"Michaela, run! Don't stop!"

"Kam! Get out!" I scream, as I see him next to me, punching an Enhanced.

I shove him toward Oleta, and she grabs him, pushes him out. "Where are the others?" she yells, but I can't answer. Because there are more Enhanced, pushing through the tent's entrance.

So many.

Hands seize me. So many at once. I fight and scream and spit at them. A glass vial slams into my closed mouth. Pain, and then broken glass and liquid across my throat.

No.

I kick and punch, new energy soaring through me, manage to wipe the back of my hand across my mouth. Got to get rid of the augmenter. Even the slightest taste is too much.

"You're coming with us!"

They drag me out of the tent, and I claw them, bite them, the Enhanced.

"Get the children away!" Amelia shouts. But I can't see where she is. "Leave me! Get out!"

She's in the tent?

I scream and punch two Enhanced men at the same time. Snarls and growls fill my ears, and—

White light flashes to the right. Seer light. Oleta.

"No!" a voice shouts.

"Kam! Where's Kam?" Oleta's voice. Distant. I think. Or something's wrong with my ears. "Run!"

I kick another Enhanced One, try to get my bearings.

Where are they coming from? A dull ache throbs through my foot, and I curse. We're going to have to run, get away. I look for the others—but they're all just shapes. Adults.

The children have gone? Run away, just as Oleta told them?

But where are Oleta and Amelia? Have they gone too? I search the chaos. But it's just me and the Enhanced Ones here. The Enhanced approaching toward me from three different sides.

Pain races through my arm.

I grab a broken branch and slam it into an advancing Enhanced One. "You going to try that again?" I yell.

"Surrender," they say. And it's pathetic, how they think I'll obey their command.

"Inga!" a voice screams.

Amelia.

I turn in a flash, see her in the shadows. See—

She's injured.

My blood turns cold.

Need to get her out of here.

"Don't get any closer!" I yell at the Enhanced, and I wave the branch around like it's the most powerful weapon ever.

I retreat toward Amelia, my eyes on the Enhanced. I scream at them, proper battle cries, and they take a step forward. All of them together. Shit. They're talking. Discussing tactics.

"We need to run now," I hiss at Amelia. A quick glance shows me she's favoring one side over the other as she tries to stand.

I wrap my free arm around her, keep hold of the branch. We need to get out of here. I have to get Amelia away.

"Run!" I yell at her. "Now!"

"I can't!" she shouts.

"You can!" I snarl.

And I partly pull her, partly drag her as her legs buckle.

"Come on!"

And then—then Oleta's here, and her hands are on Amelia. Healing and—

I whirl around and attack the Enhanced with the branch. Two of them are close, and I get them easily. Sweat lines my back and forehead, drips down into my eyes, stings.

I hear more shouts.

"Let's go!" Oleta yells, and then we're running, the three of us. We push Amelia ahead—and they're right behind us.

We're only just going fast enough.

"Get her out of here," I tell Oleta. "I'm going to hold them off!"

"There's twenty of them," she shouts. "You need me as well."

"No, just keep Amelia alive and Untamed. Just do that! Go!"

Oleta nods, and then she pulls Amelia away.

I turn back to the Enhanced.

"Who's next? Because you know who I am, right?" I yell, my throat raw. Adrenaline and energy pound through me, harder and harder. "You've heard of us—the ruthless killers, trained as children, right?"

"You're outnumbered," one of them shouts. "Surrender!"

A grin curves its way onto my mouth as they come at me.

There's a reason I was named as the best assassin. A reason that still applies now.

And fighting out here is different to inside the tent. Fighting, without having the distraction of where the rest of my group is, is easy.

It is like a dance. My movements are fluid and strong as I snap life from them.

Bodies fall, and this is it—this is the euphoria I long for. I need this. I am a killer. I am the Night Slayer.

I impale the next mirror man with the tree branch and pull it straight back out. Blood spurts, and his scream is deafening.

"We need Tranquility!" one of them shouts. "Get the dart gun."

Augmenters and a dart gun. My mouth dries. *No.*

I focus on the Enhanced retreating. Two of them. And only two left alive here.

My head spins as I do the calculations.

Then I lunge at the two nearest, screaming and shouting. My head connects with one of theirs in a loud thwack, and I see stars for a second. I drop the branch, and my hands go to her neck. I break it effortlessly.

"No!" the remaining one shouts, and the other two farther behind have slowed. They're looking at me. Looking at the monster I am.

I pounce on the nearest one. She doesn't put up a fight at all.

"Please, no." *Fear.*

"Oh, you're not supposed to feel fear." I laugh as I snap her neck and focus my gaze on the other two.

They run.

I wipe the sweat from my forehead and take in my surroundings. Look for movement.

But there are no Enhanced Ones left in the immediate area, not now those last two have run off. There'll be more. I know that. More nearby.

I turn and run. I need to find Amelia and Oleta and the littles.

My breaths burst from me, ragged, deeper, racking through me. Lactic acid burns my thighs. Pain flits through my left ankle. Damn it. Now the adrenaline's subsiding, I'm feeling everything. A tree branch tries to grab me, snags on my clothes.

I run and run, trying to work out which way the others went through the trees. Because they have to be nearby. But did they go left or right? All the trees look the same.

Sweat drips down my forehead, my back, my arms. Pain tightens my stomach. I sprint harder and faster and—

Amelia could be dead, and Oleta and the littles too. Or converted. There could be more Enhanced Ones who've found them.

No, they're not going to be dead or converted. I'd have heard screams or something. And I'd know it.

They're alive.

"Amelia," I call, but my breathing is ragged, and it swallows up her name.

They're dead. Because everyone dies around you.

No. They're not!

I scream and force myself to go faster. My thighs burn and—and I see the land ahead, the way it just falls away, ends.

"Inga! Stop!" a voice cries—a voice that—

I turn, skidding and—

Oleta.

"Stop!" she screams.

But I can't stop.

I can't stop myself as I fly off the edge of the cliff.

THIRTY-FIVE

"PREPARE A TEAM," BRIDIE SAYS. "It's going to be a long trip. At least a ten-day journey. We're going to D'Elinous."

I stare at her. "What?"

D'Elinous. That's my village. My family are there.

"Brighid has reported a recent surge in Rijikarii in many of its residents," Bridie says. "And Oleta keeps saying we need more recruits."

I stare at her, harder. "Brighid is there?"

"Of course Brighid is there," Bridie says. "I've got observers in quite a few villages—especially ones where we get good recruits from. Rijikarii gathers in areas, chooses the same families often."

I go cold. Bridie's got Brighid, an observer, in my village? Watching my people? I flex my fingers, think of the next child she brings. A child who won't know me or recognize me, born in the last few years?

"Now, organize a team, Inga. I want to set off at first light tomorrow. We're going to need strong fighters. I'm anticipating trouble."

"What kind of trouble?"

"From the recruits," Bridie says. "They're older than

251

I'd like, these ones, and there's four of them. Brighid says the Rijikarii in these four has increased substantially in the last year, in a similar way to how Petra tells me it has been increasing in you, though for slightly longer with you, given that we nurture Rijikarii here. Now, these four new'uns will put up a fight, I'm sure. But we need them. We need more highers. And I think if we bring these four here, your own energy will increase further too. We can have a reunion party. You'd like that, wouldn't you?"

A reunion party?

I know these four planned recruits?

"Who is it?" I ask. "Which four?"

Nausea grabs me. My sister. It's going to be my sister. Everything I already know about Rijikarii energy tells me it runs in families.

It's going to be my sister. She's going to be one of them.

On the other side of the hut, Oleta smirks at me. There's a knowing look in her eyes—she orchestrated this. I know it.

Blind hatred fills me.

Bridie counts on her fingers as she speaks. "Kacey, Redala, Elf, and Keelie."

My breaths come too quickly. I touch my necklace of teeth—for comfort. Only it doesn't bring any.

Not my sister. Not Gweneira.

But Keelie and Elf—my cousins.

And Kacey? Caia-Lu's niece.

Redala—the name is vaguely familiar, but I can't think of the person.

Oleta smiles sweetly at me, and I know this is it, her revenge.

"Get a team briefed, Inga," Bridie says. "I don't want any delays or problems when we leave. And you're staying here. Until I'm back, you're in charge of this camp."

THIRTY-SIX

THE WORLD HURTLES PAST ME. Flashes of color in darkness and moonlight, and—

I hit the ground. Rocks. Limestone and siltstone.

Pain in my ribs, and my eyes are everywhere at once. I see the forest far below rushing up to me and Oleta at the top of the rock face above me. I see the moon, so bright in the sky, see the hazy patterns across its surface. I see the ocean, far, far away. The beautiful sea that takes and takes and takes.

I see Amelia. See her running through the conifers, stumbling. Her eyes are still Untamed. She's alive, Untamed, yes. The children aren't with her. Where are they? Where—

Movement.

In the trees, behind.

Enhanced Ones. More Enhanced.

Shit.

They're behind Amelia, and their eyes are flashing fragments of moonlight and broken darkness, leaves and twigs.

Amelia's only a few hundred yards ahead of the enemy, stumbling. Her pace is slowing, and she stops, tries to catch her breath for a moment, then she's hurrying along again, a frantic look over her shoulder before she urges herself to go faster.

The trees whisper as she passes them. She turns her head, looking back, and—

She freezes, then crouches down as much as her curving spine will allow. The coverage around her is thick. Her whole being quivers, and her lips move soundlessly as she waits.

The darkness is a cloak. She tilts her head to the sky and the moon, and her words are blessed with their shapes as she murmurs the Gods' and Goddesses' songs and prayers.

Her gnarled fingers clasp together. "Please, Mighty Divine Ones, revered Gods and Goddesses who keep us safe, Spirits of Land and Water, if I am to be found, Inga and Oleta and the babies must be free. Please, keep them safe. Keep Inga safe."

Amelia turns and looks around again. The woods seem to be alive. Every blade of grass rustles, and the sounds are louder than her prayers, her wishes. She mumbles over and over, asking the Gods and Goddesses and spirits to please listen to her, that she doesn't know where Inga went, but to keep her safe.

"Oh, Wise Ones, please, help my Inga and—"

I see the Enhanced Ones. See them going for her. See their twisted smiles.

"Amelia, run!" I scream.

But she doesn't. She's still praying, and her breath wheezes as she inhales in between every couple of words.

"Run!" I shout, but she can't see me, and I'm not here and—

My ribs—fresh pain, and my spine and....

A thousand colors in front of my eyes, piercing me, twisting inside me. Something hot and burning in my heart and—

Then it seeps away, the heat, like it's been drained. And there's nothing.

The world has gone, and I feel nothing.

THIRTY-SEVEN

"THEY'RE HERE!" SAMIRA YELLS, FROM *near the* entrance of our hut.

I rush outside. Keelie, Elf, Kacey, and Redala. I'm going to see them. People from my village. And two are my cousins. Will they recognize me?

The truck squeals to a halt, tires throwing up sand and grit. Bridie throws her door open and jumps out, her face like thunder. Not the expression that she left with, ten days earlier.

I strain my neck, trying to see my family, my people, and—

"Bring her to me now!" Bridie bellows.

I stare at her. "What? Who?"

Behind me, the other assassins are gathering. I can see them hovering in my peripheral vision.

"Petra!" Bridie screams as the rest of our people get out of the truck. And it's just us. Not the others, not my people.

They got away?

Bridie's group wasn't successful?

I hone in on Oleta, widen my eyes at her in question—not that I expect her to answer me. But I need to know what happened. Oleta's not looking at me though, she's staring at

255

Bridie, horror on her face.

"Bring Petra here now!" Bridie yells.

"Mother, what is—" Samira starts, but she stops when Bridie growls.

A few seconds later, Hunter leads Petra forward. She's still in her chains, and the metal jangles.

"No! Don't hurt her," Oleta shouts.

Bridie grabs Petra and hurls her to the floor. "Thought you'd be clever, did you?"

"She didn't do anything!" Oleta yells, racing forward. She grabs Bridie's arm, but Bridie backhands her. Oleta falls—and I race forward, somehow manage to grab her in time and stop her hitting the ground, my hatred for her forgotten.

"What's going on?" I ask her, but she shoves me away.

"The Enhanced got there before we did," Zak says. "Complete conversion attack. No Untamed left."

No Untamed left?

My heart drops. My family?

"And it was you!" Bridie snarls at Petra. "Thought you'd be clever, did you? Tell that abomination of a sister of yours where D'Elinous is so they could get to them first?"

"I didn't!" Petra cries, just as Oleta shouts, "She wouldn't! We can't contact Anita!"

"Don't lie!" Bridie screams. "Powerful triplets like you! Of course you can contact her! And you thought you could rise against me, halt my plans, you thought you could play me?"

Petra whimpers.

"And you thought you'd take my only daughter away from me without any consequences?" Bridie grunts.

"Brighid got away!" Petra yells.

"So it was you!" Bridie pounces on her.

"Who else got away?" I shout.

"No one," Petra says.

Bridie snorts. "Setting up a conversion attack on your own people is akin to murder. Worse than murder. We needed those fighters. D'Elinous had one of the best sources of Rijikarii I've ever seen, and Brighid believed it was originating from that old Seer."

The old Seer? Caia-Lu? It has to be.

"You've taken all that away from us. Not just the recruits I wanted, but the knowledge we could've gained. Well, you need to be taught a lesson. Come on."

Bridie drags Petra by her chains.

Oleta screams, but Hunter and another instructor grab her, hold her back.

I watch Petra go. Watch her shaking.

And her words haunt me. No one got away.

My family. They're Enhanced or dead.

But I think either's better than them becoming what I am.

"You have to let me see her!" Oleta shrieks at Bridie. But the older woman just smirks.

"Do you really think I'm that stupid? Why would I let you go and heal that traitor?"

I pause in the doorway, watching.

"She's my sister!"

"No, she's nothing," Bridie says. *"And we've got work to do. You're working with me."*

"No, I'm going to see Petra—"

"If you disobey me and visit her, I'll kill her, and I'll make you watch." Bridie's voice is low.

Oleta flinches.

"Now, come on." Bridie grabs her arm and pulls Oleta out.

I sidle past them in the doorway and lock my gaze onto Oleta.

"I'll check her," I whisper, just quiet enough for Bridie not to hear.

The muscles in Oleta's face tighten, and then she nods once, quickly, before disappearing after Bridie.

Petra's face is so swollen, she can't open her eyes. Her skin is bruised, and there are four deep cuts on the right side of her face.

She's lying in a pool of what must be her own blood.

I clear my throat. She doesn't react.

But she's alive, I can feel a pulse in her wrist, and I focus on that. That's what I have to tell Oleta.

"It'll be okay," I whisper, my voice cracking. Shivers run through me.

I am lying. How can it ever be okay?

"It is okay," Petra whispers, the sound barely audible. "Your family got away."

THIRTY-EIGHT

I OPEN MY EYES. I am on my back, and the moon is bright, above me, broken only by a lone branch reaching out. I blink, grimace. Sharp pain curves behind my eyes, circles them, and I wince. The small movement is enough to send arrows through me.

No.

No.

No.

My body—the fall… I fell and….

A dull pain has wrapped around the back of my head, but the muscles in my neck work, allow me to lift my head an inch or so up. The pain of the movement is severe, but I can *feel*. Feeling is important. My breaths are heavy and labored as I check I can move my arms, my legs. I tense the muscles in my hands, my stomach, my back.

I—I think I'm okay?

Twisting my neck hurts more than expected, squeezes sharp pins of nausea through me. My stomach turns, and I look at the rock face rising next to me. I… I fell. The edge of the mountain, the rock face and… I blink. I fell…fell all this way?

259

Damn, *I fell off a cliff.*

And I am *alive.* What the… I *fell* from that height—at least three hundred feet—and I am *alive.* I am conscious.

I take a deep breath, register every bit of pain throughout my body. I must've done some serious damage. I'm on my back now. Does that mean I landed on it? But I can feel my hands and feet, and I did turn my neck. So no serious damage?

I wait for the pain in my back to numb a little, then I force myself to sit upright. Every muscle in my body screams. My eyes smart. A prickly feeling dances over my nose.

No. I will not cry.

Dark spots hover in front of me, look like tiny people floating. I can hear…pressure. There's pressure in my ears. Blood pounding. The left side of my head feels heavier than my right, and I lift my left hand up to it. My fingers come away sticky, wet, and the side of my face below my eye feels weird. But touching it doesn't hurt. Not any more than it already was.

I frown as I stare at my arms. The left sleeve of my denim jacket has gone completely, and my skin is covered in new cuts and abrasions. Dried blood and fresh blood. How long have I been lying here? It's still nighttime, at least.

I look around. Grass and vegetation to my right, with trees—dark shapes in the night. The exposed rock face is to my left. There's moisture in the air, but everything feels too quiet beyond the pressure, the roaring in my ears. Has the fall done something to my hearing?

Damn it.

Suddenly, I become aware of the strange taste in my mouth. It's dark and dangerous, rusty, but sharp. I spit out blood. The moonlight gets brighter, makes my blood look lighter, a pale pink. The kind of color Amelia likes.

Amelia.

I turn, my heart pounding. The left side of my head feels heavy again, and I think I'm swaying.

"Amelia?" My voice is weak, trembles. I do not sound like me. My hands reach for the ground, to steady me, and I wrap my fingers around damp grass. Damp with my blood? Or has it rained? But I can't work out whether it has. Can't process the information needed for the deduction. "Amelia? Are you there?"

Fool! You don't shout when the Enhanced are about.

Yes, the Enhanced. Damn. What was I…? I grimace. I need to stand. Need to find Amelia. And…and Oleta. Oleta was there—at the top of the cliff…wasn't she?

My vision wobbles as I force myself to stand. Pain circles my lower back, and my right thigh feels cold, numb. But I'm standing. I'm doing it. My head—it shouldn't feel so heavy. I try to think. Concussion. Is this…?

Amelia. Concentrate on Amelia. On family.

Something pops in my lower back as I take a step, and I stop, feel winded. The ground beneath my feet seems to get softer. I'm sinking!

No.

I can't be.

I stare at the grass. It's still there. It's my head. Hell, I've done something bad. I look back at the mountain's cliff-face. The cliff I fell from. Very bad.

And Amelia, she's going to be up there. She didn't fall. She was being chased by the Enhanced, the opposite way. And Oleta and the children… How many littles were with us? I can't think.

My mouth dries. I have to get back to them, have to find Amelia. Must find her.

"I will find you," I whisper, and the promise materializes in front of me. A snake that lassoes around my neck. Break it, and the beast bites.

I start forward, try to ignore the pain. I can deal with that later, once I know Amelia's okay. Just got to move. But how am I going to climb up there like this? How—

My boot catches on something.

I fall, hit the ground hard, breath knocked out of me. The snake around my neck loosens, whispers something to me and then—then I feel it. Pain wraps around my ribcage, flits down my spine, and zaps the insides of my legs. I breathe hard, my vision smarting, and then I'm crying, screaming a scream that doesn't sound like me, but my body vibrates with it, and the snake laughs.

I lie as still as I can, begging the Gods and Goddesses to take the pain away. To take me to Amelia, away from this place. The moon laughs, casts a brighter light down over his land.

And I...I can hear water.

Water.

A dark sense fills me. Something bad...something bad is coming.

I need to get up.

I need to run.

I need to find Amelia.

"Come on," I mutter. "You can rest later."

I use my hands to push off from the ground and wince as pain wracks through me. My wrists click, and my arms burn. Upright, I am dizzy, and waves of lightheadedness pull at me. Something wet is slipping down the side of my face again, but I tell myself not to focus on it. I must be okay—somehow—as I'm walking. That's what I concentrate on. I just need to get through this pain and find Amelia.

I blink, squint at the sky. Still dark, a darkness that makes the moon look brighter. No clouds at all. Okay. I look ahead and—

There's a figure. A woman. No flashes of mirror eyes, and she's heading straight for me, pushing back foliage, plowing through the long grass. To *me*. She's seen me.

I freeze, feel my lungs harden. I haven't got a weapon. Her eyes may look Untamed from here, but that says nothing about who she is.

She gets nearer. She's wearing a black leather jacket and black jeans, skin-tight.

I stare at her, and the strangest of feelings barrels through me. My chest tightens as I see her dark hair and curvy frame. And those eyes—

No. It can't be.

But it is.

"Keelie?"

The woman stops. "Who the hell are you?" Her eyes narrow, and, in an instant, she's produced a knife.

"It's me, Inga…"

"Inga?" She frowns. I look at her eyes for recognition—but there's nothing. She shifts her weight. Her new stance is powerful. *Of course* it would be.

"Your cousin," I say. A tingling sensation travels down my right leg. "From D'Elinous… Gweneira's my sister."

"Gwen?" Keelie's tone is neutral. I can't read her.

"Gweneira." I push my hair back. "Our mothers are half-sisters." I rub my forehead. I remember that detail, even though they always just said *sisters*. I recall a conversation where Gweneira asked why Aunt Lìxúe's mother wasn't our grandmother. Gweneira wanted to know why we didn't have any grandparents at the village, but our cousins did.

Keelie's eyes widen. "You're Sara's daughter? Hell, they *took* you. You were… It's you? Really you?"

My heart leaps, and Keelie's still speaking—I'm vaguely aware of that, but I can't focus on her actual words. Only that she's here, and I'm not alone. *Family.* I'm being reunited with them. Just as the Gods and Goddesses promised I would be. Keelie is *here.*

A new wave of pain zones in on my lower spine, and I blink rapidly. "Where's Elf?" I ask. Got to keep talking. Need the distraction. "Where's everyone else? Are you on your own?"

"Elf and Bea are alive," she says, her tone blunt. "They're not here." She shields her eyes as if there's a bright light shining down, then slides the knife back into her belt. "Mila…" She touches her chest, then frowns, looking around. "Mila's here—somewhere. And Caia-Lu—do you remember Caia-Lu? Damn, who else do you remember? How long have you been here?" But, before I can answer, she's shouting for Mila again.

I take a few steps toward her. My gait is uneven. Shaky. "Keelie? Who's Mila?"

"My sister—she's twelve. About this high, dark hair, mixed race too. Yeah, she was born after you were taken. She's… She was right with me, but now she's not. I'm supposed to be looking after her. Need to find her. Come on." She grabs my arm, pulls me along.

"Hey!" It's automatic. My arm strikes out toward her, slaps her away. Pain reverberates through my back, arms, and legs at the movement, swiftly followed by more nausea.

Keelie stops, stares at me.

"I don't like being touched," I say.

She nods. "Sorry." Then she frowns. "But, hell, what has happened? I was there, with her and a couple others—and now I'm…." Her eyes widen as she looks at me. "This doesn't normally happen," she says. "We don't just…jump about. I mean, it's pretty much just living like normal—but here instead, in the New World."

Something in my ears crackles. "The *what*?"

"The New World," Keelie says. She lets out a short laugh. "Wait, have you only just got here? We're dead, Inga."

I stare at her. I'm not dead. I can't be dead.

You fell off a cliff.

But I'm alive—I can feel it. I know I am. I wouldn't be in this much pain, if I was dead, surely?

Keelie tilts her head slightly to one side. "Maybe that's why I ended up here with you, so suddenly. The realm tries to group people together, family, you see? Doesn't want them to feel lonely…."

I hold up my hands. "I'm not dead." I wave my hands, as if that proves it. But it does. I can feel it.

I didn't die.

Keelie frowns. "What happened?"

I tell her about the Enhanced and how they ambushed us. "Amelia and I got separated, and the Enhanced chased us. Then I lost her, fell off that cliff up there—and I think Oleta saw me. But they're still up there. I need to find Amelia. And the littles—the children."

They need my protection.

But they're not going to be weak and vulnerable. They're trained killers.

Except they're still drugged or *something*.

"Wait. You're still *with* the assassins?" Keelie's eyes flash. "Or, rather, were."

"No." I shake my head, then regret the movement. "I've been killing them since I escaped. That was six years ago. Me and Oleta, together, we got away." My shoulders tighten. "I'm still trying to take out the head of the unit though."

Take out Gweneira… But how I can do that? She's my sister.

But she *shot* me.

She didn't kill you though.

Keelie's eyebrows shoot up. "Killing them?" She rubs her hands together. "I killed a lot of Enhanced." A far-away look takes over her eyes.

My eyes narrow. "You still remember how to do it?"

"Kill?" She gives me an odd look.

I nod. "Because chances are the Enhanced are still about. And we need to find, maybe even rescue, Amelia, Oleta, and the littles."

Keelie laughs. "Inga, there are no Enhanced here. The New World is *just* for Untamed."

I shake my head. "This isn't the New World."

"It is," she insists. "You're *dead*. I'm dead. We're both here."

"I'm not dead." I grit my teeth. Not with this amount

of pain.

"You have to be. *I'm* dead. I know I am. I was shot." Keelie points to her stomach. "And when I died, I found my sister—Mila—she was waiting for me. And we got to the New World. Now *we're* together too. So you're dead, Inga. Accept it and move on. Pretending isn't going to make any difference."

I glare at her, not sure I like this version of my cousin. In our other meetings, she's always been nicer. But what if that was just me? All in my head?

I breathe hard. "No. This is the real world."

"The New World *looks* like the real world."

"I'm not dead!" I shout the words. "Look, you must've come back to life or something."

"Just me?" She raises her eyebrows. "Back to life?"

"Yes," I snap, feel wetness creeping down my back. Sweat or blood?

"Hell, do you realize how crazy you sound right now?" Keelie snorts.

I glare at her.

"You know, our family worshipped you," she says. "You were always mentioned. Except Sara—she'd never say your name. But Gwen talked about you a lot."

"*Gweneira,*" I correct. She doesn't shorten her name. That's one of the things I can count on. One of the few memories I have of *before*.

"Gwen." Keelie gives me an odd look. "And she didn't mention how bloody stubborn you are."

"Stubborn?" I stare at her, throw my hands up in the air—and immediately regret it. Oh damn, the pain.

"Cool tattoos," Keelie says. She's seen my arm. The sleeveless one. Despite the blood and cuts, some of the marks are clear.

Cool? I stare at her, but she's not giving me a knowing glance or looking sly or *anything*. And she still seems relaxed—though she thinks we're both dead, and I can't therefore hurt her? But *still*. I frown. Doesn't she know what my tattoos mean? Bridie's gang wasn't a group that just played at what they did.

We were real, bad. They trained me to be the worst.

And I am the worst.

I think of Renee and swallow hard, darkness rising from the pit inside me.

"What do they mean? Your tattoos?" Keelie steps closer, bowing her head so she's staring right at my arm. She's careful not to touch me, I notice that though.

I freeze, become very aware of the inky marks.

"Inga?" Keelie looks up at me, long lashes blinking.

"Nothing," I say.

"Nothing?" She pouts. "But tattoos *always* mean something to the person."

"They're to do with my past," I mutter.

"That assassin gang?"

I give her a long look. I don't like her tone—it's too curious, too amused. Like she doesn't believe the horrors.

Maybe she doesn't know....

She shrugs. "If you don't want to say, fine. Just being friendly. That's all."

"Well, I'm getting up there." I nod at the rock face. "I need to find Amelia and Oleta, like I said."

"They're not going to be there—even if they died too." Keelie clears her throat noisily, then spits phlegm on the ground.

I roll my eyes. She still thinks we're dead.

"Because their families will be with them," she continues. "Well, any family who's also here. They'd probably want some time before we try and find them anyway, and, sometimes, you just can't. The New World houses a hell of a lot of Untamed. Yet we only see the ones who are important to us—usually family...."

I drown out her words and grit my teeth as I turn toward the cliff.

"Well that's mature, ignoring me. You should listen to me. I know the New World...."

I continue. Slowly. Keelie makes a huffing sound. I

think she's right behind me.

I pause, shift my weight so it's primarily on my right leg and grimace as new pain wracks through me. I lift my hand to my eyes, rub them, then stare up at the rock. Looks like a sheer drop. Not going to be the easiest of climbs. And in the dark too. Plus, I'm injured.

"You're going to need help getting up there," Keelie says.

I turn to her. "Are you going to help me then?"

She snorts. "You know, you could be nicer."

"So could you."

Keelie huffs, loudly. "This better not take long because I need to find Mila." A pause. "Can I put my arm around you then, to help?

After a moment, I nod. She is family. True family. And she's the first step to the big reunion. With the rest of my family. Elf, will he be next? Gweneira, I've already seen—but that can't be *it*.

Won't be it. Not if I need to kill her....

My stomach twists. Sharp pain.

Keelie sighs dramatically as she puts her arm around me. "Have you got any weapons? Or is it just my knife?"

I raise my eyebrows. "Finally agree this is the real world, then? Good."

"What?"

"You only need weapons in the real world." Despite my pain, I feel triumphant.

Her eyes narrow. "The New World isn't what we were taught it was, Inga. Bad people are here too. They're just not Enhanced. Doesn't mean all Untamed are good."

Yes. I press my lips together. I know all about that.

"So, weapons?"

I shake my head. "No, nothing on me. Amelia and Oleta might still have theirs." They both had knives before, didn't they? But they could've lost their weapons in the fight against the Enhanced. "We'll go that way." I point to the right of the cliff. In the darkness, I can just about make out a route up its looming shape.

Keelie wrinkles her nose. "That doesn't look an easy way up."

"We're not wasting time walking right round and up the slope," I say. "We need to get to Amelia. Look, she's old, and there are Enhanced up there. I'm not leaving her."

"I told you. There are no Enhanced *here*." Keelie's eyes flash. "The New World—"

I cut her off. "Unless you agree we're alive, just shut up about the New World. Otherwise this conversation is never going to end, and it's getting bloody annoying already."

She doesn't say anything more, just helps me walk.

We reach the bottom of the cliff and there's a tightness in my chest that won't go away. I can hear my heart beating in my ears, along with a slight rushing sound. Maybe I hit my head when I fell. Is this what a concussion feels like?

"You'd better go first," Keelie says. "I can push you up."

"I don't need your help."

She rolls her eyes. "Accept my help or neither of us is going to get up there. And I'll tell you what, we better not fall. I don't want your idiocy to mean I get a broken leg or something."

I glare at her. "There's nothing stopping *you* going the sensible route." My voice is loaded.

She rolls her eyes. "Why would I let you have all the fun? Now, come on." She nods at me and then cups her hands together, ready to give me a leg up.

CLIMBING IS PAINFUL, AND, BY the time we reach the top, my back and legs are on fire. For several moments, all I can do is lie on the ground, feel the grass and mud sticking to me. I struggle to lift my head.

"Look out for Enhanced," I mutter to Keelie, who's standing. "Get your knife out."

"There are no Enhanced here," she says, her voice low. But she still gets the weapon out. "I already told you. We're just wasting time. I need to find Mila."

Damn. She's annoying.

"What's happened with Gweneira then?" I ask, bracing myself as more pain cascades down my spine. "Gwen?"

I suppress the urge to sigh. "My sister." Does Keelie even know which group Gweneira's in charge of now?

"Yeah, *Gwen*." Keelie gives me an odd look. "She stopped using her full name ages ago." Then she freezes—remembering that I wasn't there at that point? That's if Gweneira even did use a shortened name. She loved her name. Didn't she?

Keelie looks down at me. "Uh, there was a conversion

attack at D'Elinous, when I was eleven."

"I know," I say.

"You know?"

I nod.

"How?"

"Bridie, our leader, had her eye on you. She wanted to recruit you too. They found the village had been destroyed. Saw some bodies, but Petra—one of the Seers—said you'd got away."

Keelie's eyes widen slightly, and the rest of her expression slackens. "Well, uh, I got away during the attack. Me and Elf, Bea, and Mila. My parents did too—but not for long. They sacrificed themselves so we could…" She swallows hard. "Or should I say my mum and *Owen* sacrificed themselves."

I stare at her, no idea what she's on about. "But Gweneira got away with you," I say. "And my mother too."

Keelie shakes her head. "They didn't. I think my siblings and I were the only survivors. If you didn't see their bodies, it means the Enhanced got them. Conversion." Her voice is low. "I'm sorry."

I shake my head. "No. That didn't happen. Gweneira is still alive and Untamed." And my mum—she has to be out there too. Petra said my *family* got away. Not just my cousins. So, it includes my mother, and I know my sister's alive.

Keelie's giving me a look that makes it clear she doesn't believe me. I open my mouth, about to tell her about seeing my sister, when a lump forms in my throat.

I can't do it.

I can't say the words.

I just… I can't.

For a moment, the trees to my right blur. I blink quickly.

I don't want to talk about it. Don't want to think of Gweneira being the new Bridie. Being evil, wrong. No, she can't be—she was only there because she was trying to find me. She's a spy. Has to be.

Only she's still there. And whenever it was that she joined, she'd have discovered then that you were no longer with the assassins.

But she'd have suspected I was the Night Slayer. She'd know I'd come after the remaining assassins. That's what she was waiting for. For me to find her again. My sister.

But she left with them. She may not have killed me, but she shot me.

She's with them now.

And it hurts. Hurts a lot. And I can't tell Keelie that. Just can't.

"Come on." I point to the right, to where the trees thicken. "That way. We need to find Amelia and the others. They could be hurt."

Keelie rolls her eyes. "Aren't you going to call for them?"

"Are you insane?" I stare at her. "And let the Enhanced know we're about?"

The corners of her mouth twitch. "We've been talking this whole time, anyway."

"There's a difference between talking quietly and yelling the others' names."

Keelie snorts. "If you say so."

I glare at her. "There *is* a difference. And I'm not taking the risk."

We walk and walk. The pain in my leg gets worse and worse, but I'm used to pain. Pain makes someone stronger, and I am the strongest. I *am*.

The air gets damper the farther we go into the trees. Insects buzz. It's getting light now, almost properly light.

"How long is this going to take?" Keelie says after a little while. She's sweating, and has taken off her leather jacket. It's tied around her waist. "I've really got to find Mila."

"Well, go on then." I don't try and hide my annoyance. "You go off and find her."

"And leave you, alone and unaccustomed to the New World? Huh. Caia-Lu would be right on my back about that."

"It's not the New World. Mila isn't here—unless she's come back to life too. How long are you going to keep saying all this?"

"Until you accept reality and—"

A bright flash burns my eyes, makes me startle.

"What the hell was that?" My whisper is low. Rushing sounds fill my ears as I stare ahead.

"What?" Keelie looks at me, her knife ready. "I didn't see anything."

"Enhanced," I whisper as I point. And it's mainly leaves and branches and stems I can see. But there's a mirror there too. They're there. They're hiding, watching us?

"Inga, I—" Keelie says, just as the mirror flashes again. Bright enough to leave murky marks on my retinas.

My heart beats faster, faster, faster.

"Hell," Keelie says. "They're here. They're actually *here*." She grabs my shoulder, pushes me behind her.

"Hey! I can fight!" I hiss. "I'm an assassin for the Gods' sake!"

"You're injured. And I've killed plenty." She holds me back with one arm extended out.

I stretch onto my tiptoes, looking ahead. Then I take in the scene around me. One of Bridie's rules for impromptu killings: *know your surroundings*. Trees. Their branches are too thick and strong to break easily. The pieces on the ground look half-rotten. There's a rough-looking rock to my right, but that's too big to lift and throw. Nearer Keelie, there's a handful of gravel, but it's been pressed into the ground—under the foot of an Enhanced One? The ground itself is firm, but slightly wet in places. Not so much here though. Looks boggier over there, to the right.

But they're here.

I clench my hands into fists, feel the joints click.

"They're not moving," Keelie says. "They must know we're here."

"They're waiting to ambush us, when we walk past." I breathe deeply. It's obvious. I can see the eyes just about, through foliage and leaves. We can play at this game too. I start counting. *One eye, two, three, four, five.* But two of the eyes are far apart. "I think there's at least three individuals."

My mind spins. There are two of us, and I'm injured—probably worse than I care to admit. The Enhanced will have seen us both. We need to be clever about this.

"Okay, here's what we do," I say. "We pretend we've forgotten something. Supplies—whatever. We'll talk about it in loud voices. Then you go back to get whatever it is. They'll most likely all come for me then. I'll be sitting right here." I point at the rock. I lean down and roll up the leg of my leggings, exposing more blood and bruising. Got to make sure as many of my injuries are visible, make me seem like an easy picking. I groan as loudly as I can before talking, my voice low again. "They'll come for me with their augmenters and conversion plans, and that's when you creep up. I'll wait until you are level—they won't know you're back so soon if you're quiet—and then we'll both strike. Are you sure you're good at fighting?"

"Am I good at fighting?" Keelie shifts her weight from foot to foot then laughs. "I can take out an army if I have to."

The corners of my mouth twitch. No wonder Bridie wanted her. "Okay, are you ready?"

"Don't you need a weapon?" she asks.

I give her a look. "I am an assassin. I *am* the weapon."

"You're injured."

I shake my head. "I've been training all my life. Now, tell me about how you're going to go back to get what we've forgotten. Water—that's it. That's convincing."

A slow grin creeps across her face.

"Get in character," I snap, then I straighten out my leg and groan again. "Damn, this hurts," I say loudly. I glance down at it, then at my arm—the one missing the sleeve from the jacket. In the early morning light, it does look quite savage. "Have you got the sterile water?"

"The water?"

Watching Keelie as she pretends to have forgotten our water would be hilarious if this wasn't a dangerous situation. She claps a hand to her mouth.

"You've forgotten it?" I yell. "Well that was bloody stupid. Look at my leg! I can't walk back there!"

"I'll go. Don't worry. You stay here. That rock—sit over there. Come on."

She makes a show of helping me over to it, and I cringe. We're overdoing this. The Enhanced will have seen me walking much better when we got here. But it's too late now.

"Here, keep warm," Keelie says, untying the leather jacket from her waist. She drapes it over my leg. The weight of it burns my skin. "I won't be long."

She bounds off—too bouncy, too quickly. I grimace. She's acting too obvious. Anyone can tell adrenaline's coursing through her veins, and it wouldn't be if what she'd said she was doing was true.

Damn. It's like working with an amateur.

I stretch out my leg. Looking pained isn't difficult. Now that I'm focusing on my injuries, everything feels worse. Pain throbs through me, but I can't let it distract me, I know that. I keep one eye on the Enhanced Ones' eyes.

They haven't moved.

Give it a minute.

I flex my fingers, work out which moves will be best. A swift kick to the skull, chest, or neck is usually enough to knock them out. Sometimes, it's enough to kill, depending on the kick and the person. If they've got a weak heart or something—though unlikely for the Enhanced Ones, of course. But kicking is probably out of the question. My leg may not be as bad as I'm making out, but it's bad, and there's definitely something wrong with my lower back. If I'm going to kick, I need to do it properly first time, but sudden moves are going to be out of the question. And I can only kick one at a time, and chances are all three of them—or more—are going to come at me at once, trying to cram their poisons into my mouth. I may have Keelie for backup, but who knows what skills my cousin really has.

Maybe you shouldn't have been so confident when she asked if you needed a weapon. Her knife would come in handy.

No. I can still do this.

I take off my ripped jacket, ignore the knowing eyes of my owl. I can use the jacket—one sleeve is still intact and the body of it is fine. If I loop it around an Enhanced One's neck, I can strangle them. Probably could strangle without it—my arms seem to be okay, mainly. I roll my shoulders carefully, still concentrating on the flashes from the mirror eyes in my peripheral vision. The movement of my head makes me think they're on the move, a couple of times. But they're not. Still waiting.

Yes. I flex my fingers. My arms are the least injured. I can get decent punches in. If I can take two of the Enhanced Ones out while Keelie gets the third—or distracts them—then we can manage it.

If there are more than three of them, all coming for me at the same time, things will get trickier. But not impossible. If needed, I can try a kick.

And it's unlikely the Enhanced will fight back. Most don't. Most are scared of violence. They'll just want me to swallow their colorful liquids so they can convert me to their lifestyle.

I glance up to the left, where the eyes are.

Still haven't moved.

I twist my head back to see if Keelie's back in sight. She's not. Gone completely? Left me?

My heart does a fluttery thing for a moment—the first family member I've seen in years, and she's gone? Then I remind myself it doesn't matter. If she flakes, it's best I'm not with her. Trust is a valuable thing, and she'd need to be worthy of mine.

I tap my fingers on the rock as I wait.

Somewhere nearby, a wheatear calls, the first birdsong of the dawn, and its notes send chills down my spine. I've never been a fan of birds.

I start counting. *One, two, three....*

An insect flies at me, and I bat it away.

Seven, eight, nine....

My neck creaks as I look to the left again. More pain. The Enhanced still haven't moved. Huh. Why haven't they moved? Enhanced Ones are predictable—or at least they should be. Their top priority is to convert us. And here I am, alone and injured, apparently vulnerable.

I press my lips together.

Ten.

My breaths get faster. What are they doing? I flex my fingers, then bat away another insect just as it starts going for my ear.

I concentrate on the counting, while keeping an eye out for any movement.

I get to fifty. And nothing.

Then a hundred.

I pull a hand through my hair, then lift Keelie's jacket from the edge of my lap. My legs and back throb as I stand.

I lift a hand to my eyes, shield them, even though the early morning light isn't that bright, and look in the direction the Enhanced are.

Except what if they're not?

What if the flashes I saw are something else? Dew, or the gluey kind of sap some plants produce, catching the light in several places, reflecting it back?

I breathe out hard, look around again. Still no sign of Keelie.

"Okay, then," I mutter. I fold the two jackets over my arm, and I set off toward the Enhanced Ones.

What if it is them?

But what if it isn't? I'm just wasting time. I need to be looking for Amelia. Time is precious. If she's injured....

I push that thought away, step over a clump of spiky vegetation. Thorns prickle my most injured leg. I didn't roll my leggings back down.

I plow forward—and I reach them.

They're Enhanced Ones all right.

And then I see it.

They're not moving because they can't.

Vines and ropes bind them to tree trunks in upright positions, and they're all gagged. Four of them. Only one of them has his head slumped over. That will be why I didn't see his eyes.

The one nearest to me is breathing—I see the rise and fall of her chest, how it strains and slackens against the rope with every breath. But she hasn't reacted. None of them have, but they're all alive, all breathing. Just staring at me. Eyes inviting me closer.

I speak louder.

Nothing.

No reaction.

Must be drugged?

A slow grin crosses my face—I know it does. I feel it. This is going to be fun.

"Hello, dear ones." My voice is a croon. "Now, how would you like to die? Shall we see what's on the menu?"

I put my jacket back on, then place Keelie's on the ground. It's got a couple metal studs on it—I hadn't noticed before—but they're the kind of things that hurt if they're swung at you.

"Inga?"

I look up as Keelie crashes into the area, her knife ready.

"What the hell are you doing?" She stops as she sees

them. "You tied them up?"

"No, someone else did. Oleta, I bet. Must be." But why didn't she kill them? I frown. Unless she wanted to have fun too? Maybe she's gone to find things. Things to make the killings more fun.

I rub my hands together. In that case, these are *her* Enhanced. They're not mine to kill. Oleta's already claimed them.

"Don't kill them," I say to Keelie.

"What the—"

"They're Oleta's." I explain the rules, how we always did things.

"You're mad," Keelie says, stepping back. "You're—" Her eyes widen, and her face pales. "Inga?"

"What?" I step up toward her and—

And I see it.

I see the body.

My heart drops.

An elderly woman. Eyes open. Untamed.

Amelia.

AMELIA. *DEAD.* LIKE RENEE AND—

I scream as I fall, hit her body. My elbow in her ribs. She doesn't move.

Of course she doesn't move! She can't move!

"No!" I'm screaming, a guttural sound. And I don't care. Nothing else matters. She's my family. Amelia is—

She can't be! No!

"Inga, stop!" Keelie's shouting, and she shoves me aside. "She's still alive! We need to help her. Be careful!"

"What?" My chest shudders.

"She's alive—look, breathing!" She grabs Amelia's wrist, and she's feeling for a pulse. "Shit, I don't know how to do this."

"You don't know healing or medicine?" I hiss.

"No, do you?"

"No! So, what are you even here for?" I look up at the sky. The Gods and Goddesses, they'd know this was going to happen, wouldn't they? So why unite me with Keelie who doesn't know a damn thing about healing either? Surely out of everyone it could've been, there'd be someone who'd know something who could've ended up here with me?

"It's okay." Keelie wipes sweat from her forehead with the back of her hand, then turns her fierce eyes on me. "Pull yourself together, screaming and crying like a baby isn't going to help."

"I'm not screaming and crying like a baby."

"You are. Now shut up and help me. Bea knows healing stuff. I'm trying to remember." She shuts her eyes for a second, and the vein in her forehead twitches before she opens them again. "Pass me my jacket. We need to keep her warm."

I pass the leather jacket to her, and she drapes it over Amelia's body, before feeling her wrist again.

"Try her neck," she says to me.

My fingers shake as I press them against Amelia's neck, find I have to press deeper because of the saggy folds of wrinkled skin. I wince.

Keelie snorts. "You don't look like an assassin now."

I glare at her, follow the glare with a few choice words.

"Hey, you're supposed to be finding a pulse. Concentrate."

I focus on Amelia's neck. But all I can feel is my own heartbeat. It pulses through me, with the roaring in my ears. My breaths get louder, faster. My stomach tightens. Pain circles my heart.

I stare at Amelia's face.

Open your eyes, I will her. *Breathe. Please be okay—*

"Got it," Keelie mutters.

"What?" A pulse? My own gets faster.

"I think so. But it's weak. She's weak." She sits back on her heels, then looks around.

"So, help her," I say.

"I don't know what to do."

I curse, then pull a hand through my hair. "Oleta," I say. "We need Oleta. You stay here with Amelia. I'm going to go and find her. She can't be far away."

"Oleta?" Keelie frowns. "The one you said was an

assassin with you?"

"She's got healing powers. A Seer." I wince as my left leg throbs more. "I won't be long. She can't have gone far. Not with the littles."

If she's still got them with her….

If they're not all Enhanced.

But, no, this is Oleta. The wildcat. Fierce. Protective. I've just got to find her.

I turn and run—or at least try to. Savage pain wraps around my leg, and I gasp. My eyes smart.

"Hey, shouldn't I be going to find her?" Keelie calls.

"No—you don't know her. She won't trust you."

I limp through the woods, concentrate on my breaths. So long as I'm breathing I will do this.

The adrenaline pounding through me numbs the pain in my back and legs to an extent, but my head begins to ache more. I grit my teeth. I've just got to get to Oleta. She's got to be nearby. She has to be. And the children. They wouldn't just leave.

But maybe they would. Oleta saw me fall from the cliff edge, and if she thinks Amelia's dead, she'd have no reason to stay.

No. she's a healer. She'd know Amelia wasn't dead. She mustn't have found Amelia or know she's injured and—

Something hits my back. Hard.

I plummet forward, hit the ground. Grit and mud in my mouth. Weight lands on top of me, and—

My neck. My back. So much pain. I let out a guttural cry, see dark shapes swirling in my vision. Fresh pain lassoes me.

The enemy, they're here and—

"*Inga?*" says a voice.

A hand touches my side, then the person's rolling me over.

I look up. Blurry vision. Dark hair, dark skin, above me. Oleta. Gradually she comes into focus. Twigs and debris stick to her hair. There's a cut on her cheek.

"You're still alive? Untamed?" Oleta's eyebrows

shoot up. "I saw you *run off a cliff.*"

I try to nod and then shake my head, barely able to breathe. My lungs…something's not… I can't….

Oleta pulls me up, and the world seems to rock. "Sorry about that. Thought you were an Enhanced." She laughs. "Dramatic exit and all that. Here, let me heal you. And how the hell did you survive that?"

I shake my head, try to catch my breath. "No. Amelia," I choke out. "She's…heal her. Me, later." I look past her. "Where are the…littles?"

Oleta's frozen, her hands partly reaching out toward me. "The littles are back there." She jerks her head to the right, behind her.

"Alive?" I pant. My ears feel too hot, and one of them feels wet too. Hot and wet.

"Of course they're alive." Oleta gives me a look. "Do you think Enhanced Ones would beat me?"

"Just get to Amelia now." My chest burns, and my head…it's…something's not right, something's got worse. "Go that way…now, Oleta… Call for Keelie… She and Amelia are by—"

"Who the fuck's Keelie?"

"My cousin." A tightening sensation fills my head. "Can't explain it all now. But she's with Amelia… We can trust her. Just run that way… Go now! She and Amelia are the only ones about…though your Enhanced are tied up still—"

"My Enhanced?"

My temples thud as I stare at Oleta. My vision doubles for a moment, and there are two of her. "You didn't tie them up? They're…not yours?" I shake my head. "Just go to Amelia. I'll bring the littles and catch up." We can work out what's going on with those Enhanced later.

Oleta nods, eyes fierce, and leaves, kicks up dirt behind her.

I breathe deeply, then turn to the right, where Oleta indicated the littles were. My vision blurs, then twists, gets too sharp as I peer into the foliage, try to see them.

But of course they'd be hidden.

I take a step forward. Nausea threatens me, and my head spins. "Kam?" I can hardly get his name out. My voice, it's too weak. And, damn, what were the other names? Michelle? But I can't think, haven't got time. "It's Inga, come on." I can't tell if I'm speaking. My ears, my head, my body's not right. "We've got to go."

For a moment, I think they're not here. Or not going to respond. But then a tiny hand pushes back a wall of foliage and the dark-haired girl climbs out. Her eyes are wild. She looks scared. Nothing like how I'd expect an assassin-in-training to be. I frown. How new is she?

Kam is next, then the other two. The four of them rush to me. The dark-haired girl clings to my bad leg, and I wince.

"Okay, are you all right?" I feel strange, like I don't know what to say, how to interact with them. I am not maternal. Not like Oleta.

A dull ache grips my shoulder blades.

The littles all nod, and then the dark-haired girl asks for *Olie*.

"Yes, we're going to her now." I turn, try not to fall over as dizziness and lightheadedness grab me. This will be the hard part. "Let's go. Come on."

By the time we reach the clearing, I can hardly see a thing. My head pounds, my stomach's threatening to expel its contents, and my back's seizing up. I can't feel my foot properly, and my right arm feels like it's falling off.

I make out the rough shapes of Amelia and Oleta—Amelia appears to be sitting up—before I sink to the ground. My breaths are short and sharp, and each one feels like a kick to the chest.

"Inga!"

I'm not sure who shouts, but then Oleta and Amelia are both around me, supporting me in a half-sitting position against their bodies. The children are moving around too fast. I catch a glimpse of mirrors—the Enhanced are still here, tied up.

"Inga, you survived!" Amelia's voice. But it's not right—it makes the colors of the trees too bright and garish. Neon greens, oranges, and yellows. And they're moving around me, dancing.

"Of course I did," I pant, closing my eyes, trying to stop the swirling colors.

"I don't know how the hell you managed that," Oleta says. "Hey, open your eyes, and lie back. Come on."

They help me lie down, and I try to keep my eyes open. My stomach turns, and there's more pain in my lower back.

"You'll feel better in a moment." Oleta leans over me, places her forefingers against my temples, and hums a little.

The neon colors around me grow stronger—but only for a second. Then they begin to dull, and I feel the magic in Oleta, how it seeps into me. My spine pulses, and more nausea pulls through me.

"Sorry," Oleta says. "This is going to take some time."

"Is she going to be okay?" Amelia asks, worry in her voice. "What can I do?"

I miss Oleta's answer because another wave of pain pulls through me. But it's not as strong as the previous ones. I stare up into Oleta's face as she works. She presses her lips together, and I focus on her expression, the utter concentration in it. My pain changes, gets a little fainter, while feeling floods back into my right arm.

A bird flies overhead. I hear the littles talking, somewhere to my right. Then I frown.

"Where's Keelie?" My voice sounds strange, and I

try to lift my head. Need to see her.

"Checking the area," Oleta says, breathless. She presses her fingers more firmly against my temples. "Stay still."

"You trust her?" I frown. "Just like that? To check the area, check that we're safe?"

"You said she was trustworthy. And I trust you. And she's definitely related to you—annoying as hell. Now, be quiet and stay still."

I try my best to relax as Oleta continues healing me, and Amelia talks in a soothing voice. The process seems to take forever.

Keelie returns just as Oleta's finishing with my leg, and a smile breaks across her face as she sees the children. Kam watches her distrustfully but the other three run up to her.

I turn and get a proper look at the Enhanced. They're still alive. Still watching us, still gagged and bound.

"What do we do about them?" I ask, flexing my neck. The pain really has gone, but I don't feel quite right. Not sore exactly, but I can't put my finger on it. Just…different.

Oleta laughs. "You're an assassin, and you're asking that?"

"No, why would someone tie them up and not kill them?"

Oleta's eyes widen and she pulls the dark-haired girl closer to her. "It's the assassins. Shit—I need to contact Petra."

"What?" I stand up. "The assassins wouldn't tie up the Enhanced. They'd kill them right away."

"No, they're going to take them back to their camp— they've got littles to train." Oleta's words get faster. "Remember? First proper lesson is always killing a bound Enhanced and learning anatomy that way… Now, be quiet, I need to contact Petra."

She takes a deep breath, then closes her eyes. She sways a little.

"What's happening?" Keelie asks me.

I wave at her to be quiet. My focus is on Oleta. Her face is smooth, but her hands clench into tight fists.

"Forty-one," she says.

"Forty-one?" Amelia says.

"Forty-one assassins?" My eyebrows shoot up. All looking for us?

"They're in this forest, looking for us," Oleta says, opening her eyes. For a moment, her pupils are tiny points, then they expand. "Petra can't get a lock on where exactly we are—she's hurt. They're torturing her. But they know we're here, in this forest, somewhere. And this—" She gestures at the Enhanced. "They're too close. That's what this means. We've got to move, fast."

I push my hair back slowly. "No, this is brilliant. The assassins are going to come back *here* then, to collect their Enhanced." I start to smile. "We can kill them, ambush them. This is brilliant."

"No," Oleta says. "There are forty-one of them. Did you not listen? We have to *move*. We have to keep our littles safe."

"But this is too good an opportunity," I say. "We have to take out all the assassins, and we could get a huge chunk in one go."

"No, Inga," Amelia says. "Oleta's right. If assassins are in this area, we need to move. You and Oleta are the only fighters—"

"I can fight," Keelie says.

Amelia shoots her a look. "Our priority is protecting the children." Her nostrils flare as she looks back at me. "And Inga, we need you with us. Not dead."

I throw my hands in the air. As if they'd kill me. "But the assassins are close."

"*If* it was them that tied the Enhanced up," Amelia says. "Oleta, did Petra say they did that?"

"I didn't have time to ask. Could only be quick, and she said they're in this forest."

"The forest is huge," Amelia says. "They could be nowhere near us."

"How do you explain that then?" Oleta points at the Enhanced.

"Could be other Untamed that've done this," Keelie says. "There's got to be more around, like me, come back to life. And, ages ago, didn't our people just try and reconvert them, tying them up and starving them of augmenters? Maybe it's those Untamed that are here."

"What?" Oleta stares at her. "Come back to life?"

"I died," Keelie says. "Shot right here." She points at her stomach. "I was in the New World until, what, an hour ago? Now, I'm back."

Huh. Well thank the Gods she finally believes it.

"Are you sure?" Amelia says.

Keelie nods. "I'm sure as hell not messing about. I thought this was the New World—until Inga and I found the Enhanced."

Amelia frowns. "Oh no."

"What?" I look toward her, find that she's staring at Keelie with a grave expression on her face.

"Something's gone wrong with the worlds' boundaries. This place—it must be this place."

"What do you mean gone wrong?" Keelie asks.

"It's unstable—the worlds are unstable. The balance is off. Must be. But it can't be permanent."

"What?" Keelie says.

"The worlds will seal when equilibrium is restored," Amelia says. "It has to—at some point. My mother taught me about the balances of energies. We need to move now—before something else happens." Amelia glances at me and Oleta. "Kill those Enhanced quietly. We can't afford for them to live, regardless of who tied them up."

"I want to kill one of them," Keelie says.

Oleta shakes her head. "You aren't an assassin."

"I can kill, believe me." She folds her arms, a defiant look on her face.

"Okay, you take one. Oleta and I will have the others," I say, ignoring the look Oleta gives me.

"Amelia, take the littles away." I don't know why I feel the need to say that, when all four of the littles were being trained as killers anyway. They may not have done their own kills yet, but if the assassin camps were anything like the ones I grew up in, they'd likely have already been exposed to murder.

Then again, I don't know how Gweneira runs things.

Oleta, Keelie, and I step up to the Enhanced Ones. Bar my first kill in the cave, never have I had to kill any adults who've been as helpless as this, literally tied up. It's easier even than those new assassins I killed at Royston's Rock who didn't even try to fight back.

Keelie lets out a euphoric cry as she stabs one of the women. Oleta and I are silent as we kill, Oleta using her knife on two while I go for strangulation as the means of death for the fourth.

"And now we go," Oleta says. She's jumpy and looks over her shoulder several times—back at the dead Enhanced—as the three of us catch up with Amelia and the littles.

"I can't believe we all survived," Amelia mutters.

"Survived?" Keelie snorts. "I can't believe I *came back to life*. Now, where are we? This forest isn't near Nbutai, it's too cold. I need to find Elf."

"We need to get as far away as possible," Oleta says. She's got two of the children by their hands.

"We still need to find Renee," Amelia says. "She's got to be somewhere."

"It's too late," Oleta says, her tone harsh. "If she was alive, the Enhanced would've found her. We've got to get away from here. There are assassins about—I'm telling you."

"Contact Petra again," I tell her. "Find out where *exactly* they are. If they're by the river or any streams, or if there are any notable trees around them or something."

"Notable trees?" Oleta stares at me.

"We need some way to work out how close they

are to us," I say, but how easy is it going to be to do that? Most parts of the forest we've been in so far have looked so similar, bar the area with the river.

"We're *not* going after them with the littles in tow," Oleta says through gritted teeth.

I snort. If the assassins are close to us, it would make sense to go and take them out, rather than wait for them to ambush us.

But are they even here? I breathe deeply. I don't feel like assassins are closing in on me. I'd expect to feel jumpy or like I was being watched. I'm intuitive, after all. And I feel nothing. But I can't take that to mean that we really are the only ones in this forest.

"Uh, hello, I asked where we are?" Keelie rolls her eyes.

"Can you just be quiet?" I glare at her. "Oleta? Contact Petra now."

"I can do it as we walk. We *have* to keep moving."

We move. Oleta tries to contact Petra, but keeps sighing. Amelia shoots me worried glances, and Michaela keeps glancing up at Oleta and asking if she's safe.

"I can't get through to her." Oleta's whole face pinches inward as she looks at me, like she's trying not to cry. "She's just… I can't… She's too injured."

I stare at her. Crying? "You're *scared*?"

She sniffs loudly and turns accusatory eyes to me. "No." She pushes Michaela over to Amelia, with the rest of the children, then steps closer to me.

"You are." I resist the urge to laugh. "What's happened to you? Ever since we rescued those littles, you've not wanted to meet assassins again. You've been scared."

"I don't want them getting the littles back," she says.

"So, you think we're no longer the best assassins around, capable of protecting four children? It's not like they even disobey what we say. We can protect them easily. And there are, what, forty assassins?"

"Forty-one."

I snort. "We can do this. Or, at least, the old you could've."

Oleta sighs, then pushes her hair back. "Fine. I am scared. I am fucking terrified now, and it doesn't make sense, okay? I know we're good at fighting. I know we're strong, and if anyone is going to be scared, it should be them. But I *am* scared. I can't help it." She shakes her head. "I just feel it. It must be the pressure of having these four with us, and I didn't think I'd feel like it, but I do."

"The four littles who *you* wanted to rescue," I say. "That was your decision. Or do you think they are spies? Is that why you're scared?"

"Do you have to keep saying I'm scared?" Her eyes flash. "But, no, they're not spies. They're safe. No, it's something to do with the actual assassins out there." She sniffs again. "I'll keep trying Petra."

"Anything?" I ask Oleta, hours later. "Did you get through to her?"

We've walked a long way, and, though we haven't got our tent now, we've found a small cave-like overhang against another cliff-base. There are a lot of cliff-faces and caves in this mountainous area, and we pause for a moment in the sheltered space. The littles are getting grouchy, and Kam keeps complaining that his stomach hurts. But all our stomachs ache for food.

Oleta shakes her head, eyes on Amelia and the littles. They're near the entrance of the overhang. The two of us are as far back as possible, in the shadows of the cave.

"This isn't right. It's normally not hard to get through to Petra. They must have really hurt her with the torture."

I press my tongue against the roof of my mouth. "If the assassins are in this part of the forest, we have to confront them, not keep running. Have a fight on our own terms, rather than them finding us through Petra and us having no warning. We've got more power, if we choose when the confrontation happens."

"No." Panic fills Oleta's eyes. "They're too close. I can feel it."

"But I can't feel them."

"You're not a Seer."

I sigh, then I shake my head. "No. I'm doing this. I'm going to go and find them."

She grabs my arm, fast. "We need more distance in between us and them, and we need to get the littles somewhere safe, before we do anything. I'm not risking them getting the children back—because that's going to be what they're after."

"The children who they let us take?" I snort.

"Yes, but—"

"Oh dear," Amelia says, and we turn, see her crouching next to one of the littles as he projectile vomits everywhere.

It's Kam.

The other children squeal, and then Michaela's running toward Oleta and me.

"Olie, Olie!"

"It's okay, Michaela," Oleta says to her. "I've got you."

Amelia beckons me over, and I hold my breath as I help her clean up Kam. His eyes have dulled, and even his blond hair looks flatter. Less life in it.

"Must be dodgy water or something," I say.

"Or just what children do," Amelia says. "Babies and toddlers vomit a lot. Lots of bugs. Best keep an eye on the other three."

Kam becomes clingy, and he still is clingy when Oleta insists we move on again. I end up carrying him, and Oleta and I walk together at the back of the group. I watch her as she tries to contact Petra, over and over.

No success.

"You've got until the end of the day to get the littles farther away," I tell her. "Then I'm looking for the assassins. And you're not stopping me." Irritation has already built high inside me. That's what we're supposed to do—confront our enemy. We don't run and hide, even if she is scared.

"That's not enough time," she hisses. "We need to get the littles away from this forest—and we only seem to be getting deeper into it."

"I'm not running forever."

Kam mumbles something nonsensical as he burrows his head in my neck. His face is hot.

"You're burning up," I say. "Poor Kam."

Then I freeze.

Oleta looks at me and stops.

"He's burning up." I hold him tighter and look down at his face. His eyes are closed. He's still murmuring, but he doesn't respond when I say his name.

My chest tightens. It's happening again.

"No…" Oleta's eyes widen. "It can't be. I told you, I'm stronger now. Better grip on my powers. This hasn't happened since I was a child."

My head spins. "When did you heal me and Amelia? How many hours ago was it?" And I'm trying to do the calculations, work it out.

"But this didn't happen before," she says. "With Falkes and…."

"It didn't happen at first when Bridie made you heal us either." I take a deep breath and hug Kam tighter. "Who knows? It could be random? Or maybe the effects have been building in Kam for a while."

"Is Michaela going to get ill too?" Oleta's bottom lip wobbles. "And the other two?"

"I don't know." I look back at Kam's face, then I shout for Amelia.

I explain what's happened as our group gathers back together.

"Pass Kam to me," Amelia says, and I hand him

over. He's drenched my shirt with sweat.

"High fever," Amelia says, and then she's looking under Kam's eyelids. She swears under her breath.

"What is it?"

"Bloodshot eyes. Extremely bad. This is progressing quickly, and his breathing is too rapid. Okay, we're going to need to stop. She rattles off a list of things she needs to do to help Kam.

Oleta grimaces. "We can't stop—the assassins are out here. We have to keep on the move."

"For the Gods' sake," I say. "*We* are assassins too. They won't hurt any of us. I'll make sure of it."

"But—" Oleta says.

Amelia glares at her. "If we don't stop, Kam could die."

FORTY-ONE

OLETA LOOKS AT ME FOR a long time. "Bridie's hurt too many people… Caro, Ty, Harmony, you."

"Me?"

"You've got the scars from where she burned you," Oleta says. "And this… This is too much." She shakes her head. "We can't let Bridie do this to us."

She looks at me for a long moment. "We're powerful, Inga. You, me, and Petra. The most powerful ones here."

I lean in closer. My heart beats faster. "Are you meaning…?"

"Yes." Oleta nods.

Adrenaline pounds through me.

"We could take out Bridie, once and for all."

Hearing the words from Oleta makes it real. But it is treason. I know this. If someone were to hear us and report us, we'd be tortured for a long, long time. Maybe even die from it.

I look at Oleta. Is she sincere? Or is she trying to get me to be treasonous? Has Bridie asked her to do this to see where my allegiance lies?

But why would Oleta go along with that, given what Bridie has done to her sister?

My chest tightens as I think of how badly beaten Petra was.

Oleta looks at me. "Bridie knows it. She knows that together, we're dangerous. It's why she separated me and Petra, and then pitted you against me, had you usurp me. She's scared of what we could be if we work together."

"Together?"

"The three of us. You, me, and Petra." Her eyes sparkle. "We can do it. We can kill Bridie."

FORTY-TWO

"KAM'S GETTING WORSE," KEELIE SAYS to me, her voice low. "There's no way we're going to be able to move on tonight, like Oleta wants to."

"That's fine," I say. I'm going to go after the assassins tonight anyway. Adrenaline pounds through me at the thought.

We found a stream not far away, and we're collecting water for Amelia to use in her healing. Keelie and I probably have the easiest things to collect—water and moss. There's even moss by the stream too, clinging to rocks. I peel a good amount off.

"Flint," Keelie says, picking a chunk of stone up. "A sharp edge. Could be useful."

"Good," I say.

We look for more flint—anything with a sharp edge is more than useful—and then return to the others with the water.

In the half hour since we've stopped, Kam has got a lot worse. And it's making me nervous. Is he going to die? Before, some of the littles did.

"He's definitely too sick to move again," Amelia says. "If we try, I fear we will lose him."

Oleta gulps. "The assassins will find us."

"They won't. But we'll be prepared anyway," I say. "Look, I'm going to wait until it's dark, then I'll hunt the assassins. We've still got several hours until then, so we'll make sure you're all prepared here, in case the assassins get here. Not that they will manage that. I'll get all of them. Don't worry." I nod at the children, but they don't look worried.

"Now," I continue. "Our priority is weapons. We need to make them. We've got two knives and wood all around us. We can make spears. We got some sharp flint at that stream, and there's probably more. Maybe we can knap something." I think of Renee, how she taught me some basics, and my heart feels heavy. "And we need to set up snares too. Can make them out of the vines and underwire in our bras, okay?"

Amelia nods.

"We'll set the snares up around this area, not just to catch game, but any assassins too." I look at each of them. "Then, when I go out to hunt them down, Keelie and Oleta, you take turns keeping guard while the others sleep. Even do patrols. You'll each have your knives, so just kill any you see and raise the alarm for the others. Decide on a bird call, and use it."

"You're not going to have a knife when you're out there?" Amelia looks at me.

"I don't need a knife to kill. And it's best that you're fully protected. I'll take a spear and anything I manage to knap into a blade or something." I glance at Oleta. She nods slowly. "Come on, we know how to do this. We're the best assassins Bridie ever had. We're going to protect our group. They haven't got a chance."

"And I can fight too," Keelie says. "I know I'm not one of you, but I *am* strong. And I am a killer."

I nod. There was a reason Bridie wanted Keelie as one of her new recruits. "And this is just in case any assassins *actually* reach you. They won't. I'm going to get them. Now, come on, we need to make weapons and set snares."

"We also need to construct some sort of shelter over Kam," Amelia says. "And a fire."

"No fire," I say. "That means smoke. We're not giving the assassins clues as to where we are."

Amelia nods, and then we're dividing up the jobs. Keelie gives us her bra before heading back to the stream to get stones for knapping, and Oleta and I extract wire from it and ours. Amelia's in non-wired. It's a shame we lost most of our supplies when the Enhanced burst into out tent as I know there were a couple of wired bras in the bags. But, still, we get a fair amount of wire from what we have.

"Hey, can you collect those vines?" I ask Michaela and Zita, and they nod.

"We need to get wood," I tell Oleta. "Give me your knife."

"You're going to blunt the blade," she says.

"We've got flint, we can sharpen it."

The next couple of hours pass in a blur. I saw off branches with the knife and we shape them into poles for the spears. Keelie and Joshua set up snares, and Amelia and Oleta make the shelter from branches and leaves. Keelie gathered quite a few chunks of flint and other rocks, and I work on them as best as I can, transforming them into heads for the spears and handheld blades, but I'm no master. Not by any stretch of the imagination. But we create more weapons we can use.

The whole time, we find ourselves explaining what we're doing to the littles, showing them how to do it. Most of my survival skills are ones I learned from Amelia and Renee, upon joining Falkes's group. The only things the assassins really taught us was how to kill—both people and game.

I carry Kam into the shelter when we're done and the evening's near. Still some light though. I want to go after the assassins in the dark.

Amelia tends to Kam, and I take Joshua and Zita out to look for more edible berries nearby. We're all low on energy. Not ideal. Michaela didn't want to join us, just wanted to stay close to Oleta, and she's trying to make another blade. Not that she knows anything about knapping.

"Is Kam going to be all right?" Zita asks, tugging at her plaits. I don't know who did her hair like that, but it was loose and free only a few hours ago. My guess is Keelie.

"Of course he will." My voice is cheery and hopeful. It doesn't sound like me at all. But it's amazing how these children are changing me—and amazing how worried I am by Kam's condition. I never thought I'd feel like this about a child. Especially a child assassin. And, to think, I didn't want to rescue any of them.

But maybe if we hadn't, the assassins wouldn't be hunting us.

Nah. Of course they would. They know I'm the Night Slayer. They'll be hunting me as much as I am them.

Except I'm not now.

But I will be.

I'm going to kill them all.

Even my darling sister.

"Are these edible too?" Zita asks me. In her hands, she's holding brighter blue berries.

"I'm not sure. We'd better check with Amelia first. Don't eat any until then."

We return to the makeshift camp. Amelia's holding one of the new spear poles while Keelie binds a flint-point to it with the vines. The sun is starting to set, and rays filter through the trees, catching Keelie's form in a way that illuminates her and makes her look otherworldly.

Huh. Well, she is back from the dead.

Back from the dead.

I suppress a laugh. Because that doesn't just happen. We all know that. But it has happened. And I think of what Amelia said about the worlds merging....

I freeze, then jolt, feel like I've been electrocuted.

Back from the dead.

Keelie isn't the first ghost I've seen.

Sweat trickles down my back.

And Oleta—Oleta's worried about the assassins. Says they're coming after us. And she's *scared*.

There was only ever one assassin who could make Oleta fearful.

One assassin whom I've already seen—that glimpse. It wasn't madness.

It was real.

Bridie is back.

My pounding heart gets faster.

Hell, Bridie's after us. She's in this forest.

"Inga?" Amelia looks up at me. "What is it?"

Oleta appears. "They here?"

I shake my head. "No—but Keelie's not the only one back from the New World. Bridie is too."

"What?"

"I saw her before." And I try to explain, and it doesn't just mean Bridie's back. Hell, it could be all the assassins. Every single one of them who died, who I killed. And those ones I saw with Bridie before—that's only a fraction of the number.

"Why the fuck didn't you tell me you'd seen her?"

"Because she's dead, and I thought people stayed dead!"

Oleta breathes hard. "We need to move the littles then. Bridie could be close. We need to get the littles out of here. If she's here—and all the others you've killed—that changes everything."

Footsteps.

We hear them.

My blood runs cold. She's here. Already.

No.

Oleta and I look at each other.

"Weapons," I mutter, and then we're all going for them. I grab a spear. One of the flint blades is in my pocket from earlier.

"Get behind us," Oleta hisses at Michaela and Zita.

A quick flick of my head tells me Joshua's already standing there. And Kam's still in the shelter, must be.

We peer out into the gloom of the trees. The strange, eerie light of the sunset. The coming darkness.

It's silent now—except for the blood pounding in my ears. I listen harder and harder, holding my breath so I can hear better and…and there's nothing? No footsteps?

I glance at Oleta, and she nods.

"Stay here," I say to Amelia and Keelie. "Protect the littles."

Oleta and I move in unison, working together as a pair, like we did so many times before. We fall back into the pattern, covering each other, being ready. My grip is tight on both my spear and flint blade at all times. Oleta holds her knife out ready. She's got a flint blade too.

And—and there's no one here. We keep walking.

We glance at each other, but we all heard the footsteps. That wasn't imagined.

"What do we do?" I whisper under my breath.

"Check farther that way. Then we're moving on, all of us," Oleta says. "We have—"

A figure lunges toward us.

Oleta screams, and I shout as the person hits me. My spear falls, and the person's weight knocks me down. My head thumps against something, and I look up at their face and—

"Falkes?"

FORTY-THREE

"WHERE ARE THEY?" FALKES GROWLS, pinning me down against the forest floor. "What have you done with them?"

For a moment, all I can do is stare at him. Because he looks terrible. He looks *feral*.

Then he spits in my face.

I shove him off me, and Oleta grabs him by the throat. Fire dances in her eyes, and he's shouting and—

"Lexa?"

I see her behind Oleta and Falkes, partly hidden by a tree, and she's pointing a gun at me.

"Lexa, what's going on?" I glance at where my spear and flint blade lie on the ground, then hold my hands up, because you don't mess around with guns.

"You took them!" Falkes screams. "Johnny and Callum. You fucking took them!"

"What?" I yell.

"You're bloody assassins—active still!" Lexa shouts, her words slurring, and she steps closer with the Luger. It's still trained on me.

"We're not—we didn't," I shout back. "Who took

them? When?"

"When you left. When do you think?" Falkes snarls.

"Just hold on," Oleta shouts.

"Mummy?"

I turn to see Michaela standing there, and Oleta rushes toward her, sweeps her up and hugs her close.

Mummy?

"You!" Falkes shakes his fist at Oleta. The gesture almost looks comical. "How many children have you taken?"

"We haven't got Johnny and Callum," I say. "Lexa, lower the gun! We never took them—and Michaela's one we rescued from the assassins. One of their recruits and—"

I stare at Oleta, how she's holding Michaela. At how they've both got the same eyes. And I think how Oleta was always more focused on Michaela than the others....

Michaela, run! Don't stop!

Is Michaela going to get ill too?

It's okay, Michaela, I've got you.

And *Olie.* Michaela's name for Oleta. The only child to use that name—the new name a compromise?

I take a step back. Falkes and Lexa are still shouting at me, but I can't hear their words. It's a fog that flies over me, because this is important.

Oleta looks up at me, her gaze startled like she's a deer about to be caught. Why didn't she tell me?

She mouths something at me, and then Falkes is shouting louder and louder.

"Shut up!" I turn on him. "And Lexa, put that gun *down.* We're on your side. I'll get the boys back. We know where the assassins are."

Or at least we know they're in this forest too, but it's only a matter of time before Oleta hears from Petra again. Or until we find the assassins.

But Oleta is Michaela's mother.

My head aches.

This changes things.

And the—

My eyes widen.

Oh, God.

Keelie skids into the clearing, spear in hand. Her eyes dart from me to Oleta holding Michaela and then to Falkes and Lexa. "What the hell's going on? Who are you?"

"No, you stay away from us!" Lexa shouts, pointing the gun at her. "We know what you are!"

"She's not an assassin," I yell. "She's my cousin. Never been an assassin! Everyone, calm down." But I hardly feel calm.

The rescue…Petra's help…the children…how easy it was to get them…too easy…except Johnny and Callum were *taken*.

I stare at Oleta. "It was you, wasn't it?"

The assassins left the children for us. And Oleta told Amelia I'd killed Stephen, knowing that Amelia and Renee would take us all away, leaving the bus with the boys in it?

She needed me away from them.

Because the assassins never give something.

Especially with children.

It's always an exchange.

"I'm so sorry about the boys," Oleta says to Lexa. "But I had to. My daughter… They had my daughter… I couldn't leave her with them, but she was with her friends—and none of them are fighters. I was only supposed to take Michaela. Two untrained children in exchange for her. But then there were four of them. I didn't know Petra was leaving the others there with Michaela, but of course she would. And how could I take my daughter but leave the others?"

Lexa lunges for Oleta, but, somehow, I intercept and grab her—and get the Luger. I toss it onto the ground farther away. Keelie retrieves it. Behind her, I see Amelia appearing. She's holding Kam, and Zita and Joshua are standing close to her. What the hell? Why are they here? If it was the assassins here, they'd have just made my job ten times harder.

Lexa struggles against me, but then stops, and I'm left holding her upright, bracing myself under her weight as her whisky-filled breaths rush down my forehead with every breath she exhales.

"We're on your side," I say. "We are not assassins."

But I look around Lexa, at Oleta, and I feel it—the betrayal. All this time, she knew the assassins had Johnny and Callum. She knew what they were going through. And she thought that was okay? Just to save her daughter?

Damn. I should've realized it. Gweneira and the others even let me and Oleta leave, alive. She shot me, but not to kill. Because that was part of the deal that Oleta had made? Said it had to be a simple exchange, and no attempts on our lives? And they listened to her—maybe because of Petra? Only it wasn't a simple exchange, because Petra left more children for us, knowing Oleta wouldn't leave them.

I look at Falkes, my gaze steely. "I'm going to get Johnny and Callum back. But, first, tell me exactly what happened."

"We woke up after the Turning, and they were there. So many assassins, surrounding the bus," Falkes says.

We've moved back to our camp, and Amelia is tending to Kam again. He looks about the same. Lexa's sitting on a fallen tree trunk, just behind Falkes, and Joshua's watching her with big eyes. Oleta's huddled up on the floor, clinging to Michaela, while Keelie sorts through the weapons.

"They broke into the bus and dragged the boys out. Stephen was gone, and it was chaos."

"Your people killed Minnow," Lexa says in a low

voice. Her eyes are daggers trained on me. "They shot her because she wouldn't get out of the way when they tried to get her boys."

Falkes looks back at me. "The assassins took them. Loaded them into trucks."

"And they'd slashed our tires. We followed on foot for a bit, but we lost them. I saw you there though." Lexa points at Oleta.

Oleta doesn't answer, just keeps rocking and clinging to Michaela. There's a glassy look in her eyes, the kind of look I saw in Petra so many times. And I thought the sisters were different—that Oleta was stronger, that that look only belonged to Petra.

But now… Well, now I see they're the same.

"It wasn't Oleta," I say. "Her sister's still with the assassins. Petra. They look really similar."

"Huh." Falkes snorts. "Convenient."

"But Petra's on our side. She's feeding us intel on the assassins—she's got a Seer link with Oleta." I straighten up, hands on my hips. So long as we can trust Petra. "We know the assassins are after us." And it has to because of the littles. Oleta was only supposed to take one with us, Michaela, in exchange for Minnow's boys. The assassins want the other three children back.

"We'll get Johnny and Callum back." I look directly at Lexa, then Falkes. "That is a promise, and I don't break my promises."

Amelia clears her throat. "What—what happened to Stephen?"

I shoot a glance at her. She knows what happened to him. But she widens her eyes at me. Then I get it. It's a question we'd ask if we didn't already know his fate. Amelia's protecting me.

Falkes shakes his head. "We don't know."

I frown. They didn't find his body? They didn't go to the camp? But it's not exactly something I can ask.

"Where's Renee?" Lexa asks.

"Missing," Amelia says.

"Okay." I clear my throat. "It was what? Four days ago the assassins took Johnny and Callum?" I think that's right. Four days since Oleta broke her deal with the assassins. I move toward Oleta, touch her shoulder. She jolts and looks at me. "Find out from Petra which band has the boys and where they are, and I'll get them back."

Oleta stares at me, her arms tightening around Michaela. "I'm not giving up my daughter or any of the littles."

"I'm not asking you to. *I'm* going to get the boys back. I need to know which band has got them and where they are. Keep trying Petra until you get through to her, and get that info." I gesture to Falkes and Lexa. "You, Amelia, and Keelie are going to take these four littles far away and keep them safe. And you as well, Oleta," I add. She's not going to agree to leave her daughter now, and I can't have a distracted partner with me.

"So you're going after the assassins on your own?" Amelia asks.

I nod, just as Falkes says, "The hell she is."

I stare at him. "What?"

"You're an assassin, and I don't trust you as far as I can throw you."

I resist the urge to snort. With his puny arms, that wouldn't be far at all. "I'm getting the boys back," I say.

"And I'm coming with you."

I grit my teeth. "You're not trained. We're going to be up against forty-one assassins, if not more. We've no idea where their main camp is yet. If they call in reinforcements, you're going to be dead."

"I can use a gun."

I snicker. "And you think we can't?"

"Inga, I am coming with you," Falkes hisses. He points at Keelie. "She's your cousin?"

"Yes."

"Then I'm going to kill her if you leave me behind."

Keelie snorts. "I'd like to see you try."

"Falkes, this is dangerous—"

He points a knife at Keelie. She's still grinning. Does she not think she can die again? Stab wounds aren't a joke. And Oleta can't heal us anymore.

"Let him go with you," Amelia says, her voice low. "We're wasting time now when we should be preparing."

I sigh hard and look at Falkes. "Then we're going to have to give you some training. And quickly." I turn to Oleta. "Get that intel from Petra. I want to leave in an hour."

ADRENALINE COURSES THROUGH ME, AND I can't stop smiling. Oleta's in a trance. In the moonlight, I can just about see her eyelids fluttering; she's got through to Petra.

And I can feel it—this is the start of the end. This night will end it all. Be the night we get the boys back, the night I take down all the assassins.

"Make the next ones a bit bigger," I say, watching as Lexa draws assassin marks onto Falkes's arms with Minnow's eyeliner, copying from Oleta's and mine. Her drawings are crude, not the right shade of blue, and, to a trained eye, clearly not actual assassin marks, but I'm counting on the darkness to help. Making him look like one of us, as much as we can, is important. We need to get in among the assassins at the camp unnoticed, with the least chance of them attacking him. Chances are Falkes is going to insist on sticking by my side, and I can't have him drawing unnecessary attention to us.

Oleta opens her eyes and blinks several times.

"Well?" I ask her.

"Callum and Johnny are in the forest too," she says.

"This forest?" Falkes asks.

"Yes. But Petra says it's *all* the assassins here now. There's the forty-one who were here before, and others have arrived since, but there are a lot more who've… come back."

"From the dead?" I ask. The night air feels heavy, like it's pressing down on us. Even the moon up there almost looks like it could fall.

Lexa and Falkes look shocked, and Amelia quickly explains.

Oleta looks at me. "It's all of them, Inga. Every single one we've killed. And they're all working together now, coming after us."

"That's no problem," I say, but my voice is quiet. Still, we can do this.

"Petra says they've got a lot of trucks, at least eight that she's aware of," Oleta says. "They're not setting up any sort of camp in this forest, just on the move the whole time. All the trucks. The boys are currently in the red one, but they keep moving them around. They're also pretty near us. I've got directions."

I nod as she recounts what Petra's told her. Most of it seems to be about traveling south.

"I've got a compass," Falkes says.

"They're desperate for our exact location, here," Oleta says. "They've got a Seer trying to siphon the info out of Petra. She's holding up as best as she can, but she doesn't know how long she can last and is telling us to run and get as far away as possible. Which I told her we would all be doing, so she doesn't know about you and Falkes going after them."

Good. I nod. The element of surprise. What Petra doesn't know, the assassins can't extract from her. We need all the advantages we can get. "But we need as much distance between you and us as possible, in case things go wrong. So you have to leave immediately."

I hate even considering it—the possibility that I won't manage it. But I've got to prepare for the worst-case scenario. And if we don't end the assassins, I don't want Oleta and the littles nearby.

"You've got to get overseas," I say. "Bridie never liked crossing the waters much, so hopefully that hasn't changed."

Oleta's arms tighten around Michaela.

I continue. "Once we get to the assassins, I'll find Petra, get her to update you. If all goes to plan, it'll be me, Falkes, the boys, and Petra returning in a couple days' time. We'll find you then. But you can't wait for us. You keep going." I look at Michaela for a second, then back at Oleta. "She's really your daughter?"

Just the thought of Oleta having a child makes me uncomfortable. She's a *mother*.

Oleta nods.

"How'd the assassins get her?"

She presses her lips together for a long moment, then breathes out hard. Her breath fogs the darkness. "It was Zak. Petra knew about Michaela, and he got the info out of her. Sasha was looking after Michaela when they killed her and took my daughter." She runs a shaky hand through her hair. "Petra told me it was an ultimatum: join them again and have my daughter freed or watch my daughter take my place."

"Damn," I say.

"As lovely as this catch up is," Falkes says, "we need to talk about the plan."

Oleta and I both shoot him dark looks.

"It's a shame we don't know these lands well, else we could arrange a meeting point." Falkes says. "Meeting points are always better than relying on communication from a person who could get killed."

"No. Meeting points are too risky," I say. "That info could be weeded out of any of us and the rest would be doomed. We meet at a spontaneous place. Lexa, that's enough marks now." I halt her as she's about to start another on Falkes's arm.

She frowns. There's something about the moonlight that makes her eyes look bigger. "But you and Oleta have loads. He needs to fit in."

"Exactly. Oleta and I were the best. Most of the new assassins we've seen only have a handful, if that. We're relying on the original assassins not knowing all the newcomers yet. Because that's who you're going to be. Now, have we got everything?"

Keelie slings a survival bag my way. It's Lexa's. She and Falkes had a decent amount of supplies with them. I check the contents, straining my eyes a little: a foil blanket, dried meat, a water flask, another knife, and a basic medical kit. I've got two of the blades I made from flint in the pocket of my jacket.

"I want the gun as well," I say, looking at Lexa.

After a moment, she nods. Hands it to me, along with a magazine. Falkes makes a move to intercept them, but I am quicker. I glare at him as I tuck the Luger into my waistband and pocket the ammunition.

"Take this," Amelia says, and she's handing me her oversized cardigan. "It's cold tonight."

"No. You'll need it."

"We've got the blankets Lexa brought. I'll be fine."

Amelia gives me a stern look until I put on the cardigan, over the top of my ripped jacket. It is like a hug, and it smells of Amelia. I shoulder the survival bag.

"Be careful." Amelia clasps my hands for a long moment. There's a sadness in her eyes, and it really gets to me. Because this is the last time I'm going to see her—something just tells me that. "And be brilliant."

Be brilliant.

No one's ever said that to me before, and there's something about it that strikes a chord deep inside me.

"See you soon." Keelie flashes me a quick smile. "I'll look after everyone here."

Without a word, Oleta retreats into the shelter with Michaela. Amelia places a hand on my arm when I'm about to follow. Need to say goodbye to Kam as well.

"Just go," Amelia whispers. "The sooner this is done, the sooner we'll all be back together."

Falkes says goodbye to Lexa—a kiss that makes me

raise my eyebrows—and then we're leaving. The two of us.

"Wish we had a torch," he mutters. "Can barely see this compass."

"A torch would mean we're seen for miles around."

"Wouldn't be *miles* with all the trees' coverage." He grunts with every breath he takes, and every ninth step has him clearing his throat. Annoying, or what?

"Can you stop that?" I shoot him a glare.

He sniffs loudly, then wipes his nose on his sleeve. "Stop what?"

"Being so noisy. We need to sneak up on the assassins, ideally."

"I thought we're pretending to be them?" He gives me a look—one that suggests I don't know what I'm doing. Huh.

"We are." I exhale hard. "But we don't want to draw attention to ourselves."

"Watch your tone with me," Falkes snaps, and I frown. I didn't even use a bad tone. No, that's just him trying to assert his dominance, obtain the position of authority between the two of us.

Across the next hour, we walk through more and more woodland, following the route that Petra relayed to us through Oleta.

"That way," I say, pointing to the left. The ground there looks a little more solid, and I've already stepped in a few places that were too boggy.

Falkes turns and trips over something, probably a root.

I swear under my breath and roll my eyes as he sprawls out on the ground. Huh. That man couldn't look less like an assassin if he tried. We're always ultra-aware of our surroundings. Always.

Falkes is going to mess everything up.

I tap my foot as I wait for him to pick himself up and find the compass again. He does—but not quickly, starts whimpering and clutching his arm. And this is a supposed leader. I snort.

"We've got to hurry," I say. "I want to reach them before it's morning again. We need to go faster."

We go quicker and—

Humming.

I stop.

"What's that?"

Falkes turns to me, but it's too dark to see his expression.

The humming gets louder. A deep whirring. I see a faint light, flickering. A headlight, through the trees?

"Vehicles." I turn to Falkes. "We shouldn't be that close."

Petra said it would be several hours. Unless it's not them... Other Untamed?

But no, I just know it's them: the assassins.

The light is getting brighter, and there are more of them now, and the sounds of the engines are louder too.

They're too close. We're only halfway to them. They're coming for us—for Oleta and the children? They got the info out of Petra so soon?

My chest tightens. We have to stop them.

I will stop them.

Headlights slice through the trees, then I see the bodies of the vehicles. Trucks. Eight of them, moving through the trees like monsters. Branches crash into them, but of course they're fearless. Tires squeal, the engines grow louder, throatier.

"They're surrounding us," Falkes says, a note of alarm in his voice.

"Just stay calm." I pull out the Luger and a knife.

Headlights flash all around us. I clock at least two assassins in the front of each truck. And the red truck—the truck Johnny and Callum are in? I can't see it. I can't see any children.

Headlights burn my eyes as all the trucks skid to a stop.

The door of the nearest opens. She steps out slowly, carefully. Each movement planned.

Bridie.

"Well, well, well." Her voice is slow. She looks me up and down, then Falkes. "Who's this? Oh." Her lips turn down at the corners, and she gives Falkes a side-eyed look, clearly not impressed. "A pretender."

More figures appear from the other trucks.

"I'm not pretending," Falkes hisses and yanks the gun from me.

"Hey!" I yell at him.

"I know how to use this!" Falkes snaps and—

A gunshot rings out. The bullet ricochets off a tree. Fragments of debris fly.

Bridie laughs. "Yes, you've proven you're a man or whatever it is you're trying to do." She flicks her hand at the other assassins. "Get him."

They dart forward like arrows. I try to protect Falkes—I really do, or at least, I tell myself I do. But my instinct isn't there with him.

I look from truck to truck as Falkes screams and curses me. But there's no sign of Petra. I hold onto my knife tighter, but I don't make an attack with it, not yet. I need to be clever about this.

"Shut up," an assassin snarls at Falkes, and I turn just in time to see him being hit over the head with a bat. He falls like a sack of potatoes.

Oh, damn. Useless walrus, he is.

An assassin approaches him, quick as lightning, crouches next to him.

"Don't move him." My words are dark, and I don't even care what happens to Falkes, I'm just trying to prove that I've got power, status here. Giving orders screams authority.

The assassin picks up the Luger Falkes dropped but doesn't touch him. *Good.*

"Look at you." Bridie lets out a low whistle. "Thinking you can command my people."

"They're not your people," I say. "You're dead."

They're Gweneira's group now. I scan the faces around us. Where is she? But all these assassins here—I don't recognize any apart from Bridie. These are all newcomers too?

Bridie cackles. "Dead? Yet here I am." She takes a step closer to me.

I lift my head, stare her straight in the eyes. The darkness makes her eyes look gray. "And here you are." I say. "How great is it that I'll get to kill you for a second time?" My words drip venom.

Bridie's eyes narrow. "No, Inga, you're going to join us."

"Join you? What kind of pathetic slug do you think I am?"

"My assassins never leave me." Bridie tilts her head to one side, and I hear her neck crack. "You are in this for life—and beyond."

"Oh, really? Well, here's what I think of that." I step up to her and spit at her face. Get her left cheek. And it feels damn good.

She wipes my saliva away in a slow movement, her gaze never leaving mine. "I have ways and means of getting what I want. Never forget that."

I laugh. "I'm not a brainwashed little girl anymore, Bridie. You'd do well to remember that." In my head, I am a mesh of energy and thoughts as I work out the best way to handle this situation. I'm obviously outnumbered, but there's always something you can do.

"Would I?" Bridie tuts. "Because the way I see it, *I* have all the power here. My men outnumber you. And I have the person you love most in the world."

How stupid is she? She really thinks that my sister still means anything to me? No. Any family relation to her died the moment she took over leadership. Gweneira means nothing to me.

But what if she's been working for Bridie's group against her will?

I shift my weight from foot to foot. Bridie may have been dead, but Brighid, Bridie's daughter, is a powerful Seer, can make people do things. I bet she's behind Gweneira's actions.

But, no, whatever woman they've molded Gweneira into, she's not my sister anymore.

"You think you can control me just like that?" I raise my eyebrows. "Come on, Bridie, you're going to have to do better than that."

I glance to the right. There are only two trucks there, less assassins. If I'm going to run, that direction's my best bet. Only I don't like running away, and I'd be leaving Falkes.

"Bring her out!" Bridie yells.

The assassins to my left move fast, dragging a figure out of the truck to my right. A woman and—

It's not my sister.

"Inga, run!" Amelia yells.

Amelia.

My stomach twists as I stare at her. Her hair's a mess, and there's dried blood on her face. They got to her? They got to them? When? How? My head spins. The children. Michaela and Kam and Joshua and Zita—they've got them all back? How have they had time to drive past me, get them, and get back here? Unless the assassin bands were spread out. Petra didn't say they were all together, she just said they were in this forest, didn't she? And she gave me directions to the group that had Johnny and Callum.

Shit. I just assumed all the assassins were together. But they're not, they can't be, and this forest is huge. There are probably more assassins still out there too.

Fire pulls through me. I lift my knife, line my aim perfectly with Bridie's face. I am good at dagger-throwing, and she knows it. My hand does not shake. "Let Amelia go. Let them all go." I speak the words through gritted teeth.

"I don't think you're in any position to cast orders around here," Bridie says, that smarmy smile on her face. "I think you need to relearn the hierarchy."

"I'll kill you. Don't think I won't do it. Because I already have. You know I'm not messing about."

"And you know *I'm* not messing about," Bridie says. "Remember Caro? Your dear friend? Well, Inga, you either join me willingly or I forcibly take you and Granny here dies."

Granny.

It makes me laugh, and it shouldn't make me laugh. But the sound bursts from me. A cackle.

"Don't do it," Amelia shouts.

I stare Bridie right in the eye. "Do you really think you can do anything to make me join you again? You should know better than to think that one of your girls can form emotional attachments that can be used against them. You think Amelia means anything to me? You made me into a cold monster, and there's nothing you can do to make me join you."

Bridie cackles. "Do you hear that, Amelia? She's finally admitted it. You mean nothing to her. I suppose that shouldn't really shock us, considering Inga lied to you, pretending to be a Seer. Oh, and she murdered your daughter. What was her name? Renee, was it?"

Amelia gasps.

I freeze, jolt, then look at Amelia. Then Bridie. She knows? How does she know?

"Oh, Amelia, you didn't know?" Bridie laughs as she takes soft steps toward Amelia. "Tiny Inga *murdered* your daughter. Poor, poor Renee."

The moonlight grows brighter, and Amelia's eyes swivel to me, wide.

I shake my head. No. She can't find out. Not like this.

"No?" Bridie cries, looking at me. "You're not even going to lie?" She points at Amelia. "Inga shot Renee. Shot her like she was a reindeer, then got rid of the body. She didn't even let you say goodbye to her, and she didn't send the body off—"

"I did!" I scream, and Amelia jolts, looks at me.

She shakes her head. Eyes shaking. "You killed her?"

"Yes, learn what a lovely little girl Inga really is."

Bridie cackles again. "She's not your family. She's part of my group. And, Inga, you are joining me. Seize her!"

Assassins spring forth, and hands grab me.

I fight them, stab two of them, and Amelia's screaming and—

I see it in slow motion.

See how Bridie pulls Amelia against her body. See how she holds her shoulders and chest against her own. See her other arm wrap around Amelia's head. See her snap Amelia's neck.

I scream and scream and—

"Did you really think you could win against me?" Bridie yells. "Did you really think you could find a new family? Because love and family are weaknesses, and they just give me more ways to hurt you."

Red blurs my vision.

I lunge toward her, somehow break free of the hands holding me. My knife's gone now, and I haven't got time to get a blade out of my jacket pocket, but I don't care. I go for Bridie's neck.

Fury pulls through me.

Bridie screams.

I scream.

And—

Pain in my head.

The last thing I see is my grandmother's body, before everything goes dark.

FORTY-FIVE

IN THE DISTANCE, NEW ALESKL is overcast. The most lifeless of the Enhanced Ones' towns I've ever seen.

Is this going to work? The question drums through me. It will *work*. If we all stick to the plan. I look at Oleta, sitting ahead of me. She'll do it, won't she? But she's not the most unreliable part of the plan. Harmony's got to do her part too. And Grace and Samira. They have to. It was a risk bringing them in on the plan, but Petra said we needed them, that we could trust them. We've got to get everything right. There's no margin for error. If we don't do it exactly as planned, we die. It's as simple as that. And the thought sends adrenaline crashing through me.

We're going to do this.

I'm going to do this.

I look at Bridie and Oleta in the front of the truck. It's got three levels of seating. I'm at the back with Clara. Zak and Hunter are in the middle. In the truck bed are some littles. And behind us are two more trucks.

I didn't want the littles to come, told Bridie it was too much of a risk counting on them. And we didn't really need them, not when there are over a hundred of us, but she insisted, said it would be good for some to be involved. And

I know better than to argue with Bridie. Still, most of the littles are back at the camps. That's good.

Oleta's going to tell Petra when it's done, tell her to get the rest of our camp's littles ready as much as she can from her chains, and then we'll go back. The weakest assassins have been left behind, and if we take out everyone who's going on this mission, we'll have no trouble at our camp.

But I wonder what will happen at the other camps. Their assassins won't be returning either. What will their littles do? They won't know to revolt against the few adults who've been left behind with them—if any have. And there'll be no highers to guide or look after them, not when all highers are being deployed for this mission. I try not to think about how one tattooed skull is the difference between a little and a higher. A life I'm trying to save and a life I'm ignoring.

"This is the biggest thing we've ever attempted to do," Bridie says.

I smile. Isn't it just?

We drive as close as we can, and then we all congregate out by the rocks, just out of sight of the town. A cool wind blows in, caresses the back of my neck. It is welcome. I'm already sweating, due to the amount of ammunition harnesses and weapons strapped under my coat.

"We all ready?" Bridie looks around at us. There's pride in her eyes.

Zak nods. "We're going to take back this town. The Untamed are going to get New Aleskl."

The others cheer.

I catch Oleta's eye and smile. We're going to do more than that.

Bridie goes over the plan one more time, talking fast and low. Oleta and I are both leading teams—our own band has been split into two—and the other units from our camp are being led by Zak, Clara, and the other seniors under Bridie's command. Almost every unit consists of an aunt or uncle— or in Oleta's case, a former aunt—seconds-in-commands, instructors, a couple from the logistics teams, highers, and a couple of the units have some littles as well.

But we're not the only ones here.

Bridie holds her radio up to her face. "Everyone ready?"

"I'm in place, Mother." Brighid's voice crackles through it. She became leader of the eastern-most camp, a year or so after D'Elinous was taken by the Enhanced.

"Good," Bridie grunts, then she's speaking into the radio again, checking with the other four camps.

"A lot could go wrong," one of the logistics guys says, and, immediately, he's frowned at.

But he's right. It's the first time all six camps have worked together like this. It's a massive operation—and Bridie thinks the biggest problem will be our timing. Huh.

Brighid will lead her people in from the north. They'll attack the pharmacy and seal off the labs and weapons areas, before heading to the meeting point. The other camps will approach from the east and west, while our camp leads in from the south, covering several routes. I'm supposed to take my squad straight into the heart of the town—that's where we're all meeting. The town center is a huge complex, with grand architecture and many buildings surrounding it. There'll be at least a hundred assassins congregating there—plus our children—and that's where the killing spree will begin. An expanding typhoon that will grow and grow, until we've covered the whole town.

"Excellent," Bridie says into the radio.

We stand in our units, our bands forgotten. I've got five littles with me, ranging from five-years-old to eight. Bridie insisted came along.

"When we meet again, this town will be ours," Bridie says.

The assassins cheer. I cheer. Oleta cheers.

I've got a radio, as has Oleta, and we share one last look before she departs. We're all on strict timing. Oleta's taking the main route through to the town center, while I'm leading my squad around to the right first, loosely following the route Clara's taking her team too. We can't all be marching to the target area together in one go. That would draw too much attention.

The littles have their guns, as do I.

"We're killing everyone," one of the boys says, a huge

smile on his face. "And then we'll be free."

"And then you'll be free." I smile.

When it's time, I follow Clara's team, at a fair distance. We're all wearing dark glasses, and I feel too hot under mine.

Gravel crunches under my boots as we reach the town. Stone-colored buildings, with overlaid tracery, fill the space. Statues stand in front of shops, and blocks of apartments stretch up. There are plenty of Enhanced about, walking the streets, and we mix in with the crowds. The aromas of a bakery sweep over us, and I notice one of the littles having a look at the bread rolls in the window.

I nudge him. "Keep focus."

He shoots a dagger look at me as we cross under a bridge, skirting around an open-air market.

We get a good way into the town, before an alarm blares out.

Damn. I inhale sharply. The logistics team said all the alarms in New Aleskl are on the same circuit. One of us has been spotted. Probably the teams going for the pharmacy and labs. That part of the town has higher security.

Shouts fill the air as the Enhanced race around, suddenly propelled into life, searching for the intruders. Damn. So much for all the assassins easily getting to the town center

"Copy them," I hiss at the littles just as, ahead, I spot Clara and her team matching the Enhanced Ones' movements.

We run. My steps are light, and adrenaline floods through my system. The ammunition harnesses shift a little as I move, pretend to look for Untamed.

The crowd sweeps us toward the town center. The top of the clock tower comes into view, rising above the other buildings. The architecture's predominantly all of the same design here. Makes the town look both sturdy and fragile.

"More are here!" a woman cries, sticks her arm out in front of me. "Got the glasses too!"

I crash into her, knock her down, as she screams. More Enhanced turn toward me, appearing from all angles. I pull my gun out. It's already loaded, and the safety's off. I fire it. The gunshots echo.

The Enhanced scream.

Sweat drips down my back as I move and duck out of the way of an augmenter. The brave Enhanced One who thought he could cram it down my throat gets a swift death. I turn, looking for my littles, see them fighting.

Clara's here too, to my right, with her posse. She's got a pistol in each hand and shoots wildly.

More gunshots rain down, try to drown out the blaring siren.

"That way!" Clara yells as she runs toward the center of the town, her unit following her. I see several other figures—assassins from other camps—running that way too. They're getting here.

We've all studied the maps of New Aleskl over the last few weeks, know the place like the backs of our hands, and the littles and I blend into the army of assassins heading for the town center. My head pounds, and there's a rushing in my ears, but I try to keep listening. Need to keep listening, hear past the gunshots and alarm. Need to hear Oleta's signal. It'll be soon. Won't it? But I can't think how long it's been.

"Positions now!" Clara yells, because we all know where we're supposed to be in the town center. My place is outside the tourist information office, under an overhang with carved dragons in it.

My littles start to run to their designated areas and—

A crow caws overhead.

Yes.

Energy thuds through me. This is it.

"Get over there!" I shout at the littles.

They skid, turn, look at me. Two of them have lost their glasses already.

"But the center's where we're all meeting!" the smallest boy cries, not seeing the Enhanced behind him. "We've got to go over there!"

I shoot the mirror man, heart pounding, then yell at them, "No! Over there now!"

I point in the opposite direction. Because they can't be in the town center. Not the littles. Not the ones Bridie put me in charge of. Not when I know the real plan.

I am scary, I am intimidating, and thank the Gods I am because they listen to me, though they're slow, and—

One of my boys starts to make a break for it, turning back, going for the town center.

I snake out, grab his arm, and—

The blast throws us back.

Screams twist in my ears, and air whizzes past me. I land, still holding onto the boy by his arm, the wind knocked out of me. Smoke and stone fragments fill my vision, and the air is thick with dust. Light flashes in the sky, and something else booms. *More chunks of stone fly, and something hits my arm. Sharp pain.*

A severed arm flies through the air.

I pull myself to my feet, quick. The boy stares at me, eyes wide. I do a quick head-count of my other littles. Good. We're all here.

The Enhanced are screaming, running around.

A smile tugs at my lips. Yes. Oleta did it. I pray she got away in time. But how many littles were in the center? How many did we just sacrifice for that?

"Go that way!" I snarl at the children, pointing the way.

"That's...that's not the plan!" one of them cries out, alarm in her voice. "We need the buildings, we need a town!" But she looks lost—because there's no town center now.

"We don't need a town," I snarl. "Now, listen to me, and do exactly what I say if you want to live." I point behind me. "Get out of the town. Run. And keep running. Run past the trucks. You shouldn't see any assassins that way, but if you do, shoot them. You're children—*you're not supposed to be in this lifestyle. You're innocent. So run."*

"But Bridie said—"

"Bridie's dead," I snarl. I point to where the explosion was, ignoring the pain in my arm. "She'd have been there." That was the plan. To get Bridie and as many other assassins from all the camps in one place, eradicate them in one fell swoop. And though we were seen by the Enhanced and alarms went off, most of us must've been there, Bridie included. Oleta wouldn't have blown up the square if not. "She's gone. The assassins have gone. And you need to

run."

It'll be easier for the littles than those of us who are older. They've got limited—if any—assassin marks on them. Other Untamed will accept them.

"Go!"

They run.

I turn, run toward the site of the explosion. Enhanced Ones are flocking there, terror-stricken, trying to help one another. We got plenty of them in the blast too. Some are trying to keep order, keep people away, and, in the confusion, they mustn't notice I'm Untamed—because none are focused on apprehending or converting me.

I've got to get closer.

Got to find her body.

Bridie's.

Got to be sure she's dead.

And Oleta—I need to find her. I promised Petra I'd look out for her, given Oleta had the dangerous job. We couldn't get hold of explosives, and, though Oleta said she could do it with her Seer powers, it required her to be near the target site.

Petra warned us that summoning that amount of energy would weaken Oleta, said she'd transfer her own powers to Oleta too, to help, to try and make sure Oleta survives the explosion. But it all depends on how far away Oleta got. And whether a building fell on her.

"Come on," I yell at myself. Oleta's got to be alive, and Bridie's got to be dead.

I pick my way over bodies. Enhanced Ones. Broken mirrors.

And assassin marks. I find them, at last. Myrtle and George. And another man. Two women from another camp. And then I'm in the center of the town square, climbing over rubble and blackened bodies. Twenty, thirty, forty dead assassins. I lose count.

Oleta is not among these dead. Neither is Bridie.

I curse. Sweat drips into my eyes, makes them sting.

But there's more rubble to check and—

"Inga!"

I look up.

"She's over there!" Oleta yells, and she's holding onto her leg as blood slides down it. "Bridie didn't get the full force of the blast." Her eyes widen, and she swears as she points to the right. "Two units are there. I'll go and sort them. You kill Bridie."

Steel fills my nerves, and I run.

My heart pounds, and I feel the beat throughout my whole body.

A building collapses to my right. More screams.

I run, ducking as chunks of stone fly through the air. Something hits my shoulder, but it's not enough to make me stop.

I find more bodies. Killed from Oleta's blast. Assassins and Enhanced Ones. Two birds, one stone.

I keep running.

And—and I see her.

Bridie's crawling on her hands and knees, matted gray hair tangling down over her right shoulder.

She's barely got a scratch on her, but she's moving slowly.

I run faster, jump in front of her. My gun is ready.

Bridie looks up and sees me. Her eyes widen. "You." Her word shakes. Her whole being shakes. "You devil. You did this. You and Oleta and—"

"Say goodbye to this world, Bridie." My tone is slow, but sharp, delicious. I taste blood in my mouth—don't know what it's from, but it doesn't matter.

All that matters is that I kill her.

And I will.

But the gun—no. That's too easy.

I slide the firearm into my belt, keep my eyes on Bridie the whole time, see how hope lights up her face. Just for a moment. Then I pull out my knife.

Yes. She needs to suffer. Suffer as she's made me suffer, made so many of us suffer.

The blade glints in the air.

"What are you going to do?" Bridie yells. "This isn't going to get rid of the assassins. We're strong. All the people back at the camp, and the littles—we will keep going, you

can't stop us by taking out me."

"Oh, it's not just you we're killing," I say. "You're not that special. We're getting everyone."

"You and Oleta?" She snorts. "Two girls who have got too big for their boots."

I shake my head, my smile unfurling. "You don't get it, do you? It's not just me and Oleta. It's Petra and Harmony and Samira and Grace too. It's all of us who you've ruined, and we're ending this now."

"My people are everywhere—"

"Not anymore." I laugh. "This isn't some last-minute plan, Bridie. Aren't you going to realize it? This is the end. The end for you and your cronies. All your strongest assassins were on this mission. A shame we blew them up. And, right after I kill you, Oleta and I are going back to the camp. Your people there are pathetic, won't be much of a problem for us. And we're getting all the children, and we're starting again."

"You're stalling," Bridie hisses. "Telling me your plans! Because you, Tiny Inga, don't want to do this. You can't do this, not to me. I'm your mother."

"You're nothing." I spit in her face. "You're absolutely nothing to me. Your reign is over, Bridie."

I lean in closer, savoring the moment. Because this is it.

I smile as I stab her. The blade slides easily into the fleshy pad of her upper arm. She lets out a guttural yell. I wiggle the blade a little.

Sweat runs down her face. "That's not going to kill me!"

"Oh, that wasn't supposed to kill you," I say, crouching in front of her. "That was for my childhood that you took." I grin as I get the knife ready again, then I stab her again. "And this is for all the other childhoods you've taken."

She screams, and—

Movement. To my right.

I turn, heart pounding. Two Enhanced Ones. I pull my gun out, sort them out.

Bridie screams at me, grabs my arm, but I kick her. Damn, she's weak already. And I've still got a lot to do before she's released from this life.

"This is for Caro," I say, my voice soft as I plunge the knife between her ribs, pierce the lungs, or maybe her upper stomach. I don't care.

Blood bubbles from her mouth, and she tries to fight me. She really does. But she's pathetic.

And I'm not going to stop.

I keep stabbing her. Over and over again.

FORTY-SIX

MY HEAD THRUMS, AND, SLOWLY, I open my eyes. My eyelids are too heavy, and my lashes seem to scratch.

I blink, groggy, staring at my legs. The leggings. Stained. I can see the stains on them. Blood and dirt. Gods, Minnow won't be happy.

Minnow's dead.

I jolt.

I'm cross-legged, my torso slumped forward. Hard stone beneath me. I lift my head and—

Pain grabs me.

I let out a cry.

My arms scream. They're sticking out, my elbows. They're bare… My cardigan—Amelia's cardigan, it's gone! And my jacket. Just my T-shirt and—

Amelia.

It all comes back. How Bridie killed her.

I gasp, pain twisting through me.

No. She can't be dead.

But she is.

I saw it.

My head pounds, and I try to think.

My hands—I can just about feel them, numb, against my mid-back. And metal, around my wrists. Manacles?

I twist my head, ignoring the way the throbbing pain takes over my body, getting stronger and stronger, a pulse of its own, as I look behind me. A huge rock, square. Crudely cut. I get a glimpse of the manacles around my wrists, and the chains that are attached to them. Chains that wrap round and round the square rock.

My legs are numb, and I try to think. I need to stand. Need to get out of this…cave. I'm in a cave.

The assassins have me. I squint, look around. The walls are just gray, extend as far as I can see, around the corner—I can't see the exit.

I don't recognize this cave. But, then again, would I recognize? I rarely went in the caves at Royston's Rock and Bluejay. But this could be any cave, anywhere. I look up and see the sky in several places, through gaps in the roof. Daylight, outside.

I take a deep breath and count to ten. I need to get out of here. Is it possible to stand from a cross-legged position when your hands are tied securely behind you?

I lean as far to my left as my protesting arms allow, then concentrate on my legs, on uncrossing them. Pain whips through them, but I do it. Sweat drips down my face, and I press my manacled hands against the rock, try to use it as leverage of some sort as I stretch my legs out, then bend my knees so the soles of my feet are flat on the ground.

I grit my teeth as more pain grabs me, and tears fill my eyes when hot lassoing pain closes around my head. Seer damage. Has to be. Brighid is a strong Seer. She'd be working with Bridie, I know it. Because Petra wouldn't do this, would she?

She would if they forced her to.

Pain rolls through my back and arms as I try to lift my torso up, need to get my weight on my feet. Need to stand. But it feels like my shoulders are going to dislocate. I take a deep breath and pull on my wrists. Need more slack with the chains. But nothing happens.

I swear under my breath, then try again. This time I manage to get into a crouching position, but I know I can't sustain this for long. It's putting too much pressure on my shoulders and arms, feels like my bones are going to snap. I flex my fingers, then turn and look at the rock. Can I lift it when I stand? But I know the answer: no. It's too big, too sturdy.

I twist farther; the chains are wrapped around the square form. And now I'm in a crouched position, the height of the rock only goes to my mid-back. I lift my hands as best as I can, still craning my neck to see behind me. The length of the chain, it's just wrapped *around* the rock. I frown. Is the final loop of the chain, ending at the manacles, locked firmly onto previous wraps of the chain or is just around the rock and can it be loosened?

I cry out as I move my hands. Pain cricks my neck—but the chains move.

Yes.

I can unwind the length of the chain from the rock. I just need to get a bit more height.

I force myself to stand, scream as pain grabs me. I lift my manacled hands higher, and to the left and backward, over the rock. The chain makes a noise, movement and—

I stumble with the momentum and force as the chain lifts over the corner of the rock. It pulls me backward against the hard stone, and something grates against my back. But I've done it. Done the hardest bit.

A smile fights its way to my face, and I move my hands to the other corner, lifting the weight of the chain. It gets easier as I unwind the fetters from around the rock, until there's no more to unwind. Just the metal fastening in the stone, blinking at me.

I stand fully, breathing deeply. Lightheadedness threatens to grab me, but I'm in a better position now.

Good. I take a deep breath. My hands are still behind my back, but with the slack chain, they're not forced against my spine now.

I pull my arms down as much as I can. I'm small and flexible, but I've got long arms. Can I step through my arms, get my manacled wrists in front of me? That would put me in a stronger position to try and detach the other end of the chain from the stone, as well as relieve some of the pressure on my arms.

Yes. I think I can do it.

I move my hands as low as I can. They reach my bottom. I grit my teeth. If I strain my arms, I think I can do it. But sitting down is best. With all the grace of a muskox, I sink to my knees, then onto the side of my right thigh. I stretch out my legs in front of me, then bend them at the knees.

My muscles and joints protest as I force my wrists down, get them underneath me. My shoulders click as I slide my hands forward, under me, and pain makes me shake. Sweat drips down into my eyes, stings. But I do it. My bound hands are now under my thighs. Good.

I hug my knees to my chest as I lift my feet up a little and slide my manacled wrists under them. My shoulders protest at the movement, but it works.

I breathe deeply, heart and lungs pounding as I stare at my bound hands in front of me with the chain snaking from them. I did it. The owl on my arm looks smug.

I turn to move, but dizziness grabs me, and my shoulders and chest ache. My left arm's going numb. *Damn it.*

But I've got to move. I know that. Just a few inches to the left. The chains—I don't know how I'll get out of them, but I need to move, need to get out. Have to get out.

I turn and see a body. A crawling sensation prickles over my skin. How didn't I see her before?

She's three or four feet away. Her dark hair is

splayed out on the stone, and the blood—there's so much blood. I swear. How didn't I notice I wasn't alone?

I crawl toward her, my heart pounding as I put every bit of energy into reaching her. Got to reach her.

"Petra," I whisper, and my voice cracks. Her name seems to scratch my throat.

My chains are just long enough to reach her, and I touch her arm. Cool. But not cold. Not dead. The skin on her wrists, around her manacles, is rough and blistered.

"Petra? Petra, can you hear me?" I try to shake her, but pain lashes through me. More sweat drips into my eyes. "Petra, we need to get out of here."

Her eyes flutter a little, open. The whites of them are bloodshot. Her pupils are too narrow. She looks at me, and I sense her recognition before she shakes her head. Her eyelids close, and her breathing gets shallower.

"Petra?" I shout, but she doesn't stir again, and I keep shouting. Got to wake her up. I need her powers to get out. *We* need her powers.

But I can't wake her up.

Sweat drips down my back as I turn away from her, look around the cave. There's got to be something I can do. I test the chains, forcing myself to move to the right, as far as they will allow me. I can almost reach the wall—but not quite.

I brace myself as I try the other direction, but I get nowhere near the wall. But if Petra's chains are the same length as mine, she'd be able to, I'm sure. I'm not sure what the significance of that is, but it's information and I need to collect information. Information is always power.

I listen hard. Outside, I can't hear anything. The air is too quiet.

"Hello?" I call out, and maybe I shouldn't be making a sound, because they're going to know I've unwound my chains so I can move. But if someone comes, I'd hear them, right? I could drape the chains back around the rock….

But what about my wrists? They're in front of my body now. Not behind.

I swallow hard.

I can fight though, even with my wrists bound.

And I need to get out of here.

It's a risk I'll have to take.

And maybe if there's a child or something, he or she can help me.

I take a deep breath, give Petra another glance, then shout again. "I need help! Petra needs help!" If an assassin comes in and focuses on Petra, maybe I can take them out before they realize I've partially freed myself.

I shout until my throat is roar and the words don't seem to make sense. But no one comes. Bridie doesn't come. The hairs on the back of my arms are on end. Why isn't she coming? It doesn't make sense. She'd want to hurt me. But she's just tied me up and left me here?

Left me to die here?

A slow and painful death?

I lick my lips and take another deep breath. There's always a way out. I've just got to think. And I know Bridie, know her well. Know the way she thinks. That meeting in the woods wasn't going to be the last time I saw her.

Something bigger is coming.

And, when it does, Petra and I have got to be prepared.

FORTY-SEVEN

I STAB BRIDIE, OVER AND *over.*

"It's done!" Oleta's arms are around me, and she's pulling me back. "She's dead!"

I fight her, screaming, screaming at her and at Bridie. Bridie's lifeless, blood-covered body.

"Come on!" Oleta yells. And she's strong, hauls me back. She's healed herself.

I stop fighting her, let her pull me back over the rubble, then watch as Oleta yanks the necklace of teeth from Bridie's neck. She pulls a gold key off it and pockets it.

"What the hell are you staring at?" I yell at the mirror men around us. They're just standing there, watching the spectacle—Untamed turning on Untamed—no doubt terrified by this display of violence. They should be trying to convert us.

But they're not.

"Come on!" Oleta yells.

"Did you kill the others?" I'm breathless.

"Yes! But we've got to get back to camp. Zak and Clara got away—took one of the trucks! They could know Petra's involved and be going for her."

I stare at her. "When did they leave?"

We have to get back before them. Taking out Bridie and the big figures is only the beginning. We've got to free the other littles and Petra. We've got to get back there before any of the assassins here do.

But how the hell did Zak and Clara survive the blast? The last I saw of Clara she was heading for the town square. The area that Oleta blew up.

"Minutes ago, if that!" Oleta yells.

We run. The Enhanced don't even try to stop us. Pathetic slugs.

Oleta and I head for the trucks.

"Did the littles get away?" I yell at her, breathless. "Did you see them?"

"Some ran that way!" She points wildly to the right. "Samira's with them—she'll look after them! And she got nine more of the assassins."

"Good." I grunt, and then we're at the trucks. I pull open the driver's door of the black truck. "Slash the tires of the others!" I shout at Oleta, but she's already doing it.

Two littles appear. They're terror-stricken and crying. They're not from my unit, or even our camp. No, these are from one of the others. Oleta's?

And I look around—for the aunts and uncles and seconds-in-commands, for anyone—but no one else is here.

"Get in!" Oleta yells at them. "Things are changing now."

Oh, things sure as hell are changing.

Forty-five minutes later we approach the temporary camp. It's almost a copy of Bluejay, complete with a cave to keep Petra in.

I'm driving and squint at the makeshift buildings with lines of washing strung up between them. Is anything going on? Have they heard what's happened?

"Can't see the other truck, Zak and Clara's." Oleta's voice is low. "Are they not coming back?"

"Maybe they're fleeing," I say, steering over rough ground. "Realize they're outnumbered now Bridie's out of the picture."

"Maybe," Oleta says. Her tone sounds like she's speaking through gritted teeth. "But we're going to have to work quickly."

"Obviously."

"I'll get the littles," she says. "And Petra. You take out the other adults."

"No problem at all."

I slam on the brakes, stop the truck, jump out. Slight pain edges into my feet but I ignore it. I've done too much to be bothered by pain now.

I run for the huts where the adults usually congregate. Not that there are many left here now. Just the weak ones.

Martin, a weedy man with perhaps the worst shot I've ever seen, steps out. He sees me—sees my blood-covered form—and starts to say something.

My gun is ready, and I shoot him before he's even finished his sentence.

He falls.

Figures run, everywhere.

Children, assassins.

Oleta flies past me.

I run after her. Something slaps against my chest, and I look down. My necklace of teeth. Repulsion pulls through me, and I grab it, pull it so hard the thread breaks. The teeth of all my victims fly like bullets, finally freed.

"What the fuck are you doing?"

I look up, see Zak.

Damn. He's here already.

I point my gun at him, pull the trigger and—

Nothing.

Shit.

No ammo left.

Blood pounds in my ears.

Zak laughs.

Run.

I run, zigzagging as I get more ammunition out of my harness. Has he got a gun? I don't know. My breaths pound through me.

Oleta screams something, and she's here and there's white light in her hands, bolts of energy licking forth. Her powers.

"Get Petra out!" she yells, and she throws something at me. The key.

I grab it from the mud and blood-soaked grass. It's hot.

Then Oleta shoots white light at a hut. An empty hut? I don't know.

Petra. Yes.

I run, duck as something flies through the air. A dark shape.

A child screams, and then more gunshots are going.

I race behind the huts to the cave they keep Petra in, duck just in time to avoid smacking my head against the low roof of the entranceway as I career in.

"Petra! Now!" I yell. "We've got to go now! I've got the key."

I skid to a stop in front of her and—

"Petra?"

She's not moving. She's just....

I scream her name, crash into her as I throw myself down. Shake her.

She stirs, fear on her face.

"I can't!" she cries. "I—"

"What?"

"I can't leave! Brighid is back! She knows, and she's—" Footsteps.

"They're coming! Come on!" I hiss, jabbing the key into the lock on the chains. Bridie had it all strengthened by another Seer a long time ago so Petra couldn't use her own powers on them to free herself, and only this key can free her.

"I can't leave this cave!" Petra yells. Her words echo in the cave and seem to speed up.

"You can! I've got the key!" And it clicks in the lock, freeing her. The chains hang down, and I pull at her hand.

"No," she hisses, eyes flashing. "Just get the other littles out!"

Shouts from outside fill the air.

"You've got to go now!" Petra shouts. "You've got to save the children!"

"No!" I roar. "Come on!"

"I can't! Go! Or you're not getting out of here!"

Adrenaline fills me.

"Run!" Petra yells. "You have to run now!"

I run. The soles of my shoes slap the stone floor. The bright light outside blinds me, and I stumble. A hand grabs me. Oleta's.

"Where is she?" she yells.

"She won't—"

Another gunshot. I blanch, and I run.

The children. They're ahead.

I run, grab a fistful of a child's hair. Can't tell who it is.

I've just got to go.

"Inga!" Oleta yells.

But I don't stop, just keep yelling, yelling at the children. "Come with me!"

And they do.

We go.

We scatter into the world, free.

FORTY-EIGHT

PETRA WAKES AS EVENING DRAWS in. She murmurs something then lets out a strangled sound as her eyes snap open.

"You're really here?" Her voice is slow as she stares at me.

I nod. My neck clicks. "Where is this? Which camp?"

"Yalton," she says. Awake, she looks a lot more like Oleta. Her chains aren't wrapped around anything, and there's not another square rock in here. Only that one for me. It must be anchored to the ground or something—maybe with Seer powers—because I tried to drag it along the floor, but I couldn't.

"Yalton?"

"It's a new one, only a couple years old," Petra whispers.

I breathe deeply. "How far away are we from Oleta and the Untamed I was with?"

Petra blinks slowly. "Day's journey, maybe… They don't let me know much about where places are now." She breathes deeply and looks into my eyes. "Inga, did Oleta and Michaela get away?"

"I think so," I say. And I have to believe it, have to

hope it. That it was just Amelia that Bridie caught. Because if it wasn't, if Bridie had more of my group, she'd be taunting me with them. Not leaving me alone with Petra.

"Good." Petra nods. "Michaela has to be safe."

I nod back and stare at the ground for a moment. All the dried blood around Petra. "Are you injured?" I flinch at the question. *Of course* she's injured.

"I'm okay," Petra says. She pushes her hair back from her face. "Inga… I'm sorry. They've got powerful Seers. I couldn't… They got the information out of me, about where Oleta was, and they made me track you separately. I couldn't stop them coming after you."

"It's okay." I want to reach for her, comfort her—and that's not like me at all, or maybe it is. Maybe I really have changed. "It's going to be okay. We're going to get out of here. We'll find Oleta and the others."

"You will, but I won't." She looks down.

"What? Petra!" I stare at her. "You're getting out of here."

She shakes her head. "I'm not. I can't leave. Inga, Brighid's bound my soul to hers. It doesn't matter what I do, I'm never going to be free."

"Bound your soul?"

She exhales. "I'm hers. I can't leave the cave, unless she gives me permission."

I snort. "Well, I'm going to kill her, so then you'll be free. We'll get you out of here, I promise."

"We will?" Hope sparks in her eyes.

"Of course."

A slow clapping makes me jump. Petra squeals, and I turn to the front of the cave, where a figure now stands.

Fire boils my blood.

"How touching." Bridie's voice is amused. "Forgiveness and hope, and all those other weak beliefs that get Untamed killed."

I stand up, brace my hands together in front of me. I make a large fist with them both, and the chains jangle as I move myself in front of Petra. A weak pain wraps around my skull, but I breathe through it. I am strong.

"Oh, Tiny Inga, stop that." Bridie strides toward us. "You can't beat me."

I glare at her—and all I can see is how easily she snapped Amelia's neck. "You want to bet?"

Bridie chuckles, then her face smooths out, and her eyes glisten with darkness. "Do you know why you're here?"

"Because you're a bastard," I snap.

Petra whimpers.

"No, it is because the two of you are traitors." Bridie's voice is low. "And do you know what I do with traitors now?" She advances nearer. And I can't have her nearer. I don't want to look at the woman who killed my grandmother.

"Get any closer, and I'm going to kill you!" I scream, adrenaline filling me, numbing my pain.

"Again?" Bride laughs. "Well, let's hope you do a better job this time. Wouldn't want me coming back to life again. But you didn't answer my question. What do we do with traitors?"

"Kill them," Petra says, her voice shaking, and I think of what she did to Fi.

"Kill them?" Bridie imitates her tone and then laughs. "Well, technically, yes, we did do that. But not for you two. Death would be too nice for you. And I want you alive. Petra, dear, I'd be stupid to give up a Seer. And, you, Inga, well… Death would be a reward. And I don't want to reward you. So, what do I do? Quite the conundrum, don't you think?"

"Let us go!" I scream at her.

"Let you go? You're even more stupid than I remember. I'm *never* letting you go. You're mine. You don't leave me. You never leave me." She clicks her tongue. "But you've both proven yourself too dangerous and unreliable. I can't ever send you out there again. But death would be too easy—death is nice. Did you know that? I quite enjoyed it."

I glare at her.

"So, we've decided we're going to hurt you, instead. Hurt you more than you've ever experienced before."

Petra starts crying—loudly—and the sound annoys me.

Bridie smirks, then raises her voice. "Come, daughter, join me in this."

"No, not Brighid!" Petra screams. "Don't bring Brighid—please don't bring—"

We see her shadow first, stretching out across the stone floor as she walks through the out-of-sight entrance of the cave. The shadow gets nearer. I get ready to fight even though I don't know how I'll go up against Brighid in my injured, weaponless state. Not when she's a Seer. Not when—

She steps into view.

My heart pounds.

It's not Brighid. This woman....

"Gweneira?" I stare at her. My sister. Not Brighid, Bridie's daughter... But she's wearing Brighid's cloak.

My head spins.

Gweneira laughs. "You still haven't realized?"

"Realized?" My voice wobbles, and Bridie laughs.

Gweneira spits at me. "I'm not your sister. Your precious Gweneira died when you were a baby. Drowned."

FORTY-NINE

"BRIGHID TOOK YOUR SISTER'S PLACE," Bridie says. "I needed eyes on the inside. To get you, Inga, to observe the old Seer, and to keep an eye on your cousins. Shame that we lost them." She turns to stare at Petra, and something passes between them—something I don't understand. "*Isn't it*, Petra? Once a traitor, always a traitor."

"Being Enhanced is better than this, and I'd do it again in an instant," Petra hisses.

"What's going on?" I shake my head.

I look at my sister—only it's not her. It's…Brighid. But she looks like Gweneira. Unless… No, the Gweneira I knew would have always been Brighid. Who knows what my sister looked like? Only, no, she must've looked like this. Brighid must've modeled her appearance on her, else everyone would've known the girl found on the shore the next day wasn't Gweneira.

Brighid laughs and adjusts her cloak.

My head feels too heavy as I stare at her, and I'm tuning out Bridie's and Petra's shouts. I can only concentrate on the woman—my fake sister—in front of me. "You fought for me," I shout, looking at her.

"When the assassins took me, *you* were fighting."

Brighid rolls her eyes. "Because Sara or anyone could've been nearby and watching—and I was playing my part."

Playing her part? Pretending to be my sister?

"Did Mum know?" I yell at her. "Did she know who you were?"

I take a deep breath as I wait for the answer.

Brighid smirks. "Who knows what that batty woman thought? Sara was desperate for her precious Gweneira to be alive, and she was so happy when I showed up." She shrugs. "Maybe she knew, maybe she didn't. All she cared was that she had her firstborn with her again."

I stare at her. "But others must've noticed. You may have looked like Gweneira, but your personality would be different."

"It's only natural that drowning would change a person."

I stamp my foot, and pain snakes up my leg. Of course. That was how the story of Gweneira's drowning always ended, with comments on how traumatized my 'sister' was.

I look at Brighid. "Change back," I command.

"What?" She takes a step toward me.

"Don't hide behind my sister's image now."

"You think I want to look like her still?" She snorts. "I'm stuck looking like this now. Even had to get my tattoos redone on this body. But, shut up now. I want to watch this." She gestures at Petra, who's screaming. And there's blood—so much more blood, fresh.

I jolt.

Bridie's attacked her? In that time? And I missed it?

"Teach this traitor a lesson she won't forget," Bridie instructs Brighid.

"Gladly," Brighid says.

I go cold, and Petra's screaming, begging for Brighid not to do it.

Brighid is a Seer. Every assassin knows that Bridie's

daughter is a Seer. A powerful one.

Brighid grins, and then Petra's summoning white light. A bolt of it. She sends it forward, but Brighid deflects it, then conjures her own. A beam of it that she directs straight toward Petra.

Petra shrieks—an inhuman sound—and I try to run for her. Got to help her! Have to help her!

"I don't think so."

I turn, heart pounding. See Bridie. Right next to me. A wooden club in her hands. I duck as she swings it, and I trip, stumble, fall. My bound hands prevent me from catching myself. Pain in my chest as I hit the stone.

Petra screams again, and I roll over and—

Bridie stands over me.

She lifts her club.

She brings it down on my legs.

And—and there's nothing.

I DRIFT IN AND OUT of pain, and I'm running… No, I'm floating. Floating above the camp, flying, watching the assassins and the recruits. And this doesn't make sense…only it does. It is happening.

I am flying.

I see Johnny and Callum, and they're playing with Kam and Michaela and Joshua and Zita. And Keelie's there, and so is Elf, and my mother….

And Gweneira. Or is she Brighid? I can't tell, but whoever it is asks how I am and tilts my head up with her cold hand, so I stare into her eyes. And I'm not floating now.

There's grass beneath me, and things are changing, and it's all happening too quickly and—

"Prepare for an extra demonstration at tonight's festival," Bridie says. "I want everyone to see what happens to those who betray me."

Pain ravages down my legs. A flash of an image fills my mind. Bridie and the club.

"They're broken," says the woman who might be my sister but probably is Brighid.

And then her face twists, and it's a spirit, an evil

spirit and—

—and I need something to defend myself with.

But….

"Fight this! Come on, fight this!"

The words echo around me. An elderly woman's voice. A slight accent. And it's familiar.

Caia-Lu? But I can't think.

"Do not die on me!"

"No," I say. "Bridie won't let me."

I open my eyes. Awake. I'm awake. Pain, so much pain.

But I'm here. The cave.

I turn my head, and just the movement sends fire to my legs. I groan, gasp. My eyes water. My legs… Too much pain and—

Where's Petra? The stone floor is wet with blood in the place she was….

"Petra?" My voice wobbles.

I'm the only one here. The only….

The chains. They've gone. I'm not bound. Not a prisoner?

Get out.

I look toward the cave's exit. Can't see anyone.

Move!

I try to get up, but I can't. I— My legs. They won't….

No. My breathing quickens. Was that why they took my chains off? To taunt me with freedom that I can't possibly obtain now. Nausea pulls through me. I can't be trapped here!

No. I won't be.

My arms. I've still got my arms.

They're working.

I swallow hard, pull myself forward. My shoulders

and back protests, and my right arm is significantly weaker—and colder—than it should be. But I do it. I drag myself forward. Inch by inch, until I'm at the front of the cave. I turn to the left, blink as I see the outside world. Bright daylight and—

Too bright. My eyes smart, and my head reverberates with pain. I look down, blinking, stare at the cuts on my arms and the dried blood. The snowy owl has been dyed red.

A cool wind blows over me, and I look up. My neck creaks.

I'm high up.

The cave's entrance overlooks the camp.

I grit my teeth as I take it all in. The huts are pretty much in the usual formation, and there are trees to the left of the buildings. Some cover. I make a note of it. Several trucks sit behind the huts, and a group of adults stands far to the right, by a smoldering hearth. Two children—probably highers—hang clothes on lines stretching between the huts. They're the only people I can see, but I can feel there are more present. Probably inside the huts.

I take a deep breath, then force myself on. I've got to get out. This might be my only chance.

A truck. I need a truck.

But can I drive? I pull on my legs, try to tense my muscles. My right leg responds more than my left. Damn. I can't drive a manual car, but maybe an automatic? And some of the trucks were automatics before. I pray they're still like it, and, that, somehow, I manage to get one and get away in it.

I crawl forward, down the slope. Coldness seeps into my hands and knees, and my head rings with one thought: escape.

I've got to get away.

But what about Petra? Where is she? My breaths catch in my throat.

And—and Falkes? I haven't even thought about him, but....

If he's here, he'll be dead. I know that.

And I've got to get away.

I count under my breath as I crawl forward, using my counting as a distraction from the torrents of pain—even if it is Bridie's technique. I can do this. Gravel digs into me as I crawl forward, and it seems to take me hours, but I do it. I reach the first hut, and I hear a sound. A cry. A child's cry.

The children.

Johnny and Callum. Are they still here?

My heart thumps. Energy catapults itself through me. Johnny and Callum, I promised I'd rescue them. And—and I'm here and that could be them.

I pull myself to the right, toward the entrance of the hut, where there are shrubs and—

A man walks into view.

Damn.

It's Hunter.

I push myself back, hold my breath. My body locks up. He's going to find me, he's going to hurt me. He's going to….

He walks right past me. Doesn't look down. Doesn't look back. He's humming a ditty.

My heart thuds as I watch him go into a hut, a little farther away.

Move.

Electric-shock-like pain fizzles down my spine, and I gasp. Sweat sticks my shirt to my back, and I pull myself into the hut, slowly, carefully, as quietly as possible.

It's dark inside, takes a moment or so for my eyes to adjust, and I listen for sounds.

Nothing.

I crawl in farther. No one in here. Just fuel cans. So many of them. And a box of matches. Huh. That's stupid having them together.

Not this hut.

I move back out, cautious, wincing as gravel rolls under my knees. Got to find the boys. Have to. I can't leave without trying, I know that.

The child's cry gets stronger, and I follow it to the next hut, all the while keeping a lookout for movement. Because they're going to find me. Any moment now, they're going to find me.

My back aches, and my hands are sore as I pull myself inside, looking.

Breathing. I can hear breathing.

I freeze. Are there adults in here?

No, the breathing is *scared*.

I edge forward.

"Inga?"

I jolt, look up. Johnny stares at me. He's tied up, and his face is tear-stricken.

"It's okay," I say. "I've got you. I'm getting you out."

But you can barely move yourself!

I ignore the voice.

"Where's Callum?"

Johnny's face crumples.

"Don't cry," I hiss. Okay. He's tied up. The ropes don't look that strong. Not enough to keep me bound, but a child, yes.

I force myself to move faster, toward him. The moment we're in touching distance, he wraps his hands around my arms, pulls me closer. He's shaking.

I push him back a bit, need to see the ropes. *There.*

"Are there any weapons in here?" I ask him. "You seen anything that can cut this?"

Johnny shakes his head, teary-eyed.

"Okay." I wrap my hands around the rope, the part that's frayed the most. My knuckles press into his stomach as I pour my remaining energy into breaking it.

It snaps.

Johnny cries, and then he's clinging to me. Actually clinging in a way he never did before. Little arms around me.

"We've got to go," I say. "Help me walk." I try to stand. I need to stand. Need to see if I can, and—

I freeze as I hear it: footsteps on the gravel. Getting closer. Going to come in here?

Johnny watches me, his eyes wide.

We listen.

The footsteps get quieter for a moment, then louder again.

Johnny whimpers. "They're going to come in here!"

I look around. A weapon. Need a weapon. My hand closes around a rubber ball. I stare at it. A toy? They have toys for their littles now?

"Inga!" Johnny cries.

"Shut up," I hiss, but he's said my name and he said it too loudly, and, outside, the footsteps quicken.

Closer, closer, closer.

"Get behind me," I hiss at Johnny, as the assassins move closer. A shadow falls in front of the doorway.

It's going to be Bridie. It's going to be her, it's—

"Inga!"

My chest tightens, and it can't be.

Figures. Two of them.

"Keelie? Oleta?" My eyes widen as they rush in. "What are you doing here?"

"Helping you!" Keelie yells, waving a gun about. One I don't recognize.

"What's going on?" Oleta hisses. Then she sees Johnny and squeals, pulls him away from me and toward her, into a tight hug. He shakes, and she looks over his shoulder at me. "I lost connection with Petra. Where is she?"

"I don't know." I wipe sweat from my forehead. "Bridie had her tortured—by Brighid. Brighid is here." I glance at Keelie. "Is it just you here? What about the assassins? Did they see you?"

"Lexa's not far," Oleta says. Then she's pushing Johnny toward Keelie, while she moves to me. Her hands touch my temples, and I feel her powers as she heals me.

"No," I say, wincing as the pain in my legs shifts. "You can't heal me, not when it causes—"

"You'd rather stay here?" she snaps. "We've got no choice. Where's Callum?"

"I don't know," I pant, trying to give her a look to warn her.

"Okay," Oleta says. "I'll look for him once I've finished your legs. And Petra too. What about Falkes? And Bridie took Amelia—is she here?"

"Amelia's dead." I choke out the words. "I don't know about Falkes, but he probably is too."

"We'll search the camp," Keelie says. "And then we'll—"

"Yes, get all the littles out here, ready," a female voice shouts. "Even the new boy."

Keelie, Oleta, and I stare at each other. Johnny's bottom lip wobbles.

My mouth dries. They're going to come in here.

"Out, now!" Oleta yells, jumping up. She shoves Johnny toward the door, then hisses at me and Keelie, for us to follow.

Keelie pulls me to my feet, and I stumble. I can walk, though it's painful, and the four of us look outside. My heart beats too quickly, and there's a dull pain in my head as I look out. More assassins, out there. To the left.

"Run that way," Oleta says. "They're going for the other huts first." She glances at me. "Ready?"

I nod. Yes.

We run, the four of us, crouching low and holding onto each other. I taste blood at the back of my mouth, stumble against Keelie as she stops suddenly.

"There!" She points at the linen on the line. "Cover."

I frown. We're here already? Where those children were hanging up the washing? I thought that was… over there? But huge sheets sway in the breeze, right near us.

We rush toward them, duck under them. The fabric is heavier than it looks, scratches the back of my neck.

"Okay," Oleta says, looking around over her shoulder. There are more huts, but it's the backs of them. No windows. "Right, the trees are that way. Lexa is—"

We all hear the engines at the same moment. Throaty, heavy rumbles. Oleta's eyes widen, and Keelie curses. Johnny turns to look at me—looking for direction, guidance. From *me*.

"We've got to move," I say. "Got to get out of here. Find Lexa. The plan doesn't change."

No. We've just got to act quicker.

I push Johnny toward the direction Oleta said the trees were, and Keelie follows. I look to Oleta, but she doesn't move. I hiss her name.

She shakes her head. "I'm not leaving Petra."

"You've got to," I say. "We've got to get out of here."

Fire dances in her eyes. "Don't tell me to leave my sister. You left her before when you shouldn't have, but I'm not the same as you. I have a conscience, and I'm finding—"

"Quiet," Johnny hisses.

"What?" Oleta and I both turn on him. He's still here? And Keelie is too. They didn't leave?

"Footsteps," he says. He's standing with his back against the huge sheet. He looks so small. "They're looking for me."

I listen, hear the movement of gravel amid the roar of the engines. The other side of this linen? Johnny turns tear-laden eyes to me.

"It'll be okay," I whisper. "Weapons?" I look at Keelie and Oleta.

They've each got a gun, but then Keelie produces a second from her belt. She hands it to me. A small, modified pistol. It's one of the assassins' guns. I look at the other two pistols. They're the same. Hell, Keelie and Oleta managed to pilfer three firearms from them?

But there's no time to think about that now.

I strain my ears, listen as hard as I can. The gravel—I can't hear it now. But the engines are louder.

"I'll check if they're coming this way," Keelie says.

Before I can say a word, she's moving forward. She

pushes back an edge of the sheet, looks left and right, slowly.

She ducks back in. "There's a hell of a lot of people out there now."

"How many?" I ask.

She shrugs. "Sixty, seventy. And there's more getting out of the trucks. Loads of them."

Oleta glances at me. "That's a lot…that's more than one camp."

"One's got a black cloak on," Keelie says. "Looks pathetic, like she's trying too hard to be scary."

"Brighid," I say.

"They're just talking, I think," Keelie says. "But I saw more vehicles driving up too. Looks like they're coming here as well."

"How many vehicles?" I ask.

Keelie shrugs. "Ten? Twenty?"

"That's not very specific." Oleta shoots her look. "Ten or twenty—which is it?"

The roof of my mouth dries.

They're *gathering* here.

A festival.

Bridie's words…that dream….

I breathe hard. "It's everyone. The festival—Bridie's having it tonight." I look at Oleta, and she flinches. "Right, you need to get out of here now. We'll have to forget about getting anyone else out—we don't even know they're alive."

"Yes, a fine day for it." Bridie's voice.

I flinch. Bridie—so close. The other side of the linen? Nausea presses its soft fingers into me, tries to make me squirm.

Go. I mouth the word at Oleta. If she goes, so will Keelie and Johnny.

But Oleta shakes her head. "I can't leave Petra. I—"

"You have to. If you want to see Michaela again, you've got to leave now," I whisper. "And Petra's dead. I'm pretty sure of it." The lie rolls easily from me. It could be the truth—though Bridie's promise that death would be too easy makes it unlikely. But I've got to make sure Oleta goes. They have to get out.

On the other side of the linen, I hear Bridie's voice again. She says something about the trucks.

Keelie looks at me. "They're going to see us the moment we step out there. There are too many around now."

"Oleta's a Seer. She can protect us," I say. "And I'll distract them."

"No, Inga—" Keelie cries.

But I'm already pushing through the linen.

Oh, I'll do more than distract them.

I'm going to end them all.

FIFTY-ONE

I FORCE MYSELF TO RUN as best as I can, though my body protests. Blood rushes in my ears. I skid on the gravel, see Bridie and Brighid as they turn toward me. The other assassins here I don't recognize. A lot of them. And more behind them. So many more.

Bridie's eyes widen. "Inga?"

I lift the gun and pull the trigger.

Bridie screams, and Brighid leaps toward me. Shouts fill my ears, and I whirl around, duck as a bolt of white light flies from Brighid's fingertips. I squeeze the trigger again—another gunshot. Get another of the assassins.

Bridie's writhing about on the floor, blood pouring from her stomach.

"You think you can beat us?" Brighid snarls, her cloak fluttering in the wind. Anger fills her eyes.

"Yes," I say, and I point the gun at her. Pull the trigger and—

White light blasts toward me, hits my shoulder. I scream, fall backward. Something hits my side and back, and—

Screams fill the air. Somewhere, I get a glimpse

of Keelie and Oleta running with Johnny. Another gunshot goes off.

Blood fills my mouth, and I turn, spit it out, try to think, try to feel. I'm not hurt. Not seriously, anyway. Arms and legs, I can feel them. And this is nothing compared to when I fell down the rock face.

I grab my gun from the ground where it fell, jump up, and turn. Brighid's advancing toward me, and I shoot her three more times. She defects each bullet with flashes of white light and—

"Enhanced!" a voice cries.

I jolt, look up, and—

Mirror eyes. Dark skin and dark hair and—

Oleta? Petra? No. *Anita.*

The third sister. She's here.

My stomach curdles.

Kill her. The desire is there—just as it is for any being with mirror eyes. But she looks like Oleta and Petra, and they're my family.

A bolt of light hits me, and I stumble. Pain in my side. I gasp. Brighid cackles. Somewhere behind her, Bridie's crawling away, two more assassins covering her as the Enhanced try to get her.

I pull the trigger on the gun, pointing it at Bridie. My shot gets her, and she slumps forward. Hands reach out for me, and I duck, push myself forward. I've lost sight of Brighid. There are suddenly so many Enhanced Ones about.

"Join us, and this will stop," Anita shouts at an assassin, and her voice sounds like Oleta's and Petra's, but it's different too.

"No!" someone shouts, and—and there are screams. Gunshots.

More assassins are here, pouring in on the enemy—so many Enhanced Ones. Here, now. Petra contacted Anita again, called them in—just like she did at D'Elinous, to save my cousins from this life.

My heart pounds. I have to kill the Enhanced. They're going to convert us all. That's my purpose.

That's what I do.

That's what we all do.

I lift my gun, train it on an Enhanced One.

But my fingers freeze. If I kill the Enhanced, the assassins will remain. They won't be converted.

My head spins, and I look at the mirror men and women. Look at them fighting the assassins. The Enhanced outnumber us. The Enhanced *will* win. And maybe—maybe that's better. Because the Enhanced can get rid of the evil in the assassins, right? They only feel good things. And if I could only feel good things—

No!

What am I thinking? Untamed never surrender.

I step back, fire several bullets at the mirror men and women, and—

I feel my expression slacken as I take it all in. The Enhanced *and* the assassins are in the same place. Just like before, with the explosion Oleta and Petra orchestrated.

I look around, but I can't see the Seer sisters. Oleta has gone? Is Petra still chained up somewhere? Or dead? But I need one of them, need an explosion, and—

My eyes widen.

Yes.

I turn, dive toward the other hut I saw the inside of, ignore the way a voice in my head calls me a coward for running from the Enhanced.

You never run away from the enemy.

But I'm not.

"Join us, and you'll be happy again."

Three Enhanced Ones loom up in front of me, seemingly out of nowhere. I fire my gun, skid to the right, narrowly avoid the hands of another and—

A gunshot, right next to me.

I turn, see Zak with a gun. He aims at the next Enhanced. Not me.

Run.

I reach the hut. The one with the fuel cans. The air is

tangy inside, and I shove my gun under my waistband, and grab two cans. I kick their lids off and douse the hut. Then I grab the box of matches. Damn. I haven't got any pockets. I freeze for a moment, thinking, then slide the matchbox under my waistband too. The leggings are tight enough to hold it in place.

I retrieve more cans, take them outside. I duck out of the way of more Enhanced Ones, force myself to run as I splash the fuel everywhere. My breaths come in sharp bursts, and pain's setting in again, but I don't stop.

Not got long, and an Enhanced could grab me at any second.

But this has got to work. They're all here. *All* the assassins, for the festival. Suddenly I don't care about the Enhanced. Sure, it's convenient they'll die too, but it's the assassins' deaths I want.

I shake the cans until they're empty, then discard them, race back for more. Sweat drips down my back, and my eyes sting from the fumes as I drench the huts and all the flammable materials with fuel. I splash more fuel on the long grass outside the huts, then the linens drying on one of the lines.

This is going to work.

I taste petrol at the back of my mouth, and I smile.

An Enhanced One appears in front of me, and I drop the fuel and grab my pistol just in time, shoot him. My aim is off, but I still get him in the leg. Adrenaline pounds through me, and the urge to correct my aim and kill him is there—but I ignore it.

This is more important, what I'm doing. *This* will get results.

I put the gun back under the waistband of my leggings and run to the edge of the camp, lugging the remaining cans with me. Got to get to the edge. Should've started there, made a circle around the perimeter. But it's too late now.

I get to the edge of the camp. My hands burn. A cold, icy wind kisses the back of my neck. I look at the fight in the camp: the Enhanced against the assassins. Oleta and Keelie, did they get away? Have they had enough time? And Lexa and Johnny?

But Petra's in there—if she's alive.

My heart bleeds, heavy. Time's slipping away. More Enhanced—I can see their vehicles approaching from the land on the opposite side of the camp. They're coming. They're going to get the assassins, convert them, if I don't do this.

Some assassins will become even more deadly as Enhanced Ones.

And some will get away, Untamed. I know it. They'll reform the group, ruin more children, more lives.

They need to die. All the assassins have to die. This has to end.

"This will end."

The voice. The one I heard before? My mind is foggy. Caia-Lu. Her voice....

"Do it!"

I pull the matchbox out from under my waistband. My fingers shake as I open it, pull a match out. I strike it. The flame seems too bright.

I throw it as far as I can, toward the camp.

Flames erupt immediately. Heat blasts over me, and I lift my arms to my face, try to shield them, and—

Figures. Running. Mirror eyes flashing.

So many, trying to get away. Screaming.

But the flames are big, engulfing, growing, and—

The sky cracks, a deafening boom.

"Inga! Come on!" a voice cries.

I look up. Keelie.

She's suddenly here, pulling me toward her, and a truck. What? We've taken a truck?

She pulls me in, across the backseat, and I bang my head, scrape my shin, hear Oleta's and Johnny's voices. I grunt, and Lexa's shouting but I can't make out the words. All I can see are the flames. The burning camp. The burning assassins and Enhanced Ones.

And I did that.

"You all right?" Lexa shouts, and I see her in the driver's seat. She puts her foot down, and we're speeding up as Keelie slams the door shut.

We drive at trucks hurtling toward us and away from us. The Enhanced, not the assassins. It's chaos. They're everywhere. Mirror eyes flashing.

"Where's Petra?" Oleta yells at me. "Did you see her?"

"Stop!" Keelie yells.

Lexa slams on the brakes, and I fly forward between the two front seats, hit the dashboard. Lexa grabs me, hauls me back and—

"What are you doing?" Oleta screams as Keelie opens her door. "There are Enhanced out there."

"Don't surrender!" I shout as I see figures out there—Enhanced Ones on foot. "We can get away from this!"

"No, that's him!" Keelie yells, pointing at the Enhanced. "Red! How the fuck did he survive? Hell, I've got to do this!" She pulls my gun from my waistband, races out the truck, and—

"What the—?" Oleta yells, and Keelie's running.

My head spins. Red? That's *Red*? Redala. From D'Elinous? That man in front of us? He's *Enhanced*.

"Get her back in the truck," Lexa yells at me.

"No! Just drive!" Oleta shouts. "We've got to get to Michaela and the others—they're unprotected, and so many Enhanced around."

The children. *Right*. Michaela, Kam, Joshua, and Zita.

"But we can't leave Keelie!" I yell. She's my family.

"We've got to!"

"No!" I scramble toward the door, jump out. Hot air hits me—and debris. Grit in the air.

I race after Keelie, adrenaline pounding through my system. And, somehow, I get to her before she gets to the man. To Red?

I grab Keelie's shoulder, haul her back. "What the hell are you doing?" I fight her as she tries to surge forward. "Don't run to Enhanced!"

"He's not just any Enhanced!"

"He's not the boy we knew," I yell, grabbing the gun back from her. I point it at the men—at Red? "He's the enemy."

"I know!" Keelie growls. "I died because of him, and—"

The land behind us explodes.

Pain—my ears. My head. A splitting sensation inside me, and I hit the ground.

Screams fill the air, and the air's so thick. I can't breathe. Can't—

Orange in the sky, and red. And black. The air's *black*. Smoke.

Everywhere and—

"The worlds are ripping!" Keelie screams, and she's next to me, on the ground. Her face contorts, and she screams again. "It's the New World!"

Pain twists down my spine as I focus on the sky. On the smoke rising from the assassins' camp. But it's not just smoke billowing up. It's a gyre, a whirlwind of destruction, pulling things up and—

There are shapes too, shapes flying upward.

Bodies.

The *assassins*. Bridie and Hunter, I see them, see them clearly as they're sucked up into the sky, and—

The Enhanced scream. They're running, jumping aboard their trucks as they drive. Drive away. But the gyre isn't trying to suck them up to the New World. It's just the Untamed. It's a vortex for us, sucking up everything Untamed, and—

"It's coming this way!" I scream, and—

I look around. The gun's there. I move forward to grab it and—and Keelie's twenty feet away. What the hell? When did she move? I pull myself to my feet. She's racing after Red, but the vortex moves toward her. It's going too fast.

"Keelie!" I roar.

She looks back at me, starts to say something and—

I scream as she's swept up into the gyre.

My lungs burn, and I'm shrieking as she hurtles upward, her body somersaulting.

"Stop!" I shout, as if that will make a difference. But it doesn't stop me shouting. And I keep shouting, and a hand lands on my shoulder.

I whirl around, come face-to-face with Oleta.

"It's righting the worlds!" she yells. "Look! The assassins it's taking are already dead!"

"But—Keelie!" My voice cracks.

"She was already dead! She's supposed to be there! It's taking back everyone who got through! It's got to seal, remember what Amelia said?"

Amelia? I blink, clueless. The air is too hot, burning me. I push my hair back, turn, see the truck closer. Johnny's face is pressed against the window, Lexa's too.

"The worlds will seal when equilibrium is restored," Oleta shouts above the rushing sounds all around us. "It's got to be how it's supposed to be."

And as we watch, the vortex turns, changes direction. Goes for more of the assassins. Bodies hurtle up. Flames spiral with them, and then the pathway to the New World is *alight*. A tunnel of fire.

Roaring sounds fill my ears as Oleta and I cling to each other, watch the destruction. The vortex snakes around, as if it's looking for more people it can send back.

"It's got everyone, hasn't it?" I look at the camp—what remains of it. A blackened pile of debris. No one alive is in there, I know it. And the only people in the wider area, apart from us, are Enhanced, and it won't go for them.

"There's someone here!" Oleta cries. "Where's the gun?"

I turn, see a figure emerging *through* the bottom of the vortex. For a moment, I think it's Keelie, but the figure changes. It's an elderly woman. My eyes widen.

Caia-Lu.

I recognize her with a jolt. She looks the same.

"The gun, Inga!" Oleta shouts. "Where is it?"

I look down at the ground. Where was it I saw it? But I can't see it now, and then Caia-Lu is running toward us. Her speed is remarkable, given she's old—only she doesn't move like she's old. She moves like she's weightless. Before I can even think what to do, she clasps my hands in hers.

"I'm so sorry." She's crying, tears pouring down her face.

"What?" Oleta yells, grabs my arms and tries to haul me back from Caia-Lu. "Let go of her!" She lifts her free arm, to strike Caia-Lu, and I yell at her not to.

My breaths stutter. This is too much. I don't understand. I look down at Caia-Lu's hands around mine. Her skin is warm.

Caia-Lu pants hard as she looks at Oleta. "I am the one who introduced Rijikarii to the world, when I was a young girl." The air whips around us, tries to carry her words away as more heat pulses past us. "I made a deal with a spirit to save a loved one, and Rijikarii exploded everywhere. When I became a Seer, my Goddess told me that many born at D'Elinous and other Untamed settlements would carry Rijikarii and be subjected to its effects."

"What the hell?" Oleta tries to pull me back farther, but I stumble.

Caia-Lu keeps me from falling, then lets go of my hands. "It got you both—it is attracted to those who are naturally defiant and courageous and determined, but also to those who are strong," she yells, her voice hoarse. She looks behind her, her hair whipping around, before her eyes settle back on me. "Rijikarii means that death follows these people around, and many carrying Rijikarii energy will cause accidental deaths. You have to know I am sorry for this curse you carried—and how your demises came so soon."

Our demises?

"What?" Oleta says. "No. We're still alive."

Caia-Lu shakes her head. "I tried to save you. I really did! But I can't overrule Rijikarii. It broke the balance between the worlds—and all these people kept coming back. There has to be the right balance of Rijikarii in both the New World and the mortal world—"

Caia-Lu screams, and the air shrieks, grabs us. Oleta yells. Caia-Lu is ripped from us, flies through the air, back into the vortex. Her screams fill my ears, make them bleed.

And then the vortex turns toward us.

"Run!" Oleta yells.

We turn and run and—

Caia-Lu's words play over in my head: *Your demises came so soon.*

What? I didn't die!

I'm not dead!

But lightning *hit* me.

And I fell *off a mountain.*

And Gweneira—no, Brighid—*shot* me.

And Oleta—the animal attack.

"It's us," I say. "It's looking for us. It can't close until we're gone."

Oleta's face contorts with alarm. "No! I have to stay here! Michaela and—"

"It's going to destroy the world," I yell over the roar of the flames and the wind.

And it's coming for us. The burning path to the New World. We are the last ones here, who shouldn't be.

"It will seal after us," I shout, and I don't know how I know, but I do know. It's got to take us! We're the last two left!"

The last two who rose from the dead.

The last two assassins.

I grab Oleta's hand. "Come on! This is to protect the littles! This is to keep Michaela alive. Equilibrium has to be restored."

Her eyes are wide, filled with tears. She holds her hand out to me, and I take it.

We run into the burning vortex.

Flames grab me.

Pain in my head, my arms, my legs.

Oleta shrieks. I shriek. And we're flying upward. She squeezes my fingers, and we're screaming, both screaming.

Pain fills my body, and—

"Oleta!" I scream, as she's ripped away.

I try to turn, try to look for her, but I can't. You can't do anything when a vortex is taking you to the New World.

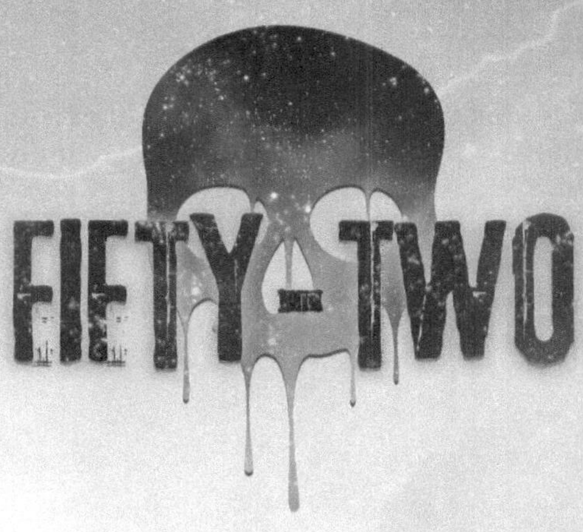

ENERGY PULSES THROUGH ME, AND I scream and scream and—

Pain, so much pain… My arms, legs….

Rushing sounds fill my ears, and I can't hear… Can't breathe. My lungs, they're too….

I scream, and Bridie, she's here—her face, in front of me.

On fire.

She's on fire.

"We won't have you here!" a voice snarls, and I turn, hairs on the back of my neck rising.

That voice, that voice is bad, I can just tell. I know it.

Got to get away.

"Oh, Inga." A face—a beautiful woman's face—in front of me. Soft words and whispers. "Well done. And thank you."

Cool fingers. My forehead.

And others are here. Caia-Lu and—

"Mummy?"

I stare at her, and it *is* her. My mother. Blond hair brighter than I remember, and dark eyes full of kindness, and—

And this isn't real.
Her face swims.
It is cold here.
So cold.
Darkness.
"Inga!" a voice cries.

I open my eyes.

Grass. I'm lying on grass and—the smell. Oh Gods, the smell. Burnt flesh and smoke and—

"Inga? Inga?" Oleta's face hovers above me.

I jump up. She pulls back just in time so we don't clash heads.

"What? Where are we?" I look around. This is the New World? My chest tightens. I'm breathing too quickly, can't catch my breath. Not properly.

But it looks the same. This place—it's the same. The burned mess of the camp over there, and Lexa's in the truck with Johnny, right next to us. And…and the Enhanced, they're driving away, retreating.

"It's okay, Little Sister. It didn't take us!" Oleta cries. "It was a Goddess. A bloody *Goddess* saved us, sent us back."

"What?" I stare at her. Nothing makes sense. And my legs feel weird, too soft. Like they can't really be what's supporting me, keeping me from falling.

"But look!" Oleta points at the sky, and it's…it's normal. No break. No vortex. No…no nothing. Just *sky*.

I stare at it, feel a tightening sensation across my scalp. This… No.

I turn around, looking everywhere.

"Inga? Oleta? Come on," Lexa shouts from the truck.

I'm rooted to the spot. I can't move. I look down at

my hands, stare at them. They feel real, substantial.

And this is all real?

This is the mortal world. I didn't die?

I breathe out hard. But the vortex… It was *taking* us. And Caia-Lu, her words.

I tried to save you. I really did! But I can't overrule Rijikarii. It broke the balance between the worlds—and all these people kept coming back. There has to be the right balance of Rijikarii in both the New World and the mortal world—

I jolt. Bridie was here because of me and Oleta. They all were. Oleta and I didn't die when we should've, opening a channel between the worlds, and they came back.

But…but we're still here.

And a Goddess saved us? That's what Oleta said. That's….

I blink, shake my head. This is all too much.

"Inga, we've got to go," Oleta shouts. "We hid the littles, and we need to get back to them."

"Yes," I say, but my word is too quiet for her to hear. I swallow hard, then step toward the truck.

Yes. We've got littles to find, children to look after. To keep alive. To keep Untamed. To keep free.

END OF BOOK TWO

THE DANGEROUS ONES SERIES
WILL CONTINUE WITH

THE THREAT OF THE HUNT

ACKNOWLEDGEMENTS

For a long time, *This Vicious Way* was a book I didn't know I would write. It is, after all, a sequel to a book that I'd never intended to have a sequel. *A Dangerous Game* was written as a standalone, but Inga just crept up on me and demanded I write her story.

Of course, there are so many people I owe my gratitude and thanks to for this book.

To my wonderful critique partners: Sarah Mensinga, S.E. Anderson, Stacey Trombley, Rachael Bundy, Dawn Metcalf, Janelle Alexander, Megan Eccles, Maria Sinclair, Lizzy Burnett, and Isvari Maranwe Mohan—thank you for your countless reads of multiple drafts. Thank you for your suggestions and questions regarding plot and character. And thank you for being my cheerleaders when writing this. You have all really helped me to shape this book into something I'm so proud of, and I look forward to working with you all again.

Michelle Dunbar, as always, you've blown me away with your spectacular editing advice. You never cease to amaze me. I can't believe this is the fourth book we've worked together on.

Molly Phipps—what can I say? You've once again amazed me with your outstanding designs skills. The cover and interior art in this book suit Inga's story perfectly. Thank you.

To Sarah Mensinga and Stacey Trombley: thank you for providing such amazing blurbs for this book.

To Mum, Dad, and Sam: thank you for absolutely everything. I can't put into words how much your support means to me.

To the rest of my family and friends: thank you.

And, lastly, to my readers: I know so many of you

loved Keelie's story in *A Dangerous Game*, and thank you for telling me. Hearing from you is always wonderful, and, who knows, maybe if I hadn't heard how much you enjoyed that book, I'd never have turned it into the start of a series and *This Vicious Way* wouldn't exist. So, thank you.

ABOUT THE AUTHOR

MADELINE DYER lives on a farm in the southwest of England, where she hangs out with her Shetland ponies and writes young adult books—sometimes, at the same time. She holds a BA Honors degree in English from the University of Exeter, and several presses have published her fiction. Madeline has a strong love for anything dystopian, ghostly, or paranormal, and she can frequently be found exploring wild places. At least one notebook is known to follow her wherever she goes. *A Dangerous Game* is her fourth novel.

Find Madeline online:
Twitter: @MadelineDyerUK
Instagram: @MadelineDyerUK
Facebook: MadelineDyerAuthor
Website: www.MadelineDyer.co.uk

Sign up to Madeline's Newsletter:
http://madelinedyer.co.uk/newsletter/

www.ingramcontent.com/pod-product-compliance
Lightning Source LLC
Chambersburg PA
CBHW030358200726
48286CB00015B/1522